BRADFORD
Brawler

BRAWLER!

Tuck in those titties, ladies. Shit is about to get real!

CHAPTER 1
Brielle

Brielle Ashford, you're under arrest for the brutal attack, rape, and attempted murder of Miss Addison Morgan.

The words circle my head as I pace through the small mirrored room. I don't understand what's happening. One minute I was sitting in class, determined to spend every minute ignoring Tanner, and the next thing I know, I've been arrested for the attack on his younger sister.

What the fuck is happening?

It's been four hours, and no one has told me a damn thing. I've been left alone, waiting, scared, and panicked. No one has come for me, no one has even bothered to tell me what's going on. Only one woman asked me if I required my lawyer, but I'm only eighteen. I don't have a lawyer, especially not one Mom or I can afford.

This isn't right. I'm innocent, and no matter how many times I scream it at the stupid two-way mirror, I fear my pleas are falling on deaf ears. They've already made up their minds. To them, the word guilty is already stamped across my forehead.

What the hell am I supposed to do?

This isn't some ridiculous shoplifting charge or a slap on the wrist. A crime like this means prison time. This is life or death. This is my whole fucking world and it's caving in before my very eyes, and I'm drowning in it. I don't know how to save myself.

My hands push back through my hair as I pace the room for the millionth time, my heart racing with fear. I try to hold my tears at bay, try to swallow over the lump in my throat, but there's no use. Until this bullshit gets sorted out, I won't be able to calm down.

This shit stinks of Colby, and the minute I get out of here, he better watch himself. I will not go down for this, and there's no way in hell I'm going to allow him to walk free. One way or another, he will be punished, but now, the only issue is who gets to be the one to do it. I know Tanner wants to put him in the ground, and maybe he'll get his chance, but not before I get my hands on him first.

Fuck, I've never felt rage like this before. It's like a searing hot poker piercing straight through my spine and boiling me from the inside out. Is this what it's like for Tanner when he loses himself?

I stop pacing and stare at my reflection through the two-way mirror, knowing they're just standing there, thinking they have me right where they want me.

The words go round in circles.

Brielle Ashford, you're under arrest for the brutal attack, rape, and attempted murder of Miss Addison Morgan.

Shit.

A soft click sounds through the room, and I whip around, watching as two officers make their way into the small interrogation room. I recognize one of them from my arrest—the guy who initially cuffed me after slamming me down against my desk, the guy who belongs to the voice that's been circling my head for the past two hours.

The other guy is wearing a suit, and I can only assume that he's some kind of detective. He holds a folder and tablet under his arm and gives me a tight smile while the arresting officer just scowls. Though I suppose I should be grateful that the other cop from school isn't here because after pulling his gun on Tanner in the middle of a classroom full of students, I have a few choice words that are bound to get me in even more trouble.

"Miss Ashford," the detective says, moving toward the small table in the center of the room. "Please take a seat."

My gaze flicks between the two as I cautiously make my way toward the table, keeping my hands right where they can see them. I've seen plenty of cop shows. I know what they're thinking of me, despite their lack of evidence. I mean, surely there can't be any, seeing as though I literally had nothing to do with it.

Dropping down into my seat, I place my hands on the table and try to ignore the rapid thump of my pulse beating in my ears. "I don't know what's going on here, but I have nothing to do with this," I start.

"I am Detective Steven Jones, and this is Officer Williams. We'll be conducting your interview today," he states, unbuttoning his suit jacket before making himself comfortable in the chair directly opposite me. The officer hangs back by the door, his back up against the wall, glaring at me as though I'm the scum of the earth. "Before we get started," the detective continues, "is there anything we can get for you? Water? Coffee?"

A smirk pulls at my lips, and I berate myself before the words even sail out of my mouth. "What you mean to ask is, would I like to give you a DNA sample, and my answer is no. Though, you have absolutely no reason to need it. I didn't do anything, but while I'm here, we might as well discuss the abusive manner of your arresting officers."

"I don't have time for games, Miss Ashford."

"In what world would you assume I want to be here playing games with you?" I demand. "The officer behind you slammed me down on a desk despite me having a broken rib, which you would already know if any of you did your homework before storming into a school full of minors. But while we're on the topic of minors, how about the other officer pulling his gun on a student in a classroom full of them, or the fact that your officers disclosed confidential information about a rape victim to her whole school? Where do we stand on that? Because I know damn well that your department is going to have one hell of a mess to clean up after that. Can you imagine the pissed off parents coming for your neck? Hell, Addison's mom alone would burn this department to the ground for that."

The detective watches me for a long moment, his eyes narrowed as if trying to decide if I can be trusted, and after a moment too long, he looks back at Officer Williams. "Is this true?"

He shakes his head and scoffs. "Absolutely not. The girl is exaggerating. She was arrested as per standard procedure."

I laugh and relax back into my chair. "You want to rethink that answer? We're living in a world where people don't know how to put their phones away. What's the bet that at least five of my classmates were recording the whole arrest? Plus, don't you guys have to wear body cameras?"

His gaze hardens and Detective Jones lets out a sigh. "Get out of my interrogation room, Williams. I want both you and Harris waiting in my office the moment I'm through here," he says, reaching for his folder and opening it as the other asshole sends me a scathing glare before striding out of the interrogation room. The detective turns his stare back to me, his gaze narrowed, unsure what to make of me. "Do you know why you're here, Miss Ashford?"

I shake my head. "Honestly, no. I know that your officers fed me some bullshit about being under arrest for what happened to Addison, but I know damn well they were talking shit because I had nothing to do with it."

"Really now?" he questions. "Because I have two sworn statements from witnesses who claim you had everything to do with it."

Two. It's like a bullet right to the heart. I know one of those statements is from Colby, which means the other would be from Erica.

"Your witnesses are full of shit and are setting me up for a crime they've already admitted to me they had everything to do with."

Detective Jones thumbs through his folder before pulling out a photo and sliding it across the table. "This is you on the night Miss Morgan was attacked," he says.

My gaze drops to the image, and I see myself smiling. The girl here is almost a stranger to me. She was caught up with a guy who treated her like shit and all she wanted was to enjoy her night. "Yes, that's me at the party," I tell him, taking in the maroon dress and the soft loose curls that I'd spent an hour perfecting. "But there were also hundreds of kids at the party. This doesn't prove anything."

The detective reaches across the table and points to someone in the background of the photograph. "Is this Miss Morgan behind you?"

I lean in and search the picture, seeing four or five girls standing behind me, one of them with eyes that are so familiar it makes my chest ache. "I couldn't be sure," I tell him. "I've never met her before, though this girl in particular looks a lot like her brother, Tanner."

"Right, so you were at the party while Miss Morgan was also present?"

"Yes, as well as hundreds of other kids—kids like Colby Jacobs and Erica Sawyer, the people who are actually responsible for hurting Addison."

"What makes you say that?"

"Because Colby admitted it to me and then warned me if I don't keep my mouth shut, I'll be next," I say with a scoff. "He ran me off the road, held me down, and warned me to keep quiet. That's how I got this broken rib. He attacked me, and then went to the hospital and tried to kill Addison by tearing out her breathing tube."

"And Erica?"

"She told me that she and Colby were responsible for giving Addison drugs and then Colby raped her. She said that when she walked in, she saw Addison on the ground seizing and that they just left her there before taking off."

The detective leans back in his chair, and I can tell from the look in his eyes he doesn't believe a word I am saying. "Let's talk about this broken rib," he says. "I assume after you crashed your car, you went to the hospital?"

My brows furrow. "It wasn't a car crash. Colby intentionally rammed me off the road and wrapped my Honda around a tree. He dragged me out of my car, into the bushes, and held me down with his hands around my throat." I point to my throat. "You can still see the bruises."

"Miss Ashford, answer the question. Did you attend the hospital last night?"

"Yes. Yes, of course I did. Tanner scared off Colby, and he rode with me to the hospital. I was seen quickly and discharged around eight in the evening."

"We have checked the records, Miss Ashford. The hospital holds no discharge papers for you. You were still at the hospital last night, weren't you? You were right there waiting and in the dead of night, you slipped into Addison's room and pulled her tubes from her throat."

My eyes widen in horror, my stomach twisting with nausea. "No, I would never do that," I rush out. "Why are you doing this to me? Why are you trying to pin this on me when I had nothing to do with it?

Colby and Erica are out there, and you're letting them get away with it."

"Tell me what happened last night, Brielle."

I clench my jaw, frustration pulsing through my veins. "I was discharged at eight and I certainly did sign all the correct paperwork. Tanner was with me all night. His cousin, Jax Morgan, picked us up from the hospital and we went back to his place where we hung out with all of our friends. There are multiple witnesses who can place me at Tanner's house. They left after midnight and Tanner took me home and stayed with me there." I let out a sigh and meet his stare. "I'm being set up to take the fall. I swear to you, I didn't do this."

I'm met with the kind of silence that scares the shit out of me, and my heart begins to race even faster. I can't go to prison. I'm not strong enough to be the top dog, and I won't handle becoming someone's bitch. I can't do it.

The detective drops his gaze to the tablet on the table and presses something on the screen before turning it around and showing me the screen. A video plays from inside Addison's hospital room, and I watch as a person creeps into the room and closes the door behind them. They're wearing a black hoodie that has the hood pulled right up over their head and they're avoiding the cameras with ease.

It's clearly a man from the height and build, a man I recognize to be Colby. I watch as he rushes across the room and stops in front of Addison's lifeless body before looking over her as if wondering what to do.

My stomach rolls, knowing what's coming next, and a tear falls from my eye.

Colby pauses, his hands hovering over her and then in a flash like lightning, he grabs the tubes coming from her throat and tears them out. An alarm sounds and I watch as he panics before racing out of the room. "Is the person in this video you, Miss Ashford?"

My eyes bug out of my head. "Excuse me?"

"Is this you?"

"Absolutely not," I say, flying to my feet. "That's Colby Jacobs. How can you be so dense to assume that could possibly be a woman in that video? That guy is over six foot and packed with muscle. I'm barely five foot four."

He lets out a heavy breath and places the tablet down, letting the screen go blank. He glances toward the two-way mirror and raises his brow before turning back to me. "Sit down, Miss Ashford. We are not nearly done with you."

"Pray tell," I scoff, taking my seat. "What other bullshit evidence do you want to try and pin on me?"

Jones thumbs through more of his papers before finding a photograph and sliding it across the table. "Is this you?" he questions.

My gaze drops to the image to find myself and Erica sitting in a gutter, and the very first thing I notice is that I'm wearing the same maroon dress from his earlier photo. Not only that, there's a small bag of pills clutched in my hand that I've never seen before.

Erica and I were drunk as skunks, laughing as I smoked pot for the first and only time. I threw up immediately after this and regretted it straight away. "Yes," I say slowly, not understanding what this has to do with anything. "This is me, but I've never seen that bag of pills a day in my life. This was taken the first weekend of the summer, weeks before that party."

"The timestamp on that photograph would suggest otherwise."

My gaze drops again, and I take in the numbers along the bottom and read the date. My brows furrow and I shake my head, trying to do the math. "No, this isn't right," I tell him, my panic only getting worse. "This photo was taken weeks before. Check my phone. I have it stored in my gallery, but it's different. This photo has been messed with."

"Are you telling me the evidence is lying? That the camera is lying?" he questions, his voice slowly raising. "This photo was taken on the night Addison Morgan was attacked and we have photo evidence of you holding the drugs which put the victim into a coma."

"NO, THAT'S NOT—"

"You drugged her, ensured she was attacked, and then left her there."

"No, I didn't, I—"

He grabs his tablet and brings up another video, flipping it around and showing me the screen with the volume turned up. "It was all Brielle's idea," Erica sobs, sitting in a room similar to this. "She's been jealous of Addison for as long as I can remember, and when she showed up at the party, she just … I tried to tell her to stop, but there's no stopping Brielle when she's out for blood. She slipped the pills into her drink and dragged her into the room. Her and Colby … they … he would do anything she asked of him. He was in love with her, and when she told him to hurt Addison, he did, no questions asked. The poor girl … I tried to stop them, I swear." She drops her head into her hands as ugly heaving sobs tear from her chest, tears falling down her face. "By the time I got into the room, it was already too late. Addison was on the ground, naked. They raped her and just left her for dead. She was having a seizure and I … I was scared I was going to get in trouble, so I ran."

My heart shatters into a million pieces. Thirteen years of friendship gone in a matter of seconds.

How could she do that to me? After everything we've been through.

I shake my head, tears streaming down my face. "She's lying," I cry, my voice barely audible. "I was out enjoying the party. I didn't do drugs that night, and I sure as hell didn't concoct some brutal attack plan with Colby. That photo is fabricated. There wasn't even a bag of pills. That joint was the first one I'd ever had and the only. I swear to you, this wasn't me. Colby and Erica did this, and they're trying to make me take the fall. I'll do whatever you want. A lie detector test, I'll wear a wire. Whatever it takes, just please … you're going to let them get away."

"I am not questioning Colby Jacobs' involvement in this. His DNA confirms that he was responsible for the rape of Addison Morgan, and he will be dealt with. However, right now, what I am questioning is what kind of involvement *you* had in this attack. You were the brains of this attack, and Colby was the brawn. You set Addison up, and you used Colby as your pawn to do it."

I shake my head, his every word killing me, but before he can continue, the door flies open and Orlando—my brand-new stepdaddy—comes striding in, his face full of anger. He stares at me in repulsion. "Don't say another word. We're leaving."

I stand, my eyes wide as the detective whips around to face Orlando. "Excuse you. I was not through with my interrogation."

"Don't play with me, Jones," Orlando spits. "I'm Miss Ashford's lawyer. I have reviewed your evidence and your case. You've got nothing. Now unless you plan on charging my client, you have no grounds to hold her."

Detective Jones slouches in his chair, anger burning through his stare, and as Orlando holds the door open, I don't let my opportunity go to waste. I push past the small table and toward Orlando before turning back to Detective Jones. "For the record, the two officers who stormed my classroom today will be facing charges of their own for the way they handled my arrest, and unlike you, I won't need to fabricate evidence to make it happen."

And without another word, I storm out of the interrogation room, knowing damn well that the race is only just getting started.

CHAPTER 2
Brielle

The door slams behind me, and I've barely walked into Orlando's mansion before my mother is coming at me. Her hand lashes out and smacks across my face, and before I can even flinch or register the pain, her ugly words are thrown at me. "How dare you embarrass me like that," she seethes, her whole body shaking with rage. "I knew that Colby Jacobs was a piece of work, but this? How could you do such a thing? I raised you better than this."

She waves her arms, putting on a show for her new husband as my hand comes to the side of my face, feeling the throbbing sting left behind from her hit. "Are you kidding me right now?" I demand, my eyes wide with disbelief. "You really think I had anything to do with this? You're my mother."

"The evidence is right there, Brielle," Mom spits. "You don't think I remember all the late nights over the summer, all the times that boy snuck into my home? And now look. How am I supposed to live knowing that my daughter committed such a crime? I have to walk out of this house every day and hold my head up while that woman next door watches me, knowing exactly what my child did to hers. I've never been so humiliated in my life. Rape? RAPE? And you had the audacity to say such awful things about Jensen when all along you were the one behind that attack. I'm disgusted with you, Brielle. I don't even recognize you anymore."

I gape at her, my world crumbling around me. "I didn't do it, and if you were any kind of parent, you would be able to see that I'm telling the truth. I was at that party, but it had nothing to do with me. It was Colby and Erica. They were hooking up behind my back all summer. Erica and Colby gave her the drugs, she told me only a few days ago, and I told her if she didn't come clean to the cops that I would do it for her. Then Colby rammed his car into mine to ensure my silence. Why don't you believe me?"

"It's like a big web of lies with you, Brielle. I never know what to believe anymore."

I step into her, my eyes wide and full of fear, unable to comprehend the idea of her thinking I'm guilty in any part of this. "Mom," I whisper, reaching for her, only to have her flinch away from me. "I didn't do this. I promise you. I know you and I have had our issues over the past few weeks, but I'm still the little girl you raised. I … I swear to you, Mom. Erica is lying. They did it together, and they're setting me up to take the fall, and I … I don't know what to do. I'm scared."

Something flashes in her eyes, and for a moment I think I can see the mother I remember from Hope Falls, but her gaze darkens once again, her arms crossing over her chest. "How long have you known about this?" she questions.

My brows furrow and I shake my head, confused. "What do you mean? When the cops showed up at school and arrested me, that was the first of it."

"I don't mean your arrest. Erica and Colby. When did you first learn that Colby and Erica were involved?"

"I learned it was Colby the same time everyone else did."

"And Erica?"

"Only a few days ago."

"Why didn't you say anything?"

My eyes bug out of my head. "I did. The minute I knew what Colby had done, I came down here and spoke to both you and Orlando about it, and you acted like I was throwing an innocent man under the bus. As for Erica, I told her to hand herself in. That's why Colby rammed his Charger into my Civic the other day. He was trying to ensure my silence, then after that, he tried to pull the same shit on Addison. He tore her breathing tube right out of her throat. You know me, Mom. You know I could never do something like that. Don't you see? They're setting me up for it. All the evidence they had was fabricated."

Mom takes a step back from me, turning away and pressing her hands to her temples, and I listen as she takes slow, calming breaths. "I just don't know what to do with you, Brielle. We came all the way back from Paris, cut our honeymoon short only for it to be thrown in our faces."

I scoff. "After everything that happened to Addison, you have the nerve to make this all about you. Wow, Mom. You hit a new low today. You have a chance here to support your daughter, to stand by my side and help me clear my name, but instead, you can't even look at me and are talking shit about cutting your honeymoon short. Who are you?"

She spins back around, jamming her fingers right into my chest. "Who am I?" she spits. "Who am I? I'm the woman they will stare at, whisper about, and bar from attending events because my daughter attacked one of their own. I will never be able to fit into this world, and I have you to thank for it."

"YOU WERE NEVER GOING TO FIT INTO THIS WORLD," I roar. "They're already talking about you. You're the joke of every conversation, the pitiful woman who can't see through Orlando's bullshit. Can't you see how they laugh at you? You're the town gold-digger and everybody knows it. That's all on you, Mom. You did that all by yourself."

Her hand cracks against my face again, and I stumble back a step, tasting blood in my mouth. "How dare you," my mother seethes. "After everything I've done for you."

Anger burns through my veins as I launch myself at her, only to have a strong hand curl around my arm and yank me back. Jensen pushes in front of me, giving me a hard shove back as he stands between me and my mother. "Instead of tearing shreds off your daughter, don't you think your time would be better spent trying to figure out how the hell you're going to clear her name? Take it from someone who's already been falsely accused of rape. Everything you want is going to slip right through your fingertips unless you start doing something about it. Every second you're here trying to beat the shit out of your daughter, is another second someone is spreading another lie. So do yourself a favor, stepmother, and start figuring out how the hell this bullshit isn't going to destroy another life."

Mom glares at Jensen but seeing the fight leave her, he steps out from between us and moves deeper into the house. I wait for him to turn back, to give me some kind of weird stare suggesting I'm now in his debt, but it never comes, and before I can think on it longer, Mom's fingers curl around my arm. She drags me through the house and into the formal dining room before yanking out a chair and shoving me into it.

"Right," she says. "You will talk until I tell you to stop, not sparing a single detail, and only after that, will I decide what I'm going to do with you."

I stare at her, the rage threatening to take control.

How can my own mother not have my back right now? She really has become a stranger.

"Now, Brielle," she demands.

Curling my hands into balls on my lap, I spill every last detail, relaying the exact conversations and filling her in on everything I can possibly remember. By the time the sun is sinking in the sky and the formal dining room darkens, Orlando is stepping through to join his new bride.

"I take it things have calmed down in here?" he questions, looking at Mom as though he actually cares for her.

She shakes her head. "I just don't know what I'm going to do," she says, putting on her show. "It's clear she is lying to me. I know she didn't hurt that girl, but I just don't believe her when she said she had nothing to do with this. I don't know what I've done to deserve this. Perhaps she's acting out because we've been moving so fast."

I scoff, unable to believe what I'm hearing as I watch Orlando's hand fall to my mom's shoulder and squeeze in support. "All teenage girls act out at some point. You'll get her name cleared and then we'll be able to go on as we were. Everything is going to be okay."

"Thank you, my dear," Mom says. "I don't know where I would be without your help. I'm sure I'm probably panicking for nothing. You'll have this taken care of in no time."

Orlando's hand falls away from her shoulder, and he takes a hesitant step back. "Me?" he questions. "Oh, no. There's been a mix up here, Cora. I will support you through all of this, but I cannot take Brielle on as a client. I am representing Colby Jacobs. It's a conflict of interest. I'd be happy to find you another lawyer."

My stomach sinks as a weight drops down on my shoulders. "Wait. What do you mean you won't represent me?" I question, fear rocking through me. "You came into the police station and told them I was your client."

"Indeed, I did," he says. "Had I not, you would still be sitting in that interrogation room. Am I mistaken in assuming you wanted to get out of there, or shall I drive you back to the precinct?"

I clench my jaw, absolutely hating this guy. Apart from his money and silver fox status, the asshole has no redeeming qualities about himself. I can't understand what my mother sees in him.

Orlando smirks at me, taking my silence as a win. "That's what I thought," he says, moving back to my mother's side. "Now, if you will excuse us, your mother and I are due out for dinner and I need to salvage what's left of our plans."

Rolling my eyes, I push up from my chair and start making my way out of the formal dining room when I hear Mom's and Orlando's conversation behind me. "You're really not going to represent my daughter in this? You know how grateful I would be."

"I'm sorry, Cora. My hands are tied. I'm representing a conflicting party."

"You can't get out of it? I know those people, Orlando. They don't have the funds to pay for your time."

"It's a pro bono case," he says as I pause outside the formal dining room, listening in. "You know I must take a case like this every month. I have a reputation to uphold."

"Pro bono?" Mom questions. "They're not even paying you, and yet you still won't take Brielle's case? Can't you hand Colby off to someone else? This is my daughter we're talking about, your stepdaughter. Don't you see how important this is?"

Orlando sighs. "Come on, Cora. We have dinner plans. It's best we get going."

"So, that's it? That's the end of the conversation?" she questions, her chair scraping back against the marble tiles. "You're going to leave

Brielle to fend for herself over that … that vile boy?"

"I don't know what you want from me, Cora. Colby's case will bring me national attention, whether he did it or not, this is a chance to boost my name and prove again that I am the best there is," he says. "Brielle doesn't need me. Any standard lawyer will be able to take care of it. The evidence is poor, and her arrest was questionable. Now, I am more than happy to give Brielle a list of lawyers who will be able to take her case, and I am happy to pay for those fees, but what I will not do is take a backseat in Colby's case because you couldn't keep your daughter in check."

Frustration burns through me, and as my mother begins screeching at him, I take off up the stairs, knowing nothing good could possibly come from sticking around.

All I want is to crawl into a dark hole and die.

I've never felt so broken in my life. Erica was my best friend for thirteen years. I had her back every chance we got. I held her hand when she got her period for the first time and thought she was dying. It's one thing to screw around with Colby when we were still together, but this? To incriminate me for a crime she had everything to do with? No, never again. Erica has destroyed me, and there's no going back.

Everything is spiraling out of control, my world is burning around me, and I'm frantically trying to put out the flames but they just keep coming. Every time I put out a fire, another twice as big shows up at my back. Every turn I take, I am blindsided, and I can't take it anymore.

Tanner is … well, he's Tanner. Self-explanatory. He's an ass and he fucked up, and all I want is to fall into his arms and hear him tell me that everything is going to be alright, but not after what happened at the track. He crushed me in a way I wasn't prepared for. He needed an outlet and I allowed myself to be that for him, but I wasn't ready for just how much it was going to sting.

I need to distance myself from him. He's not good for me. Shit, the flames Erica and Colby have ignited are nothing compared to the inferno Tanner could cause.

Pushing through to my bedroom, I come to an immediate stop, my heart shattering as I fall to my knees and break.

I LEAN, you LEAN.

The words scrawled across my mirror kill me, and all the pent-up aggression, pain, and fear break through the surface and claim me. Hot tears spring to my eyes, and I drop my face into my hands, sobbing uncontrollably.

Tanner's words are like a searing blade struck right through my chest. He's trying to tell me he's got me, that no matter what, he'll have my back, and that he's sorry. I saw it in his eyes this morning. He wants to forget about everything and go back to the way things were, where nothing has to change between us, but so much already has.

I wasn't kidding when I told him we were done.

It's already too late.

He crushed me, just as I always knew he would.

But those words. Why did he have to use *those* words? *I lean, you lean.* They come filled with the promise of so much more, and all it does is act as a reminder of the things I can't have anymore, the things my heart aches for.

If I had enough time, I could have fallen in love with Tanner Morgan. Hell, maybe I already am. But I guess I'll never know.

CHAPTER 3

TANNER

My arm rears back and I launch it forward, releasing the glass from my hand and listening as it shatters against the kitchen wall. This shouldn't be happening. Bri shouldn't have been arrested like that, and she sure as fuck shouldn't be facing charges for what happened to Addison.

I know with all my heart she had nothing to do with it. It reeks of her ex and that bitch she called a best friend.

Colby came for her neck when he rammed her into that tree and I wanted to fucking kill him, but now setting her up to take the fall … he's coming for her soul and there ain't no way in hell I'm about to let it happen. Brielle is better than this. I know things are about as fucked up between us as things can get, but that doesn't mean I'm going to let her take the fall.

She deserves better. I fucking owe her after the bullshit I said to her at the track. She had every right to walk away from me, and all I can do is beg for her forgiveness. Fuck, I will fall at her knees if that's what it takes.

I was so wrong to want her to hate me. For weeks, it was all I could think about, but seeing the pain in her eyes, seeing the way her heart broke, it shattered something within me. Now that she does hate me, I'd do fucking anything to take it back. Brielle Ashford is my girl—whether I was ready to admit it or not—and there's not a damn thing she can do to make me change my mind.

"What on earth is going on in here?" Mom demands, rushing into the kitchen after hearing the glass shatter.

I lean against the counter, bracing myself against the Italian marble as my head tips forward, trying to find the control that just keeps slipping. "It's nothing," I mutter, my fingers clenched against the counter. "I'll clean it up."

Mom stops and takes a quick glance around, her lips pressing into a hard line as she takes in the mess. "That better not have been one of my good glasses, Tanner Morgan."

Ahhh, fuck.

Mom sees the cringe creeping across my face and lets out a heavy sigh, her gaze filling with pity. She watches me a moment before moving closer, and I shake my head, holding up a hand. "No, don't come any closer," I tell her, noticing she's barefoot. "There's glass everywhere. You're going to cut up your feet."

She rolls her eyes and moves across the kitchen to the storage closet. She pulls out a broom and hands it to me before settling in on one of the breakfast stools. "Well, if it cost me one of my good glasses, then you better start talking."

Letting out a sigh, I start pushing the shattered glass into a pile, making sure to get every last piece. "I don't know where to start," I tell her. "The fact that I pushed Brielle away, or the fact that she was arrested during school for what happened to Addie."

"What? The girl from next door?" Mom breathes, her eyes coming to mine and holding them captive with her sheer concern and confusion. "What are you talking about? What does she have to do with this?"

I cringe, realizing just how much Mom doesn't know about my relationship with Brielle, but know damn well I'm not about to walk away without her knowing everything there is to know. "I've been… kinda dating her. At least, I was until I fucked it all up."

"I'm not understanding. Brielle is new here. How does she have anything to do with Addison?"

"That's just the thing, she doesn't," I explain. "She's Colby's ex. They were together at the time he attacked Addison, but I swear, Mom, she knew nothing about it. She broke up with him because he wasn't treating her right, and now … I don't know. A few days ago, her best friend admitted to having something to do with it, and Bri told her to go to the cops and tell them what she knew, otherwise she'd do it for her. The next thing we know, Colby rams her off the road and warns her to keep her mouth shut. Then in class today, two cops came in and arrested her, pinning everything on her after pulling a gun on me and all but telling the whole fucking school what happened to Addie."

Mom's back stiffens, her eyes widening. "What do you mean they pulled a gun on you?"

I give a sharp shake of my head. "That's not important," I spit. "All that matters is Bri didn't do this."

"Forget about this girl for just two seconds," Mom says, anger beginning to claim her. "You had a gun drawn on you during class and police officers disclosed confidential information about my daughter?"

"Yes."

"You need to tell me exactly what happened right this instant, Tanner."

I groan, desperately needing to get back to Brielle. "The cops came in. I thought they were coming for me after I busted through Colby's home last night, but they went for Brielle. One of them slammed her down on her desk to cuff her and said she was under arrest for the brutal attack, rape, and attempted murder of Addison," Mom gasps, cutting me off, but I keep going. "I couldn't help myself. I went to help her and by the time I had the asshole off her, the other cop had his gun drawn."

"In a classroom full of children?"

I nod and her face goes red.

Mom takes a moment, bracing her elbows against the counter and dropping her face into her hands. "What about Addie?"

I cringe, knowing this is the last thing she wants to hear. "It was like a rumor mill all day. I couldn't escape it. If people weren't talking about

Brielle's arrest or the gun, they were spreading shit about Addison. The whole school knows what happened to her," I murmur, listening as she whimpers, her heart breaking for my sister, just as mine has been all day. "No matter what I said, they all think Brielle did it, and now she's going to have to go to school tomorrow and face the whole student body who thinks she raped my sister."

Mom's lips press into a hard line as she plays with her fingers, a tell I've learned over the years that shows she's uncomfortable. "Oh, Tanner," she finally says. "You can't always protect everyone."

"I can try."

Mom nods. "If she is innocent, she'll be able to clear her name," she says. "She lives under Orlando Channing's roof, and I doubt he's about to let this all get pinned on her. She'll be okay, but do you really think seeing this girl is a smart idea? She has connections to Colby Jacobs. I'm sorry, love, but I don't think this is a good—"

"Don't even say it," I warn her, more than ready to go behind my mother's back. "You're my mom, and I love you, but she means more to me than you understand. I'm going to see her with or without your approval, and I'd really prefer not to have to lie to you. Though right now, it probably doesn't even matter. I fucked up. I pushed her away and she said we're through."

Mom stands and walks around the kitchen, putting herself right in front of me. "If she is the one for you … if you love her, then you have my approval and I will support you however I can through all of this," she says, pulling me into a tight hug and refusing to let go. "If she feels for you what you're feeling for her, then you don't need to worry. Whatever you did, you will make it right, and she will forgive you. You're a Morgan, Tanner. We don't give up."

With that, Mom pulls back out of my arms and gives me a tight smile. "Now, as for those officers who thought they could pull a gun on my child and expose my daughter's worst moment to a school full of gossips, they're about to experience the wrath of a protective mother."

She doesn't wait for my words of encouragement before she turns and takes off, leaving me to scoop up the pile of shattered glass in the corner of the kitchen. I doubt I'll see her for the rest of the night. She'll put in a complaint and demand action be taken against Bri's arresting officers, and the moment that's done, she'll be right back to Addison's bedside, holding her hand and willing her to wake from this nightmare.

Knowing that staying down here and pacing my kitchen another million times isn't helping anything, I take off up the stairs and push through to my room. Out of habit, my gaze falls to my window, and I come to a stop, finding Brielle on her knees, crying on her bedroom floor.

My heart falls right out of my chest. Seeing the anger and pain I caused last night at the track is nothing compared to the pure torment of watching her fall apart. God, I'd give anything just to hold her, to press a kiss to her temple and tell her that everything is going to be alright. Fuck, the things I'd do to Colby for bringing this down on her.

Unable to help myself, I move across my room until I'm standing right in front of the window. My fingers latch around the frame, and I slowly draw it open, desperate for her. As if sensing me here, Bri's head snaps up. Those blazing blue eyes come to mine, holding me hostage with nothing but her stare and willpower.

Tears race down her cheeks, dropping to her uniform, and it guts me, but I hold still. I need her more than I ever knew I could. Brielle stands and I swallow hard, watching as she moves toward her window.

That's right, Killer. Come to me.

A flare of hope surges through me, and my chest heaves with heavy breaths. Just a little bit closer and she'll be able to open her window.

My fingers ball into fists at my sides, the anticipation too much to handle. All I need is two seconds of her time. I just need her to hear me, to tell her that I have her back in all of this. That I know she didn't do it.

If she leans, I'm going to fucking lean too. Hell, I'll fucking jump if that's what she needs me to do.

Brielle moves in front of her window and my mind races with all the things I need to say to her. My eyes zone in on her every movement, watching as she reaches for the window. Only she keeps going, gripping the blinds instead.

No. No, baby, no. Don't do it.

Her stare hardens and, in a split moment, she yanks them closed, blocking me out. Pain rocks through my chest like a fucking dagger to the heart.

Fuck. That stung like a motherfucker.

It's nothing I didn't deserve, but one thing is for sure, she can block me out all she wants, it doesn't mean I'm going to sit back and accept it though. She's crumbling in there, and there's no way in hell I'm about to sit here and let it happen. She might not want me, but she *needs* me.

I launch myself out the window and take a few steps across the roof to the edge before jumping straight down, landing in a low crouch. I waste no time, dashing across the boundary line of the two properties before pushing my way through Channing's front door.

The sound of an argument comes flowing through from the formal dining room, and irritation pulses into my veins. I don't hang around long enough to determine what the argument is about, but the brief second I spent passing by is enough to realize that Brielle's mom is a piece of shit.

Skipping up the stairs two at a time has me in front of Brielle's bedroom door in three seconds flat, and I'm not surprised to find the door handle locked. I slip back a step to the hallway closet and push my way inside before closing the door behind me and reaching up to remove the ceiling panel for the crawl space.

I pull myself up and crawl through the roof before dropping back down inside Brielle's closet. I'm not exactly quiet, but I'm not surprised when Bri doesn't hear me coming. There are clothes everywhere and I step over them to get out of her closet.

It's insane to think it was only last night I was in here with her and everything was okay. That was before Colby tore the breathing tube from my sister's throat and before I took my anger out on the track … and on her.

So much has gone down over the past twenty-four hours, I can barely wrap my head around it, but fuck, I'd do anything to change it, to take it all back and make her pain go away.

Bri lays across her bed, her face pressed into her pillow as she silently cries, and everything inside me breaks for the millionth time today. I make my way around her room and watch as her body tenses, realizing I'm here.

She doesn't say anything and doesn't move, simply allowing me to turn off the light, kick my shoes off, and climb into her bed. I wrap my arms around her and pull her tight into my chest, right where she was always supposed to be.

This is exactly what I should have done at the track last night. I should have held her tight, should have used her to center myself and find control instead of using her feelings as a weapon against her. How will she ever forgive me for that? I don't deserve to hold her in my arms, but for whatever reason, she's not pulling away.

It's like coming home. There's not a damn fiber in my body that tells me this isn't where I belong, *where she belongs*. Brielle Ashford is mine, and without a doubt, everything I am belongs to her.

Killjoy melts into me, her head resting against my chest as she holds me like her only lifeline. It's bittersweet, holding on to her while knowing that the moment she calms herself, she's going to push me away. I don't know when I'll get the chance to hold her like this again, so I soak up every fucking second of it. Because the next time I do, it'll be because I've earned it.

Her tears fall onto my shirt, and I run my fingers through her long hair, giving her whatever it is she needs to remember that she is the strongest woman I've ever met. This bullshit isn't going to drag her down. She will rise above it and she'll fucking shine while she's at it. Hell, if she wants to fuck with the assholes who did this to her at the same time, then she knows I'm down for that too.

Bri slowly begins to calm as we lay in dead silence, and the exhaustion of her day begins to claim her. She closes her eyes, her breathing beginning to even out, and all too soon, she falls into a broken, fretful sleep.

It kills me that even in her sleep, the tears still fall down her cheeks, but I don't dare let her go. Even during this hell, I'm her calm in the storm, and as long as she'll allow me, I'll be right here, more than ready to slay every last one of her demons. Myself included.

CHAPTER 4
Brielle

I've never feared a set of school gates more than I do now. My car—and by *my car*, I mean my mother's car I stole after the douche king wrapped my Civic around a tree—has barely passed through the gates to the student parking lot, and I already feel eyes shooting lasers my way.

I swallow hard and push down the fear rising in my chest. The cops were wrong, and the second I get a chance to clear my name, everything is going to go back to how it was. I can continue being the mystery girl nobody can quite figure out. I don't want to be this scared, timid creature because the moment they see me as weak, the wolves will descend.

The students of Bradford Private will crush me if they think for even a moment I had anything to do with what happened to Addison. I'll never be able to show my face again. Jensen is proof of that. One false accusation and he was done. That can't be my life. I won't accept it.

Pulling into a parking space, I bring Mom's car to a stop and do my best to rein in the nerves pulsing through my body. My hands shake and there's an uneasy feeling in the pit of my empty stomach, one I can't seem to control.

My gaze shifts across the prestigious school, skimming over the huddled students all looking my way, scowls on their faces and venom in their eyes. Tanner stands up near the front entrance, his gaze locked on my mother's car as Riley, Hudson, and the twins loiter around him, probably talking shit.

I should have stayed home.

The driver's side door of my mother's car swings open, and I jump, more than prepared to drop a bitch. "What the—" I cut myself off finding Ilaria, Chanel, and Arizona standing in my open doorway, their sharp stares locked on mine.

"You better start talking, girl," Ilaria says, crossing her arms over her chest. "You know I've got your back, but if I'm about to go to war for you, then the least you can do is assure me that I'm not fighting a losing battle."

Arizona's lips press into a hard line, and she averts her stare as if she can't even look at me right now. "Yeah, what she said."

Letting out a heavy sigh, I reach across to the passenger seat and grab my bag before looking back up at them. "Seriously? Don't you think if even a little bit of it were true, Tanner would have already laid my ass out?"

Chanel's gaze flickers toward Ilaria's. "She has a point."

"A good fucking point," I mutter, stepping out of the car and closing the door behind me. "This was all Erica."

"I … just … can we take like, a million steps back?" Ilaria says, moving in beside me as we start making our way up to the fiery pits of hell otherwise known as the school. "I'm confused. Is all this one big lie? I thought Addison was at some big-time performing arts school, well on her way to becoming Hollywood's newest *it* girl."

I shake my head, my heart shattering at the thought of having to tell them where Addison has been all this time. I come to a stop, not wanting my words to be overheard by the gossipy assholes around us. "No. About six weeks ago, Addison was drugged and raped by Colby at a party in Hope Falls."

Ilaria's eyes bug out of her head. "Your ex?" she gasps, disgust marring her pretty features. "But … I slept with him. Don't tell me I slept with a rapist. Please, Bri, tell me there's been some kind of mix up."

"I wish I could," I murmur. "But if it makes you feel any better, I'm right there with you."

"Wait," Arizona says. "If that was six weeks ago, then where the hell has Addison been all this time? If you're innocent, can't she just tell the police?"

My gaze shifts up to Tanner still standing by the entrance of the school, his stare locked heavily on mine, so many unsaid words flowing between us. Turning back to the girls, I drop my gaze to the grass and start walking again. They fall in beside me, hanging on my every word. "The cocktail of pills she was given put Addison in a coma. She's been in the hospital ever since, just lying there, not waking up."

"Holy shit," Ilaria breathes. "Are you fucking kidding me? That's insane."

"Insane doesn't even begin to cover all the bullshit that's come from this."

"How do you mean?" Chanel asks.

"I still haven't quite worked out all the details, but I know Erica had something to do with it. She was screwing Colby behind my back, and the night of that party, she was doing pills with him when Addison turned up. I guess Colby and Tanner have some beef about something that happened years ago, and Colby saw Addison as a way to get revenge on Tanner. Erica and Colby got her fucked up on pills and then Colby raped her in the bedroom, and all this time, Erica knew all about it."

Arizona gasps, her eyes going wide. "That's what that fight was about at the track," she says. "We thought Colby was jealous because you and Tanner were getting close."

I give her a tight smile. "Bingo," I say. "Well, there's more to it than just that. Colby showed up at the track only because I put him on blast and was refusing his calls, but he had to know the second he turned up at the track, Tanner was going to destroy him."

"So, Tanner knows it was Colby?" Ilaria questions. I nod and her brows furrow. "So why did the cops arrest you for rape?"

A heaviness rests against my chest as we slowly creep closer and closer to the front of the school, all eyes on our group. "A few days ago, Erica showed up at my place and accidentally outed herself for having something to do with it. I gave her an ultimatum to tell the cops, or I would, and she played me. She gave a statement saying it was all my idea and that I was in the room, basically cheering Colby on as he raped Addison. They have all this false evidence of me holding the bag of pills—which I never did—and now they're trying to pin it on me as aiding and abetting. They're saying I was the brains behind this, and Colby was the brawn."

"Are you shitting me?" Arizona demands, gripping my arm and bringing our whole group to a stop once again. "That's fucking sick."

"You're telling me," I say. "But the cherry on top—Colby snuck into the hospital the night he wrapped my car around a tree and tore the breathing tubes out of Addison's throat, and they're trying to pin that on me too, despite the surveillance footage clearly showing a male figure."

"That's fucking bullshit," Ilaria says. "You were literally at Tanner's place with a broken rib and all of us there to back it up. Colby can't honestly think he's going to get away with all of this."

I scoff. "Who knows? Orlando's still taking his case, so I wouldn't be surprised if he walks free."

She shakes her head, anger raging in her honey-colored eyes. "What about Erica?" she asks. "That bitch needs a fucking ass beating. Just say the word and we'll jump her after school. I mean, after dance practice, of course. My mom would kill me if I skipped out on training."

Chanel scoffs. "And to think she called you her best friend for like … how long?"

"Thirteen years."

Chanel lets out a huff. "It's on. I don't care if you say no. I'm breaking her nose so bad that not even my mom's plastic surgeon could fix that mess."

"Fuck Erica," Arizona says. "What are we going to do about Addison? She's just been lying in a hospital bed for six weeks without anyone even knowing she's there." Arizona nibbles on her bottom lip, her gaze flicking toward Tanner. "Do you think Addison's parents would be down for us to visit? I mean, I know we're not exactly close, but I don't like the idea of her being alone."

"She's not alone," I tell her as we start walking again. "Tanner's mom practically lives at her bedside."

"Yeah, but it's not the same," Arizona says. "Now that everyone knows, people are going to be randomly showing up there to visit, and I wonder—"

"Wonder what?" Ilaria questions when Arizona cuts herself off.

Her lips twist with uncertainty and she pulls her gaze back from Tanner at the top of the school entrance, still staring at me with his heart on his sleeve. He should have stayed away last night, but I'm grateful he bulldozed his way into my life once again. I needed him more than ever, and he showed up for me. Even when I pushed him away, even after everything that went down. "I wonder if her mom would be cool with us going and just … freshening her up. Like painting her nails and brushing out her hair. I mean, I wasn't close with her or anything, but I knew her enough to know that she would never walk out of her house without makeup and her nails done, so like, I don't know. I think it's the least we could do for her, and then when she wakes up, she'll be happy to know that when people came to see her, she was presented in a way that she would have been comfortable with. Is that … is that okay, or am I being rude? I don't want to overstep or anything."

I step into Arizona and wrap my arms around her. "I think that's an amazing idea," I tell her. "All you can do is ask. If her mom says no, then at least she knows you had Addison's best interests at heart and that not everyone in this world is a monster. I never met her, but from what I can tell, I think she'll appreciate it."

"Awwww," Ilaria says, flinging her arm over Arizona's shoulder and pulling her into her side. "Aren't you just the biggest bundle of sweetness?"

Chanel laughs. "I really don't know how you forced your way into our lives. You're over here wanting to take care of Addison while Ilaria and I are planning to file our nails into sharp claws for when we jump Erica."

The girls laugh, and while I desperately want to join in with them, my heart is simply too heavy.

We continue making our way to the entrance, and as we finally reach the very front of school, my chest begins to ache. Tanner is so close. Only a few steps would put me right in his warm arms, and the pain in his eyes tells me just how welcomed I'd be, but it hasn't even been forty-eight hours since those vile words flew out of his mouth at the track.

My gaze drops away, feeling not only the heat from his stare, but Riley's, Jax's, and Hudson's too. The only one who takes it easy on me is Logan, but that's purely because his gaze is locked on Chanel's. I start making my way up the stairs to the main entrance and suck in a breath, unable to release it as I painfully make my way past him.

His fingers flinch at his side, and I'd do anything to cling on to them, needing him more than I ever thought possible. Instead, I keep walking, feeling a piece of me die with each new step I take.

A strange hush falls around us, and I can practically read the questions lingering in my friends' minds, wondering what the hell went down between us. I didn't get a chance to explain the hostility between me and Tanner before I was carted off in handcuffs. They're not stupid. They know there's something much deeper going on between us than just the bullshit Colby and Erica created, and I don't think it'll be long before their ability to hold their tongue fails.

He doesn't try to force my attention, but I see his need to. This morning is already going to be hell, and the last thing I need to deal with is this twisted, fucked-up mess of feelings between us. The fact that he allows me to walk by uninterrupted is a gift which brings nothing but sweet relief, but he won't be able to resist for long. He's going to want to talk, and when he does, it's not going to be pretty.

Reaching the top step, we file through the main entrance of Bradford Private, leaving the boys behind on the stairs. We've barely taken a step before Ilaria grabs my arm. "Girl, if you don't tell me what the fuck went down between you two, I'm going to go insane."

Point proven.

"It's nothing," I say, not wanting to get into it with the eyes of every last student in the corridor resting on me with scowls on their faces and the vilest thoughts spinning around their clueless minds. "We just … we're not going to work out, especially now. Being with him is only setting myself up for the worst kind of heartbreak, and I don't think I can handle it. We'll just go back to being neighbors who can't stand each other."

Ilaria scoffs and rolls her eyes. "Right, because that's exactly what you were."

Arizona shakes her head and gives me a beaming smile. "In the words of Aaliyah, *dust yourself off and try his friends* … or something like that."

"That is definitely not how that song goes," Chanel laughs.

Ilaria scoffs, a smirk cutting across her full lips. "Sounds right to me."

I roll my eyes as I reach my locker and stop to work the lock when I hear my name called from back down the corridor. "Brielle, babe. Wait up."

My cheeks blow out in frustration, and I let out a soft groan, hearing the familiar holler coming from Riley. I glance over my shoulder to find not only Riley barging through the crowd, shoving people out of his way, but Jax and Hudson right on his heels. Riley's brows raise as he catches my eye and puts up a hand, signaling for me not to take off before he gets a chance to say whatever it is he needs to say.

Ilaria laughs and presses her back against the locker beside mine, settling in for the show. "What was that thing Arizona was saying about his friends?"

"Don't even think about it," I mutter as Riley, Jax, and Hudson come barreling toward us, barely stopping before knocking us over.

"Yo, what's up?" Riley says, his lips pulling into their usual flirty smirk as my gaze roams over the subtle bruising around his eye, an after-effect of Tanner's temper tantrum at the track—something I could have avoided had I been quicker to handle it.

"What's up with you?" I question, eyeing Jax and Hudson, suspicious about what they could possibly want.

"I, uhhh, thought you were gonna take off."

I arch a brow before reaching in and grabbing my things from my locker, finding them exactly where I left them yesterday before I was dragged out of here. "Thought about it," I murmur, turning back to face Riley, willing the bell to sound. My gaze drops away and I stand awkwardly before them. "Look, I—"

"Don't stress," Riley says, reaching out and brushing the backs of his knuckles over the side of my cheek, a move that feels oddly intimate and has me shrugging back from his touch. "We're not here to give you a hard time. We know you had nothing to do with what happened to Addie. We just wanted to check on you, seeing as though Tanner ain't saying shit."

I glance away. "I'm fine."

"Really?" Jax mutters. "You can barely look us in the eyes. Two nights ago, we were chilling, discussing appropriate cum shot etiquette, and now you're acting like a fucking stranger. You're not fine."

"I'm fine."

"Bullshit."

I let out a heavy sigh and lean against my locker, holding my books to my chest as though they're some kind of security blanket. "What do you want me to say? My whole world is burning to ashes around me. My mom married Orlando, the whole school thinks I'm a rapist, and Tanner is … I don't know what he is, but *asshole* comes to mind."

Riley moves in closer, wanting our conversation to remain private. "What happened at the track," he starts, his lips pressing into a hard line. "You have to know he didn't mean it. He was just angry and didn't know how to control himself. Addison had just been attacked for a second time, and there wasn't anything he could do to help her. He's going through a lot and trying to protect everyone around him. He needs you, babe. Surely you know how much you mean to him. The things he said—"

"The things he said were unforgivable. They *hurt*, Riley. He hurt me just as he always promised he would. How am I supposed to come back from that?"

Hudson moves in closer, his heart on his sleeve. "Don't walk away from him," he murmurs, reaching for my hand and giving it a gentle squeeze. "You're the only person who can keep him grounded. Without you, I don't know if he can handle this."

I pull my hand out of his and indicate toward Riley's black eye. "I'm sorry you got hurt, but I can't willingly hand myself over to him knowing I'm going to get hurt. Especially now, after everything that went down yesterday. I can't be somebody else's rock when I can't even be one for myself."

Riley shakes his head. "That's just the thing," he murmurs. "You shouldn't have to be your own rock. You need him just as much as he needs you."

The heaviness of his words has me falling back a step, fear and unease weighing down on my chest, making it hard to breathe. I glance away, unable to handle the intensity of his stare as the bell sounds through the school, telling me to get my ass to homeroom. "I don't think you understand how much you're asking of me, Riley," I murmur, my gaze shifting over his shoulder to find Tanner moving in through the front entrance and striding down the corridor, his eyes already locked on mine. "If I allow myself to fall back into his arms, I will fall in love with him, and he will hold the power to destroy everything I am."

And with that, I turn on my heel and walk away, the fear of the unknown working its way into my body and sending my heart into overdrive.

CHAPTER 5

TANNER

Fuck this school and fuck Riley Sullivan. The bastard can go to hell.

It's been a long-ass day, watching Brielle get named and shamed for some fucked-up shit she had nothing to do with, but the moment the whispers hit me about what Riley said to her this morning … I could have strangled him. He's such a meddling bastard. I get his heart was in the right place and that he was looking out for a friend, but the asshole needs to keep his nose out of my business.

It's bad enough hearing what people are saying about her today but hearing them discuss Addison's attack so casually has me spiraling out of control. I'm going to break, and I'm trying to hold on to that sliver of consciousness, reminding me that if I lose control again, I'll lose Bri for good.

Don't get me wrong. All it took was one warning from me and the whispers about Brielle and Addie faded away, but the damage has already been done. The last thing I needed today was to hear that Riley has been trying to meddle in my relationship … or what's left of it.

Damn fucker. If he doesn't mind his own business, I'll have no other choice but to ram a goal post up his ass. Though something tells me, if he keeps getting in Brielle's face like he did this morning, she might beat me to it.

The thought of Killjoy has my gaze sailing across the school to the student parking lot, watching as she walks with Ilaria and Arizona toward her mom's beat-up, piece of shit car. Her head is down and I hate it. She rarely walks with her head down—she's the type to stand tall and proud, but today has kicked her ass. Hell, the past few days have kicked her ass and some of that blame rests on my shoulders.

I need to make this right with her. I need her to know what she means to me, and if she decides I'm all out of chances, then I have to find a way to change her mind. I'll never stop fighting for her.

Needing my head in the game for training, I force my stare to the football field before me. Hudson, Riley, and the twins are huddled in a tight group, and I've known these fuckers long enough to recognize when they're up to something. "Yo," Logan says, eyeing me over his brother's shoulder, a clear warning for the others to shut their mouths. "Where have you been?"

I shrug my shoulders and move closer to the guys, knowing damn well I'm not about to be let in on their conversation. "Whatever the fuck you're planning, forget about it. It ain't happening."

Jax scoffs, a smirk playing on his lips. "Right," he says before pulling away from the guys and moving toward the rest of our teammates. We all follow suit, and I can't help but glance up toward the student parking lot one more time. She hovers at her mom's car with the driver's door open as she talks to her friends, only her attention is on the field.

The moment she catches my stare, her gaze falls away and a pang of guilt and pain bursts through my chest. I'm an asshole.

I never should have said that shit to her. Never should have lost control.

Bri's expression hardens, and I watch as Ilaria and Arizona glance back over their shoulders, eyeing me with an odd reluctance. They have no idea what went down between us, though I know it won't be long. Those girls have a way of finding out the impossible. Hell, I should have put them in charge of finding Addie's rapist. They would have had the case closed before lunch and still had time to get their nails done.

Bri gets into the car, and I watch as her friends step away, giving her room to pull out of her parking space.

"MORGAN," my name is hollered across the field, and my gaze snaps toward Coach Wyld, finding a pissed-off expression across his aging face and the rest of my teammates already huddled around him, taking a knee. "Either get your head in the game or I'll find someone else who can."

Fuck.

"Sorry, Coach."

Hurrying along, I drop down beside Riley, and he gives me a hard stare before silently ramming his shoulder against mine. "The fuck is wrong with you?" he mutters, knowing damn well that Coach Wyld is going to have all our asses for my slight moment of distraction. When one of us fuck up, we suffer as a team.

My lips pull into a cringe. "Sorry, man," I murmur, turning my attention back to Wyld to listen to his rundown for the rest of our week.

"—versus Langford Boys Academy on Friday night. These assholes nearly got us last season, and I'm not about to let it happen again. You need to be ready. They have a strong defense, and their running back is like none other—" Wyld pauses before glancing toward Logan. "Sorry, kid. Just facts. He's good and he's in better shape than I've ever seen him. Scouts will be at this game, and I want their eyes on you, not him. You need to be ready."

Logan scoffs, the cockiness in his tone knowing no bounds. "You talking about Rockman?" he questions, watching Wyld's curt nod before his lips pull into a twisted smirk, looking more like his brother than ever before. "Oh, I'm ready. Fucker can't beat me. I've got this in the bag."

"Leave the attitude for the field, Logan," Wyld mutters before going over his game plan for today's session.

The moment he's done, he excuses the team to get started on their warmup, and just as I get back to my feet, he steps toward me. "Hold up, Morgan," he murmurs, his tone lowering.

My brows furrow, and I wait back as the rest of my teammates take off around the field. "What's up, Coach?" I ask, itching to take off. Coach Wyld rarely holds any of us back, but when he does, it's usually because he thinks we're in too deep.

"Heard what happened to your sister," he says. "How's she doing?"

My lips press into a hard line. "It's not looking great," I tell him, not bothering to sugarcoat it. "The fucker who hurt her is probably going to get away with it, and as for Addie being in a coma … I don't know. Her scans are looking good, but there's been nothing to suggest she's going to wake up. At least, not any time soon. Doctors are hopeful though."

"Shit, kid. You should have come and talked to me. I could have eased up on your training."

"With all due respect, Coach, that's exactly why I didn't tell you," I explain. "I don't need any favors, and right now, training with my team is one of the only things keeping my head on straight."

"You don't need to do that, Tanner," Coach murmurs, lowering his voice as the boys come heading back up the field. "You don't need to always have your shit together. You're allowed to break every now and then. No one is going to hold it against you if you want to sit out a few games."

I shake my head. "Being a mess at Addie's bedside ain't helping nobody," I tell him. She wouldn't want me to do that, and honestly, I don't think my mom could handle it either. With Dad still out on business, I'm all they've got.

"That's fair enough, but you need to watch yourself. Don't be taking any unnecessary risks," he warns. "Don't think for two seconds

I'm not aware of your illegal racing on the twins' property after game nights. You've always had your head screwed on right, Tanner, so I've let it go, but I don't want to see you end up wrapped around a tree and paralyzed because you needed an outlet. If you're going to keep training through this, then channel that recklessness into your game. Throw harder, run faster, be better, but don't be fucking stupid. You hear me?"

"Yeah, I hear you, Coach."

"Good, now do I even want to know why that girl you've been drooling over for the past few weeks was the one arrested for all of this?"

I shake my head, a flare of anger bursting through me. "She had nothing to do with it."

"Are you confident in that?" he questions, making me want to pulverize him. "She's new here. How well do you really know her?"

"She had nothing to do with it," I repeat, my tone full of venom. "She shouldn't have been arrested yesterday. I know exactly who attacked my sister, and one day soon, the bastard will get exactly what's coming for him."

"Don't do anything stupid, Tanner."

I scoff, wishing he'd release me to go warm up with the boys. The last thing I need is some fucked-up version of a therapy session from my coach. "Ain't no guarantees," I tell him, giving it to him straight. "If Colby Jacobs is stupid enough to show up here again, nothing will stop me from taking him out, and that's a promise."

Coach watches me for a moment, his eyes narrowing in thought.

"Jacobs?" he questions. "The captain of the Hope Falls team?" I nod and Coach glances out toward his players. "You've had issues with this kid before."

"That's right."

"Perhaps I should bench you for a few weeks," he murmurs, almost as if talking to himself. "We're still due to play Hope Falls later in the season. I can't risk having you on the field if that kid is playing."

"You want to punish me because he raped my sister?" I demand. "If anyone should be benched, it's Colby. I had to listen to her screaming for help over the phone while he forced himself inside her, and I couldn't do shit to save her. Now I'm the one who's gonna be benched? Fuck that. Colby raped her just to get at me. What happened to my sister is on my shoulders, and his lawyer is going to make sure he walks, so at the very least, the asshole should be suspended from playing for the rest of the season."

"I didn't mean that as a punishment, Tanner. I'm simply looking out for what's best for you. The last thing I want is to see you on my field beating the shit out of this kid for the world to see. You will not be throwing your future away on my watch. If skipping a few games doesn't sit right with you, then I'll figure out something else, but mark my words, Tanner, you will not be playing on the same field as Colby Jacobs."

I clench my jaw, fury burning through my veins. Taking Colby out on the field might have been my only chance to get close to him, but that simply means I have to get a little more creative. Whether Colby walks free or not, I'll still get my chance to wrap my fingers around his throat.

Watching me mentally shut down from the conversation, Coach curses and nods toward the rest of the team. "Go warm up, then we're running drills."

I don't bother with a response before taking off toward the guys, ignoring the stares from Hudson and Riley, knowing they're well aware of my conversation with Coach Wyld. Instead, I take off at a jog, pushing to the front of the group and forcing them all to pick up their pace.

Just as promised, we get stuck into drills, and two hours later, I'm fucking exhausted. Sweat drips from my brow as I make my way back into the locker room, the boys on my heels. Not gonna lie, training fucking sucked. Just as Coach said, I channeled the rage and recklessness inside of me into my training and used it to push myself harder. I flew up and down the field, letting it consume me. My passes were wild and my game was off, but once I was able to find control, I used it to my advantage. I was un-fucking-stoppable. That doesn't mean the anger is gone though.

As long as Colby is free, the anger won't subside, and as long he's trying to take my girl down with him, the fury will continue to burn.

Jax's hand comes down on my shoulder as I stop at my locker, more than ready to peel off my uniform and shower. "Whatever bullshit pep-talk Coach gave you worked like fucking magic," he says, moving past me toward his locker. "You were on fire out there."

"I'd hardly call it a fucking pep-talk," I mutter, gripping my jersey and pulling it up over my head, unable to handle much more after-training chatter than that. All I want is to get home and check in on Brielle, even if it means spying on her through the cracks of her Venetian blinds like a fucking creeper.

At the hard edge in my tone, all the guys look my way, but it's Riley who watches me the longest. "Yo, you good?" he questions.

I stare straight ahead at my locker, the conversation with Coach bringing up all the shit that I've been trying to squash all day. "Fine," I murmur, reaching for my towel and taking off toward the showers.

"Tanner?" Riley calls after me, the tone of his voice filled with the type of concern that has me desperate to escape. The last thing I want is to talk it out, and knowing Riley, that's exactly what he wants me to do. Hell, my version of therapy includes beating the shit out of heavy bags and clearing my head on a long ride. Talking it out only serves to piss me off more. Though lately, just being near one particular little killjoy seems to make me happier than anything has before. With her, everything is just … right.

Wanting to get home and put this day to rest, I make quick work of my shower. By the time I finish and wrap a towel around my waist, I find the guys huddled in the locker room, just as they were when I first walked out on the field. These fuckers are up to something, and my gut tells me I'm not going to like it.

When they spy me coming out of the showers, their conversation falls to silence, and I narrow my gaze, more than ready to drop a bastard if that's what I have to do. "Whatever it is," I say, reaching my locker, repeating the same words I'd said to them only two short hours ago, "forget about it."

Hudson chuckles under his breath and turns toward his locker. "You're always so suspicious of everyone, man. I wonder how life would look for you if you just allowed yourself to enjoy it."

"Fuck man," I scoff as I hastily dress. "Layering on the bullshit thick today."

Logan smirks and glances toward Hudson. "Yeah, that one made you sound like a fucking loser, dude. Ease up on the deep shit. Save it for when you're trying to get your dick wet. Chicks love a man in touch with his emotions."

Hudson scoffs. "I am not in touch with my emotions. Just saying it how it is."

Jax laughs and walks across the locker room butt naked, his dick swinging from left to right. He stops by Hudson's side and throws his arm over his shoulder before leaning into him and giving him a sappy smile. His hand drops to Hudson's chest and he bats his lashes. "Don't listen to them, I love a big strong man who's in touch with his emotions. It gets me hard every single time."

Hudson blanches at Jax and shoves him hard, sending him sailing across the locker room as Jax's booming laughter bounces off the walls. "Touch me with your dick out again and I'll fucking deck you."

Jax laughs as he balances himself and cups his dick, protecting it at all costs. After all, it wouldn't be the first time one of the guys has retaliated by taking aim at his cock, but Hudson wouldn't. He's not one to waste energy on stupid shit like this. It takes some real messed-up bullshit to get Hudson to snap.

Before Jax gets a chance to bait him again, I grab my shit out of my locker before turning to the guys. "I'm out," I tell them, still suspicious of whatever the fuck they're planning. "I'll catch you fuckers tomorrow."

And with that, I stride toward the door, looking back just in time to catch Riley glancing back toward the guys with a smirk cutting across his face. "It's so fucking on."

Well … shit.

CHAPTER 6

Brielle

Homework can kiss my ass. After being arrested yesterday and not getting a chance to complete my schoolwork last night, everything has started to pile up. I'm only one day behind on homework but it's enough to make my room look like it's been assaulted by a bookstore. Hell, the fact that I've been struggling to focus really isn't helping either.

I had a game plan for tonight; get in and get it done, but so far, all I seem capable of doing is sitting here and staring at the pages, wondering about the asshole next door. Today really sucked for me, but it couldn't have been easy for him either. The whole school was talking about his sister, and I'm sure every time he heard the word rape, memories of that night came flying back to him—storming into that room to find his sister on the ground, knowing he wasn't fast enough to help her.

Knowing Erica stood by while that was happening to Addison and did nothing to help her, just the thought of it makes me sick. Hell, even Colby. One minute he was raping Addison, and the next, he was taking my hand and dragging me out of the party as though he was looking out for me. Fuck, I hate them both, and one of these days they'll be prosecuted for what they did to Addison. I just have to somehow prove I had nothing to do with it first.

Frustration overwhelms me, and I let out a heavy breath before rubbing my hands over my face and falling back onto my bed. This is useless. I'm not getting anywhere. I can't focus on a damn thing while my fate is still in the hands of a bunch of cops who can't see what's right in front of them.

How the hell did it come to this? Just as my life was starting to turn around. I had Tanner right where I wanted him, and given enough time, I could have fallen madly in love, but this? If I get charged for the assault on Addison, we'll never be able to see through this fog … not that I should want to try. Not after what he said to me at the track. I can't help but crave him though. Every moment of every day, I'm pining for him. Every chance I get, I'm staring out my window, hoping for just a glance at him, checking in to make sure he's doing okay.

I'm a woman obsessed.

Mom called me down for dinner half an hour ago, but after her dismissal yesterday and the memory of her hand stinging the side of my face, I can't bring myself to go downstairs and play the part of her doting daughter. It's all an act to her. She wants to appear as the world's best mom in front of her piece of shit husband, and I'm done letting her use me to make it happen. When I got home from school today she didn't even look at me, and after everything that's been going on, her dismissal was a relief.

My phone buzzes on my bedside table, and I groan as I roll to grab it before flopping back against the pillow and holding it above my head. There's an unread text and I quickly click on it, assuming it's Ilaria or Arizona checking in, but as I open it, regret slams through me like a freight train.

Erica - Please talk to me. We've been friends for too long to let this come between us. It was a mistake. I'm so sorry. I don't know what I was thinking. I was desperate and I knew you'd be okay. You have Channing on your side, but if I go down for this, I'll never recover. Please, Bri. You have to believe me. You're my best friend. We can get past this.

She has got to be fucking kidding me.

A laugh bubbles up my throat and my finger hovers over the delete button, only I resist. She didn't exactly admit to what she'd done in the message but I'm sure it could be used as some kind of proof to win my freedom.

A moment of weakness comes over me and I consider responding, but I won't dare offer her the relief of her own guilty conscience. She seriously screwed me over when she sat in that interrogation room and put the blame on me. I don't care if she truly did think I'd be let off with nothing more than a slap on the wrist, I'm not going down for this. No way in hell. Was it not enough that she was fucking my boyfriend behind my back?

I toss my phone to the end of my bed, and just as I start to convince myself to attempt my homework again, my bedroom door flies open. My head whips around, my eyes bugging out of my head as a gasp sails from my throat.

Riley smirks as he storms into my bedroom.

"What the fuck are you—"

It's too late. The big asshole grabs me, hauling me off my bed and over his shoulder without breaking a damn sweat. "What the hell?" I screech, trying to free myself. Only the big jock-sock locks his strong arm over the back of my legs, pinning me in place.

His hand spanks my ass. "Sorry, babe. Duty calls." And with that, he storms out of my room like a fucking hurricane and skips down the stairs two at a time. I scream, certain that today is going to be my last day on earth. Riley is a cool guy and has a big heart, but I don't trust him one bit, especially not while running down the stairs with me over his shoulder. Who the hell does that?

"Brielle?" I hear my mother's curt tone booming through the lower portion of Orlando's mansion. "What on earth is the meaning of this? Put my daughter down this instant."

Ahhh, fuck.

"RUN, RILEY. RUUUUUNNNNNNN!"

Riley's booming laugh tears through the mansion, and I grip onto his sides as he flies out the front door, my ribs aching, but damn it, it's worth it to get out of here. "BRIELLE," my mom screeches after us, the anger in her tone sending a wave of exhilaration pulsing through my veins.

The door slams behind Riley as I laugh, the excitement of my breakout sending a thrill shooting through my veins, only it falls away the second I realize Riley is cutting across the lawn and onto Tanner's property, rather than heading for his truck that's parked on the curb.

"Riley," I warn, pulling against his tight grip on my body. "Where are you taking me?"

He cackles like a little bitch, and I drum my fists against his back, panic searing through my chest as he races up toward the front door of Tanner's home. "Damn it, Riley. Put me down. I am not going in there."

"And I'm not spending another day being the awkward buffer between you and Tanner," he tells me, grabbing the door handle and giving it a quick twist. "You two are clearly crazy about one another, and you're both too fucking stubborn to admit it, so you've left me no choice."

Riley pushes through the front door and heads straight for the stairs. "I swear to God, Riley. Turn your bitch ass around right now. Otherwise, I'll have no choice but to drop you again."

"Ahhhh," he says, a chuckle in his tone. "But you'd have to catch me first, and unfortunately for you, with these tiny little legs, you're just not quick enough to catch a stud like me."

"RILEY!"

He booms down the hallway, murmuring something about Flash

2.0, and all too soon, Tanner's dreaded bedroom door appears. Riley wastes no time barging through it, and I cringe hearing Tanner across the room. "The fuck are you doing?" Tanner demands. "Get your dirty fucking hands off my girl."

"Your girl? You've got a lot of nerve calling me your girl, Jockstrap," I say to Riley's ass, my head spinning from hanging upside down. I can't see anything, so I shove my elbow into Riley's ass and push against it, using it to prop myself up while secretly loving the way Riley groans with pain.

Tanner is across the room, glaring daggers at me, and I glare straight back, fighting my desire to run to him. I would love to bask in the safety of his strong arms, but I'd also love to tear his boxers up over his head until he cries like a little bitch.

Riley smacks my ass and grips me around the waist before hauling me off his shoulder. He puts me back on my feet and holds me against his chest, letting me regain my balance. "I've always wondered what it'd be like to have you take a ride on the Riley express, but this wasn't exactly what I had in mind."

Tanner steps into my back, placing his hands just below Riley's on my waist and yanks me back away from him. "I told you to get your fucking hands off my girl."

Riley just smirks as I whip around and shoot daggers at Tanner. "What did I say about calling me your girl? I'm not your fucking gi—"

"See that's just the thing," Riley sings from behind me, slowly backing away until he's standing in the open door, his fingers hovering over the handle. "You are his girl. I know it, the boys know it, the whole fucking school seems to know it apart from you two. You're both too fucking stubborn to try and make it work." He glances at Tanner. "You're too busy fucking moping about with your dick in your hand, and you," he says, looking back at me, "are too busy punishing him over what he said that you can't see how fucking sorry he is. So, until you two can figure it out, you're not coming out of this room, even if it means locking you in here for days on end. We're fucking prepared. We brought snacks."

"Who's *we?*" Tanner snaps.

Riley grins wide and nods toward the window, so smug with himself, it makes me want to pour milkshakes down his throat for hours on end, just to watch as his stupid lactose intolerant body begins to fail him and gives him the worst case of diarrhea known to man.

Tanner and I spin around to see Jax outside Tanner's window, his hands gripping the glass, that same smug expression written across his face, showing that this bullshit has been planned out. "Sorry, fuckers," he says, his fingers playing with the lock just inside the window. He glances toward Tanner. "You brought this shit on yourself. She's a fucking firecracker, and if you don't hold on to her, then you better be prepared for someone else to take your place."

And with that, Jax gives one more dopey grin before closing the window, making sure it clicks into place, the key nowhere to be seen. He gives me a curt nod and laughs before sliding down the roof and disappearing out of sight.

I spin around and storm toward Riley, knowing damn well what he plans to do. "No, absolutely not. You cannot lock me in here with that donkey fucker."

"Donkey fucker?" Tanner demands, making no attempt to try and do anything about this situation.

I glare at him and let out a huff. "Will you do something about this?"

Tanner shrugs his shoulders, looking as though he's almost enjoying this. "What can I do? I'm nothing but a donkey fucker."

I groan, my frustration getting the better of me. "You are infuriating, Tanner Morgan," I spit before looking back at Riley. "Let me out of here right now, and I won't tie you down and pluck every single one of your pubes with a pair of rusty tweezers, even the ones up under your ball sack."

"Ooooh," Riley says, his eyes lighting with excitement. "I just got a little hard. I'm not letting you out of here, but after you and asswipe have made up, do you think we could give it a try anyway? I promise, I'll only scream if you want me to."

"Get the fuck out of here," Tanner grunts.

Riley nods and steps back out of Tanner's room. "My pleasure." He pulls the door closed, and I listen as he locks it from the outside. "I'm ordering dinner. I'll bring it up when it gets here," he calls through the closed door. "Oh, and we'll be downstairs, so if you crazy little monkeys decide to get it on, can you screw loud enough so we can hear? I need something to visualize while I'm jerking off on your mom's good couch."

Tanner clenches his jaw and grabs one of his textbooks off his desk and launches it at the closed door. We hear Riley's gasp followed by a booming laugh as he takes off down the hall, and the moment his laugh fades away and we're truly alone, a strange tension fills the air.

Tanner leans back against his desk, bracing himself as I stand awkwardly in the middle of his room. I don't say a word, but the weight of his stare is enough to drive me insane. I can't do this. There's too much to talk through, and I'm not even a little bit ready.

Turning on my heel, I storm toward his private bathroom and glance up at the small window above the toilet. Maybe Riley isn't as bright as he thinks he is. It'll be tight, but with the right amount of wriggling, I should be able to free myself from this hell. It won't be my finest hour, but it's better than being trapped in here with Tanner.

Now, the only question is, how the hell do I get up there? Stupid rich people and their high ceilings. I might just be able to reach it by standing on the toilet, but even then, I probably don't have the strength to haul myself up and through it. Hell, not to mention what will happen when I reach the other side. Am I setting myself up to fall to my death?

What have I got to lose?

Bracing my hand against the cold tiles, I step onto the toilet and reach up to the window, only just managing to get my fingers around the bottom of the glass to open it.

"Really?" Tanner asks. "That's your grand plan?"

"Better than being trapped in here with you."

"Me being the donkey fucker?"

Rolling my eyes, I glance back over my shoulder at the asshole, hating just how good he looks as he braces himself against the doorframe with just a sliver of skin showing at the bottom of his shirt. My mouth waters. I hate how attracted I am to him. If he wasn't my cup of tea, hating him would come so much easier. "Shut up about the donkey fucker. It's all I could think of, but if you prefer, I could go back to calling you jockstrap. Take your pick."

Tanner groans. "Would you get down from there? You're going to fall."

"Oh, that's nice you actually care. And here I was thinking that I'm just some bitch you fuck every now and then," I say, repeating his insults from the track.

Tanner sighs and pushes off the doorframe before striding toward me. He reaches up and curls his arms around me, yanking me off the top of the toilet before moving to the counter and dropping my ass to the edge of the expensive marble. He pushes between my legs, his big fingers curling around the back of my neck and forcing my eyes to his.

Silence surrounds us as I'm left to drown in his intense stare. My heart races and I know I'm going to break. He's too much, too important. How did I let him become my world like this?

Tanner's thumb trails along the side of my jaw, and all I can think about is the way he held me in his arms last night. I didn't ask him to come over, but he did anyway. He knew how much I needed him, and despite everything, he was still there for me. Despite everything … he owns my heart.

"Tanner," I whisper, reaching up and stopping his thumb from moving across my jaw, feeling the seriousness of our situation weighing down on me, all insults and jokes aside. "We can't do this. You're going to break me, and I … I can't handle it. I won't survive it."

He shakes his head, refusing to accept this is over, and honestly, I don't want him to. I want him to fight for us because, as much as I know we won't work together, I also know living without him might just hurt me more. I'm not ready to give up on this, even though I know I should. "Don't say that," he says, moving in even closer so that our bodies are pressed together, his heart beating right alongside mine. "What I said at the track, you have to know I didn't mean it. You and me … you're so much more to me than just the new girl next door, and I'll do whatever it takes for you to understand that."

"Tanner …"

"Don't give up on us," he begs. "I know we never had the big defining conversation and put a title on what this is, but I know you feel it just as much as I do. You know this is real and I'm not ready for it to be over. I'm not giving up. Give me a chance, Killer. Let me make it up to you. I fucked up out on that track. I should have leaned on you. I should have trusted that you would be able to ground me like you did that night on my bike, but instead, I wanted everyone to hurt like I was, and in that moment, nothing else mattered. I couldn't control myself. All I could see was Addison in the hospital and everything inside of me broke."

Tanner pauses and drops his forehead to mine, his chest heaving with heavy breaths. "Please, Killer," he whispers. "Give me a chance to make this right. I know I don't deserve you, and I know just how badly I screwed up. But the thought of you walking away before we even get a chance to see where this could go … fuck, Bri. I don't want to live in a world where I don't have you beside me."

My gaze drops as his hands fall to my shoulders and slowly make their way down to my hands, clutching them tight as though he'll never let them go. "You said all I'll ever be is a whore shaking her ass for a dollar."

Tanner cringes, his whole face scrunching with pain. "Fuck, babe," he says, his grip tightening on my hands as his forehead drops to my shoulder. "Surely you know I don't really think that. Just the thought of another man looking at you tears me to shreds."

"You said I was the reason you weren't at the hospital with Addison," I remind him. "I know that's not true and that you were just trying to lash out to ease your own guilt, but words like that sting, Tanner. Do you have any idea how much guilt I've carried over that? I never asked you to stay with me, and I sure as hell would never try to take you away from the time you spend with your sister."

Tanner grabs my face, forcing my eyes to his as he holds me close, his lips barely a whisper from mine. "I know that," he insists. "Trust me, I fucking know that, and I will never stop being sorry for everything I said, and I sure as fuck won't apologize for spending the night with you, especially after Colby wrapped you around a fucking tree. That was my decision and mine alone. The blame is on me. I never should have said that to you."

I shake my head, agreeing with him wholeheartedly. "You couldn't have known Colby was going to attack your sister. You can't blame yourself for not being able to predict the future. He snuck into her room the minute your mom stepped out, so whether you were there or not, he still would have found his moment to attack."

Tanner presses his lips into a hard line. "I should have been there."

"Don't do that to yourself," I tell him. "I know you want to always protect the people you care about, but you can't always be everybody's hero. The world doesn't work like that."

He lets out a heavy sigh, refusing to hear me. "Tell me you'll forgive me, or at the very least, that it's not over."

I lean into him and press my lips to his ever so gently, wanting so much more but refusing to allow it. I pull back, breaking our kiss. "It's not over, Tanner," I tell him, my hands finding his again. "How could it ever be over?"

His brows furrow, searching my eyes. "But yesterday before class, you said—"

"I know what I said," I tell him, remembering the exact moment I told him I was done. "But that doesn't mean you're off the hook. You hurt me, Tanner. You lost control and used me as your punching bag, and I can't just forget the things you said to me. You broke me, and it's going to take time for that to heal. But I understand your situation, and while I want to pulverize you into dust right now, I also don't think it's completely fair to hold it against you. It was a mistake made out of desperation, and I just hope the next time you lose control, you'll have the sense to work with me, rather than against me."

"I swear to you, Killjoy," he promises. "No matter what happens between you and me or with my sister, I won't lose control like that again."

"You can't promise me that, especially now that everything is getting even more screwed up."

His lips press into a hard line and he nods. "Maybe not," he says, understanding the situation all too well. "But I can promise to work on myself. I saw how much I hurt you, and trust me, it didn't feel good. I don't ever want to make you feel like that again."

I nod and bring his hands to my chest, needing him close. "I'm not ready to just jump straight back into where we were before."

"I get it," he says. "You need time, but at least now I know I can sneak into your room without getting my head chopped off."

An ugly scoff catches in my throat. "Don't count on it," I laugh.

Tanner leans into me and presses his lips to mine. "Don't act like you don't love it," he laughs, wrapping his arms around me and lifting me off the counter. He walks out of the bathroom, and we crash onto his bed, my arms wrapped tightly around his neck. Tanner kisses me again, much deeper than before, and it's just enough to satisfy the need I've felt for him over the past few days.

I've been such a mess. My life has been rapidly falling apart, but now with Tanner back in my arms and the promise of trying again, a little flame of hope ignites within me. As long as I have him at the end of the day, I know that whatever I must face with Erica and Colby's false allegations, I'll be alright.

Not wanting to push his luck, Tanner pulls back and meets my stare as he braces himself on his elbows above me, the rest of our limbs tangled in a desperate mess. "We're going to be okay, Bri."

My lips press into a hard line, the weight of my situation coming back to me. "I don't know," I tell him. "Orlando is refusing to take my case because it's a conflict of interest with Colby, and my mom … she thinks I really had something to do with it, no matter how many times I go over it. She's already treating me like a criminal."

"The fuck do you mean he won't take your case?" Tanner demands, grabbing me and rolling us until I'm straddled over his hips. "He won't drop Colby as a client to defend you?"

I shake my head. "Nope. Apparently, Colby's case is big enough to have his name in lights. He's doing it all for publicity, but he said he'd set me up with someone else."

"That's not the point," he says. "He married your mom. He should have your back no matter what."

"You'd think," I scoff. "I can't wait 'til my brother gets back from boot camp. He'd have no issue putting Orlando in his place for this. Hell, Mom and Erica too."

"Is it true Erica set you up? I thought maybe Colby had done it."

"Nope," I say. "Well … kinda. He confirmed Erica's story, but she's the one who gave them my name. I saw the footage of her statement. She completely threw me under the bus and fabricated evidence to go along with it. I can prove she was lying, but it doesn't make it suck any less." I let out a heavy breath before meeting his gaze again. "On the plus side, the detective told me they were able to match Colby's DNA to the rape kit they took from Addison and was confident he'd go down for it. Though, he was also confident that I'd go down for it. He was claiming I was in the room with Colby and just sat back and watched it all go down. They think I put him up to it."

Tanner sits up and rests against the headboard of his bed, pulling me into his chest and holding me tight. "Don't worry, Bri. We're going to get this sorted out, and Colby is going to suffer for it. I swear to you, I won't let anything happen to you. You're not going down for this."

I nod against his chest just as we hear the faintest click of the lock. The door creaks open and Riley's head pokes through the small gap, his eyes brimming with hesitation. "I haven't heard any screaming," he says, his gaze narrowing as he looks at us on the bed.

"You better be here to free us, otherwise, I'm going to castrate you," I warn him.

His hand slips through the gap and he holds out a takeout container. I immediately smell noodles and my stomach growls after skipping dinner with my mom. "I thought you guys might be hungry, but seeing as though things are looking better, maybe you'd wanna join me? Jax bailed twenty minutes ago, and I've been sitting downstairs by myself. Though, I haven't heard any fucking yet ... so maybe things aren't going as well as I thought."

I roll my eyes and climb off Tanner's lap before barging past Riley and grabbing the noodles in the process. "Things were going just fine until you shoved your big head through the door," I tell him. "And for the record, you're lucky I'm hungry, otherwise, your balls would be mine."

Riley grins wide, reminding me that the fucker must be into some twisted kinks. And with that, I make my way downstairs with the boys on my heels, my stomach rumbling, and my shattered heart slowly piecing itself back together.

CHAPTER 7

TANNER

Logan's good, I'll give him that.

I watch him through the rearview mirror as his black Camaro tears around the track behind me. The dirt from my tires cloud around him, almost like an insult. He's the only competitor who's ever been able to stay so close on my ass, the only one to give me a run for my money, but he's never been able to beat me.

We do the same dance every few months when Logan's ego outgrows his abilities. He gets in my face and forces me onto the track, and I oblige simply to remind him why I still hold the title. He wants to be the best, he craves it, but it's nothing but a title for him, which is why he'll never take it from me. For me, this is the fucking air I breathe. The speed, the adrenaline, the win. It comes as easy as waking up in the morning. Whether I'm on my bike or in the Mustang, I will always win.

And Logan fucking hates it.

A laugh rumbles up my chest as I catch the slightest glimpse of his expression through the rearview mirror, and all too soon, the dust cloud from my tires completely claims him. I shouldn't gloat, but I can't help it. Logan is such a sore loser when it comes to racing. He's going to spend the rest of his night sulking. Not even Chanel will be able to pull him out of this one. Hell, tonight was game night and we dominated. Logan was on fire, more so than usual. It's as though he were one with the ball. Langford Boys Academy didn't stand a chance with Logan on the field, and it's the cockiness from tonight's win that prompted this race. He simply doesn't know when to stop.

My gaze falls from the rearview mirror as I reach the top of the track, and I immediately find Brielle in the crowd. She stands with her friends and the boys, her sharp glare already locked on mine. She hasn't even begun to forgive me a little bit, but just the fact that she's willing to try is enough for me.

She holds my stare, her arms crossed over her chest as though she'd rather be anywhere but here. Her only problem is that she can fool everyone around her but me. Her thighs press together, and the longer she feels my returning stare, the more hooded her eyes become. She fucking loves this little game of cat and mouse we play. She can't resist it, just as I can't resist her.

The momentum of my Mustang speeding past her nearly knocks her off her feet. It sends a wave of exhilaration across her face, and she lives for it, which only makes me want her more.

She's a fucking spitfire. A goddess. Even when her stare is so fucking lethal it kills.

I fly around the top half of the track, easing up on the gas for just a moment to let Logan think he has a chance. He barrels in beside me, and just when he thinks he'll pass, I hit it hard, shooting the Mustang out in front, and crossing the finish line first, each of us beating our personal best times.

I hit the brakes and stop just in time before running headfirst into the flood of Bradford's most delinquent seniors. Before I even get my door open, they're already surrounding me, their cheers loud enough to vibrate through the car. I'm yanked out of the Mustang as bodies crowd me, but I'm only interested in one person.

Weaving through the crowd, I make my way to Logan, who's getting just as much attention as I am. After all, he was the king of tonight's game, and that win puts us one step closer to claiming the championship, a feat no one's going to dismiss simply because I kicked his ass on the track. "You good, bro?" I ask, stepping into his side and clapping my hand on his shoulder, trying to hold back my smirk at the venomous glare he shoots my way.

Logan shrugs off my hand. "Just once," he says, "it'd be nice to see you in my rearview mirror."

"You and I both know that'll never happen," I laugh as we make our way through the crowd, heading back toward our usual spot where we know we'll find everyone waiting for us.

"It'll happen," he assures me. "You can't be the reigning champion forever."

"Watch me."

Logan rolls his eyes as I watch up ahead and see the four girls cutting across the track. I nod toward them, catching Logan's attention. "You saw Chanel during that race, right?" I question, a smirk cutting across my face. "She was about ready to put her ass in the air, waiting for you to come ram her from behind, car and all."

Logan shoves me hard. "Fuck off, man," he mutters, his gaze shifting to the ground, but not quick enough to hide the cheesy-as-fuck grin stretching across his face. This asshole has got it bad. "Better than having my girl look like she wanted to stab me through the eye."

I shake my head. "Don't go worrying yourself about me and Brielle. We'll be fine. Besides, the best part about a fight is the angry make-up sex afterward."

Logan scoffs. "Assuming she's the type to go for angry make-up sex. Some chicks aren't into it. Who knows. Maybe she'll prefer to talk it out instead."

A shiver of fear trails down my spine at the thought, but I quickly shake it off. Logan's wrong. I know Killjoy better than I know myself, despite only being in her life for a few weeks. She's the type to want angry sex, followed by make-up sex, and then a splash of *we're all good* sex to finish it off. And just to make a point, she'll probably demand a bit of *just because I said so* sex in the middle of the night, and I am more than okay with that.

"Truth be told," I say, watching her every step. "As long as I get to call her mine at the end of the day, I'm good. You though, I don't know if Chanel is going to afford you the same luxury."

Logan clenches his jaw and is about to throw shade right back at me when a girl steps in front of me, her hands bracing against my chest and forcing me to stop. "Hey Tanner," she says, looking up with big doe eyes as though she doesn't already know I'm into Bri.

My face twists with the horrid reminder of how I used this girl to make Bri jealous, and my dick all but shrivels up inside me. I shove her hands off me and force her back a step. "What do you want, Jules?" I ask, glancing over her head to where Bri makes herself comfortable against Jax's Silverado, her eyes narrowing on the back of Jules' head.

She tries to move into me again as Logan continues up the hill to our spot, deciding I should deal with this shit on my own. "I thought you'd be down to hang out," she purrs, reaching for my chest again. "You know, now that whore is out of the way and going down for what she did to your sister."

I move closer to her, anger spiking deep in my gut. "The fuck did you say to me?"

Jules flinches, confusion spreading across her face. Her brows furrow and she nervously raises her chin to meet my stare. "I just thought maybe you'd need some company tonight. We can go out into the woods, and I'll give you anything you want. I swear, after I'm through with you, that whore will be the last thing on your mind."

"Brielle didn't hurt my sister," I growl, my tone lowering with venom. "And if you ever disrespect her again, I'll tear you to shreds with my fucking teeth. Is that clear?"

Jules' eyes bug out of her head, but I have no time for it, especially when Brielle is waiting for me. I move around her, and before I even get two steps away, Jules seems to have recovered. "Don't you walk away from me, Tanner Morgan. That girl is trash," she calls after me, her voice loud enough to travel up the hill to where Brielle is standing, leaving me no choice but to turn back around. "When will you get it? She's not good enough for you. None of these bitches are. She's a Hope Falls gold-digger just like her mom, and she has her claws so deep inside you that you can't even tell your head from your ass. She's dragging you down, and whether she gets charged for what happened to your sister or not, she'll never be able to move past it. Everyone will always remember her as the chick who raped Addison, no matter what."

I clench my jaw, my hands shaking with anger. "Are you done?" I question, trying to swallow down the rage. I promised Bri that I would work on myself, that I wouldn't lose control like I did last week, and I'm sure as hell not about to fuck with that.

"Done?" Jules laughs. "Not even close. I won't be done until you finally see that she's not right for you. She's a social climber, but she'll never be what you need. Not like I am. You and I both know it. There's a status-quo around here, and you need to stick to your own kind." Jules pauses and takes a step toward me, her eyes softening with desire as she attempts to touch me again. "That night you asked me to come over. You wanted me. I saw it in your eyes. Just admit it. There's no logical reason for you to be holding back from me. We'd be perfect together."

A wave of blonde hair cuts in front of me, and before I get a chance to respond, Brielle's shoving into Jules' shoulders so hard the bitch goes flying back. Jules screams as my brows fly up, and not a second later, Jules falls to the ground, her ass landing hard with a heavy thump.

"What the fuck is wrong with you?" Brielle demands, hovering over Jules as she stares up at her in shock. A roar of laughter comes from the top of the hill, Jax and Riley's tones the loudest of them all, but Bri doesn't seem to notice. "No means no. If this were the other way around and you weren't such a thirsty hoe for my boyfriend, you'd be the first to claim he was sexually harassing you. Read the fucking room, whorebag. He's not interested."

Brielle spins around, her cheeks red with frustration as she grips my hand and storms away. I laugh and her sharp gaze snaps up to mine. "What?" she spits.

"Boyfriend?"

Brielle rolls her eyes and keeps marching back toward our group, dragging me along beside her. "Would you have preferred I called you the bastard next door or a regular donkey fucker?"

I stop walking and pull back on her hand, circling her until she crashes right into my chest. Using my other hand, I take her chin between my fingers and raise her gaze to meet mine. I lower my voice, making sure I have her undivided attention. "You called me your boyfriend."

Brielle huffs and glances away. "It was the only title I could think of to lay claim on your stupid ass so that dumb bitch would see that we're more than just ... I don't know what. But don't get things twisted here, just because I'm giving you a chance to make things right, doesn't mean I'm automatically yours."

"I know that," I tell her, snaking my arm around her waist, "but that doesn't mean that hearing that word on your pretty lips didn't get me hard as fuck."

Her gaze drops between us, and just to prove my point, I gently grind my hips and let her feel just how worked up she's got me. A devilish grin cuts across her face as she raises her gaze back to mine. "Sucks to be you, doesn't it?" she tells me, her eyes sparkling with mirth. "I hope you enjoy blue balls."

And with that, she releases my hand and steps out of my arms before heading straight back up the hill to our group.

I follow behind her, my stare glued to her perfect ass, unable to stop picturing the way it looks when I fuck her from behind. She's got me right where she wants me. When this whole thing started, we were playing by my rules, but now, I'm not even sure we're playing the same game. Brielle Ashford now holds every last card in the palm of her hand, but I wouldn't have it any other way.

Fuck, I'm such a sucker for this chick. I don't even recognize myself anymore. But if I'm completely honest, I think I like who I am with her. She makes me feel as though I have the whole fucking world at my feet. As though I could take on anything and survive.

I reach the top of the hill just in time to catch the end of Riley's question. "—your ribs healing?"

I drop down beside Jax who has some random chick on his lap and glance toward Bri as she raises the side of her tank, showing off the bruises left by Colby's boot. The sight of the marks that fucker left on her body sends pain slicing through me, and the guys must feel the same because I hear them sucking sharp breaths through their teeth.

Bri shrugs her shoulders. "It still hurts like a bitch," she says, settling her tank back into place, "but it's easier to manage now. I think the bruising makes it look worse than it really is."

"Fuck, babe," Jax says, his arm tightening around the random chick, who eats up his affection like a fucking buffet. "Are you sure you should be out tonight? Don't try to bluff us. We've all had broken ribs, plenty of them, and they fucking suck. I know that's hurting more than you're letting on."

Bri shakes her head. "Honestly, I'd rather sit here in pain with you guys than be stuck at home with my mom. At least you guys have the decency to believe I didn't hurt Addison."

Hudson leans forward in his chair, his elbows braced against his knees as he briefly glances toward me. He holds my stare for a moment before he swivels his gaze back to Bri. "Your mom really thinks you did it?"

She falls back against Jax's Silverado, propping her foot against the tire. "I don't know. It's been so hard to read her lately. All week she's been looking at me like I'm a stranger and there's this disgust in her eyes. She hasn't outright accused me of anything after we talked it all through, but I can't help but feel that she thinks I'm guilty."

"Shit," Ilaria murmurs from beside her as she reaches for another drink. "You can always come and stay with me. We have a pool house. It's full of Mom's old crap, but we can clear it out if you want to stay."

"Thanks," she says, giving Ilaria a tight smile while the idea of her moving away makes something ache in my chest. "I'll keep that in mind, but honestly, I think a big move like that might make things worse."

"Okay, well the offer still stands. There's no expiration on that," Ilaria says as Chanel and Arizona nod in agreement, wanting what's best for Brielle.

"You know," Riley says in a tone that has me sighing as he smirks at my girl. "You have a bruise. I have a bruise. We were practically made for one another. So, if you really do wanna find somewhere to crash, my place is looking pretty fucking good."

I shoot him a hard stare, but the fucker just grins back at me, knowing all too well how to push my buttons.

Asshole.

Bri though, she doesn't even crack a smile at his stupid joke. Instead, her gaze falls to the ground, almost as though she's trying to fade away. Nobody even seems to notice, but I notice every fucking thing she does.

My brows furrow as I move across the grass and rest my hands on her shoulders, brushing my thumb across her soft skin. "Hey," I murmur, her stare lifting to mine. "What's wrong?"

She shakes her head, her hand coming to rest over mine on her shoulder, and honestly, I'm not entirely sure she's aware she's done it. "Nothing, I just … all this talk about my mom and Addison—"

"It's heavy," I finish for her.

Bri nods and I pull her into my chest, wrapping her in my arms and hoping I can somehow ease her pain. "I haven't been able to stop thinking about it all week," she murmurs into my chest, her words muffled by my shirt, keeping our conversation private. "Every day it's just … always on my mind, and I can't seem to shake it. It's turning me into a moody bitch. This isn't who I am, Tanner. Pushing Jules like that, that's not me. Not to mention, I've been snappy with everyone, especially you."

"To be fair, I kinda deserve it," I tell her. "Though, just for the record, watching you get all worked up is hot as fuck."

I can almost feel the way she rolls her eyes. "You're not supposed to be getting off on my pain," she mutters, her tone filled with irritation, but the grin stretching across her face tells a different story.

"You wanna get out of here?" I ask, my hand moving over her back. "You can crash at my place if you don't want to go home. Or I can stay with you at yours."

She shakes her head. "No, it's fine. It's your big night. You just won your game and kicked Logan's ass on the track. I don't want you cutting your night short for me. You should stay and enjoy yourself."

"No amount of wins can make me enjoy my night while you're over there in your own personal hell," I tell her. "Besides, I'd prefer to take you back to my place, and if you're lucky, I might even show you a few tricks I've learned to help get your mind off things."

Her brow arches and she glances up at me. "Oh, yeah?" she questions. "What kind of tricks could the famous Tanner Morgan possibly know that he hasn't already shown me?"

"Don't you worry your gorgeous little head about that," I say, a grin pulling at my lips. "I've got all sorts of tricks hidden up my sleeve, tricks that will blow your mind."

"And here I was thinking you were nothing but muscles and a pretty face," she says, stretching up onto her tippy toes, her eyes locked on mine, hooded and full of desire. "But for the record, it's not my mind that needs to be blown."

Well fuck.

Her wish is my command.

CHAPTER 8
Brielle

The Mustang idles in Tanner's driveway, and I go to reach for the door when his fingers gently curl around my elbow. "Hold up a second," Tanner murmurs, his tone stopping me faster than his hold ever could.

I pause and let my hand fall from the door. We're cloaked in darkness from the starless sky, and the subtle lines on his face are impossible to read, even in the close confines of the Mustang.

It's well after one in the morning, and it's been one hell of a long night. While our friends are still out, determined to party into the early hours of Saturday morning, I couldn't be happier to be home … at least, home with Tanner. The last thing I want is to walk back into Channing's mansion and have to pretend it feels like home to me.

Pretend the stranger wearing my mother's face isn't one of the people helping to burn my world to ashes. Pretend as though every time I step through that door a little piece of my heart doesn't die.

The ride home was silent, and I couldn't help but wonder if Tanner was purposely taking his time. The further we drove, the more he seemed to sink inside his own head, hostage to his thoughts, and it killed me wanting to know what was going on. I suppose I won't have to wait long to find out.

I twist in my seat, getting comfortable as his hand falls from my elbow and drops to my thigh.

"What's up?" I ask, my eyes locked on his through the darkness.

Tanner shakes his head and reaches for me with both hands, gripping my waist and hauling me over the center console until I'm perfectly straddled over his lap, being careful not to jostle me in any way that's going to send a wave of pain shooting through my healing ribs. Both his hands rest at my waist, his thumbs slowly brushing over my skin, leaving a trail of goosebumps. "I hate that we're not together," he tells me, his voice thick with regret as those dark eyes pierce right through to my soul, holding me captive in the best way.

I sink into him, my heart shattering for having to keep him at an arm's distance when we both know that's not really what I want, and it sure as hell isn't what I need, but I simply can't risk it. He has the power to break me like no other, and until I'm confident that won't happen again, I can't risk my heart. "I know," I tell him, my fingers threading through his, holding on to him with everything I am, desperate for the way he makes me feel so at ease. Without even trying, he has the ability to calm me, to be the light in the middle of a hurricane. "But if you want to be technical, we were never actually together in the first place. You were just the asshole next door who couldn't resist me, no matter how hard you tried."

Tanner's lips pull into a smirk. "You've never been so wrong," he tells me, his eyes sparkling with silent laughter. "We have been together since the moment you told me to shove Riley's cock down my throat, you just didn't know it."

A laugh bubbles up my throat as I lean into him, brushing my lips over his. "Ahhh, so is that all it takes to convince the King of Bradford to stop being such a manwhore playboy? Interesting. Who would have known the thought of sucking off your best friend was such a turn-on for you."

Tanner's eyes bug out of his head as he tightens his arms around me, pulling me closer to his body. "That's not what I meant, and you know it," he says. "It's that smart fucking mouth of yours."

"Oh yeah?" I question. "Is that all?"

"It's so much more," he murmurs, his eyes sparkling as his hands trail down my back to grab my ass, firmly squeezing and making me even more desperate for him. "It's this. It's your reaction to me, the way your body craves me just as I crave you. It's the way you so quickly put me in my place but then turn around and need me to tell you that everything is going to be okay. It's that fire that burns in your eyes and the way you've so effortlessly fit into my life. You light up every time you look at me, even when you're screaming about how much you despise me. And your fucking smile, Killer. Fucking hell. You're the most gorgeous woman I've ever laid my eyes on, and you're making me feel things that … that I don't understand."

My arms fall around his neck as I kiss him again, my heart racing faster than ever before. I pull back to meet his soft stare, his warm eyes taking me in as though I'm some kind of mystical goddess. Biting down on my bottom lip, a nervous wave crashes through the pit of my stomach. "Are you falling in love with me, Tanner Morgan?"

His lips pull into a cocky smirk as his hand sails up my spine until his fingers are curling around the back of my neck. "Wouldn't you like to know?"

Holding his stare, I shake my head as a soft smile pulls at my lips. "You're a mystery to me," I murmur just as he draws me back in. His lips press to mine, kissing me gently at first before deepening the kiss. The words he refuses to say out loud are clear in his actions, clear in the way he holds me.

Tanner Morgan is in love with me, and there's no denying it.

"Come on," he says a moment later. "Let me take you inside, and I can show you all these tricks that are going to blow your mind."

I laugh and shake my head. "Uh-uh, Mr. Jockstar. You're not getting off the hook that easily. You think you can whisper something sweet in my ear and expect me to spread my legs? That's not how these things work."

A pout rests over his delicious lips and he gives a subtle shrug of his shoulders. "That's how it's worked for me in the past."

"Seriously?" I grumble. "You want to flaunt how much of a manwhore you were before meeting me?"

Tanner laughs, his fingers brushing over my skin. "Are you jealous, Killer?"

"Jealous of a bunch of girls who got tossed aside before you'd even finished wiping the cum off the end of your dick? Nah, I'm good."

Tanner smirks and draws me back in, his fingers clutching at the back of my neck. "You fucking amaze me, Bri," he murmurs, his lips gently moving over mine. "But don't be fooled, I have every intention of wearing you down until you can't possibly resist me."

"I don't know," I whisper. "My tolerance threshold for dealing with horny assholes is pretty high. Take Riley for example."

"Good point," he says. "But the difference between me and Riley is that he gives up far too easily. One shot to the balls and he's down. That's not me, baby. I'll be there night and day, getting under your skin, wearing you down until you don't know whether you want to shoot me or fuck me."

"You should know better," I murmur, leaning in even closer, letting him feel my body pressing up against his, letting him feel the way my nipples harden through the flimsy fabric of my bralette. "When it comes to me, I'll always shoot first."

His lips capture mine and he kisses me deeply, his tongue fighting mine for dominance. I melt into him. Tanner and I have never had any issues when it comes to being intimate. It's our inability to handle situations like adults that brings us down. This right here, we've always been compatible.

My body heats and my core clenches, desperation and need

slamming through my body as I begin to grind over him. Tanner grows hard beneath me, and I know I should stop before I end up screwing him in the driver's seat of his Mustang, but to stop would be criminal. He tastes too good, and the promise of what's to come … shit. It'll be like fireworks on the Fourth of July.

A soft moan escapes my lips, and Tanner's fingers dig into my hips, a troubled groan rumbling through his chest as he breaks our kiss. "If you don't get out of here right this fucking second, I'm going to bend you over my hood and fuck you until you scream, Killer. The whole fucking neighborhood will be watching, wanting what's mine."

I grind down against him, my pussy so wet and ready. His hand circles to my back and slips into the back of my pants, squeezing my bare ass so hard that I'm forced to rock my hips over him again. "Fuck, Tanner," I groan, my head tipping back.

He doesn't skip an opportunity and presses his lips to the base of my throat, working his tongue over me, making that desperation burn me from the inside out. "We can't, Killer," he murmurs between kisses. "Trust me, I want to disrespect you in every fucking way, but you said no. We're not doing this."

I shake my head, my heart warming at his need to protect my word. "It's just you and me here," I murmur. "Disrespect me, Tanner. I want you to fuck me on the hood until I scream. No one needs to know. It'll be our dirty little secret."

Tanner laughs and grabs both of my hands in one of his, holding me back before I get the chance to jump him. "Don't tempt me," he says, his eyes sparkling with excitement. "Besides, is it wrong that I'm kinda looking forward to the challenge?"

My eyes widen, understanding dawning. "You think I'll give in."

Tanner laughs and motions toward me, using our current state as a perfect example. "I mean, fuck babe. The resistance you're showing right now is blowing me the fuck away. I don't think I'll ever be able to break you."

Sarcasm laces his tone and I give him a hard stare. "Okay, Mr. Donkey Fucker. You're on. I'll stick to my word. No hot, kinky fuckery for you."

Tanner laughs. "I'm regretting it already."

"Good," I mutter, purposefully scooting back on his lap so that his rock-hard cock isn't pressing against my clit, turning me into his personal cheerleader.

"Come on," he says, his hands moving over mine until our fingers are laced. "I'll take you up to your room, and I might even reward you with a kiss goodnight."

I scoff, my eyes meeting his with silent laughter. "Oh, I see how it is. I'm good enough to kiss, but not good enough to fuck."

Tanner blanches, his eyes widening for just a moment before quickly realizing I'm screwing with him. "You're trouble, Brielle Ashford," he says, reaching for the door and letting the cool night breeze rush into the warm car. "And for what it's worth, when the time comes, and you're finally ready to let me back in, I will be making up for lost time, so you better be prepared."

I laugh as a grin stretches across my lips. "I'll be sure to bring the lube."

Tanner winks and it sends a bolt of electricity pulsing right through my body. "And I'll bring the edible underwear."

He scoops me up off his lap and, in one easy motion, steps out of the Mustang before placing me down on the driveway. Tanner holds my waist, making sure I have my balance before slipping his hand into mine. Just as promised, he walks me over to my house and goes as far as to personally deliver me to my room.

I stand at my door, leaning against the frame as his warm eyes take me in, his hands lingering on my skin. "Just say the word and I'll stay."

My lips press into a hard line and I shake my head. "That's okay," I tell him, moving closer into him, unable to resist the comfort of his warmth and strong arms … not to mention that heavenly scent that washes over me every time he's near. "You were right to tell me to stop. I don't want to rush into this and then end up moving past all our issues without actually resolving them. I know we've only known each other for a few weeks, but I don't think it gets better than this. I don't want to fuck it up because I can't control this need to jump you."

Tanner laughs. "I can't say I ever saw that being an issue, yet here we are."

I roll my eyes and playfully smack his chest. "Get out of here before I'm forced to jump you and not in the way you like."

Tanner takes a step back, his eyes sparkling with laughter as he salutes me, obeying my every command. "Whatever you say, boss."

He takes off down the hallway, and as I close my door behind me, I hear his muffled laughter coming through the walls. This might have been goodnight, but it certainly wasn't goodbye. There's no way that was the last of Tanner Morgan I'll be seeing tonight. I know with every fiber of my soul that he won't be able to resist watching me through his bedroom window, and I won't be able to resist welcoming it as he does.

Moving through my room, I peel off my clothes, switching them out for my pajamas. I slide beneath the blankets on my bed, and pull them right over my shoulders. I can't help but glance up, watching as the light switches on in Tanner's room, and just as I expected, his eyes immediately come to mine.

My heart races and a stupid grin stretches across my face. Despite not needing to be shy with Tanner, I find myself pulling my blanket even higher, covering my face, and only leaving a sliver to peek through the top. My lights are out, so I doubt he can even see, but just the thought of his eyes on me makes my body squirm with need.

He moves around his room, reaching over his head and gripping the fabric of his shirt before shrugging out of it and putting his sculpted body on display. His gaze lingers on me, and I watch as he pops the button of his pants, letting them fall from his narrow hips.

My mouth waters.

Holy hell, I'm in so much trouble.

All too soon, Tanner disappears from the window and his room falls into darkness. A hollow disappointment takes root deep in my chest, and I let out a heavy sigh, not wanting tonight to be over. Though, that's ridiculous since I was the one so ready to cut my night short.

Tanner came through for me. Every step of the way, he's had my back. I was having a shit night, struggling with my inner demons, and without even trying, he managed to pull me out of the darkness, making it easier to breathe. Tanner Morgan truly is something special. Maybe I'm a fool to be pushing him away. Though to be completely honest, I don't think he's going to let me do that, and more so, I don't think I want to.

I'm a sucker for all things Tanner Morgan. There's no doubt in my mind he's going to pull me back in, and when he does, that's it between us. It's final. There's no walking away. I might as well sign a marriage certificate.

My eyes begin to grow heavy, and just as I start drifting to sleep, my phone chimes on my bedside table. I take a moment, wondering if I should just leave it for the morning, but my lack of self-control has me reaching for the phone.

It's cool in my hand, and the moment I find a text from Tanner, my whole body begins to warm. I press on the unread message and a grin stretches across my face finding he's sent a video. I open that bad boy faster than I've opened anything in my life.

Tanner's face appears on my screen, covered in darkness, and a rush of adrenaline pulses through my veins. His strong arm is propped behind his head and his dark eyes are hooded with desire. "Ask and you shall receive, Killer," he murmurs, his deep tone flowing through my room like the sweetest caress. "One cum shot video coming right up."

"Holy fuck," I breathe, my eyes widening as my whole body freezes with anticipation.

There's no way. Me and the girls joked with the guys about dick pics being a thing of the past, that what we really want is cum shot videos but … no! A thrill shoots through me and my head snaps to the window. His room is still dark, but I feel his heavy, intense gaze locked on me like a vice.

Rustling on the video draws my attention back to the screen, and I watch as the camera slowly pans down his sculpted body, the moonlight casting the softest glow over his abs. It keeps going, trailing lower down his delicious body until it finally stops, his rock-hard cock standing at attention and his strong fist clutched at his base.

"Oh, my fucking God." The anticipation is too much, my eyes glued to the screen like a starving whore, desperate for him all over again. I clench my thighs, but it's not nearly enough to ease the ache building between my legs.

The moonlight is just bright enough to capture the angry veins working their way up his thick shaft all the way to his tip, and my mouth waters, but not as much as when his hand begins to move. Slow at first, lazily working his way up and down his cock.

"What were the stipulations of your cum shot video?" he questions, his voice so deep and rumbly that it sounds almost as though he were under the blankets with me. "You wanted to hear me groaning your name while I come? Wanted to know it was your sweet cunt I was picturing?"

Tanner groans, his pace starting to increase as I hear his heavy breathing coming through the phone. His thumb circles his tip, and I can't take it anymore. My hand slips down the front of my pajama shorts, my aching clit desperate for his touch.

"You're touching yourself, aren't you, Killer? You're such a greedy whore for me, just the way I like it."

Holy mother of all things sweet and juicy. This man … How the hell did he know? It's as though he knows me better than I know myself, he can read me like a book, anticipate my every move.

My fingers rub tight circles over my clit, matching his speed as my breath becomes just as heavy as his. His thumb circles his tip again, and my desperation gets the best of me. Fuck, I'd throw myself out the window just to feel him pushing inside me. I need him like never before.

"That's right, Killer. Picture me touching you, picture me inside you, filling you, stretching you."

I suck in a breath, that familiar sensation already building between my legs. I'm wound so tight, but I'll hold on for him. I don't want to come a second too soon.

I match his pace, my eyes glued to the screen as every little grunt has me falling to pieces.

"Fuck, Killer. I've got to have you. I need to taste that sweet little cunt."

"Oh, fuck," I breathe, biting down on my bottom lip.

He's close. So fucking close.

His breathing catches, and the lowest moan sails through the phone, causing a needy squeak to tear from my throat. I'm right on the edge, right there with him as his grip tightens and he pumps faster. I match his rhythm, panting with desperation until he finally comes.

"Fuuuuuuck, Brielle. You're fucking mine, Killer," he groans low, his hot seed spurting from his cock as I'm pushed right over the edge.

My eyes widen, the sight of this man coming undone feeds the raw desperation inside of me.

My orgasm explodes through me, sending hot pulses of pleasure rocking through my body.

"Oh, fuck, Tanner," I moan, unable to catch my breath.

I don't stop, slowly rubbing my clit as my pussy convulses, my high working its way through my body. I keep my eyes locked on the phone, and not a moment later, Tanner's face appears on the screen, the corner of his lip pulled up in a boyish grin. "How was that for a cum shot video?" he murmurs, his breath coming in hard pants as those dark, dreamy eyes seem to stare straight through the phone and into my soul. "Just so you know, I don't do anything for free. I'll be expecting a video in return. Though, take your time. I know you're probably worn out after spending the last ten minutes fucking yourself while thinking about me."

And just like that, the screen goes black, and I stare at it in wonder.

What the fuck just happened?

That big bastard.

A breathy laugh tears from my throat, and I throw the blankets back before storming across my room. Gripping the edge of my window, I wrench it open with a balled-up pair of socks in my hands. I don't know when I picked them up, but one minute they're on the floor, and the next, they're flying out my window and slamming against the frame of Tanner's. "Open up, you big bastard," I call through the night.

I watch as Tanner flies out of bed and crosses to the window with a cocky smirk resting on his full lips. The window slides back effortlessly and just like that, I'm face-to-face with the one man who could destroy me. "Is there something you need?" he questions, acting as though he didn't just send me the most erotic video I've ever seen … you know, except for that shit I've seen on Pornhub that I definitely don't watch, and I definitely don't get off to.

"I … I … I don't even know what to say," I mutter, blinking rapidly and fumbling over my words, a little starstruck from his performance.

Tanner crosses his arms over his chest and leans against the window frame, smugness wafting off him. "Considering those gorgeous, flushed cheeks of yours, I'm assuming that you more than finished … the video, that is," he adds as an afterthought.

"Like you wouldn't know, you dirty perv," I throw back at him. "I could feel your stare on me the whole time. You watched every second. I wouldn't be surprised if you've got binoculars stashed in your bedside drawer."

Tanner laughs, his eyes filled with the darkest secrets. "Baby, you're not prepared for the shit I've got stashed in my bedside drawer."

Hooooooly shit.

My cheeks flame to the point of pain, and all the fucker can do is grin. So instead of chickening out like a little bitch, I reach up to grip the bottom of the window and grin right back at him. "I think the things I'm prepared for might just shock you, Tanner Morgan," I say, letting him see the twisted desire in my eyes. "Now, be a good little perv and go to bed, and while you're at it, you can dream about all the ways I'm going to return the favor."

And with that, I close the window and race back to my bed before pulling the blanket right up over my head. I grab my phone and save the video to a locked gallery, but only after watching it three more times. A grin pulls at my lips as I turn the camera on myself. That big asshole isn't going to know what hit him.

CHAPTER 9
Brielle

The blistering sun shines down over Bradford, and I adjust myself on the pool lounger. Summer is supposed to be over. It shouldn't be this hot. I have boob sweat. BOOB SWEAT! Chicks with minimal breasticles aren't supposed to get boob sweat. What the fuck is going on here?

Ilaria stands in the pool, her arms resting on the tiled edge as she looks up at me, her long hair swaying around her shoulders in the water. "I swear to all things holy, Brielle. If you bail on the twins' party tonight, I'm personally going to sew your vagina closed with a knitting needle."

Chanel scoffs from beside me, having to pause her cocktail sipping just to berate me. "Girl, it's social suicide if you don't go. Though, I suppose that shit doesn't really bother you."

Arizona laughs across the other side of the pool, pulling up her bikini straps to check the process of her suntan, though it looks more like a burn to me. "You're the social climber around here," Arizona says to Chanel. "This is Marjorie we're talking about. She'd probably skip the party simply because it is social suicide. Bri's an old, introverted soul who doesn't give a shit about anything. The only reason she went to the races last night is because she's wet for the captain."

I laugh and shrug my shoulders. "The girl has a point."

Chanel rolls her eyes. "Well, I don't care," she says, turning her attention back to me. "You're coming whether you want to or not. I swear if anyone knows how to throw a party, it's Jax Morgan."

"Not Logan?" I ask, my brow arching in interest.

Ilaria scoffs. "Hell no. Logan wouldn't know how to throw a party if it inserted itself up his ass and he had to shit it out again," she laughs, her gaze flicking toward Chanel who clearly doesn't like us talking shit about the guy she's madly in love with, though I'm not entirely sure she's aware of that. "Logan lets Jax do all the work so he can take all the credit, but everyone knows Jax is the brains of the operation when it comes to parties, which is saying a lot. Jax is never the brains of any operation."

A laugh rumbles through my chest. I've never heard such a truer statement.

Chanel rolls her eyes. "Can we all lay off Logan now? He's not as bad as you're making him out to be."

Arizona laughs. "You're just saying that because you're the one reaping the rewards. Tell me, how long have you two been screwing in secret before we figured it out?"

Chanel glances away, sipping on her straw as if trying to buy herself a minute to come up with a perfectly good explanation as to why she kept us all in the dark about her budding relationship with Logan. Though to be fair, I'm almost certain the girls already knew and just decided not to say anything until Chanel was ready.

A smug smile spreads across her face and she turns back to me. "So," she says, releasing the straw from between her lips. "What are you wearing to the party?"

I can't help but laugh. This girl would do or say anything to avoid discussing the ins and outs of her relationship with Logan, though I'm not sure if relationship is the right word for it. They're definitely more than just fuck buddies, but they hate each other enough for it to be the worst kind of toxic … but then, didn't Tanner and I start the same way? Not that Tanner and I are anything solid right now. At least, not until he breaks down my resolve and forces me to face the fact that I don't want to be without him.

"I'm not going to the party."

Ilaria scoffs and shakes her head. "You're going to the party."

"I'm not."

"I won't hesitate to cut a bitch," Ilaria says. "You're coming to the party, we're going to have a few drinks and dance while watching Chanel and Logan get into an argument over something ridiculous, and then I'm going to find someone to screw in the pool house, and you're going to let Tanner take you home and fuck you until you can't see straight."

I press my lips into a hard line, becoming all too aware that I have no choice in the matter. My gaze lifts to Arizona's across the pool. "And what about you? What filthy activity will you be doing while this bitch is forcing me to have a good night?"

Arizona grins, her gaze darkening as she pushes off the edge of the pool and makes her way toward us. She presses in beside Ilaria, putting arms up on the tiled edge as she bites down on her bottom lip, a flash of nervousness in her eyes. "You really want to know?" she questions, lowering her tone as though it's some kind of big secret.

I scoot closer on the sun lounger, not wanting to miss a damn thing as Chanel sits up, her eyes narrowing on her best friend. "Oh no," she says, slowly shaking her head. "What messed-up bullshit are you planning?"

Arizona smirks wider, her eyes squinting with the force of her grin. "So, last night at the races," she starts. "I sort of promised Jax a birthday present in the form of sexual favors—"

"Annnnnnd?" Ilaria prompts, none of this out of the ordinary by even a little bit.

"Well, when I got home last night, I was thinking that sexual favors aren't anything special when it comes to Jax. We've been fucking on and off for years. When it comes to me and him, he's seen it all, so I needed something better ... something surprising."

My eyes widen. "What does—" the sound of Tanner's Mustang pulling into the next-door driveway cuts me off, and a thrill shoots through me, the memory of his cum shot video far too prominent in my mind. I take a second, waiting for him to cut the engine just so I can hear myself think. Riley's voice sails over the fence from Tanner's front yard, and I make sure to lower my voice even more, definitely not wanting our conversation overheard by those ears. "What does that even mean? This is Jax we're talking about. I don't think anything could surprise him when it comes to sex."

Ilaria chokes on a laugh. "I mean, you could attach tassels to your tits and jiggle them around."

Arizona grins wide. "No, I was thinking of something a little more literal."

My brows furrow as I watch her with suspicion. "How much more literal does it get than surprise titty tassels?"

She shakes her head, the apples of her cheeks pushing up high with her beaming grin. "He'd be expecting something like that. He already knows it's something sexual, so he'll be prepared for sexy lingerie or a lap dance. I wanna catch him off guard, right when he least expects it."

"Dare I ask how you're going to do that?" Chanel questions.

Arizona's eyes sparkle with excitement. "I'm going to suck him off right in the middle of his party while his friends are around. And what's best is no one will have a damn clue. It'll be our dirty little secret."

"Oh, God," Ilaria laughs, pushing back into the pool and treading water. "You're insane. There's no way you'll be able to pull that off without anyone noticing. Do you have any idea how many people are going to be there tonight? Plus, Jax is kinda the birthday boy and a big deal around here. All eyes will be on him."

"I know," Arizona grins. "Isn't it exciting?"

"Holy Shit, Ari," Chanel laughs, scooping up her cocktail again. "You're asking for trouble. Are you sure there's nothing more between you two?"

Arizona's eyes bug out of her head, looking more appalled than ever before. "Are you insane? Jax Morgan is not the kind of guy a girl wants to fall for. Sucking him off during a party is exciting, but actually falling for him is the real trouble."

"Oh, hot chicks in bikinis? Don't mind if I do," comes a cocky tone from behind us. My head whips around to find Riley hovering in the open bifold doors, looking out over the pool as though he has every right to crash our girls' day. He strides out to the entertaining area and scoops my cocktail right out of my hand before lifting the whole thing to his lips, bypassing the fancy straw.

After chugging nearly the whole drink in one go, Riley pulls the glass away and licks his lips. "Mmmm, passionfruit?" he questions before going in for the rest.

He places the glass down on the end of my sun lounger before reaching for the one to my left and yanking it closer. Riley shrugs out of his shirt, drops it to the ground and makes himself comfortable beside me. "So, what's going on? What are we talking about?" he questions, ready to soak up some rays.

I gape at him before turning to the girls to make sure they're seeing this too. "Ummmm, don't you have somewhere to be?" I ask.

Riley shrugs his shoulders before propping his hand behind his head, making it easier to see the two bikini-clad goddesses in the pool.

A smirk pulls at his lips. "I'm right where I'm supposed to be," he murmurs.

I let out a heavy sigh and reach for my empty glass before leaning down beside me and grabbing the cocktail jug. "Have it your way," I say, filling my glass. "But remember what happened last time you touched something that wasn't yours to touch."

"Oh, I know," he says with a cheesy wink. "You can drop me like that any day. I swear, I won't tell Tanner. It'll be our secret."

I shake my head and glance toward Arizona. "You two should date. You'd be perfect for each other."

In the same second, both their faces scrunch up in disgust, and Arizona even goes as far as taking a few steps further away. "No thanks, he's probably riddled with STDs."

Riley scoffs, his lips still pulled into a cocky smirk. "Yet you have no issue whoring out to Jax. Hmmm, peculiar."

Arizona sends a wave of water sailing over Riley, getting me and Chanel in the process. "You're a grade A asshole, Riley. No one can ever say that you don't excel at anything."

Chanel shrieks, flying up off the lounger as water drips off her, but I can't seem to find the same level of outrage. My boob sweat kinda likes the cold bite of the water.

Riley laughs, not even bothered a little bit by the water soaking his body and holds his hand to his heart. "I think that's the nicest thing you've ever said to me."

Arizona groans as the rest of us watch on in amusement. "Oh my God, Riley, you are so frustrating. Why are you even here?"

"Good fucking question," a deep grumble comes from behind us.

I glance over my shoulder to find Tanner hovering in the open doorway, gripping the top of the frame and looking like some kind of Adonis. His eyes scan over the yard, and as they settle on me, his lips twitch, the corners pulling into the slightest, knowing smirk, flooding me with heat. The image of his video has been playing on repeat in my head non-stop, and the fucker knows it. Hell, I've had to take care of business three times already just today, and it isn't even lunchtime yet.

"Ugh," Riley groans. "If it isn't the fun police."

Tanner's gaze scans back to Riley's, watching as his best friend all but dangles over the backrest of the sun lounger. "Fun police?" he scoffs. "You said you'd help me work on the Mustang. I went inside for two fucking seconds and come out to find you gone."

Riley shrugs. "What do you want from me, man? The girls practically begged me to come over. It's not my fault they all want me. What was I supposed to do? I didn't want to be rude."

Chanel scoffs and throws a jam-filled donut right at Riley's chest. "You're so full of it, Sullivan," she says, watching as the donut splatters against his skin.

Riley gapes at the mess of jam before slowly raising his gaze to Chanel. "You did not just do that," he rumbles, sitting up from the sun lounger and letting the donut fall into his lap.

Chanel swallows hard, her eyes widening as she cautiously climbs off her lounger, putting more space between them. "Don't even think about it," she warns, throwing up a hand, knowing damn well what's coming her way.

Riley springs off his lounger, moving across the backyard like a fucking ninja as Chanel lets out an ear-shattering squeal. She takes off at a million miles an hour darting in front of me, but her speed is no match for the star athlete. He launches at her, flying through the air and collecting her around the waist, sending the two of them into the deep cold water with a ferocious splash. Water flies up around them and I brace myself for the epic splash.

They surface a moment later, Chanel gasping for breath as Riley's booming laugh sails through the yard. "ASSHOLE!" she screeches, blinking rapidly and trying to save her false lashes as she flails toward the edge, her teeth chattering from the cold water.

She hauls herself out of the pool as Riley cuts through the water, going the long way to take the proper exit, only stopping in front of Ilaria and grabbing her waist. He pulls her in flush against his chest and the sudden movement has a rush of breath escaping her lips. "Hey, babe," he murmurs, his tone low as her hand presses against his defined chest.

Ilaria shakes her head and looks up at his hooded stare with a firm one of her own. "You have a better chance of fucking Rihanna than getting your dick inside me."

Riley laughs and ducks his head down low, pressing a kiss to her cheek. "It was worth a try," he says before making his way out of the pool, dripping everywhere. He stops by my side and reaches down, hauling the towel out from under my ass in one easy swipe.

"Hey!" I whine just as a set of large warm hands press down over my shoulders, gently squeezing and making my stomach swirl with anticipation.

"If you're done striking out," Tanner says to Riley over my head, "we have shit to do."

"Striking out?" Riley laughs. "Man, that was just the warmup. You know how it is with these chicks, you have to warm them up first. Trust me, I'll have them eating out of my hand by the end of the night."

With that, Riley turns and looks back at Ilaria, catching her horrified stare before winking at her, his intentions for the night perfectly clear. "See ya 'round, babe," he murmurs before striding back through the bi-fold doors and leaving a trail of water behind him.

"Oh, hell no," Ilaria gasps, her eyes wide with fear. "I changed my mind. We're not going to the party."

Tanner laughs. "Whether you're at the party or not," he says. "You and I both know Riley will still find his way between your legs. He'll wear you down and you won't be able to resist him. Just accept it, it's written in concrete. You'll be his newest obsession, but that's not really the worst thing, is it? At least he's not frothing at the mouth over Bri anymore."

I scoff. Clearly Tanner is blind. It hasn't even been twenty-four hours since the last time Riley hit on me, but the more it happens, the more I realize that Riley simply can't help it. He's harmless. He likes to make girls smile, and the easiest way to do that is to make them feel like the most gorgeous and desired woman in the room. Not going to lie, Riley has a gift for it. He'll make someone very happy one day, though something tells me when that happens, he'll be a force to be reckoned with. There won't be any games. He'll claim what he wants and won't ever look back.

The girls laugh at Ilaria's pain, but I'm far too distracted as Tanner leans down, his warm lips hovering just millimeters from mine as his dark, hooded eyes roam over my face. "I'm out," he tells me, his fingers moving to my face and brushing my unruly hair behind my ear. I'm captured in the moment and lean in, needing his lips on mine, but I don't dare close the gap. After all, there's nothing Tanner wants more than to break me, and I'm not about to let that happen, my desperation be damned. I have a video stored safely on my phone to tide me over until I finally give in and accept that Tanner Morgan is my future … until then, these games will keep me more than entertained.

A grin pulls at the corner of my lips. "Then what are you waiting for?" I ask. "You're not going to break me. I thought I already told you just how high my tolerance level was for horny assholes like you."

"Uh huh," he grumbles, his gaze dipping down my bikini-clad body. "We'll see about that."

I press my thighs together, softly panting. He's got me right where he wants me, and he knows it. I'm all talk. The fucker isn't even trying, but something tells me the moment he gets me alone and decides the games are over, I'll give right into him.

"I don't think you have any idea who you're messing with, Tanner Morgan," I say, my words certainly not reflecting the desperation I feel inside.

Tanner winks and I melt.

I fucking melt.

Goddamn it.

"Wear that lacy black thong tonight," he murmurs, his voice lowering and sending an electric current right through to my core. "I wanna rip it off with my teeth."

Holy Mcfluggalugging. Yes, sir.

I suck in a breath, my heart racing, and I curl my hands into fists at my side, determined not to reach out and grab him. "I believe you were leaving," I murmur, my voice breaking and certainly not sounding as unaffected as I intended.

Tanner grins, his soft laugh speaking right to my soul. Without another word, he pulls away from me and leaves the way he came, giving me a chance to finally breathe.

I sink down into my sun lounger, my head right where my ass is supposed to be as my wide gaze stares at the cloudless blue sky. "Fuck me," I breathe, completely ruined by the man I once vowed to despise.

"Fuck you?" Ilaria mutters. "Fuck me! That was so fucking hot I nearly came in the pool."

"Right?" Arizona scoffs. "You're an idiot if you don't hold on to that big bastard with both hands and ride him like a fucking cowgirl until the end of time. If you're not going to, then move the fuck over, girl. There's a whole line of desperate seniors waiting to be looked at like that by the famous Tanner Morgan. Hell, if you weren't so clearly in love with the guy, I'd be the first in line."

An unladylike grunt tears from the back of my throat. "Please, if I weren't stealing Tanner's attention, Jules would be all over him like a rash."

"So true," Chanel laughs. "But seriously, what the hell are you waiting for? You can't still be angry about what happened last week at the track. He apologized for that, and I could be wrong, but I thought you forgave him?"

"I did," I mutter, biting the inside of my cheek, trying to figure it out. "It's just a weird time. I'm under investigation for the attack on his sister, and I want to clear my name before I allow myself to give in. When I fall in love with him, I want us both to go into this with a clean slate. I don't want anything holding us back or getting in the way. Plus, he said some things at the track, and while he apologized for it, it doesn't make those words hurt any less. He has things he needs to work on and his sister to think about while I have my own shit going on."

Ilaria shakes her head. "You're both idiots," she says. "You've both got shit going on, shit that other people our age couldn't even begin to understand. You should be finding comfort in one another instead of keeping each other at arm's length."

I shrug my shoulders. "I mean, I think we sort of do that. We just haven't given it an official title. He still calls me his, despite how much I argue against it. I think in his mind, we're already a done deal, but he's just giving me that time and space I need to come back to him."

Chanel sulks, her bottom lip pouting out. "Why the hell can't Logan be like that? He's such an asshole."

We all laugh as Arizona and Ilaria get out of the pool and come to join us on the sun loungers. "Speaking of your case," Arizona says, reaching for the cocktail jug and filling her glass. "What's going on with that? Have you heard anything?"

I shake my head. "Nada," I tell her. "Orlando set me up with some big-time lawyer. I have a meeting with him after school on Monday, so I'm hoping I can give him all the original versions of the images Erica photoshopped and then he'll be able to clear my name. The evidence they had against me was so ridiculous that it shouldn't be hard, but I don't know how these things usually work. I don't know if it's a quick thing or if it'll take months."

"I'm sure it'll be quick," Ilaria encourages. "But if you're nervous, you can get ready at my place for the party tonight. We can brainstorm all the questions you'll need to ask and make a list so you're prepared and you'll come out of your meeting feeling good about it all."

"No amount of questions will ever make me feel good about this situation."

Ilaria rolls her eyes. "You know what I mean."

Chanel reaches for the cocktail jug at Arizona's side. "I just can't believe they haven't charged Colby yet. I mean, didn't they confirm his DNA matched the sample found in the rape kit?"

"Yeah," I say with a disgusted scoff. "I'm sure if they could actually find the asshole, he'd be in custody. But there's gotta be more to it than that, right? I feel like it's such an open and closed case that it shouldn't be taking this long. From what I can tell, Tanner's parents are throwing money at every available resource to get this case closed, but it just keeps stalling. There has to be something more, something the cops aren't sharing."

"I don't know," Ilaria says. "I don't know shit about the justice system, but my mom used to watch Law & Order all the time and they would always say that they needed every little scrap of evidence to make sure the bad dude was actually convicted and not let off on a technicality."

A heavy sigh pulls from deep within my chest. "I'm sure getting assholes like Colby off on a technicality is Orlando's specialty."

"Exactly," Ilaria says. "The cops are probably just making sure they have all their i's dotted and t's crossed before submitting anything. Besides, I'm sure they're still investigating Erica's part in all of this."

"Maybe," I murmur. "I told them everything I remember from that night and what Erica said to me the other week. I just hope they're taking it seriously and don't think I was just talking shit out of desperation to save myself."

"Who knows?" Chanel says, giving me an encouraging smile. "I'm sure once your lawyer submits your evidence and your name is cleared, they'll be able to see Erica for the spineless, rotten bitch she is."

"Cheers to that," Ilaria says, reaching for her glass and holding it up.

We all clink our glasses together, and while a tight smile rests on my face, it doesn't reflect the pain circling my chest at the mention of Erica's betrayal. Thirteen years of friendship thrown away in a matter of seconds. I don't think I'll ever recover from that.

Chanel was right—Erica is nothing but a spineless, rotten bitch and soon enough, karma is going to catch up with her. When it does, I'll be the first one in line to watch her burn.

CHAPTER 10
Brielle

What in the ever-loving hell is this?

I walk into Jax and Logan's home, gaping at the sheer size of the luxurious, modern foyer before me. I knew the twins' family had money, but I didn't think it was anything like this. The place is a freaking mansion on steroids.

The lights are dimmed for the party, but that doesn't even begin to conceal just how truly big it is. The ceilings are at least twenty feet high with a massive staircase to the left that splits off into two directions halfway up, with a stunning wrought iron railing following it around.

The second level of the home overlooks the foyer, only going to show just how big this place really is. It's impressive and if it weren't for all the people, I'd already be snooping around. Though one thing is for sure, it would definitely get lonely and cold in a place like this. My heart almost breaks for Jax and Logan … almost.

Music vibrates through the floor as bodies barrel through the front door behind me. I stand with Ilaria, both of us looking around in awe, despite the fact she's probably been here a million times before.

We spent the afternoon in her oversized closet going over everything for the lawyer. We made sure I had all my evidence lined up and ready while she yanked skimpy dresses off hangers and held them up against her body. She must have tried at least fifty outfits before finally rushing into her father's closet and grabbing one of his white button-down dress shirts and pairing it with the most stunning black corset I've ever seen. The sleeves were rolled up, and after spending twenty minutes trying to get into a pair of thigh-high boots, she was ready.

Not going to lie, she looks fucking gorgeous and makes me feel severely underdressed in my high-waisted shorts and cropped tank. Though, she did lend me a pair of boots, and I'm a little obsessed.

"This place is incredible," I call over the loud, thumping music.

Ilaria grabs my hand and starts weaving through the bodies. "Right, just wait until you see the rest of it," she says, eyeing every guy she squeezes past as a potential candidate for her night of screwing around. "Jax is a showoff, so you can guarantee that any party he throws will be the biggest and best this place has ever seen."

I can't help but laugh. Why am I so not surprised by that?

"You know," she says, glancing back at me, her eyes sparkling with excitement. "I heard they might have even invited some guys from

Broken Hill. You know those brothers I was telling you about from there? Nate and Jesse Ryder?" She pauses looking expectantly at me, so I quickly nod, kinda remembering her saying something about them during one of the boys' football games. "Apparently, the older brother, Nate, is super into racing as well. Could probably go pro if he wanted to."

"No way," I say, kind of excited by the thought as she drags me through the mansion, bypassing all the partygoers and beelining for the backdoor. "Like, as good as Tanner?"

Ilaria scoffs. "I don't think anyone could be as good as Tanner on the track. Though, I'm sure if you asked the Broken Hill crew, they'd probably say differently. I guess no one will really know until you get them on the track together."

Excitement drums through my veins at the thought of watching Tanner go head-to-head with another racing legend, and I find myself walking just a little bit faster, desperate to see him again. I don't think the rush of being near him will ever go away. The way his eyes clock me every time I walk into a room is addictive, but nothing is better than the way he watches me after that. It's as though he's mentally preparing a list of all the filthy things he's going to do with me, imagining exactly how he's going to bend me over, how he's going to slide inside of me, and how his handprint is going to decorate my ass for hours afterward.

Fuck, I'm getting wet just thinking about it.

We step out into the night, and I gape at my surroundings. The pool is a fucking oasis. It looks like a private beach with a rock formation waterfall built high at one end that doubles as a platform to jump off.

Hell, it even looks like there's a cave built beneath it, creating a private spa area, one that I have every intention of getting Tanner alone in.

There's a swim up bar that's staffed and another that's currently hosting a game of poker, but the pool area is nothing compared to the rest of the outdoor setting. It's like nothing I've ever seen before, and to be completely honest, I'm feeling just a little intimidated by it all. Jax and Logan don't just have money, they're freaking loaded. I wonder what they must think of my shitty home back in Hope Falls. I bet they laughed when they first saw me pull up in my falling-apart Honda.

A wave of unease settles into the pit of my stomach, but the moment I hear Chanel's high-pitched tone cut through the night, a wide smile spreads across my face and the unease fades away. "WHERE THE HELL HAVE YOUR BITCH ASSES BEEN?" she squeals from way across the party, her voice somehow traveling over the music and all the twins' guests.

I find Chanel and Arizona immediately, wide grins on their pretty faces, both already looking as though they're ten drinks in. Arizona's hand flies up into the sky, holding a glass of who the hell knows what. "TIME TO PARTAAAAAYYYYYY!"

Ilaria tugs on my hand and the two of us weave through the bodies again, cutting across the designated dancing area and nearly sprinting past the pool as the football team tries to drench us. I barely take two steps before I feel his stare and goosebumps spread across my skin.

I glance over my shoulder as Ilaria drags me toward the girls and find him sitting beside the massive built-in fire pit, looking fucking delicious in his loose tank, his strong, tattooed arms on display and those dark, devious eyes only for me. Tanner sits with a few guys I haven't seen before, and while they talk animatedly among each other, Tanner seems to have completely zoned out.

He stands and excuses himself from the group, making his way across the party, ducking and weaving past the thirsty girls who reach for him. We reach Chanel and Arizona and I position myself so that I can keep my heavy stare on Tanner.

His eyes darken the closer he gets, and a shiver sails right down my spine.

Tanner is hungry, and from the looks of it, I'm his meal.

"What happened to the pink latex dress?" Ilaria asks, glancing at Arizona as Chanel cuts across to the bar behind us and grabs strawberry daiquiris for me and Ilaria. "This is cute, but I thought you were planning something extra saucy to entice the birthday boy."

Not wanting to be rude, I turn my attention toward the girls and watch as Arizona glances down her body and smirks. "Yeah, apparently my cousin raided my closet and stole it, so I thought I'd wear black because I'm in mourning for all the faces that have been buried between my legs."

A choking laugh bursts from my throat as Ilaria holds up her daiquiri toward Arizona. "Cheers to that, girl."

As the girls talk among themselves, my gaze shifts back toward the crowd, searching for Tanner once again, only he must have slipped away. If he were actually coming for me, he should be here by now as he was only a few steps away. But he's nowhere to be seen.

My brows furrow as I search the crowd. "What are you looking for?" Chanel asks, capturing my attention again.

I shake my head. "It's nothing," I say, shrugging it off. "I just thought I should go say happy birthday to the twins, but I'm sure I'll see them at some point. Besides, with an audience like this, they're both eventually going to do something to draw attention to themselves."

"Speaking of," Ilaria smirks, glancing at Arizona. "Are you ready for the performance of a lifetime?"

"Fuck yeah," she says, stretching her neck to the left then right and bouncing her shoulders. "I'm warmed up and ready to go. Just waiting for the perfect moment to pounce."

Chanel laughs. "I stand by what I said this morning, you're asking for trouble."

"Nah," Arizona says. "He'll fucking love it, and even if I get caught, what does it really matter? Everyone knows I love dick, and it's almost expected of Jax at this point."

Chanel shakes her head. "This is going to be a disaster."

A hard body presses into my back and I suck in a breath, more than ready to slam my elbow back into the asshole when that familiar scent washes over me. A smile tugs at my lips as his mouth grazes the side of my neck, and I can't help but press my body harder against his.

Tanner's hand circles my waist as his other plucks the strawberry daiquiri out of my hand. He lifts the glass to his lips and annihilates every last drop before silently handing the glass off to Ilaria, leaving both our hands free.

The girls smirk at me, and not a second later, Tanner drags me back into the crowd.

My whole body melts.

The music is pumped up, and as his hips begin to grind against my ass, I bite down on my bottom lip. Tanner Morgan wants to dance.

He spins me in his arms until his strong chest presses against mine. His hands roam to my ass, and his knee pushes between my thighs. A low moan escapes my lips as our bodies begin to move together, dancing as one and making me wish we were alone.

My hand slips up the front of his shirt, devouring his chest as though it's mine to take. Though, I guess it kind of is. Tanner doesn't say a word, just watches my body move against his while I watch the hunger intensify in his dark eyes.

His hands roam over my body as I grind down against his strong thigh, and I can no longer resist him. My hand curls around the back of his neck, pulling him down to me, and the second I can, I close the gap between us and kiss him with everything I've got.

I don't hold back and neither does he. Our tongues fight for dominance as I claim everything he is. Tanner Morgan is mine without a doubt, though that doesn't change the fact that we each have some things to work through. Plus, the whole being accused of aiding and abetting his sister's attacker is kind of a sore point at the moment.

His knee moves back and forward, and as his hands touch me in all the right places, a familiar ache begins to build deep in my core. I pull away from Tanner's kiss and meet his stare, but as he moves his knee again, I suck in a deep breath.

His eyes are hooded, and it doesn't take a genius to realize this was his plan all along. "What's the matter?" he rumbles, his voice vibrating through his chest, so deep and low it starves me for more.

"I swear to God," I gasp as his hand squeezes my ass and forces my hips to rock against his thigh. "If you make me come in front of all these people …"

Tanner smirks, his eyes like molten lava. "Just say the word and I'll stop."

I glance around, realizing no one is paying any attention to us, but can I really do this? Hell fucking yes, I can. I need this more than I need my next breath.

Rather than responding, I simply pull him back in, our faces barely a breath away. I let him do his thing, keeping my eyes locked on his as he watches me back, watches the way pleasure rocks through my body. His hands move across my skin, knowing exactly where and how to touch me, and the more his thigh moves against my pussy, the more desperate I become.

My nails dig into his chest, feeling his heart beating beneath my palm as my other arm snakes around his neck, needing him so much closer. "Tanner," I pant, right on the edge as his forehead presses against mine, closing us into our own little bubble, the rest of the party quickly fading away.

"Give it to me, Killer," he murmurs. "Give me what I want."

He pushes me harder, bringing me right to the edge and just as the music changes again, I come hard. I suck in a gasp as my orgasm tears through me, and before I can take another breath, Tanner's lips are on mine. He kisses me deeply as my high rocks through my body, the walls of my pussy convulsing.

"Holy shit," I say, pulling back and trying to catch my breath. I meet his amused stare, finding him smirking with pride. "I can't believe you just did that."

"Me?" he questions, his smirk only growing wider as his eyes sparkle with mischief. "I didn't do a damn thing, Killer. That was all you."

My cheeks flame and I smile up at him. "You're an asshole."

"I think the words you're looking for are *thank you*."

"Now, why would I go and thank you if it was all me?" I tease. "If anything, you should be thanking me for the show."

"In that case," he murmurs, pulling me back in and brushing his lips over mine, "I'll be sure to give you the thanks you deserve when I get you home."

"Oh, no, no," I laugh, swatting at his sculpted chest. "That won't be necessary, big guy. I got what I needed now. I suppose you'll have to deal with those blue balls for one more night … or you could simply get yourself off again. Though, you know how I appreciate a good cum shot video. If you're going to play, make sure you capture every moment of it."

Tanner laughs and captures my lips in his, his hands squeezing my ass. "You're fucking trouble."

I meet his stare, a grin pulling at the corner of my lips. "Do you have a tripod? I think I should get you a tripod. That way you can use both hands and I'll be able to see your face as well as your giant—"

"BRIELLLLLLLLLE," Riley's roar sails through the party as his strong hand curls around my waist, tearing me out of Tanner's arms.

He spins me around wildly before dropping me back to my feet and hooking his arm over my shoulder. "Where the fuck have you been, babe? Are you enjoying the party?"

I shove his heavy arm off my shoulder and shuffle back into Tanner's chest only for his arms to immediately circle my waist. "Can't complain," I tell him. "It's been pretty … thrilling so far."

"Damn straight it has," he says. "Come on. You two are fucking boring over here. There's a party and I'm not about to let this fucker hoard you all night. Let's get fucked up, and after that, we can snoop through Jax's things. You know, I heard he has a sex dungeon in here somewhere."

My eyes bug out of my head, and I gape up at the big asshole. "Bullshit," I say as Tanner shakes his head. "Nah, there's no fucking way."

"Cross my heart and hope to die," Riley vows. "Now let's go."

Riley drags me off the dance floor with Tanner following behind, irritated to have our moment bombarded. But while I love spending time with Tanner, I can't lie, I'm excited about the idea of getting fucked up and enjoying my night with people who I trust to keep me safe and out of trouble. At least, only the bad kind of trouble. I'm open to anything else, especially if it involves Tanner.

CHAPTER 11

Brielle

We make our way over to the fancy fire pit, and now that I've had a closer look, I think I'm in love. The pit is sunken and has gorgeous lanterns around the outside, creating a border around us, and even though we're out in the open, surrounded by party guests, I feel like it's somewhat private.

The cushioned seating is inviting, and I drop down beside Hudson only to have Tanner yank me back up and take my place. He pulls me down into his lap and I melt into him, my arm looping around his neck as his hand rests against my thigh.

The girls join us a moment later, their hands filled to the brim with daiquiris and shots, and I'm not surprised when Riley pounces on them, hoarding a few for himself before handing them out and sending some dude I don't know out for more.

I've barely been here for half an hour, and already this party beats anything I've ever seen. Hope Falls parties are clearly the bare minimum when it comes to letting loose.

Jax is missing in action, but Logan sits across the fire pit pretending to enjoy himself, though he looks like he's about to throw up. Seeing his eyes locked on Chanel, I can only guess what's on his mind.

The girls are laughing between themselves, and with Riley talking shit to Hudson, I turn to Tanner. "You know, I heard there's some big-time dude in Broken Hill who could whoop your ass on the track."

"Who? Nate Ryder?" he questions. My grin widens, confirming his thoughts. "That motherfucker is like none other on the track. He'd kick my ass a million times over. Though I think the better question is, how do you know him?"

"Jealous?" I question. He gives me a blank stare, and I glance toward Ilaria, but can't help noticing the way Arizona throws back shot after shot. "Ilaria's got a hard-on for him and his brother, Jesse. She talks about them every chance she gets."

Tanner laughs and nods toward the poker game in the middle of the pool to a bunch of guys I've never met before. "That's them in the pool," he says, bringing my attention to the two guys at the left of the table, each of them looking like the best kind of snack, but to me, no one compares to Tanner. There are a few guys surrounding them and a bunch of girls who look like they'd claw the eyes out of anyone who gets too close. But there's no questioning it, the way the big guy watches the girl in the black bikini, it's clear they're meant to be together.

"A lot of us racers are pretty tight," Tanner explains. "Plus, I think Nate is Logan's man crush. I caught him googling the asshole once, and he makes a point to invite him and his brother to all of our parties. Though, I think Ilaria should find someone a little more attainable. They're practically hitched to their girls. She doesn't stand a chance in hell."

"Hmmm," I tease, arching a brow in interest as my gaze feasts over the brothers. "Maybe I've chosen the wrong asshole to sink my claws into. They're hot."

"Watch it, Killer," he warns, his tone low and threatening in my ear, sending a wave of exhilaration pulsing through me.

"Hey," Arizona calls, her gaze locked on the party guests around us. "Any of you seen Jax around?"

A smirk pulls at my lips as Hudson responds. "Nah, I think the fucker found some chick early on and has been working his way between her legs. You know how he is. He'll show up at probably the most inconvenient time."

The guys scoff with laughter as my gaze falls to Arizona, watching as her face falls. "Oh, okay," she says, reaching for her drink before glancing back at us and giving everyone a tight, forced smile, the determination slowly coming back to her. My brows furrow as I notice the way she looks longingly back toward the crowd, and I can't help but wonder if there's something more there between her and Jax. At least, on her end maybe. Jax's position with women is clear. He knows what he wants and gets it without trying to break their hearts, and I thought Arizona was down with that. She's always claimed he was a manwhore and could never want something more, joking about him being a walking STD, but now … I'm not so sure.

A heaviness claims my heart, and I can't help but notice how Ilaria watches her in the same way, but my concerns are pushed aside when Logan mutters something to himself and slams his beer down a little too hard. "Fuck it," he says and stands, forcing a chorus of nervous sighs out of the boys.

All eyes fall toward him, watching as he moves toward the fire before stepping up onto the edge of it, the flames close to the back of his legs. He turns to face Chanel and a grin stretches across my face.

"I can't fucking take it anymore," Logan announces to everyone in earshot. "Chanel, you fucking infuriate me. Just hearing you sitting over here, laughing with your friends while purposely avoiding my stare is the single most humiliating thing I have ever endured. So, tell me why the fuck I can't get you out of my head? Why have I been simping for you for over a fucking year, babe? Why am I in love with you?"

Chanel stands, craning her neck to meet his hard stare while glaring at the guy. "Are you kidding me?" she demands, frustration clear on her features. "You think because it's your birthday, I'm just going to stand here and let you talk to me like that in front of all these people? What the fuck, Logan?"

Riley cringes. "She has a good fucking point, man. I don't think this is coming out right."

Logan groans, ignoring Riley as he glares right back at Chanel. "What do you mean, *what the fuck?* I'm standing here telling you I'm in love with you and you're throwing it back in my face."

"Do you even hear yourself?" Chanel demands. "You literally just told me how infuriating it is to have me sitting so close to you and how humiliated you are because I haven't looked your way in a while, and you think you can make it all good by throwing a quick *I'm in love with you* on the end while making it sound like the worst thing in the world?"

"What? No," Logan says, my eyes wide as I watch the exchange like the hottest new mini-series to hit the market. "That's not what I was trying to do."

Tanner laughs and pretends to cough. "Bail."

I shove my elbow back into his stomach, silently telling him to keep out of it. If Logan wants to die tonight then we might as well allow him to dig his own grave.

"Pray tell, Logan," Chanel says, crossing her arms over her chest as a crowd gathers. "What the hell were you trying to do?"

"Can't you see?" Logan says, jumping down from the edge of the fire and putting himself right in front of her. "I'm trying to tell you that I can't go on like this anymore. That I'm so fucking in love with you that being this close without being able to call you mine is killing me. I want you, Chanel. I want to be with you, and not just for tonight. I want to be the idiot waiting by my cell, hoping you call. Fuck, babe. I already do that. You're turning me into a fucking whipped pussy, but I fucking love it. I'm done fighting with you every day, done with the constant arguing because we're both too fucking stubborn to make something of this."

Chanel stares at him, completely speechless as her arms slowly fall from across her chest. "You better not be fucking with me because that's so messed up."

Logan shakes his head, his voice lowering and making it hard to hear over the music. "I'm not fucking with you, Chanel. I want to make this work. I've been waiting a year for you to come around, and I don't want to wait anymore."

"You're serious," she murmurs, inching in closer, her big eyes only for him. Logan nods and her brows furrow. "But I like the way we fight."

"I know," he says, his hands falling to her waist. "That doesn't have to change. Hell, I'm sure we'll probably fight more. But I want it all, including the fucking angry sex that comes afterward."

"Logan," she hisses, insisting he keep his voice down, but it's a little too late for that.

Nervousness flickers over his face. "Please don't say no in front of all these people. I'm already embarrassed enough. Just smile and nod and then tell me to fuck off later."

Chanel laughs and places her hands on his chest, sliding one of them up around his neck. "You're an asshole," she tells him, her eyes sparkling with happiness. "But I swear, if the fighting stops and you become all lovey-dovey on me, I'll break up with your ass so fast."

"Wait," Logan says, his whole body tensing. "Does that mean yes?"

"Yes, you big mor—"

Logan kisses her so fast that she doesn't even get to finish her insult, and the gathered crowd cheers for the new couple. "HELL

YEAH!" Ilaria shouts, throwing herself to her feet. "SHOTS ALL ROUND."

Happiness bursts through my chest as Tanner's arms lock tighter around me, and before I know it, Logan's hands curl around Chanel's ass and lift her off the ground. I suppose the party is over for them as he strides through the crowded bystanders, more than ready to get her naked.

The guys laugh and Riley shakes his head. "Fuck, I thought he'd never find the balls."

"Nah, I knew he had the balls," Hudson says. "I just thought he'd fuck it up before he got to the end."

Tanner takes my waist, twisting me on his lap until we're face-to-face. "If they can figure it out, then surely we can too."

"Yeah but … It's Logan and Chanel. I'm not sure their version of figuring it out is exactly the same as ours. They'll be arguing with each other and broken up by the end of the night."

"True," he says. "But then they'll fuck and make up, just like couples are supposed to do."

I press my lips into a hard line, knowing just how right he is but still so nervous about completely handing over my heart. "Don't push your luck, Morgan."

"Can't help it," he mutters, his eyes lighting up like the Fourth of July. "You're the hot sauce to my wings, my ride or die, baby. We're supposed to go together. I lean, you lean."

My heart flutters as nervousness creeps into my veins. I hate it when he says stuff like that. I'm so used to him being the broody douche canoe full of assholish comments that it always throws me off guard to see this softer side of him. But on the other hand, I love it. Like, really fucking love it.

"Tanner Morgan, are you going soft on me?"

Tanner gasps, feigning outrage. "The very idea that I could ever go soft on you offends me."

I groan and roll my eyes. "That's not what I meant, and you know it."

"You know, bro," Riley says, leaning into Tanner's side. "If you're having problems in that department, you can talk to me. Otherwise, they have pills for that sort of stuff. Sort your shit out."

"Great," Tanner groans. "The whole fucking football team is going to think I have a limp dick now."

I grin back at him, wide eyed and as innocent as ever. "I can always show them your cum shot video," I suggest, being my usual helpful self.

Tanner's arm scoops beneath my legs and he makes a show of lifting me up. "Take it back or you're going in the pool."

"You wouldn't dare," I challenge, narrowing my stare. Tanner just looks back at me, his brow slowly arching before I realize just how serious he is. "Okay, okay," I rush out, my hand gripping onto the seat behind his back. "I swear, it's for my eyes only."

"What's for your eyes only?" Arizona questions, leaning down to place her empty glass at her feet.

"Tanner's cum shot video," Riley responds.

"The fuck, man," Tanner says. "Do you have to listen to every private conversation around you?"

"Can't help it," he says with a slight shrug of his shoulders. "It's a gift."

"Finally," Arizona says, cutting off the boys' bickering as she glances out toward the pool, watching as Jax protrudes from the hidden cave beneath the waterfall. She stands and a stupid grin stretches across her face.

Ilaria shakes her head, and I can't help the laugh that bubbles up my throat. I know I shouldn't watch what's about to go down, but the cold hard truth is that it will turn into a trainwreck, and I simply can't look away. I mean, how? There's no way she can pull this off in such a huge crowd, and where exactly does she think she can do it? There are people everywhere, plus she wants it to be a birthday surprise, so it's not as though she can just lure him into a hiding spot. Though judging by the way she's been sitting here, mostly in silence, I can only assume that she's been planning out every second of this. I think she was hoping that it would be spontaneous, and it will be for him, but for her, this is planned right down to the second.

"Alright, ladies," she says, watching as he swims to the side and hoists himself out of the pool, water rushing off his sculpted body as though he's in some kind of underwear commercial. "You're about to witness something incredible."

Arizona makes her move, taking a few steps toward the pool when a girl swims out of the cave, struggling to hold her bikini together. She meets Jax at the side and he bends down, scooping her effortlessly out of the water, bringing Arizona to a standstill.

The girl stands chest to chest with Jax, and he reaches around to help her do up her bikini top, fastening it before dropping his hands to her ass. His fingers slip into the wet material and squeeze as she giggles and presses in even closer.

Arizona's face falls, and just when I think she's holding herself together, Jax kisses the girl, deep and passionately.

Arizona backs up a step, looking as though something inside of her is breaking. "I'm such a fucking idiot," she says before turning and rushing back toward the house.

"Shit," Tanner mutters, having seen the whole exchange and being able to read Arizona just as well as I can.

I go to get up when Ilaria holds out a hand. "I'll go," she says, her heart breaking for her long-time friend.

I quickly nod and Ilaria takes off, but not before Jax and his new toy start making their way toward us. "Yo," Jax says, a cocky smirk playing on his lips as he stands behind the fire pit, his toy under his arm. "Was that Ari running inside?"

"Mmmhmm," I say, unable to meet his eye, wanting to hate him for breaking Arizona's heart. Though she has been incredible at hiding her feelings from all of us, maybe Jax never realized she wanted more than casual sex or that he even had the power to break her heart the way he has.

"What's wrong?" he asks, his brows furrowing, watching after her with real concern on his handsome face. "She sick or something?"

"Or something," Hudson murmurs. "I'm sure she's fine. She'll be back. There are still shots and chick drinks to be had. I doubt she'll skip out on those."

Jax laughs and rubs his chest as his new friend pushes her tits up against him. "Where's Logan at?" Jax asks.

"Shacked up," Riley says, "The fucker finally grew a pair of balls and asked Chanel out. They're probably upstairs fucking as we speak."

"No way," Jax laughs. "You're fucking with me."

"I swear it on my goldfish's grave."

Jax grumbles something under his breath, and while I can't hear it, I get the distinct feeling he's not exactly over the moon about this new revelation. "What's the matter?" I question. "You don't like Chanel?"

"Nah, that's not it," he says. "Chanel's probably one of the only chicks around here who'll actually be good for his oversized ego. I just … worry about him. He goes too hard too fast sometimes. Don't want the fucker getting hurt."

I nod just as the girl lifts up onto her tippy toes and nuzzles her face into Jax's neck before raising her chin and whispering something into his ear. He glances down at her, his brows arching high. "Already?" he questions, making her eyes sparkle with excitement, our conversation already long forgotten.

The girl nods and Jax looks back at his boys. "Duty calls," he grins stupidly before saluting us all and letting the girl drag him away. "Hey," he calls back to us over the music when he's a few feet away, that same stupid smirk still playing on his lips. "When Ari gets back, remind her that she promised me something and I'll be coming to collect. Don't let her run off again."

My scoff is far too loud, and for the first time since meeting Jax,

I want to pulverize him. I bet the asshole thinks he's being secretive by wording it like that. It's one thing to have a healthy fuck buddy relationship, but this almost feels … wrong, especially now that it's obvious she feels something more for him. Screwing one girl only to jump to Arizona a few hours later is tacky. Don't get me wrong, we've all done ridiculous things to earn a guy's attention, to be the apple of his eye if only for a few minutes, but this isn't okay. I can't stand the idea of him using her like that.

"Hey," Tanner says, his hand squeezing mine. "He doesn't know how she feels. I'm sure if he did, he wouldn't be rubbing it in her face like that. He cares about Arizona. He wouldn't want her getting hurt. You know Jax, he has a big heart, even though he doesn't like to show it."

"Yeah, I know, but it doesn't change the fact that he's literally about to fuck the pool chick again and then still wants to screw Arizona in the same night," I murmur, keeping my tone lower so that Riley can't overhear this one. "I'm not down with that. I mean, how would you feel if I screwed around with some random guy at a party and then crawled into your bed expecting to fuck?"

Tanner's eyes darken, but before he can respond, I shake my head. "No, don't answer that," I tell him, pressing my lips into a hard line. "I shouldn't be judging it. I don't know the twisted little ins and outs of their relationship. Maybe this is just normal for them and she's usually cool with it, only now there's added feelings and it changes things. I mean, she talks about him being a manwhore all the time, so surely she's watched him hook up with chicks at parties only to be the one he goes home with at the end of the night."

Tanner nods. "Honestly, I think it happens more than any of us know," he tells me. "She's seen him with other chicks all the time. This is the first she's ever shied away from it though."

I let out a heavy sigh, wishing I knew where in this big ass mansion Ilaria took her, but Hudson was right about one thing. When there's still a good time to be had, Arizona won't waste it. I'm sure after she shakes it off, she'll be back, and in good Arizona fashion, she'll find someone else to screw around with, and just to prove some kind of point, she'll be sure to do it right in front of Jax.

The thought lightens my mood, and when Tanner places a hand on my thigh, I turn back to him with a challenging grin. "Ever jumped off the roof and supermanned into a pool?"

His eyes narrow and he glances up toward the roof before focusing back on me. "Noooo," he says slowly, suspicion radiating out of him.

My grin widens and I realize I'm going to need a few more shots to get through the night. Throwing caution to the wind, I stand up and take his hand, dragging him to his feet, knowing damn well he won't be able to resist. "Want to?"

He glances up to the roof again, knowing damn well we won't make that jump, but we sure as fuck will make it from the roof of the pool house.

"Don't be a chicken, Mr. Morgan."

He finally lets out a sigh. "Fine, but there better be something in it for me."

I sashay away, letting Tanner follow after me with both Riley and

Hudson coming along for the ride. "Do a backflip and I might just think about it," I tell him just as he catches up, scoops me off my feet, throws me over his shoulder, and slaps my ass with a thrilling spank.

CHAPTER 12
Brielle

The cafeteria table feels cool beneath my head as I try to drown out the noise of senior lunch.

The twins' party was a mistake.

No, I take that back. It was awesome, but I went way too hard. Even now, over a day and a half later, I'm still hungover as fuck, and not a damn thing seems to help. Though, my embarrassment over how the night ended could be the biggest reason I'm not ready to face the world.

Our group was the last standing, which was surprising since the girls and I had gotten wickedly drunk. Chanel was already fighting with Logan at that point, and Jax was all broody.

I don't know who suggested getting into the pool at five in the morning, but I'm blaming them for the unholy mess I made.

Tanner and I had snuck into the swim-up bar, and I was so close to losing our little challenge and giving in to his advances. But then my stomach churned. Not wanting to throw up all over my half-naked, nearly-boyfriend, I flew to my feet and launched myself over the bar. Unfortunately, in my desperation, I turned the wrong way, and instead of throwing up all over the pavement, I blew chunks directly into the pool.

I thought there would be no other moment in my life more humiliating than the great wax incident of ninth grade, until I woke up in the twins' guest room to the sound of workmen cleaning the pool. No one has mentioned it, but at some point, it's going to come up just like my guts did.

The cold table soothes my aching head as I listen to Chanel's recap of her last two days for the hundredth time. "Can you believe it?" she says, grabbing her apple and slamming it down on the table, the vibrations traveling right through my skull. "Two days. Two freaking days and the asshole still hasn't talked to me. I mean, why even bother asking me out in the first place? He's such a dick. I swear, give me something so I can strangle him. The swamp turd needs a foot up his ass."

Ilaria laughs and shakes her head. "You know at some point, you two are going to have to learn how to communicate without screaming at each other."

"You're literally asking me to achieve the impossible," Chanel deadpans. "I don't think Logan Morgan has ever had a conversation in his life where either his ego or attitude hasn't gotten in the way. I mean, is he for real? The asshole literally always thinks he's right. I don't know what I was thinking when I agreed to be with him. This was such a mistake. I should have known, but the moron had me all swept up in his stupid, sweet words. He's like a Venus fly trap. Lures me in and then BAM! Just when I least expect it, he eats me … and not in a good way. Though don't be confused, when he does eat me, it's fucking amazing, A+ material. The guy has the tongue of a demon because nothing that feels like that could be heavenly."

I raise my head off the table and just stare at her. "Are you fucking kidding me? Go and fuck him in his car and make up already."

"What?" she screeches. "Have you not listened to a damn thing I've been saying all day? He's the one who should be making up with me. Not the other way around."

"Then fuck in your car instead."

Her brows furrow and she looks at me as if trying to work out how the hell that changes anything. "What … huh? What does it matter whose car we're in?"

"I don't know," I groan. "Go and test both theories. See what works."

Chanel rolls her eyes as Arizona drops down beside me. "Feeling any better?" she asks, grabbing a bottle of water and taking small sips.

I shake my head against the table, which turns out to be a big mistake. "Nope. You?" I ask, smirking at the reminder of how her night turned out.

"Shut up," she groans, dropping her face into her hands and

wallowing in self-pity. She was the star of the night. After Jax threw his bimbo in her face and she had a good cry, she went back to the party to have the best night of her life. She downed every shot she could get her hands on, and then, just to prove some nonexistent point, she found a random guy and gave him Jax's surprise birthday BJ instead. Nothing was better than watching the jealousy flash in Jax's eyes as he watched her crawl out from under a table with a round of applause. Though I don't think he was jealous because she was hooking up with someone else, I think it was more about that random guy getting what should have been his. Jax would screw just about any cute girl on offer, but he does not share well when it comes to his favorite toy.

Ilaria laughs. "Have you spoken to him?"

Arizona shakes her head. "Not really. He texted me yesterday asking if we were cool. He said things felt weird between us by the end of the night, but I shrugged it off and told him he must have been imagining it."

"So," I say slowly, my lips twisting with a cringe. "You've got a hard-on for Jax Morgan."

"Stooooop," she groans. "I already feel stupid enough. I mean, out of all the guys, why does it have to be him? He's literally the biggest whore I've ever met, and that's saying a lot coming from me. We literally joke about it together and then fuck some more."

Little Miss Mother Duck, Ilaria, reaches across the table and squeezes Arizona's hand. "Yeah, but at the same time, he has always treated you differently. You're the only constant for him when it comes to girls. You practically already have the relationship just without the exclusivity clause."

"And the rest of it," Arizona scoffs, clearly not agreeing with her. "When we're not together, we're practically strangers. There's no secret texting unless we want something. There's no kissing, no hand holding, none of that relationship stuff, but there is a real friendship buried in there somewhere. He cares about me, and I think since hoe-bag one and hoe-bag two have been spending so much time together," she adds, referring to me and Tanner, "it's forcing us to spend more time together. I guess I've started to feel something."

"So, what are we going to do about it?" Chanel asks.

"Nothing," Arizona says. "I don't want this. I don't want it to turn into anything. I just want it to all go away and then Jax and I can go back to how things were before. He never has to find out about this. I don't want to screw up a good thing because I went and caught feelings. That's not how I roll."

"I don't know," Chanel says. "This is why friends shouldn't have sex, one of them always starts to develop feelings, and then things are never the same. Look at me and Logan for fuck's sake. We barely tolerate each other most of the time. I think if you want to move past this, you need to stop falling into his bed for a while. Sex complicates things, and I think it's clear that Jax isn't the kind of guy to want a relationship, and honestly, neither are you, but I'm so scared you're going to get hurt. What happened at the party, that's only the beginning of it."

"And you?" Arizona asks, glancing at me. "What are your thoughts on my impending doom?"

My lip pouts out as my head pounds just a little bit harder. "I think thinking is too hard and we should just let the chips fall where they may … is that how the saying goes?" I question, raising my head off the table and immediately regretting it. "Anyway, my point is that there's literally nothing you can do about it. If you're going to develop more feelings for the guy, it's going to happen whether you want it to or not, so until you're certain that it's not going away, you shouldn't be stressing yourself. In the meantime, enjoy your senior year and invest in a vibrator instead."

Arizona gapes at me, completely horrified with the idea of having to get herself off instead of letting Jax do it. "What?" she breathes. "Manual labor?"

"Girl, trust me. Get a vibrator," Ilaria says. "There are some things that a vibrator can do that a tongue just simply can't."

Arizona's cheeks flush before she indicates to me. "Why's all the attention on me when we could be discussing the twins' pool?"

"No, absolutely not," I say. "That is not up for discussion. It's humiliating enough as it is. Though if you really want to push it, I'll have no choice but to remind you that even though I was the one who had the unfortunate incident, you were the idiots flailing around in it while you were trying to get out of the pool."

"Okay," Arizona says, her face scrunching in disgust. "I agree. It shall never be brought up again."

"Good," I say as my phone vibrates against the table.

Glancing down at the screen, I find an unread text from an unknown number and without questioning it, I open the message to immediately wish I hadn't. My gaze travels over the words and each time it does, a weight drops down over my shoulders, reminding me of the ugly reality I've been avoiding.

Unknown - Keep blaming Colby for what you did, and I'll have no choice but to find you, and when I do, it'll be lights out, you fucking whore. Don't worry, I know how you like it rough, so I'll be sure to fuck you before I slit your throat.

I swallow hard, my gaze lifting to Tanner's across the room as unease and fear rattle me. My hands begin to shake and the girls' conversation fades to white noise. My heart pounds and my eyes grow watery. I lived in Hope Falls for years and heard shit like that every day, but I've never had something so violent and ugly directed at me before.

Tanner stands, and before I know it, I'm running across the cafeteria, my phone clutched tightly in my hands. "Bri?" Ilaria calls after me.

I don't stop until I'm crushed against Tanner's chest, his strong arms wrapped around me. "What's wrong?" he demands, his gaze sharp as it sails around the cafeteria, searching for a threat. "What happened?"

I pass him my phone, and as he scans the text, his gaze darkens, and his hold becomes bruising around my waist. "Fucking Colby Jacobs," he rumbles. "It always comes back to that piece of shit. I swear to you, Killjoy, I will find whoever the fuck sent this text and destroy them. No one gets away with talking to you like that, especially after what Colby has already put you through."

Unshed tears fill my eyes as I crush my face against his strong chest. "It's going to be okay," he murmurs, his hand moving up and down my back as the rest of the guys move in, their expressions filled with concern, more than ready to jump to my defense at a moment's notice. "It'll be okay."

The bell sounds through the cafeteria and Tanner hands my phone to Riley. I watch as it's quickly passed around, and one by one, their faces become grim. "You've got biology now?" Tanner questions, his hands on my shoulders, putting the slightest space between us so that he can see my face. I nod and he glances toward Logan. "Aren't you in that class?"

"Yeah, man. I've got her. No one will touch her," Logan confirms, the reality of the situation like a weight on my chest.

"Don't take your eyes off her for a fucking second, got it?" Logan nods as Tanner glances toward Riley and Hudson. "I want this fucker found."

Jax hands my phone back to me, and I slip it into my pocket as Tanner takes my chin, forcing my freaked-out stare to him. "You have my word, Brielle. Whoever this fucker is won't get within a hundred feet of you. Go to class with Logan, stick right by his side, and then I'll drive you straight home after school."

I shake my head. "You'll be late for training," I tell him. "I'll be fine. It's just a threat. I think this guy is just trying to scare me to save Colby, but it won't work. Colby's DNA was confirmed, and not even this stupid text is going to stop me from doing my part in putting him away. It's just a scare tactic."

"I don't care what it is," he murmurs. "I don't care if it's some stupid kid having a laugh with his friends. No one gets away with talking to you like that, whether they're bluffing or not."

"Come on," Logan says, his fingers at my elbow. "We're going to be late. We'll sort this out."

I swallow hard and Tanner hastily brushes a kiss to my temple before allowing Logan to pull me away. I glance back over my shoulder, finding the girls huddled together, their concerned stares locked on my retreating form as Tanner remains right where he is, his dark, cloudy gaze filled with venom.

I've never seen this side of him. He's overprotective and scary, but he's exactly the type of person I want in my corner when receiving a text like that. Is this the version of him that Addison begged for over the phone while screaming for help? Did she know how he would drop everything to protect her? Fuck, I can't even begin to imagine how scared she must have been. And to think I was just in the next room. If I had been more aware of Colby and Erica's betrayal, maybe I could have done something to stop this. Maybe I would have known to keep a closer eye on them.

Logan walks beside me, and as we make our way out of the cafeteria, he glances at me with a grim expression. "So," he says, looking as though he's about to be sick. "How badly does Chanel want to kill me?"

Two minutes later, I walk through the door of my biology class with Logan trailing behind me. He usually sits in the very back of the classroom, doing everything he can to be invisible and avoid being called on. Only today, I'm not surprised when he drops down in the available seat beside me. "You really don't have to do that," I tell him. "You can sit in your normal spot. Nothing is going to happen."

Logan scoffs. "You really want to be the one to explain to Tanner why I wasn't glued to your ass the whole way through the lesson? I sure as fuck don't. Face the facts, Bri, today is the day we cross all those personal boundaries. I'll sit on your lap while you take a dump if I have to."

I gape at him as he smirks right back at me. "Like that's any worse than scooping chunks of your vomit out of my pool with my bare hands."

"You didn't," I gasp, humiliation draining the color from my face.

Logan laughs and turns to face the front of the room, leaving my question unanswered. But there's no way. Logan is rolling in cash. As if he would have done a dirty job like that. I heard the cleaners there first thing the next morning. Actually, maybe I should be offering to cover the cost of that. I'm sure Orlando would be happy to foot that bill.

I'm just about to offer when my biology teacher strides through the door with what looks like ketchup dripping down his shirt. He dumps his things on his desk before glancing up, his eyes locking right onto mine. "Miss Ashford," he says, giving me a friendly smile. "Principal Dormer has requested your presence in his office."

"I'm sorry," I say, my back stiffening with unease, my mind rushing through every little thing I've done since getting to this school. "In regard to what?"

"I wouldn't have a clue," he says, scrambling for something on his desk before holding it out to me. "I was under the impression it was going to be a quick meeting, so take the hall pass and hurry back. We're covering some important topics today."

Well, fuck.

I get up to make my way toward the front of the classroom when I notice Logan following behind and roll my eyes. "Seriously?" I question, glancing over my shoulder at my stalker before reaching out and taking the hall pass out of the teacher's hand. "I'll be back in two minutes. Chill out."

"Mr. Morgan," the teacher booms as Logan begins following me to the door. "Sit your ass down. I'm sure Brielle doesn't need you following her around school like a lost puppy."

"But—"

"Take your seat or your afternoon will be spent cleaning desks."

Logan grumbles something under his breath before turning on his heel and stalking back to the table, leaving me to walk out the door in peace. I make it quick, the message leaving me feeling way too uneasy despite the probability of the sender being someone from Hope Falls. I'm safe in the confines of the school. I shouldn't be worrying about it so much.

I reach Principal Dormer's office in no time and poke my head into the impressive room as I gently knock against the frame of the door.

Principal Dormer stands at his desk, shuffling through a bunch of files, and his head snaps up at my knock. "Ahh, Miss Ashford. I've been expecting you," he says, waving his hand toward the chair opposite his desk. "Please come in."

I hastily move across the room and drop into the empty chair, my hands fidgeting with the hem of my uniform. "I won't keep you long," he says, stepping back to the low-riding cabinetry behind his desk and leaning against the edge. "I wanted to check in with you after the events of last week. I understand it would be quite a lot to take in."

"Understatement of the year," I mutter.

"How are you handling everything?"

I shrug my shoulders. "It's been a huge clusterfuck if I can be so bold. The whole arrest was a joke, and the evidence they have against me is all fabricated."

"How so?"

"Well, they have images of me at the party where Addison was attacked. However, the photograph they have has been manipulated to appear as though I'm handling the drugs that Addison was given."

His brows furrow, looking thoughtful. "And you have proof of this?"

"I do," I tell him. "My … stepfather, Orlando Channing, has set me up with a lawyer who I'll be meeting with after school. So, I'm hoping that once I've supplied all my evidence, it'll be enough for the police to see the statement they were working with was false."

"I'm glad," he tells me. "I've been working with teens like yourself for twenty-odd years and it's shocking how often good students are led down a bad path. I have only the highest of hopes for you, Brielle."

"Thank you," I murmur, feeling a little odd about the whole meeting.

"Now, I'm sure you're aware that when things happen on school property, such as students getting arrested, there tends to be some … backlash from that." My brow arches and I wait impatiently for him to continue. "Your arrest has been the topic of conversation all week, and as you can understand, I have had many calls from misinformed parents. Please don't be alarmed, I do not intend to take any action against you. I'm simply informing you of what's going on."

"What is going on?" I question.

"There has been a call for your suspension. Some of the parents feel, considering the reasons for your arrest, that their children would be safer attending school if you were not here. Now, I have put my foot down and explained that you are innocent until proven guilty, and no disciplinary action will be taken against you. However," he says, a nervousness flickering in his eyes as his tone shifts, adding a higher level of authority. "I am sure you would understand that if you do happen to be charged with these horrendous accusations against you, I will be left with no choice but to expel you from Bradford Private. Is that understood?"

"Yes, sir," I say with a slight nod of my head. "I understand. Though you should know that I am completely innocent in all of this, I didn't even have a little bit to do with it. I know exactly who hurt Addison and his motivation behind it, and the police have ensured me that he will be going down for it. You don't have anything to worry about."

"Let's hope so," he says. "As for your arrest, how are you handling that? It was … unexpected, and had I known a gun would be drawn on one of my students, I would have never allowed them onto school property. I know you are still new here, but please remember that we have student counselors if you feel that you need someone to talk with."

"Thank you," I say, giving him a tight smile. "I'm okay."

"Wonderful," he murmurs, pushing off the edge of his cabinetry. "In that case, I think you should hurry back to class, and remember that my door is always open. I look forward to hearing when your name has been cleared."

And with that, I get the fuck out of there, realizing how much damage has already been done. While the police may give me the all clear, my reputation has already been destroyed.

CHAPTER 13

TANNER

My helmet rocks back and forth, balancing on the handlebar of my bike, and I don't waste another second getting off and sprinting toward Channing's front door. Brielle should have been home from her meeting with the lawyer twenty minutes ago, and I need to know how it went. I can't wait another second.

My patience is nonexistent, and that was made clear during practice. I got my ass handed to me. Usually, I take pride in my ability to keep my head in the game, but after the text that was sent to my girl today, I've struggled.

The thought of something happening to her … fuck. It's bad enough that every night before bed, the image of Bri's Honda wrapped around that fucking tree haunts me. I'll never forget that moment. It's ingrained in my brain for all of eternity. In those few seconds between throwing myself off my bike and racing around the smoking car, I think I died a million times.

It was the exact same gut-wrenching feeling that nearly brought me to my knees when my sister called me in hysterics. Only with Addison, I had to listen to her cries for what seemed like an eternity before I could get to her. I was too late then. I'm always too late, but never again.

I know the text was sent as a threat with the sole intention of scaring her. There's no doubt in my mind that the asshole on the other end is probably a fucking pussy who'd wet his pants at the thought of me showing up on his doorstep. Either way, I'm going to put an end to it, even if it's the last thing I do. Having Brielle going through life looking over her shoulder is unacceptable to me. She deserves better.

I reach for the handle of the front door just as it's yanked open from within. Jensen Channing stands before me, his eyes widening as I try to slow my momentum. Clearly he hadn't expected me to storm through his front door while he was trying to leave. "She home?" I rush out, glancing over his shoulder and trying to listen to the noises coming from inside, but he blocks my way with a narrowed gaze.

I can only imagine what he's thinking. He was there that night at the track. He heard the bullshit that came from my mouth, and he was the one who drove her home in tears. He saw the pain I left her in.

Jensen's probably not my biggest fan, but I can't exactly say I'm a fan of his, either. I don't like that he sleeps just down the hall from my girl, despite knowing he was cleared of hurting that girl last year. I don't trust him, and from the look of it, the feeling is mutual.

"Ever heard of knocking?" he spits, his lip pulling up into a slight sneer, something I've seen from him all too often.

"Waste of time," I tell him. "Is she home or not?"

Not seeing the point of arguing about this in the doorway, Jensen steps aside. "She's in her room," he mutters, rolling his eyes, probably realizing that no matter how this conversation goes, I'll be getting inside that house and to my girl. Nothing will stop me, even if it means physically removing him.

I don't give him a second thought before barging past and flying straight up the stairs two at a time. I have the brief thought to slip in through the hallway closet and hoist myself up through the crawl space to surprise her, but by the time the thought has even fully crossed my mind, I'm already barging through her door.

Killjoy gasps at seeing me and her whole body jumps with shock. "Fuck, Tanner," she breathes, her hand flying to her chest. "You can't just storm in here like that after the text I got today. You scared the shit out of me."

"My bad," I say, sucking in a deep breath and trying to calm my own nerves. I move to the end of her bed and lean over, bracing my hands on either side of her thighs before brushing a soft kiss over her lips. "How'd your meeting go?" I question, my heart racing, desperate for some sort of good news.

Bri leans back onto her hands, her eyes sparkling with happiness. "He thinks I'm going to be fine," she tells me, her words forcing a low sigh out of me. "I submitted everything I had, and he was confident they'd drop the case against me. My evidence was overwhelming and proof enough that Erica was lying. They're going to have to disregard her whole statement and she'll probably get a misdemeanor charge for lying to the cops, meaning I'll be completely off the hook."

My head falls forward as relief rocks through me. "Fuck, Killer. That's the best news I've heard all fucking week."

"You're telling me," she murmurs, her forced smile not reflecting the way she should be feeling. "I feel like I can finally breathe. I never want to have to go through something like this again. I mean, it's not officially over. My lawyer has to present it all to the cops and then he'll call me once I've officially been cleared."

"Okay, why don't you look thrilled about all of this?" I ask, moving back and leaning against her desk.

Bri lets out a heavy sigh and presses her lips into a tight line, worry marring her pretty face. "He said it's more than likely the police will still want to talk to me, specifically about Erica's involvement and the statement I made last week. I guess they have more questions or something like that. Don't get me wrong," she says. "I'll tell them anything they want to know. I want your sister to get justice for everything that happened to her, I just …"

"Feel like shit for throwing Erica under the bus the way she did you."

Bri nods, and I move across the room, scooping her off her bed before taking her place and lowering her to my lap. "Talk to me, Killjoy. I don't want you feeling like shit over this."

"I know," she murmurs. "It's just that those thirteen years of friendship actually meant something to me. She was my best friend, and I guess I'm just not over it yet. It still hurts to think about what she did. I thought she was my ride or die, and to find out she wasn't only sleeping with Colby behind my back, but that she had something to do with hurting your sister … the whole thing makes me sick."

"It's going to be okay, babe," I tell her. "It'll feel like shit, but you're doing the right thing. She can't get away with this. You just need to think of it as taking out the trash. You have new friends to lean on now, friends who actually give a shit about you."

Bri's face softens and she leans into me, her lips pressing to mine. "Thank you," she whispers, her warm lips moving against mine. "Who would have—"

My phone cuts through the serenity and Bri's words fall away as I groan and adjust my hold on her. My hand slips into my pocket, searching for my phone. I can guarantee it's the boys checking in. Everyone knew what Bri was doing this afternoon, and they were just as hungry for answers as I was. Only unlike me, they can control themselves.

I'm just about to silence the call when I see Mom's name flashing across the screen. "Shit, sorry, babe," I say, hitting accept on the call and bringing it to my ear.

"Mom, what's up? Everything okay?"

"Oh, Tanner," she says, sounding as though she's out of breath. "I just had a call from the doctor. They think this is it. She's waking up."

"For real?" I rush out, throwing myself to my feet and struggling to hold onto Bri, momentarily forgetting she was on my lap. My eyes zone in on hers, so wide and alert as she grips onto me, sensing this is an important call.

"Yes, Tanner," Mom says, sounding as though she's about to break into tears of joy. "I had to duck into your father's office to collect some papers. I'm not with her right now, and it's at least an hour drive back. I'm not going to make it in time. Please tell me you're close. I can't have my baby waking up alone."

"I'll be there," I tell her. "I'm leaving now."

"Hurry."

I throw my phone down, frantic as I search Bri's room for my shoes that are already on my goddamn feet. Bri grabs me, forcing me to focus and breathe. "What's going on?" she questions, her eyes wide and full of hope. "Is Addison okay?"

A grin stretches across my face and I all but start whooping like a fucking cowboy at his first rodeo. "She's waking up," I beam, feeling so relieved that it physically hurts. I grab Brielle and pull her into me, crushing my lips to hers in a bruising, swift kiss, wishing that I could have her in my arms for all of eternity. "I have to go."

Her warmth hasn't even left my fingers before I'm flying toward the door. "GO," she calls after me, joyous laughter in her addictive tone.

I fly down the hall before doubling back and shoving my head through the open door, the beaming grin on my face like nothing I've ever felt before. "Hey," I rush out, watching as she spins around to face me. "I fucking love you."

Brielle's eyes bug out of her head, but I don't hang around for a response. There's no way in hell I'm about to let Addie wake up alone. Not on my fucking watch. Though I'm not going to lie, it feels fucking amazing to have those words finally come out of me. It's not exactly how I'd envisioned telling her for the first time, but it'll have to do. I can make it up to her later, but right now, I have a sister to see.

I'm out the front door and catapulting myself over the boundary line in no time. My leg flies over the side of my bike and knocks my helmet off the handlebar. I consider taking off without it, but the last thing I need is to end up in the bed next to Addison. Besides, this really incredible chick told me I needed to learn how to control myself, and I think taking the extra second to do the right thing falls under the self-growth category.

My bike rumbles to life, and I take off, not even bothered by the thick black line left across my driveway. I know my father will have something to say about it, but I'll just blame the douchebag next door … or Jax.

I reach the hospital in under ten minutes and fly through the automatic double doors. I've been here so often with Mom over the past seven weeks that the nurses don't bother asking me to stop and sign in anymore. Most of the time, I follow the rules here, but today is different. I don't have time to spare.

Making my way up to the ICU, I go through the routine of washing my hands and using the anti-bacterial sanitizer, knowing damn well that if I don't, they're just going to throw me back out the door. It feels as though it takes forever, but when it's finally done, I take off like a bat out of hell.

I hurry down the hall, trying to be respectful of the other patients, and take the first right, counting the doors as I go.

Seven.

Eight.

Nine.

I shove my way through the tenth door on the left, my heart racing with anticipation, only to come to a screeching halt, finding Hudson in the seat my mother usually claims. He watches over Addison, his eyes wide, but not as fucking wide as when he turns to find me staring right back at him.

"The fuck are you doing here?" I question, my gaze flicking toward Addie and checking her over as I move deeper into her room, noting the few nurses busily going about their jobs, and making sure she has everything she needs.

Hudson stands, awkwardly hovering in the corner of the room as I move right to Addison's bedside, slipping her soft hand into mine and willing her to wake. "I, ummm … I thought I'd swing by and check on her after practice," Hudson says, his voice cracking with a strange emotion, one I've never heard from him before. "Is she really waking up?" he questions. "The nurses won't tell me shit. I had to practically bulldoze my way in here."

I glance toward him, full of suspicion before looking back at Addie. "Yeah, that's what they told Mom. She called and demanded I get my ass over here as soon as possible. She didn't want Addie waking up alone."

"She wasn't alone," Hudson says way too fast.

"The fuck is wrong with you today?" I ask.

He shakes his head, his gaze shifting to Addie again. "Nothing, I just ... I meant that I was here so if she woke up before you got here, she wouldn't have been alone."

"Right," I say, more than ready to push him for details when Addie's hand flinches in mine and my head swings back to her like one of those clowns at the fairground. "Addie?" I rush out, my body tensing with nervousness as Hudson shuffles in closer, both of us desperate to see her finally open those bright blue eyes. "Addie? Can you hear me? Please, Addie, wake the fuck up. I know you're in there, just put me out of my misery."

Her eyes flutter and I gasp like a little bitch. "Holy fuck," I rush out, shoving my elbow back against Hudson's ribs. "Did you see that? Tell me you fucking saw that?"

We both lean in closer, and I give her hand a gentle squeeze. "Come on, brat," I urge. "You got this in the bag. I swear, just open those goddamn eyes, and I'll give you whatever you want. Lamborghini on Dad's credit card? One of those Burger Bags you always talk about? Fuck, I'll even admit that I was the one who switched out the ketchup for the hot sauce during Dad's big business meeting when we were kids."

Her eyes flutter again, and I swear, I could fucking cry with happiness. This is more than we've gotten from her in a little over seven weeks now. I just hope the sister I've always known and loved is still in there somewhere, though I'm not foolish. I know things are going to be different, *she's* different now. How could she not be after what she went through? But not a day will go by where I won't remind her that she's fucking perfect. Though, I'll make sure to call her a brat every time I do. I can't have her thinking I've gone soft.

A quiet groan fills the room, and just like that, Addie's eyes open, squinting into the harsh hospital light.

"Holy fuck," I breathe, falling to my knees, my head dropping to the edge of her hospital bed as I cling to her hand with everything I've got.

Addie makes a choking noise, and my head snaps up to find panic in her eyes, but the nurse quickly rushes in, putting herself between me and Addie. "You're okay," she says in a soothing tone, working quickly to remove the breathing tube.

Addison takes a gasping breath, her eyes wide, unsure of what the fuck is going on. Her stare comes back to mine, waiting for some kind of explanation, but another nurse hurries in, giving her a thorough check and making sure she's stable. "Hi Addison," she says as she goes about her routine. "My name is Rebecca. I've been waiting to officially meet you. Do you know where you are?"

Addie glances around, her eyes flicking from left to right before coming right back to mine. She nods and Rebecca smiles. "You've been in a coma, but everything is looking good here. I'm going to call for the doctor and give you a chance to catch up."

With that, Rebecca glances toward me with an encouraging smile. "Take your time," she says, her voice low. "She's bound to have questions and she'll be confused. It's like waking from a really long sleep. She'll be groggy and tired, so offer her small sips of water and just hold her hand like you're doing. She had a very traumatic experience, and there's a good chance she remembers it, so be prepared for that."

Rebecca excuses herself and I look back toward my sister, every piece of me breaking. It's one thing holding out hope for her to come out of this, and don't get me wrong, I've never been so happy, but now she has a completely different battle to face. One that's going to tear her apart.

Addie glances toward Hudson, and before anyone can say a damn word, he backs up. "I, umm … I'm gonna give you guys some space," he says, his gaze shifting over my sister again. "I'll give your mom a call and let her know the good news so you can focus on helping her."

"Alright, thanks, man," I say, watching as he takes off like a fucking bullet.

I look back to Addie, unsure what to do. "Can you talk?" I ask nervously, creeping even closer toward her, not wanting to make any sudden movements as though it could fuck everything up and send her back into a lifeless coma, though I doubt that's even possible.

Addie swallows hard and cringes before lifting her hand to her throat. "It's sore," she says, her tone raspy and quiet, but fuck it's good to hear it. I'll take raspy and quiet over nothing any day.

"Yeah, you've had a breathing tube down there for the past few weeks. It'll be sore for a while. A few days, maybe a week. I'm not really sure." I glance over her bed, trying to figure out how to make her comfortable. "Do you need anything? I can adjust your bed so you're sitting up."

She nods and I quickly make the adjustments before filling a cup of water and topping it off with a straw. I hold it to her lips and hate how she cringes as she takes small sips. My heart breaks for her, and the hollowness deep in my gut has me desperate to make things right.

"You said weeks," she whispers, not able to use her full voice just yet.

I nod, and the more I look at her, the more I'm reminded of that night, of her terrified scream on the other end of the phone, the pain, how she begged me to help, begged me to get to her faster. "Yeah," I say, trying to hold myself together as I reach for her hand again. "Seven to be exact."

"Seven?"

I nod and watch as a heaviness creeps into her stare, and just when I thought this moment couldn't get any harder, her eyes slowly begin to fill with unshed tears. Anger bursts through my chest, and I clutch onto her hand just a little bit tighter. "You remember."

Her face scrunches with her silent pain and she nods. "All of it."

Her tears begin to fall, and I lean into her, wishing there was some way I could take away her grief, some way to take the darkness out of her soul and give her the light and happiness she deserves. "Addie, I—"

"No," she says, her voice so broken and defeated. "Don't, Tanner. I … I can't. Don't make me."

"Okay," I rush out, reaching up and brushing her hair back off her face. "I won't. We don't have to talk about it, but I'm here, Addie. Right fucking here. I'm not going anywhere."

We sit for ten minutes as I just hold her hand, listening to her broken cries and watching the way her tears fall, every last one of them breaking me further. But she needs me to be strong, needs me to be her rock, and until she's ready to face the world on her own, I'm going to continue to be that for her.

The doctor comes in and quickly checks over her, and while he doesn't specifically ask what she remembers, it's clear from the tear-stained gown, her blotchy cheeks, and her red-rimmed eyes. With Addie stable, he puts off his tests until Mom can be here and promises to return in an hour. Until then, we just sit, waiting and hoping that one day, it'll all get easier.

CHAPTER 14
Brielle

Darkness falls across my bedroom as I flip the bathroom light off and head back to bed. It's just after one in the morning, and despite my tireless efforts, sleep simply isn't in the cards for me tonight.

I haven't been able to stop my thoughts from spinning since the moment Tanner burst out of here like his ass was on fire. When he ended the call with his mom, he dashed around my room with wide, frantic eyes, and instead of dropping his phone into his pocket, it fell to the floor and slid beneath my bed. He was so full of hope but also plagued by fear, and I wanted nothing more than to be by his side, holding his hand and telling him that everything was going to be okay. It wasn't my place, though. Tanner needed to be there for Addison, and I'm sure she wouldn't have appreciated waking up to find some strange girl clinging to her big brother.

I can't imagine the things that went through her mind when she woke up. She would have been so scared and confused, and then at some point, the memories of what Colby did to her would have come rushing back, but I hope for her sake that doesn't happen. I can't imagine how it would feel to have to live it in your mind over and over again, the emotions that would come along with it, the pain and agony, the anger and self-loathing.

No woman should ever have to go through that.

Though, one thing is for sure, if Addison has woken up and does remember what happened, she's lucky to have someone like Tanner watching over her. He'll take care of her, and while he might not be able to change what happened or take her pain away, nothing will stop him from being the rock she leans on. Whatever she needs, he'll be right there to deliver—whether it's just someone to hold her hand, or Colby's severed head.

Out of habit, my gaze rises to my bedroom window to find Tanner's room still covered in darkness. He's probably going to spend the night at the hospital with his sister, which is expected. If I were Addison, I'd want somebody by my side, ready to hold my hand and remind me that no matter what, they have my back.

Pulling the blankets down, I slip back into bed and drop my head to the pillow, but I can't keep my stare off his window. I don't know when I'll see him next. I wouldn't be surprised if he stayed in the hospital all night and then skipped out on school tomorrow as well.

His coach would understand, and the boys will be there to pick up the slack during training.

But without his phone, no one can check in on him. No one can make sure he's actually sleeping or hasn't gone off the deep end again. Right now, he's busy playing the role of Addison's protector, but who's going to protect him?

Fuck.

Tearing my blanket back, I throw myself out of bed and grab his phone off my bedside table before slipping my feet into my oversized chicken feet slippers. I smirk just as I do every time I put them on. My brother bought them for me as a joke, assuming I'd never wear them, but the joke's on him because it's been two years, and I wear them all the time.

Trudging out of my room, I sneak down the stairs, not wanting to wake anyone, but I only get halfway down before coming to a startled stop, finding Jensen hovering at the bottom step, looking up at me with a raised brow.

"Where the hell do you think you're going?" he questions, his gaze sailing down to my chicken feet.

I resist rolling my eyes and give him a tight smile. "Nowhere."

"Right," he scoffs before continuing up the stairs and stopping right next to me. He gives me a knowing smirk, and I instantly want to smack it off his stupid face. "Remember, no glove, no love."

"You're infuriating," I tell him. "Has anyone ever told you that?"

Jensen winks. "All the time," he says before laughing and continuing up the stairs.

Ignoring the dipshit, I waddle the rest of the way down the stairs and hurry out into the night. It's unreasonably cold, especially considering just how hot it was over the weekend, and I immediately regret not grabbing a hoodie. I move faster, hurrying around to the side of the property to the tree between our homes.

Shoving Tanner's phone into the pocket of my sweatpants, I begin my climb, making it to the top in no time. Now that I know the easiest route to the top, scaling the big bastard isn't as hard as I once thought it was.

As usual, Tanner's window is cracked just enough to slip my fingers through and jimmy it open, and I quickly welcome myself into his room, pinching the discarded hoodie off his bed. I pull it on and find myself inhaling his scent, sending a wave of butterflies to wreak havoc in my stomach.

I am so unbelievably head over heels for this guy. I mean, look at me. I'm breaking into his bedroom at one in the morning simply because he might need his phone at some point tomorrow.

Fuck, I'm a loser, but a cool loser, not like an actual loser. I'm also a thoughtful loser, which is why I don't just put his phone on his side table, I go ahead and plug it into the charger.

Feeling proud of myself, I turn back to the window to leave when I find myself pausing and glancing back to the wall behind his bed. I mean, I'm already here. What's the harm of leaving a message while I'm at it? Besides, I'm sure he'll be happy to know I was thinking of him.

Searching through his room for something to use, I find the

tattered remains of more than half of my lipstick collection. I roll my eyes before shoving what I can salvage into my pocket and taking the cap off a bright red shade I used to love. I climb onto his bed, and just because I take wall messages seriously, I pull up the sleeve of his hoodie and get to work.

A grin cuts across my face, deciding what better way to tell him I'm here for him than writing something equally as crass as the messages he's left for me.

IF I HAD A DICK, I'D FUCK YOU SO HARD WITH IT. HOW DO YOU FEEL ABOUT A PEARL NECKLACE? ACTUALLY ... EVER HEARD OF PEGGING?

I stand back, surveying my handiwork when a throat clears from across the room. My head whips around and I gasp, finding Tanner leaning against his open doorframe, a wide grin across his devilish face. "What the fuck?" I whisper-yell, pressing my hand to my chest over my racing heart. "You scared the shit out of me."

"Well, if you weren't busy breaking into my room in the middle of the night to tell me about your dick, then I wouldn't have been able to scare you."

"Ha, ha," I murmur, jumping down from his bed and regretting the choice to wear my chicken feet.

Tanner stares intently, and I watch with a racing heart as he makes his way toward me. "I'm glad you're here," he says, stepping right into me. His gaze trails over the stolen hoodie with a smirk. His hands slip beneath the hem of the hoodie before taking my waist, and I immediately move closer, needing his touch more than I need to breathe. "I was planning on sneaking into your room to check on you."

"Check on me?" I question, my hand slipping up the front of his shirt and resting against his warm chest, feeling the heavy thump of his heart. "I should be the one checking on you. How did it go? Did Addison wake up?"

Tanner's eyes brim with relief and a weight lifts off my shoulders. "She did," he murmurs, his thumbs brushing back and forth over my skin. "It's going to be a long road though. She's broken in ways I've never seen before. But if she can make it through this, she can make it through anything."

"She's going to be okay because she has you," I tell him, making sure he truly hears me.

Tanner shakes his head before dropping his forehead to mine. "You put too much faith in me, Bri."

"No," I whisper. "You don't put enough in yourself."

Tanner takes a breath, his fingers tightening on my waist, and as the room falls into silence and his eyes remain locked on mine, a heavy tension begins to build between us, morphing this sweet moment into something much more serious.

For the past week, it's been teasing, fun, and games. Pushing each other's buttons and trying to prove a point with this ridiculous challenge, but right now, none of that matters. All I need is him.

His arms close around me, holding me as though he'll never let me go, and I feel my heart swell. I knew that sooner or later, Tanner would claim me, and I would give myself over, knowing we'd never look back.

For the past few weeks, we've been dancing around one another, feeling that exhilarating push and pull, but we've moved past that now. Tanner Morgan is my future. I want to be the woman standing at the sidelines of each of his games, the woman pushing him to do the impossible, the one he comes home to.

I want to be his world.

I pull back, the overwhelming emotion almost too much to handle, especially as those dark eyes stare longingly into mine. "Tanner," I whisper.

He leans in again, this time barely touching his lips to mine. "I know," he tells me, feeling it too. "There's no going back for me. I'm not fucking around anymore. This is as real as it gets. Addison is awake and your charges are going to be dropped. There's nothing standing in our way, nothing stopping us, and I don't know about you, but it'll fucking kill me if you've decided you don't want this."

Looping an arm around the back of his neck, I press my body right up against his. "I'm scared we're rushing into this," I tell him, searching his eyes, my heart pounding like never before. "We've only known each other for a few weeks. How can we be this serious so soon?"

"Don't doubt us," he murmurs. "Just because I haven't known you since you were a toddler or been dating for the past year doesn't mean that what I feel for you isn't real. It doesn't matter how quickly it happened or how unexpected it was, all that matters is that it did. I told you the other night in my car, the moment I saw you and you opened that smart mouth of yours, you were mine."

"This is insane."

"Maybe it is," he agrees, his eyes staring so deeply into mine, daring me to say yes.

"You told me you love me," I remind him, my hold getting tighter as I remember the way his eyes lit up as the words flew from his mouth. "On second thought, it was more like a yell," I add. "Did you mean that?"

His voice lowers, so deep and full of wonder. "Every fucking word."

A soft squeak tears out of me just as his warm lips crush to mine. He kisses me deeply, everything left unsaid being communicated through his actions instead. He kisses me with passion and hunger, and I meet his intensity, needing this more than I've ever needed anything in my life.

Tanner Morgan is mine.

His hands drop beneath my ass and lift me just enough for my legs to wrap around his waist. A thrill shoots through me as Tanner walks us across his room, a hungry growl rumbling through the back of his throat.

Before I know it, my head hits his pillow, and his body presses down on top of mine. When I pull him in closer, I tighten my legs around him, and Tanner grinds into me, his hardening cock rocking against my aching clit. I latch onto the hem of his shirt and pull it over his head, starving for the feel of his sculpted body.

He tears his hoodie off me, taking my sleep tank with it and immediately diving down to suck my pebbled nipple into his mouth.

Pleasure blasts through me as I murmur his name, my fingers threading into his hair and holding on tight as I arch my back off his bed, needing so much more.

Reading me perfectly, his tongue flicks over my nipple and my whole body jolts. "Again," I breathe.

I feel his smile against my skin as he teases me just right, his fingers brushing over my body, leaving a wake of goosebumps as his tongue flicks my nipple again. And again. And fuck yes, again.

My pussy throbs. I have to have him.

Tanner's lips come back to mine, and I reach down between us, slipping my hand inside his sweatpants. He's so fucking hard it makes my mouth water. My fingers curl around his velvety cock, slowly working my way up before swiping my thumb over his tip, enticing a groan from deep within his chest.

"Fuck, Killer," he growls, his lips pressing against my throat, right where I like it. A breathy moan sails from my lips as he raises his hips just enough to rid me of my pajama bottoms. "If you want me to stop, you need to tell me now," he says, his lips not daring to move off my skin. "I know you wanted to wait a while …"

He allows his words to trail off, and I shake my head, pushing his pants down past his hips with my other hand. "Don't you dare stop," I tell him in a breathy whisper. "I'm done waiting."

Tanner groans, and without skipping a beat, his hand trails down my body, cupping my pussy and giving a firm squeeze, relieving the ache for only a second. His grip loosens, and just as I stroke his thick cock again, he pushes two fingers deep inside me.

My back arches as a gasp sails between my lips. "Yes," I say through a clenched jaw.

His fingers curl inside me, massaging my walls as his thumb comes down on my clit, rubbing tight, lazy circles and making my eyes flutter with pleasure.

"Tanner, I—" His fingers plunge deeper, and I gasp, needing him inside me. "God, YES!"

He reads me so well and knows my body better than I know myself, but nothing is better than that deep, throaty voice in my ear. "You fucking want it, Killer? Are you ready for me?"

"Fuck, Tanner. I need you inside me," I pant. "Fuck me, please."

In one smooth motion, Tanner reaches across to his bedside drawer and pulls out a condom before tearing it open with his teeth. I take it from him and watch his eyes flutter as I roll it down his thick shaft. He growls deep, his eyes darkening with desire. He's a man starved, and I don't doubt he'll be fucking me into the early hours of the morning.

My stare locks onto his as I hitch my leg higher over his hip, ready to take him deep, but the bastard grins down at me, shaking his head as his eyes sparkle with devilish intent. "Oh, no, Killer. This ain't gonna be that easy."

Not a second later, Tanner grabs my hips and flips me over, my chest flat on the bed as my ass rides high in the air. He spanks my ass, and I suck in a breath, spreading my thighs as wide as they'll go, the anticipation damn near ready to kill me.

I feel his heavy erection against my ass and push back against him. Tanner groans, one hand on my ass cheek as the other takes his thick cock and drags it through my wetness. He does it again, and just as I think he's going to keep teasing me, he slams that thick cock deep inside my waiting cunt.

"Oh, fuck," I cry, my pussy stretching around him, taking him whole. I push back as my fingers fist into the bed sheet. Tanner draws back and slams forward again, hard, heavy thrusts giving into the raw, animalistic need we hold for one another.

Reaching between my legs, I gently rub my clit, already feeling that pulsing desire deepening inside me, growing, expanding, and desperate for more. I take it all, everything he's got, and when his hand moves to my ass and his thumb applies just enough pressure, I'm fucked.

He's giving me exactly what I need, and I clench my eyes, my orgasm building to new heights. His thumb moves in sync with the way I rub my clit, and as he moves in and out of me, his thick cock throbbing, I can't help but feel like the most desirable woman in the world.

It's a sin to feel this good, and without a doubt, Tanner and I are going to hell. Fuck, I'd burn with him for eternity if it meant getting fucked like this every day of forever.

Tanner pushes me hard, fucking me like he'll never get enough, and I cry out, hearing that delicious *slap* of his strong thighs slamming against mine. My pussy shudders as I clench around him, and with one more thrust, my world explodes with the most intense orgasm.

"Fuck, Tanner," I cry as my high rocks through me, pulsing through my veins and right through to my fingertips. My toes curl and my pussy convulses as I turn into a shaking mess, completely wrecked, but Tanner doesn't dare let up. He pushes against his thumb, stretching me just a little wider and just when I thought it was all over, my orgasm reaches new heights.

"Fuck, fuck, fuck," I moan into the mattress, concentrating on the way his velvety cock slides in and out of my pussy, his tip massaging my walls, teasing me in the most devilish way.

I come down from my high, and just when I sense Tanner about to come undone, I flip the game on him, just as he did to me.

Despite being thoroughly fucked and exhausted, I push up from the mattress, giving myself enough space to pull away from him and spin around. I come face-to-face with him, each of us on our knees as I hold his stare and free him from the confines of the condom.

Tanner watches me through a narrowed gaze as he reaches for me, but I swat him away and shake my head. "Uh-uh," I grin, my tongue rolling over my bottom lip as I continue working his thick cock. "Down boy."

"What—"

I motion to the edge of the bed. "Sit."

He arches a brow but does exactly as I've asked, and I don't waste a damn second, scrambling off the bed and dropping to my knees before him. His eyes darken as I look up at him, my tongue rolling over my lips.

"Open wide, Killer," he murmurs, his voice thick with desire.

"Tsk, tsk," I say with a hungry stare, unable to resist spreading my thighs. "I'm the one giving orders here."

Tanner grins down at me, and if it weren't for how hungry I am for him, I might have even taken my time. I lean in and keep my eyes on his as my tongue swirls over his tip, lapping up the bead of moisture as though I'll never eat again. I can't resist him and open wide, taking him deep in my throat, showing him exactly what my tongue can do.

I suck and tease, bobbing up and down as I hollow out my cheeks and almost get myself off at the needy groans tearing out of Tanner. His hand curls into my hair as I push myself further, bypassing straight past that gag reflex.

"Fucking hell, Killer," Tanner says through a clenched jaw, his whole body tensing beneath me, warning me just how close he is. I push myself harder, sucking, teasing, moaning. Whatever he wants, I'll give him. My tongue rolls over his tip, and as I take him in the back of my throat again, Tanner groans, his body stiffening as he comes hard, spurting his hot seed right down my throat.

I suck him dry, not giving in until I've tasted every last drop like a greedy whore.

Satisfaction tears through me, and as I stare up at him, licking my lips for a job well done, I see nothing but wonder in his eyes. I'm hit with a wave of pride.

Tanner reaches down and grabs me, hoisting me up until I'm straddled on his lap, my pussy grinding against him. He kisses me deeply, and when we finally come up for air, Tanner's eyes light up like a fucking Christmas tree. "What?" I ask, a wide grin stretching across my face.

Tanner just laughs, and with one smooth throw, my body crashes down against the pillow. Before I know it, he's hovering over me. "You didn't think you'd be able to suck my cock and not have me spread those pretty thighs like a fucking buffet, did you?"

"I—uhmmm." I swallow hard, unable to take my eyes off him, watching as he crawls down my body. He reaches the end of the bed, and just when I start to wonder what the fuck he's going to do, he grabs my ankles and drags me down until my ass is almost hanging off the edge. Tanner drops to his knees and spreads my thighs wide, exposing every inch of me.

He meets my stare, and I watch with bated breath as his tongue rolls over his lips. "Don't move a fucking muscle," he tells me. "This is my game now, and I'm not stopping until I've pulled every last orgasm out of you."

What's a girl to do?

Dig in and don't wait, baby. I'm yours for the taking.

CHAPTER 15
TANNER

My lip curls watching as my father, Trenton Morgan, fusses over Addison as though she were his whole world, and if it weren't for the fact she's eating up every last second of it, I would have kicked him out hours ago.

What kind of father remains on a business trip while his daughter is suffering through a coma after being drugged and raped, leaving his wife to go through hell trying to hold things together on her own?

Fuck him. I used to have respect for this prick, but not anymore. I understand business is important, but what's more important than being there for his family when they need it most? I have to give the asshole credit, the second he heard Addie was awake, he boarded a flight and was here to act like he'd been here the whole time. A regular fucking hero.

I didn't have the heart to tell her the dickhead could only spare a five-minute phone call with Mom during those long hours she waited by Addie's bedside. Hell, sometimes he forgot to call altogether. Addie's already broken after what Colby did to her, and I don't want to be the one to break her again. So for now, she gets to think she's the apple of my father's eye, and that she's the most important person in his world. I just hate that one of these days, he's going to break her heart just like he did to me when I was a kid.

My father and I have always had a strained relationship. He's an asshole, and I'm a prick. There's no middle ground between us. He was always the hand that came down with the law. He was responsible for turning me into a man, punishing me whenever I fucked up, and it shouldn't come as a surprise just how often that happened. I resented him during my younger years, and now, I just simply don't give a fuck. When he started taking these extra-long business trips and leaving us for months at a time, I had to step up and be the man of the house. And now, he's nothing but an intruder in my home.

Dad treats Mom well—when he's around—and she seems to still be madly in love with the guy. I don't understand it. I've wondered so many times why she bothers hanging on to him. At first, I thought she was sticking it out for me and Addie, but we're older now. We could handle it if she chose to leave his ass in the dust, yet she keeps up this ridiculous charade that we're some kind of happy family. But for her, I'll grin and bear it. Mom and Addie are what matter here, and as long as they still want him in their lives, then that's how it's going to be.

Dad sits at Addie's bedside, clutching her hand and laughing with her as he shares stories about how he's the hero of all his board meetings, and though I can easily see she's dying inside, desperate for real entertainment, she still laughs along with him, living off his attention like an addict.

It's been a week of this bullshit, and I'm barely holding on. The only thing keeping me grounded right now is knowing that when I go home, I'll be in Brielle's bed, between those sexy thighs, and listening to the way she cries my name as she comes on my tongue. It's fucking magical.

Addie laughs again, and I have to remind myself how fucking lucky we are that we're even blessed with the ability to hear her laugh. This could have ended in tragedy, and there was a good chance that I was never going to see her again. I should be thanking anyone who has the ability to put a smile on her face, even if it's my father, and while she's laughing with him, she's not shrinking back into that dark place or remembering the terror she felt when Colby forced himself inside of her.

A heavy smack hits the back of my head and I whip around to find my mother glaring at me. "Quit with the scowling," she says under her breath, trying not to draw attention. "You look like someone crawled up your ass with hot sauce. Is it so hard to pretend to be happy for your sister?"

I give her a blank stare. "Hot sauce? Really?"

Mom tries to hold my stare, but a wide grin cracks across her face, her eyes lighting with silent laughter and making that coldness in my chest begin to thaw. "That was a good one, right?" she says, her brows bouncing as though she's the funniest person on Earth. All I can do is shake my head. For those seven long weeks, that spark in her eyes dwindled down until I was sure I'd never see it again. I'd never seen her looking so defeated in my life, but now, she's never been happier. Which, unfortunately for me, means that she's right back to cracking the most inappropriate jokes at the worst time. I swear, this woman lives just to humiliate me.

There's a soft knock on the open door, and every conversation falls silent as all eyes zone in on Dr. Arton, the best neurologist in the country. We've been waiting for this moment all week. There has been test after test, checking Addie's brain function and motor neurons … whatever the fuck that means. But today we find out if she gets to come home.

Dr. Arton strides across the room, putting himself right at Addison's bedside and giving her a proud smile. "Passed with flying colors," he tells her, holding up the tablet that's been attached to his hand since the second we first met him. "You're going home."

Addie gasps, her hand flying to her mouth as she whips around and gapes at Mom, who's already sobbing with happiness. "Are you shitting me?" Addie questions, glancing back to the doctor.

"Language," Dad grunts before standing on Addie's other side and offering Dr. Arton his hand. "Thank you for everything you've done for my girl, Doctor. We are forever in your debt."

Dr. Arton nods and gives Dad a forced smile. "Just doing my job," he says before turning to Addison. "Now, you're not entirely off scott free. You'll need to continue taking your medications for the time being. I know you don't like them, but unfortunately, it's a necessary evil in your case. I'll need to see you every few months for scans to ensure your brain is functioning as it should. Emerging from a coma can be … difficult. It's a lot to process, missed time, confusion, memory loss. I know these aren't symptoms that have affected you, but I strongly recommend talking with a specialized therapist who deals with patients like yourself. On top of that, I'd like you to continue your physical therapy. You lost a bit of muscle mass and your body is still weak. Twice a week should be fine for now. However, when you're ready to start dancing again, you can speak with your therapist regarding a more intense schedule."

Mom nods. "Of course. Whatever we can do to make this journey easier for Addison, we'll do it."

"Wonderful. I'll leave some recommendations with the nurses' desk," Dr. Arton says, giving Mom a real smile, nothing like the forced one he'd offered my father. The doctor turns back toward Addie, looking chuffed to be telling her goodbye. "In the meantime, I'm signing off on your discharge, so while your parents fill out a bit of paperwork, you can figure out what you're going to do with all these flowers and balloons."

Addison glances around the room with a cringe, taking in the vast array of gifts she's received over the past two weeks as if only now realizing what a massive job this is going to be. "Oh, umm … yay."

I snort a laugh and shake my head as my sister glares daggers at me. "Chill out," I say, far too amused by this. "I've got the Mustang in the parking garage. You go home with Mom and Dad, and I'll sort this shit out."

"Huh," Addie says, watching me with a strange curiosity. "I should slip into a coma more often if this is the type of treatment I'm going to get from you."

"Don't even joke about it," I say, giving her a blank stare. "It's way too soon for that shit. But don't be fooled, little sister, I won't hesitate to drop your ass if the moment calls for it. I have seven weeks of missed opportunities to make up for, and who knows, they might all come at once, or I might surprise you with them one by one. Get you when you least expect it."

Addie's glare narrows and she holds my stare much better than Mom ever could. "Bring it, clown," she says, holding her arms out wide. "Go ahead and underestimate me. I've had seven weeks of sleeping. Do you have any idea how much extra energy that is than the regular eight hours a night? It's like twenty four hours a day times … wait, how many days are in seven weeks?"

Dr. Arton rolls his eyes. "There are forty-nine days in seven weeks," he clarifies, "which is something like a thousand or so hours. However, while your theory has some merit, that's not exactly how it works."

Addison grins at the doctor before turning to me, her brows bouncing. "You hear that? He said my theory has merit. I have a thousand hours of energy running through these veins. I'm like the Energizer Bunny on steroids. You can't beat me. In fact, you should be shitting yourself right about now. Sleep with one eye open, big brother."

Dr. Arton rolls his eyes and shakes his head. "Do I need to remind you that you're in a fragile state? I'm ninety percent sure you're joking, but I will go through an extensive list of what not to do if I feel it's called for."

Addison laughs. "Am I joking? Who could ever know?" she says, the apples of her cheeks pressing up with her wide smile. "Though feel free to take Tanner through that extensive list of dos and don'ts. He's got nothing better to do other than carting around a crap ton of balloons like the clown that he is."

If it weren't for how proud she looks for that quick wit of hers, I'd be more than ready to put her in her place. Though, to be honest, if this past week is anything to go by, I have a feeling Addie is about to start getting away with murder when it comes to me.

Dr. Arton grumbles something under his breath before turning toward Mom. "I think I've covered everything, so unless you have any questions, we can get Addison's discharge papers sorted out."

Mom stands and gives him a smile. "Discharge papers would be good."

With that, Dr. Arton and Mom take off down the hall toward the nurses' desk, and I watch after them, knowing the doctor's routine well enough by now. Bad news gets discussed with her in private, though I'm hoping this one time I'm wrong and that he really just wanted to escort her to the nurses' desk.

Dad gets up and starts collecting Addie's things, throwing her phone and charger into her bag before starting on the shit she's left scattered across the other half of the room. I get up and walk over to the massive display of *get well soon* cards, balloons, flowers, chocolates, and teddies. "What the fuck am I going to do with all of this?"

Dad sends a scathing glare my way. "I've had just about enough of your language, boy."

I grin. "Whatcha gonna do about it, huh?" I question. "You gonna beat it out of me like you did when I was a kid?"

He holds my stare, but it doesn't take a genius to see that he wouldn't be able to get within ten feet of me. I tower over him now, and those scrawny arms of his are barely strong enough to hold up his ego. The asshole has been terrified of me since the second I started to fill out. I see it in his eyes. He's waiting for me to break, waiting for the day I've finally had enough and put his ass in a hospital bed just like the one Addie's in.

Giving up, Dad huffs and turns before storming for the door, leaving me with a pissed off Addison. "Seriously?" she demands. "Do you really have to push his buttons like that? He's going to end up leaving again."

"Would that be such a terrible thing?" I question. "It's so chill when he's not here."

"Yeah, for you," she mutters darkly.

I roll my eyes and make my way toward her before letting out a defeated sigh. "Fine. I will try harder to be pleasant when he's around. Now, can you hurry up and tell me what the fuck I'm supposed to do with all this bullshit behind me so we can get out of here? I think burning it would be the quickest option."

Addie gapes at me. "What kind of monster are you?" she demands. "You can't burn it." She takes a moment, scanning over everything to figure out a game plan. "Ummm … can you hand out a bunch of flowers to all the nurses who were looking after me, and if there's extra you could drop them off at the women's shelter. I'm sure some of them might like a bunch of flowers. Maybe offer them the chocolates too. The balloons can just get popped. I don't think anyone will want them, and as for the stuffed bears, do you think they'll take them to the nursery?"

I look over my sister, proud as fuck of the woman she's growing into. Don't get me wrong, she sure as hell has her immature moments and can be an infuriating brat, but then there's times like this when she reminds me that she's truly an amazing person with the sweetest heart. "I can always ask, but are you sure you don't want to keep any of it?" I ask. The Addie I grew up with would have hoarded every last gift.

She presses her lips into a hard line and shakes her head. "No, it was nice of everyone to get them for me, but I don't want them. They're a blatant reminder of why I'm here and I don't want that at home. I want to start fresh and try to put it all behind me, and seeing it every day—"

"I get it," I tell her. "I'll get rid of it all."

Addie goes to stand, and I offer her my hand without thinking before quickly pulling it away. But it's already too late. She saw it. "I can get up by myself," she says, a harsh bite in her tone.

My face scrunches with a cringe. This isn't the first time I've been bitched at over the past week for trying to help her, but what am I meant to say? I love that she's doing everything she can to get back to where she was seven weeks ago, but I hate seeing her struggle and wish that she wasn't so stubborn and could just accept help when it's offered.

Dad returns a moment later with a wheelchair, and I do my best to hide a smirk as Addie glares at it. "Sorry, kid," Dad says. "Hospital policy. You have to use it until we're off the premises."

Addison reluctantly makes her way toward Dad as he positions the wheelchair so she can easily sit down, and the moment she does, Dad begins piling her bags onto her lap and the handle before doing a second walk around the room, making sure he has everything. "You know," Addie starts, watching me from across the room. "Hudson came and hung out with me yesterday."

My gaze narrows as I turn my attention back on my sister, noticing the stuffed bear she's been gripping since I got here this morning. "Why?"

"What do you mean why?" she questions, a slight hesitation in her eyes as she draws the bear back beside her, almost as if trying to hide it from view. "He's always hung out with me while you and the guys were being your usual idiotic selves. He's come a few times to check on me."

My suspicion only gets worse, and I make a note to beat the shit out of Hudson for getting too close with my sister. He knows the rules, and if I find out it's anything less than innocent, there'll be hell to pay.

"What are you trying to tell me? Do you have a thing for Hudson?" I ask, trying to focus on the flowers and not be so blatantly obvious about how twitchy this topic makes me. After all, Hudson just happened to be here when Addie was waking up, and now she's trying to tell me he's been here a few more times. Surely if there was nothing going on, he would have mentioned it.

Right?

Fuck.

Addie gapes at me. "Seriously, after … everything, do you really think I want to spend my time obsessing over boys? We're just friends. He's nice and he doesn't give me that pitying stare that I get from everyone else. Plus, he's not one of those guys who always has to fill the silence. He's happy to just sit there and stare at the wall just because it means I don't have to be alone."

I know her words are meant as a compliment and are supposed to ease the monster rearing its ugly head, but it's not working even a little bit. "You're not helping his case, Addie."

She groans. "Uggggh, you're impossible," she says. "The only reason I brought it up was because he was telling me about Jax and Logan's party and how your girlfriend got way too drunk and threw up in the pool, and you could imagine my surprise because my own freaking brother didn't say a damn word about the fact he was seeing someone. I had to pretend like I already knew."

"Addie, listen—"

"Why are you hiding her from me?"

I shake my head, my chest constricting like a million rubber bands squeezing far too tight. "I'm not hiding her from you, I swear, Addie, it's just … it's not that simple."

"I swear, Tanner. Stop trying to handle me with kid gloves. Do you like this girl?"

My gaze crosses to my father, noticing the way he goes around the room, pretending not to listen. "I more than like her."

"You're in love with her?" I nod and her brows arch high, her eyes widening in surprise. That confirmation was the last thing she ever expected. "Well, shit."

"Yeah."

"So, she lives next door, right?"

Another nod.

"Channing's latest gold-digger girlfriend?"

"Wife," I confirm. "Gold-digging wife. He married her in Paris a few weeks ago."

"Wait," she says, her brows furrowing. "What the hell, Tanner? You're seeing Channing's new wife? I mean, I know you stoop low sometimes, but this is messed up."

"What?" I demand, my eyes going wide, the flowers forgotten. "That's messed up. I'm not fucking Channing's wife, I'm dating her daughter, Brielle."

Understanding dawns on her face, and she grins slowly. "Now that makes more sense," she says, pressing her lips into a hard line to keep from laughing at my horror. "So, what's wrong with this chick? Give it to me straight, Tanner. If she's special, then you need to be upfront from the get-go."

That heaviness returns and I hate how right she is. I move across the room, perching my ass against the edge of the hospital bed and looking across at Addie. "Brielle is from Hope Falls," I start, watching as her face falls.

"She was there, wasn't she?" she questions, assuming that's the worst of it.

"Yeah, but there's more to it than that," I explain. "At the time of … the party, Bri was dating Colby Jacobs. They were together for six months or something like that, but she ended it with him toward the end of summer when she found him cheating on her. She was also best friends with Erica, the girl who—"

"The drugs."

"Yeah," I murmur, watching as Addie's gaze falls to her hands in her lap, her expression completely void of all emotion. It's almost as though there's nothing but darkness behind her eyes, but I owe it to her to be honest about Brielle, especially if she's going to be around my sister. She deserves every bit of the truth. "You need to know that a few weeks back, Erica admitted to having a hand in what happened to you, and the second that happened, Brielle cut all ties with her. There's a lot of undeserved guilt riding on Bri's shoulders. She hates that she wasn't more aware that night and that the two people she'd gone to the party with, were … you know." Addison nods and I go on. "Erica tried to have Brielle go down for what happened to save herself. She made a false statement to the police stating that Brielle was in the room with Colby. She submitted false evidence and Brielle was arrested at school for aiding and abetting the rape of a minor, drug abuse, and attempted murder."

"Attempted murder?" she asks, her head snapping back up, her brows furrowed in confusion.

I press my hand to my throat. "Your breathing tube," I remind her. "Erica tried to pin that on her too, however, the surveillance footage clearly shows a male."

My father scoffs, and I whip my head around, having forgotten the asshole was even in the room. "I've heard about enough," he says, his disgusted stare piercing straight into me like a thousand tiny knives right through my back. "Do you have no regard for your sister or what she's suffering through right now? How could you, for even one second, think that being with this girl is a good idea? She's a nobody, a poor girl from Hope Falls, with connections to the two main suspects in Addison's case. She could have had a hand in this for all we know, and you're going to parade her through our lives, rubbing it in your sister's face like a constant reminder."

I stand, towering over my father as my hands ball into fists at my side, more than ready to send this asshole to an early grave. No one talks about Brielle like that. "You don't know what the fuck you're talking about," I seethe, spitting the words through my teeth.

"I know enough," he says, standing tall and holding his ground. "You'll end it with this girl immediately. I don't want that trailer trash in my house."

And with that, Dad walks straight past me and latches onto the back of Addison's wheelchair, pushing her from the room and leaving me boiling from the inside out.

CHAPTER 16

Brielle

The ball flies across the field, and I watch with a cringe as Logan catches it, the force of Tanner's throw like a freight train slamming into Logan's chest. Hell, I can see the power behind his throw from the student parking lot.

Tanner is pissed and there's no doubt about it.

I don't know what's up with him, but he's been in a mood all day. I'm just grateful that he hasn't pushed me away, which could only mean that it's not me who's fucked up. Though, judging by the shorter, scrawnier version of Tanner who's been hanging around his home for the past week, I can only assume Tanner's mood has something to do with that.

I hate seeing him like this, but I can't push him. I don't want to be that girl who doesn't give her boyfriend space to work out his shit. If he wants to talk it through, he knows where to find me, and I'm sure that once the anger subsides, he'll find it easier to discuss. But until then, I have to be patient and hope to God that whatever this is doesn't darken his fragile heart.

I have to give credit where it's due—Tanner is holding himself together remarkably. I've seen him on the brink of losing control, and I've seen him at his worst, and this right here has got all the markers to become one of Tanner's most reckless moments. And yet, he's in control. All day I've looked into his eyes to see nothing but rage burning in their depths, and instead of allowing that rage to rule him, he's kept it bottled down, keeping calm and collected. I just hope an intense training session will do more good than harm.

Having to trust that he'll be okay, I slide into Mom's car and distantly notice that I'm one of the last students here. I must have been watching Tanner for longer than I thought. Backing out of my parking space, I work on getting my ass home.

The drive back to Orlando's place feels longer than usual. Maybe it's just my troubled mind, trying to figure out how I can help Tanner, or maybe it's just the exhaustion of everything creeping up on me. His sister returned home last night, and while I haven't met Tanner's mom, I bet she's the type to invite their extended family over for some big party or plan a nice dinner with Addison's close friends.

I wonder if Tanner's mood has something to do with Addison's health. Maybe she didn't pass all those tests with flying colors as Tanner originally suggested.

Knowing I'm only going to drive myself crazy with all these assumptions, I focus on the road in front of me. Just as I said earlier, Tanner will come to me when he's ready, and I don't want to be the one to push him. Despite how deeply I feel for him, this relationship is still new, and we're still working out one another's boundaries. Though, Tanner sure as hell loves to push mine.

I arrive back home and am just getting out of Mom's car when I hear voices from next door. My gaze snaps up to find Tanner's mom and sister, and I can't help the smile that spreads across my face. I'm nobody to her. Hell, she probably has no idea who I am, but I have never been so happy to see someone in my life.

She looks just like the female version of Tanner, only instead of packed muscle and towering height, she's lean like a dancer, maybe only five foot five. She has the same shade of dark hair, and her eyes are so similar, only hers are painted with black liner and thick mascara. There's no doubt about it, Addison Morgan is gorgeous.

Sensing my stare, Addison and her mom glance my way, and their well-mannered nature has them immediately smiling back, only there's a strange hesitation in Addison's eyes that catches me off guard. She glances across at her mother, the two of them sharing a kind of silent conversation, yet for some reason, I can't help but shake the feeling it's about me.

A strange pang settles into my gut, and I turn back to the car before reaching through the driver's door and grabbing my things. If Addison has a problem with me, or maybe if Tanner's mom doesn't like me, then I don't want to know. I'll be happier living in denial.

Closing the car door, I make my way toward Orlando's front door when a hesitant voice rings out across the yard. "Brielle, right?"

Glancing back over my shoulder, I find Addison and her mom creeping closer to the boundary line between our homes, and I pause with my arms full of books, almost using them as a security blanket. "Yeah, that's me," I say, giving them a tight smile, not wanting to be rude.

"It's lovely to finally meet you, Brielle," Tanner's mom says, "You've become quite a celebrity in our household. I've heard so much about you. This is Addison, and I'm Tanner's mom, Sara."

"Oh, um … thank you," I say, feeling a genuine kindness in her words. "I hope it's all good things."

Sara laughs. "Honestly, any young woman who has the ability to draw in my son the way you have is a celestial wonder to me. You've achieved the impossible."

My cheeks flush with the compliment, and thankfully Sara continues, releasing me from the social requirement to respond. "Listen, I know you're in your senior year, so I'm sure your afternoon is already busy with homework and whatnot, but we were wondering if you could spare a few moments to sit down with us? I consider myself to be quite the baker and have just taken chocolate muffins out of the oven."

"Oh," I say in surprise, glancing between the two to find Addison's stare focused heavily on the ground. Despite her not saying a word, I can tell she doesn't want this. But I'm backed into a corner, and I'm not about to refuse an invitation from Tanner's mother. Besides, something tells me they're not inviting me over for a slumber party. There's a purposeful reason behind this, and my curiosity is piqued. "That's not a problem at all. Give me two seconds to put these books down and I'll be right over."

Addison lifts her gaze and gives me a tight smile as though she's trying to be strong, but that's not needed with me. "Cool," she finally says before stepping closer to her mother as if needing her comfort. "We'll wait."

Nerves rattle me as I dart off toward Channing's home and slip inside, not wanting to hold them up. I drop my books down on the bottom step before glancing toward my phone. I hate going into things unprepared like this, especially something so important as meeting Tanner's family. The need to call him burns in my chest, but he's in training and won't be able to take my call. I'm going in blind and judging by the look in Addison's eyes and Tanner's mood today, something is warning me that the two are connected.

Slipping my phone into my pocket, I hurry back outside to where Sara and Addison wait, and I don't miss Sara's encouraging smile. "Right this way, love," she says, waving me toward her home.

A million things flow through my mind. Are these Morgan women secret serial killers? Am I about to walk into a trap? Hell, maybe Tanner's been keeping something from them and they think they can get it out of me. Shit. What have I gotten myself into?

Sara welcomes me into her home, and I wait for Addison to pass before following her in. They lead the way to the kitchen and offer me a seat at the island counter. Addison sits as well, leaving a space between us as Sara makes her way around the other side of the kitchen. "Can I get you a dr—" she starts, cutting herself off as she turns back to glance at me. She laughs as she takes in my expression. "Oh, honey. You look as though you're about to be interrogated. Please don't be nervous. We have absolutely no ill intentions, simply want to have a chat so that we can all be on the same page."

"Okay," I say nervously, her words doing absolutely nothing to ease the anxiety building within me.

Sara takes a plate out of a drawer before placing one of her freshly baked muffins onto it. She slides it across the counter to me before going about the same for Addison. "Dig in," she says. "They won't stay fresh forever."

Out of sheer manners, I pick at the top of the muffin before placing a bite-sized piece into my mouth. I have to give it to her, the woman bakes one hell of a good muffin. "This is the best muffin I've ever tasted."

Sara smiles wide. "Thank you. It was always my dream to open a bakery, but then I met Trenton and those dreams shifted toward marriage and babies. However, now that my babies are all grown up, I'm starting to wonder more and more about that little bakery."

"If the rest of your things are this good, I'll be the very first one in line," I promise her.

"Thank you, Brielle. That is very kind of you," she says as Addison sits silently beside me, looking as though she'd rather be anywhere but here, and as if realizing this, Sara moves this strange little meeting along. "Listen, Tanner is one of the most precious people in my life.

He's my firstborn, the child who made me a mother. I know him better than I know myself, which is how I can tell that this relationship with you is so much more than just a fling. My son is in love with you, Brielle, and while it fills my heart with joy to see him this way, it also makes me very nervous."

My back stiffens as my hand pauses over the muffin. "How so?" I ask, terrified she's about to tell me I can't see her son anymore.

"Because we are very aware of your connection to Colby Jacobs." My gaze immediately flashes toward Addison and my chest tightens, realizing exactly what this is now. "Exactly," Sara continues. "I am sure you can appreciate our hesitation due to our current situation. Right now, Addison's health and well-being is my top priority—"

"You want me to break up with Tanner," I breathe, reading the room as my heart starts to crack.

"What?" Addison cuts in with a grunt, forcing my head to whip her way. "Are you insane? We can't ask that of you without having our asses whooped by my brother. We just want to get to know you so we understand the situation between you and Colby better. I'd never ask you to break up with him for me. I haven't seen you two together before, but I can see a difference in him already. You make him happy, and I would never take that away from him because of my own issues."

The relief is like nothing I've ever known. There was no way in hell I was prepared to end things with Tanner. I would have gone to ridiculous lengths just to ensure that didn't happen. "Okay," I say. "I'm an open book, and I plan on being with Tanner for a very long time. I don't want there to be any hostility or secrets between us. So have at it, whatever you want to know, I'm willing to share."

Addison straightens in her chair, quickly glancing toward her mom who nods, giving her an encouraging smile. "Here's your chance, darling," she tells her. "She's a big part of Tanner's life, and trust me when I say, you don't want to push him away. He's your rock, Addie, but you're his little sister, and it would mean the world to him if you could open yourself up and allow her the chance to explain."

Addison nods before taking a breath, and I don't miss the way Sara takes a step back, allowing Addison to take the lead and handle this the way she's comfortable with. Her hands shake and she blinks back unshed tears. "You … you know what happened, right?" she starts, her fear radiating out of her in waves.

"Yes," I say, wanting to give as much information as possible to save her from having to physically say it. "I was there that night, at the party in Hope Falls. I'd been dating Colby for six months, and by that stage of our relationship, it wasn't great. It was near the beginning of summer, and I was already starting to distance myself from him because of his drug use. I'm not into that scene. However, my best friend Erica was, and I didn't know it at the time, but they had been sneaking around behind my back."

"Okay, so you were already planning on breaking up with him at the time of the party?"

I nod. "Yeah, it was over weeks before it actually ended. He was starting to get aggressive when he was using, and I'm not down for that shit. I just wanted to enjoy my summer, but break ups are such a downer, and with how aggressive he'd been getting, I was putting it off."

"So, when did you break up with him?"

A soft smile pulls at my lips. "The same night I met Tanner," I tell her. "Colby had dragged me to a party here in Bradford because after what happened to you, the cops were shutting down every party in Hope Falls. So, Colby brought me here to have a good time, but it took him less than twenty minutes to take a girl upstairs. I walked in on them and walked straight back out again. That was the end of it. That same night was when my mom told me we were moving in next door and I didn't see him again … at least, until Erica dragged me back into Hope Falls with the intention of confronting him."

"You were still friends with her?"

A pang of guilt cuts through my chest and I nod. "At that stage, yes. I didn't know of her involvement in your attack, and I had no reason to doubt her. We'd been friends for thirteen years, and as far as I was aware, we didn't have any secrets between us."

Addison scoffs. "Well, I guess that was a load of shit."

"Yeah," I say with a scoff of my own. "The two of them played me, and they nearly got away with it, but I swear to you, if I knew what they were doing that night, there's no way I would have just stood by and allowed it to happen. I feel sick that I was in the next room, completely oblivious to what was happening to you. If I'd just been more aware, or if I hadn't drunk so much, I—"

"Don't do that to yourself," Addison says. "This isn't your fault, and I don't want you carrying the guilt for something someone else did."

My gaze falls to the muffin, and I feel my chest beginning to tighten when Sara moves forward again, bracing her elbows against the island counter. "Tanner mentioned last week that you had been arrested for involvement in Addison's case. Now, we're aware that you truly had nothing to do with it, but how is that going? I'm assuming Orlando Channing is taking care of it? He married your mom, right?"

I shake my head. "Orlando is still representing Colby and refused to take my case because it's a conflict of interest, but he set me up with another lawyer who's confident that my name will be cleared. I'm just waiting to hear back. All the evidence that was put forward against me was manipulated so—"

"Wait," Addison says. "I'm confused. How were you arrested in any of this?"

I give her a tight smile. "Erica made a false statement claiming that I was the one who gave you the drugs and that I was in the room while … you know. She made it seem as though I was the brains behind everything and that I was putting it in Colby's head to hurt you."

She shakes her head. "That's … no. There was no one else in the room. Just me and him. That's not fair. How can she get away with saying stuff like that?"

Sara reaches across the table, taking Addie's hand. "You were in a coma, honey. You weren't there to defend yourself and set the record straight, but you are now, and the ball is in your court. I know it's going to be hard, and it'll bring up things you're not ready to face, but a statement from you will clear everything up. Brielle's name will be cleared and Colby will be put away."

"And Erica?" she says. "What's stopping her from doing this to someone else?"

Sara shakes her head. "I'm not sure, sweetheart. We will have to have a talk with our lawyer, but I'm positive there is something we can do. We won't allow her to get away with this either."

Addison takes a moment, considering her options before sparing a glance at me. She bites her lip, her eyes growing watery before turning back to her mom. "Okay," she finally says, making Sara's brows shoot up. "I'll talk to the police and make a statement. People like Bri shouldn't be getting dragged down with all of this shit, and Tanner is too, and it's not fair. I don't want Colby to get away with this, but I'm terrified that he'll try to hurt me again. He already wrapped Brielle's car around a tree and then came for me with my breathing tubes. He's already proven that he'll do whatever it takes to try and save himself."

"Oh, sweetheart," Sara says, walking around to our side of the island before wrapping her daughter in her arms, this moment meaning everything to her. The police had come to the hospital the moment Addison woke up and she refused to talk about it, not ready to discuss the heinous things Colby did to her, but this just proves how much of a fighting spirit she has. "You are the strongest person I have ever met. The way you've overcome everything over this past week shows just how resilient you are, but you don't need to be strong all the time. We're going to keep you safe, Addie. You have my word. Colby isn't going to be able to get near you. He'll be charged and locked up before you know it. We're all going to be okay."

Addison begins to cry in her mother's arms, and I look away, wanting to offer them as much privacy as possible, only I'm stuck on something Addison said. She mentioned that Tanner was now being dragged down by all of this too, and that doesn't make sense. Unless she's referring to the way he's holding all the guilt on his shoulders because of his connection to Colby's older sister. However, if something more was going on, it'd explain the aggravated mood he'd been in all day.

I itch to ask about it but now isn't exactly the right moment.

Addison takes another minute before finally pulling out of her mom's arms and wiping her eyes. "Sorry," she says, glancing toward me. "Didn't mean to make it awkward for you."

"It's fine," I tell her with a smile, popping another bite of the muffin into my mouth now that the heavy stuff has passed. "Not awkward at all."

"So … did that asshole really break your ribs?"

I nod, pulling up the side of my shirt to show her the lingering bruises. "Yep, wrapped me around a tree, strangled me, and then kicked me right in the ribs as a warning not to talk to the cops. If it weren't for Tanner showing up, I think he would have killed me."

"Fuck," she gasps, her eyes going wide as she gapes up at her mom, probably already regretting her decision to make a statement. "Maybe I shouldn't."

"No," I say. "Don't be scared. I'm not going to lie to you and tell you that Colby won't act out. He will, but you're the one with the power here. He's scrambling for his freedom, and you hold the power to put the nail in the coffin."

She presses her lips into a tight line before nervously watching me. "Do you think that maybe … you'll come with me to the police station?"

"Of course," I tell her. "I don't think they'll allow me to go in with you, but I'm happy to sit in the waiting area, and if you're up for it, we can go and have a spa day after it to get your mind off it."

Sara squeezes Addison's shoulder as Addison smiles back at me. "I think I'd like that," she tells me before biting the inside of her cheek. "I think I owe you an apology."

"Huh?" I grunt. "What the hell for?"

"I judged you too soon," she explains. "The moment Tanner mentioned that you used to be with Colby, I wanted nothing to do with you. Just the thought of being in the same room with you was making me feel sick, but you're not at all how I imagined. I should have known Tanner wasn't going to have anything to do with someone who had a hand in what happened to me. I need to give that guy more credit, but don't tell him I said that. I'll deny it until I'm blue in the face."

I can't help but laugh. I'm starting to really like Tanner's sister. "Any other questions?" I ask.

"Just one."

"Shoot."

Addison holds my stare, her eyes starting to liven up as the weight releases off her shoulders. "Are you in love with my brother?"

I gape at her, my eyes widening as Sara sucks in a breath. "Oh, Brielle, honey. You don't have to answer that," she says before focusing her attention on her daughter. "You can't just ask people that."

"Why the hell not?" Addison argues back. "She told me she was an open book and that I could ask her anything. Was I not supposed to take her quite so literally? Besides, you can't tell me you're not the least bit curious, Mom. This is Tanner we're talking about, your little baby boy, the first child of your womb. Don't you want to know if this girl he's madly in love with feels the same way?"

Sara's brow arches as she considers her daughter's argument, and I feel my face flush, knowing what's coming next.

Sara glances back at me. "I mean, who am I to argue with that logic?" she says, her lips pulling into a grin. I have to give her credit, at least she tried.

I press my lips into a hard line, desperately trying to hide the wide grin stretching across my face. I don't say a word, but my response is clear as day. "OMG!" Addison cheers, her eyes lighting up like the Fourth of July. "She totally does."

I laugh it off and bury my face in my hands. "I haven't told him that yet," I explain, "so the same rules apply. If you tell him, I'll deny it until I'm blue in the face."

Addison laughs and holds out her hand. "You have yourself a deal, Brielle Ashford," she says as I reach out and shake her hand. "Welcome to the family."

CHAPTER 17

Brielle

A grin pulls across my face as I drive into the student parking lot well past ten in the morning. I don't think I've ever been this late, but when Addison knocked on my door at seven in the morning and said she was ready to make her statement, I couldn't refuse her. Screw school, showing up for her this morning was important.

Sara came with us, and it wasn't until after Addison had made her statement and we were chilling with breakfast milkshakes that I realized Tanner had no idea what was going down. I wonder what was going through his mind when I wasn't in my room this morning or didn't show up for the start of school.

Tanner leans against the side of Logan's Dodge RAM, his arms crossed, and his heavy gaze locked on me as I make my way around the student parking lot. I bring Mom's car to a stop beside Logan's truck, and by the time I cut the engine, Tanner is opening my door, clearly having bailed on class this morning.

"Where the fuck have you been?" he questions, almost sounding hurt that he hasn't heard from me all morning, but Addison said she didn't want him to know until afterward because firstly, he'd make a big deal about it, and secondly, she wanted to mess with him over the fact that we've been spending time together.

I step out of the car and raise my chin, brushing my lips over his in a quick kiss. "Good morning to you too."

"Seriously?" he mutters, taking my books for me. "That's all you've got to say? *Good morning?* I was about ready to send out a search party. You can't just disappear on me, especially after that text you got the other day. I thought something happened to you."

"I'm sorry," I say as I lean back against Mom's car, smiling up at him. "I was sworn to secrecy, but now that it's all done, I'm allowed to tell you."

Tanner puts my books on top of the car and leans into me, his eyes narrowing on my mischievous stare. "The fuck are you talking about?" he rumbles, his deep tone vibrating through his chest and making my knees weak.

"Well," I start, unsure why I feel so nervous. "Yesterday, your mom and Addison sorta kidnapped me and—"

"The fuck?"

I stare up at him, shooting daggers. "Do you want to hear the story or not?"

Tanner groans and rolls his eyes before making a show of zipping his lips and patiently waiting for me to continue, and just to be an ass, I give him the most dazzling smile I can possibly give. "As I was saying, before I was so rudely interrupted," I continue. "They caught me when I got home from school yesterday and your mom lured me in with muffins, which is really not hard to do, and we started talking. Addison was having a hard time wrapping her head around us because of my involvement with Colby and wanted a bit of clarity with everything that's been going on. So, we spent some time getting to know one another, and I'm not going to lie, Addison might even be cooler than you."

Tanner scoffs, his lips pulling up into an impressed smile. "Not possible," he says. "But that doesn't explain where the hell you've been all morning."

"Oh, Addison and I have been hiding out in your room setting fart bomb traps to go off spontaneously through the night. Apparently, it has something to do with seven weeks of torture she needs to make up for."

Tanner gives me a blank stare, seeing right through me. "Spill it, Killjoy. Where have you really been?"

I push up onto my toes and kiss him again, unable to get used to just how good it feels to call him mine. "Well, yesterday when I was with your mom and Addison, we were talking about me being arrested and how she didn't want more people to be dragged into all of this. So she decided to make a statement if I went with her, so of course

I did. We even went and had milkshakes afterward and got our nails done. See," I say, holding up my hand for him to see the blood-red paint across my nails.

Tanner just stares at me, completely dumbfounded and unaffected by the stunning state of my nails. "Addie spoke with the cops?" he confirms.

"She did," I say with pride. "She was amazing, and I think when you get home, you need to remind her how much you love her and that you'll never let anything happen to her because she's scared shitless. She thinks Colby will try and wrap her around a tree like he did to me."

"Over my dead fucking body," he says. "Colby will never touch her again."

My hands curl around his strong biceps, holding on for dear life. "I know," I tell him, having complete faith that this is the end of it. Colby is going to get charged and locked up for good, and Addison will never have to fear him again.

Tanner looks down at me, a soft smile playing on his lips, and he goes to lean in when that smile begins to fade and his eyes narrow with suspicion. "Hold up, why didn't she tell me she was going to make a formal statement? And why the fuck are you two spending so much time together now? I don't like it."

My eyes widen just a fraction, a pang of hurt slicing through my chest. "You don't want me hanging out with Addison?" I ask, unable to hide the hurt from spreading across my face.

Tanner is quick to shake his head. "No, no, Killer. It's not that. I fucking love that you two are getting along. I just don't trust it," he says, his voice filled with suspicion. "You and Addison together … that's fucking terrifying. That's two against one, and I don't like those odds."

"Technically, it's three against one," I tell him, relief pulsing through my veins. "We've got your mom, too. We discussed prank wars over milkshakes, and your mom is all too ready to throw you under the bus. You're fucked, Tanner Morgan."

Tanner laughs and shakes his head. "Nah, you're lying," he tells me, unable to accept what he's hearing. "I'm Mom's special little guy, she wouldn't do that to me."

Reaching up, I place my hand on the side of his face, brushing my thumb over his strong jaw. "That's cute. She said you'd say that," I taunt, my condescending tone making his confidence falter. "But Addison was quick to remind her that she just woke up from a coma, and your mom was like putty in her hands."

Tanner stares back at me, realization dawning on him as he sucks in a horrified gasp. "I'm fucking screwed."

"Big time," I laugh, enjoying Tanner's horror far too much. "Your sister is some kind of evil genius. The shit she has planned for you is epic. You need to watch yourself."

Tanner lets out a heavy breath before reaching up and grabbing my books off the top of the car, simply accepting his fate. "Come on," he says with a heavy sigh as the bell for our first break sounds through the school. "Let me get your ass inside."

We start making our way up to the main entrance when I glance up at him. "Can I ask you something?"

"Of course," he says, looking down at me, his brows furrowing at the tone in my voice.

I bite the inside of my cheek, wondering how to word this, then think better of it and just allow the words to fall out like word vomit. "Yesterday when we were talking about your sister making her statement, she made a comment about you being dragged down by everything that was going on, and I just wondered what she meant by that."

Tanner's lips press into a hard line and his eyes soften. "It's really nothing," he says, his arm curling around my side and pulling me in closer as we make our way to the entrance. "Just my father's usual bullshit. He was nervous that me being with you was rubbing Addison's attack in her face, and not so subtly requested I end things with you, and I suppose that's part of the reason Addison and Mom asked you over yesterday. Addie wanted to make up her own mind about you, and considering she asked you to go to the police with her, I can only assume that she really likes you."

I nod, knowing he added the part about Addie liking me to lessen the blow of what he said about his father. But my mind is stuck there, unable to move past those comments. "Is that why you were in such a bad mood yesterday? Because your dad said we had to break up?"

"Yeah, I'm sorry about that," he says. "My father just has this gift for making my life a living hell, but don't worry, I have absolutely no plans to end this. My father can get fucked for all I care. What you and I have is far more important than his thoughts on the matter. Besides, Addie is cool with it, so there's no issue."

"Okay," I say, feeling better about it all, despite the overwhelming need to throat punch Tanner's dad.

We reach the top of the school and Tanner holds the door open for me. We walk into the busy hallway, students shoulder barging one another as they make their way out of class, desperate to eat and find their friends before being dragged back to the confines of a bland classroom.

We stop by my locker so that I can shove everything in it, but before I've even closed the door, Ilaria and Chanel are by my side with Riley quickly joining the fray. "Where the fuck have you been?" Riley demands, leaning his shoulder against my locker before taking a massive bite out of an apple, all but splitting the thing right down the center.

"Yeah," Ilaria says. "What he said."

Tanner grins, all too proud to *not* say anything. "She went with Addie to make a statement," he says, grinning from ear to ear, and Riley looks like he's about to shit himself out of pure happiness.

"Thank fuck for that," Riley says as we all break away from the lockers and make our way to the cafeteria. "So, what happens now?"

I shrug my shoulders. "Assuming everything goes as expected, my charges will officially be dropped, and Colby will be charged with rape and attempted murder. Then I'm sure there will be some kind of court case and the asshole will be locked up as he should be."

"Hey, yo, wait up," I hear coming from behind us.

I glance back to find Logan ducking and weaving through the crowded students, catching up to us just in time for Chanel to step out from behind Riley, her arms crossed over her chest and a scowl stretched across her pretty face.

Logan's eyes bug out of his head, and he comes to a screeching halt, having done everything in his power to avoid her up until this very moment. "Fuck, babe … ummm."

"Don't *babe* me, Logan Morgan. You've been avoiding me again. Just when I think we're all good, you go and fuck it up again. If you want to break up with me, just say that. Stop being such a pussy about it."

Logan glares back at her. "Tough shit because I don't want to break up with you."

"Good," she snaps back at him. "Because I don't want you to break up with me either."

"Good."

Chanel groans in frustration, clenching her jaw. "You're impossible," she spits. "I can't stand you."

"Wonderful, because I can't stand your bitch ass either."

"Good," she spits.

Logan gives her a condescending grin, irritating the shit out of her. "Good."

Chanel's frustration reaches a whole new level, and she balls her hands into tight fists, more than ready to drop his ass, but instead, she turns on her heel and storms away, leaving Logan staring after her with a dopey-ass grin across his face. "Fuck, she's incredible," he says, completely amazed by the creature otherwise known as Chanel.

I shake my head, unable to understand their twisted relationship. "You two are giving me whiplash."

"I know," Logan says. "But tonight, when I'm all alone and she's refusing to text me back, I'm going to feel like an asshole and go over to her place, and then we're going to have the most vigorous make up sex you could ever imagine. It's such a fucking rush."

"Okay," Tanner says, cutting him off before he can give us any of the sordid details. "Did you get what you were looking for?"

Logan holds out his phone to Tanner. "Why do you doubt me?" he questions. "I always come through with the goods."

Tanner immediately takes the phone and unlocks the screen before glancing over it, his brows furrowed in confusion before turning the screen toward me. "Do you know who this is?"

I look over it, finding a picture of one of the assholes I used to go to school with. "That's Roxten Hargrove. He's one of Colby's best friends and a fucking pig at that too. He's on the football team, but I don't think he's very good, not like you guys. Why? Did he do something to piss you off?"

"You could say that," Tanner scoffs. "This is the asshole who sent that text last week."

My eyes bug out of my head, glancing over the image of Roxten again. "No shit," I say, not in the least surprised. I'd wondered if the text had come from one of Colby's friends, and the moment I did, Roxten was the first to come to mind. "I should have known. The asshole is all talk, but when it comes down to it, he's a sheep. He doesn't have the balls to act on anything he says."

Tanner studies his image again before pressing his lips into a hard line. "I'm still not taking the risk," he says. "We're up against Hope

Falls next week, so I'll be more than happy to have a quiet word with the guy when I see him."

My heart lurches in my chest, squeezing with unease. "What are you going to do?"

Tanner grins wide as Riley smirks back at me, his gaze darkening with something sinister that puts me on edge. "Nothing that he doesn't deserve."

The end of the day is creeping closer and closer, and I can't get out of this class soon enough. The tension in the room is so thick it's going to suffocate me. Arizona sits on my left as Jax takes up prime position on my right. Neither of them has uttered a word to each other since the party, and I think Jax is finally starting to figure out that something has shifted between them. My only question is, how the fuck did I get stuck sitting between them?

My gaze snaps up to the clock. Twelve minutes left.

Fuck my life.

As we take notes, I can't help but glance through the window, my eyes connecting with Tanner's in the adjacent class, separated by nothing more than a row of poorly cleaned windows.

The fucker rolls his tongue over his bottom lip, his eyes darkening as a flood of heat blooms deep in my core, forcing me to clench my thighs. The asshole. He knows exactly what he's been doing because he's been doing it for the past forty-five minutes.

"Oi," Jax says, stealing my attention away from Tanner as he leans into my shoulder, pretending to take down his notes. "Would you stop trying to eye fuck Tanner and concentrate on the issue at hand? Ari's avoiding me. What's up with her? Is she acting weird to you too, or is it just me? Because I invited her over last night to … you know, and she left me hanging. She never leaves me hanging. Ari is always down to fuck. I didn't know what to do. I had to take care of business by myself."

I shove him back to his side of the desk, a shiver of disgust sailing down my spine. "I don't want to hear about your sexcapades," I tell him. "If you think she's done with your shit, then ask her yourself. I'm not doing this messenger bullshit anymore."

His face scrunches, clearly not liking the idea of handling his own shit like a man. Then I feel Arizona leaning into my other side. "Tell that knob-jockey to mind his own damn business before I shove a ten-inch dildo up his ass … with no lube!"

"I … no. I'm not telling him that!" I whisper-yell. "You two are as bad as Logan and Chanel. I'm not getting involved."

Arizona rolls her eyes and resting back into her seat, sticking her legs out as far as she can under the desk, and seeing as though she's tiny, it's not very far at all. Jax on the other hand just looks confused and leans in again. "Did she say something about a dildo? I'd prefer to fuck her with my own equipment, but if she's down to explore a little, then I don't mind."

I shove him back again. "You're so gross."

Jax laughs to himself, and I realize that the asshole was just fucking with me for a bit of entertainment. When I glance at the clock again, there are still eight minutes left.

Damn, time is moving slower than Jax's brain.

I need something to entertain myself.

Letting out a heavy sigh, I can't resist glancing across at Tanner again. Except, for the first time all lesson, his eyes are actually on his teacher and not me, taking away any hope of entertainment ... or does it?

A smirk pulls at the corners of my lips, and I pull my phone from my pocket and keep it hidden under my desk as I open a text to Tanner. My smirk widens, and I feel all sorts of giddy inside as I attach the special return favor video I recorded only for him. What better time to send it than right now?

This couldn't possibly go wrong.

I hit send and have to choke back a laugh, which only has Jax's eyes snapping back to me. I quickly lock my phone, but Jax watches me with a suspicious stare before glancing across at Tanner just as his hand slips into his pocket. "What?" he asks, the curiosity killing him. "What did you send him?"

I consider not telling him when I remember I'm talking to the least judgmental, free-spirited person I've ever met. "The girl version of a cum shot video," I tell him, watching as his brows shoot up and a devious grin crosses his lips.

Jax laughs and shakes his head before turning to watch Tanner, both our stares locked heavily on his face. He brings his phone to his lap, keeping it concealed from the teacher's view and I watch the exact moment he opens the video.

Tanner's eyes go wide, and his head snaps up, almost breaking his neck as he whips around to meet my stare. His jaw is slack, and I have to cover my mouth with my hand to keep from bursting into laughter.

Not wanting to miss a second, his gaze falls back to the video, discreetly watching every moment of it. Hell, I wouldn't be surprised if he rewound it just to start from the beginning in slow motion.

His expression begins to change as I watch his chest beginning to rise and fall a little faster. He presses down beneath the desk to adjust himself, and I'm not going to lie, watching him get hot while knowing exactly what he's looking at is getting me just as excited.

Tanner sinks lower in his chair, clenching his jaw as he's forced to adjust himself again. "He's not going to make it," Jax murmurs, just as intrigued by the show as I am, only for very different reasons. "The fucker's gonna come in his pants."

"No he won't," I laugh.

Jax shrugs and gives me a blank stare as though I should know better before turning back to watch the afternoon's entertainment. It wasn't the longest video, and I know he's gotta be getting close to the end when Jax laughs again.

"Ahh, and here we have the teenage virgin, stumbling through his first sexual encounter," he mutters low, doing his best *David Attenborough* impression. "The mating ritual of the human species is more commonly performed as a pair. It's animalistic and often very wild and raw, however here we have found an odd occurrence. What appears to be a solo performance brought on by nothing more than a visual."

Tears leak from my eyes as I do everything I can not to laugh when Tanner shoots to his feet, the front of his pants tenting as he bolts for the door, his teacher yelling in his wake.

"Oh, what is this?" Jax continues. "The teenage virgin has finally broken, coming to terms with the fact that if he does not run now, the whole class of humans will witness what is bound to be an agonizing climax. The virgin runs, his ability to process orders from his alpha hindered by the raging erection straining to be freed. Astounding. This is truly an odd occurrence indeed.

"The teen rushes down the hallway, breaking into a supply closet so he can climax into his hand and enjoy his moment of solitude before returning to his pack a lesser man. I am beyond speech, beyond words, purely wowed by this rare occasion. What could be more impressive than the display of the no-handed climax?"

I can't hold it in a second longer, and my laughter comes bursting from the seams.

My teacher whips around, a sharp glare heading straight for me and Jax. "Jaxon and Brielle, is there something you need to share with the whole class?"

"Not at all, sir," Jax says, waving him off as I struggle to contain myself. "I think we've reached the climax of our moment. Though thank you, for your offer to share. I appreciate that."

The bell sounds a moment later, dismissing the class, and Jax and I take off at the speed of light, certain that another second in this classroom is going to earn us detention. "Gotta go, babe," he says, throwing the words over his shoulder. "Coach Wyld will bust my ass wide open if I'm late for training again."

Jax rushes off, and as I wait outside the classroom doors for Arizona to catch up, a text comes through.

Tanner - I'm coming for you, Brielle Ashford. You better be ready for me.

CHAPTER 18

TANNER

Kill me now.

I step out of the locker room after training to find Hudson hovering by my bike, and the instant need to strangle him pulses through my veins. The fucker has been watching me all day, biding his time. There's something he's been meaning to tell me, and I think I know exactly what it is.

Fuck.

I was hoping this was all in my head, that the times I've caught him hanging around the hospital were innocent, and that the way he always seems to pay more attention when Addie is mentioned was simply out of respect. But this? I'm going to kill him. I'm going to fucking kill him.

I've sensed it ever since the attack. Things have shifted. The way he listens when she's mentioned, the way he seems to know the exact medical terms and what they mean, the way he stormed through the party by my side to get to her. He's the first to put his hand up whenever I want to go hunting for Colby, and he's the first to offer to take my place when I do. Don't get me wrong, Riley and the twins had my back in the same way, but there was something so intense about Hudson's approach. It's as though the thought of Addison hurting was killing him inside.

Hudson Bellamy is in love with my goddamn sister.

Taking a deep breath, I pump my hands at my sides before starting the trek down to the student parking lot. I try to calm myself, but this shit ain't gonna be pretty. It has to be done though.

Hudson watches me from the parking lot, and I see just how miserable he is. Hell, the fucker looks downright sick about what he's going to say. He's hoping that I'll put him out of his misery and welcome him into the family with open arms, but he's got to be kidding himself if that's what he wants. Addison has just been through hell, and I can guarantee the last thing she's thinking about is dating.

Absolutely not.

Hell, even before the attack, it still would have been a no from me, but now things are different. Addison is working through the kind of shit no woman should have to suffer through. She's learning how to run again, learning how to fly, and I don't want her dragged down by some guy who isn't ready for just how much of a challenge it's going to be.

Addie isn't some average chick whose biggest problem is bleaching her hair or asking daddy to buy her a new designer bag. Addison has real issues, gut-wrenching issues that are tearing her apart. If and when she's ready to share her world with someone, I need to know that someone is going to be able to handle it.

My feet hit the pavement of the parking lot, and I cross toward my bike, my hard stare locked on Hudson. He knows I know what this is about, and he knows what's coming his way.

He's three feet away.

My hand curls into a hard fist as my bag drops off my shoulder.

Two feet.

I rear back and he braces himself, prepared to take it like a man …

One foot.

CRACK!

My fist pummels against his jaw and the fucker flies back, the momentum from my swing knocking him flat on his ass. I shake out my hand as he grunts in pain, our other teammates watching as they make their way to their cars.

Hudson doesn't curse me out, doesn't try to fight back, simply accepts it like a fucking man as he gets to his feet and spits a mouthful of blood onto the pavement.

"How long?" I question, not needing to clarify what I'm asking him.

He blows out a heavy breath, swallowing the remaining blood in his mouth as he stands tall and meets me eye-to-eye. "Two years, give or take," he says, his stare unwavering, giving this conversation the respect it's owed.

"FUCK!" I let out a frustrated growl before running my hands through my hair, trying to work through the need to punch him again. I take a moment, trying to calm myself before turning back to him. "You've been in love with my sister for two fucking years and you never said a word."

"Come on, Tanner. You've known," he says, shaking his head, being real with me for once. "You might not have listened to the signs or refused to believe it, but it's always been there. Especially the last few weeks. I see it every time you look at me. You see it clear as fucking day."

"I see it," I agree with him. "But I had no idea you felt that way for two fucking years. How could you not say something?"

"It was never the right time. She's young, man. She never needed me."

"Oh, and she does now?" I scoff in disbelief.

"Yeah," he says, dead fucking serious. "She needs every last person who's in her corner. Yeah, she's got you and for now, that might be enough. You might make her feel like she's safe to sleep at night, but what about when she needs to get it off her chest? When she needs to scream about the fucked-up things he did to her? She'll never open up to you like that. You're her big brother, man. She'll never burden you with those details, and fuck knows you won't be able to handle it without losing yourself in the process."

"You don't know what the fuck you're talking about."

"Don't I?" he says, stepping closer. "Or are you just too fucking self-important to admit that she might need someone other than you?"

"Don't push me, Hudson. I'll break your fucking jaw if I have to." He takes a hesitant step back, and I let out a heavy sigh, trying to approach this rationally. "She's not ready for this. She barely woke up a week ago. The last thing she's thinking about is hooking up with you. She thinks of you as a fucking brother."

"You don't think I know that?" he questions. "I'm not telling you this because I want to sweep her off her feet and be her fucking hero. I'm telling you this because she *needs* me. She needs a friend. She needs that one person she can call when her world is crumbling around her. I'm telling you this," he says, slowing his tone to make it fucking clear. "Because when she wakes up in the middle of the night screaming because she can feel the taint of his hands on her body, I have every intention of being the first one through her fucking door. So don't insult me by assuming that I'm just out to get my dick wet or that I'd ever try to push her into a relationship she's not ready for. I love her, Tanner. I've been in love with her for two fucking years. I can wait. I'll wait as long as it takes. Five years, ten. Whatever she needs, but just know that I'm not walking away."

My hands press against my temples, unsure how to handle this. "Fuck, man," I say, shaking my head. "Why does it have to be her? She's my little sister."

Hudson scoffs. "Trust me, I've been asking myself the same fucking question for two years."

I drop to the ground, my ass hitting the pavement as I lean up against the side of Hudson's car. "You're one of my best friends," I tell him. "I respect you, you're one of the good ones, and though I don't want to admit it, I know deep down that you'd only ever want what's best for her. You'd treat her well and give her the fucking world, and don't get me wrong here, but you'll never be good enough for her. No one will."

He nods, and drops down opposite me, resting his arms against his knees as he gives me a hard stare. "I know," he says, slowly nodding. "It's in the way that you'll never be good enough for Bri. Brielle is an amazing chick, and you're a rough piece of shit, but for some damn reason, she looks at you and she sees her whole fucking world. I'm going to be that for Addie."

The thought of anyone being Addie's whole world terrifies me, and it gives them the kind of power that'll make her vulnerable. If someone were to hurt her again, I don't know if she would ever recover. "I swear, man. If you break her …"

"You have my word, Tanner. I'm not going to push her on this, and I sure as fuck won't try to start something until she's ready. She already has so much going on, physical therapy, putting Colby away, getting back into her dance classes, not to mention the ongoing trauma of what he did to her. When the time is right, I'll let her come to me."

I watch him a moment before finally nodding, that being something I can deal with. It'll give me time to get used to the idea of them together and peace of mind that he'd never pressure her into it. "You should know that every chance I get, I'm going to kick your ass."

"Trust me, I fucking know."

I drop my face into my hands while shaking my head. "Fucking hell, man. My little sister."

I can all but hear his cringe. "Don't say it like that. You make it sound like she's a fucking child."

My head snaps up and I gape at the asshole. "Isn't she?"

A grin cracks across his face and I immediately want to pulverize it. "Maybe to you."

"Man, you need to watch yourself. I will beat you senseless and claim you fell."

Hudson laughs, but he knows just how serious I am. Knowing the rest of this conversation couldn't possibly go well, I get up and grab my bag before walking the few feet to my bike. Hudson gets up with me and senses the topic of his undying love for my sister needs to be dropped, so he moves on to something that's equally as infuriating. "We're up against Hope Falls next week," he reminds me, the undercurrents in his tone expressing something much more sinister.

"I know," I tell him, straddling my bike, reading exactly what he's thinking. Colby Jacobs has been evading the cops at every turn, but there's no way in hell he's going to skip out on this game. He wants his shot to put me down, but after what he did to Addison and how he hurt Bri, I'd rather end my life than let that motherfucker best me on the field, and that goes for his friend, Roxten Hargrove as well. Neither of them are going to know what's going on. The whole fucking team for that matter. Addison is the princess of Bradford Private and now that what happened is public knowledge, she has the whole community rooting for her.

I meet Hudson's hard stare, letting him read the darkness in my eyes. "Be ready," I tell him. "Because after that game, we're going to destroy him, even if we have to hunt him down."

Hudson nods, all in. "I'm ready," he says. "Whatever it takes."

CHAPTER 19
Brielle

A loud yawn tears out of me as I walk through the door late on Saturday afternoon. The girls and I have been chilling out at Chanel's place. Even Addie tagged along, claiming she needed a girls day, but honestly, I think she only came to escape Tanner and her mom. They watch her like a hawk, constantly checking on her as though she can't possibly care for herself, which I completely understand, but being on the receiving end of that must be a lot.

Making my way through the lavish house, I take a detour to the kitchen, scanning the fridge for a bottle of water and something to eat. The girls and I lost track of time and skipped lunch when we started talking shit about the boys. Well, mostly about Jax and Logan, but there have been a few crude retorts about Riley as well.

Grabbing the leftover Chinese takeout from last night, I shove it into the microwave and hit go before searching the drawers for a fork. Just as the microwave finishes, the backdoor opens and Orlando strides through, just finishing a phone call.

Hearing me rifling through his kitchen, his head snaps up and his strained gaze locks on me. "Ah, Brielle, just the person I need to see."

My gaze narrows. What the hell is that supposed to mean?

I suppose the one good thing about Orlando Channing is that he doesn't make me jump through hoops for answers, he's straight to the point. "That was Garrett," he says, referring to the lawyer he'd set me up with. "He was just confirming that you are officially off the hook. Your evidence together with the victim's statement was all they needed to clear your name."

I brace my hands against the counter, needing to hold myself up as the relief washes through me. "Right, okay, so … wait," I pause, my brows furrowing as I meet his stare. "Why is Garrett discussing my case with you and not speaking directly to me? I didn't consent to that. Isn't there supposed to be some kind of client-lawyer confidentiality agreement?"

"Do not forget who is footing this bill," he reminds me. "Besides, I am an interested party, and the outcome of your case directly affects mine. I have a responsibility to my client to ensure that I have all the information."

"Sounds like bullshit to me," I scoff, reading between the lines. "What you mean to say is, you want to explore every little loophole so you can get Colby off on a technicality. Let's be real here, you know damn well that asshole is guilty, but your precious reputation is more important than seeing a rapist and attempted murderer locked up. You were all too comfortable with the idea of asking me to supply a false alibi. Tell me, if it came down to it in court, would you have asked me to commit perjury just to save face?"

Orlando's lip twitches as Mom walks into the kitchen, completely oblivious to the tension in the room. She's dressed in a gown, and I can only assume they're heading out for yet another gala event. Orlando glances toward her, his eyes skimming over her choice of gown with distaste before forcing a fake smile across his lips. "You look positively breathtaking, my love," he says, moving toward her and pressing a kiss to her cheek.

Mom plays the role of doting, bashful wife perfectly and bats her lashes before Orlando turns to me, his calculated stare narrowing with confidence. "You should consider a career in law, Brielle," he says. "You'd make an excellent lawyer."

And with that, he strides out of the kitchen, his head held way too high for a man with such questionable morals.

An unladylike scoff flies from my mouth, and I can't help the way my face twists with disgust. That man truly is a piece of shit. I have no idea what my mother sees in him, you know, apart from the obvious deep pockets, high society lifestyle, and silver fox status.

Mom sighs and moves toward me, setting her clutch on the counter and turning to the oven to see her reflection. Her face is a mask of indifference as she threads a pair of diamonds through her ears, the matching set to the ostentatious ring that protrudes from her finger. "What on earth was that about?" she questions, as though she hasn't spent the last two weeks assuming I was guilty.

I bite my tongue, working extra hard at keeping the nasty comments to myself. "He was just letting me know that on top of being a piece of shit who wants a rapist to walk free, the accusations against me have officially been dropped."

I give her a fake grin and without another glance her way, I take the container of Chinese takeout and make my way upstairs.

What can I say? I really tried to be nice, but I clearly lack self-discipline. Oh well, it's done now. Perhaps I've been spending too much time with Tanner and the boys. They're definitely rubbing off on me.

Making my way into my room, I come to a stop, my lips stretching into a wide grin as I find black eyeliner scrawled across my mirror in Tanner's familiar handwriting.

NICE LEGS, WHEN DO THEY OPEN?
NICE PUSSY, WHEN CAN I EAT IT?

A snorted laugh tears from the back of my throat, imagining the way Tanner would have stood here smirking at himself as he crossed out the first line and started working on the next one. He would have thought he was such a genius. The idiot is probably still chuckling to himself about just how clever he is.

Unable to tear the grin off my face, I move across my room and glance through the window, double-checking if he's in his room. I'm not surprised to find it empty, he's rarely home on a Saturday afternoon doing nothing, unless there's something wrong with the Mustang after thrashing it the night before at the races.

Just to mess with him, I put the Chinese takeout down and replace it with my phone before hashing out a text and feeling all too smug about it.

Brielle - Nice cock, when can I ride it?

Tanner - Nice ass, when can I fuck it?

Brielle - I'm down now. It's a shame you're not home, I could have used your help. Don't stress, I have plenty of reliable replacements in my bedside drawer.

I laugh, picturing his face wherever he is, regretting the life decisions that led him to miss out on a Saturday in bed. Knowing damn well I've won this round, I slip my phone back into my pocket, and as I turn to find my Chinese takeout, something out of the corner of my eye captures my attention.

My eyes bug out of my head, and I suck in a sharp breath finding Tanner out my bedroom window launching himself over the back fence. "Oh, fuck."

Laughter tears from my throat as I sprint to my door and hastily flick the lock before hurdling over my bed and slamming my closet door. My heart races, hearing Tanner's feet on the stairs, sprinting faster than humanly possible.

He goes for my bedroom door first, and I watch with bated breath as the handle wiggles, finding resistance. "Brielle Ashford," he rumbles.

"You feisty little pocket rocket, open this motherfucking door right this second."

"Oh no," I cry. "My brittle little fingers. I couldn't possibly do something like that."

The door handle wiggles again, and not a second later, I hear him down the hall, breaking in through the hallway closet and up into the crawlspace. My heart hammers erratically, excitement pounding through my veins. I had intended that text as nothing more than a tease, but now that he's here with this desperation to get to me, something tells me this is only going to end one way.

A light thud sounds from within my walk-in closet, and a gasp sails through my lips as I press my back up against the locked door, feeling all too smug with myself. "Brielle," he demands, his voice sailing through the door, so fucking close to me that a shiver sails across my skin.

Butterflies claim my stomach as I swallow hard. "Yes? Is there something you need?"

"If I get in there to find you going to town on yourself without me, I'm going to be pissed."

"What a shame you're so far away," I tease. "If only you were in here to do something about it. Though, I'm a little lost. I can't decide which toy to replace you with. Any thoughts?"

A soft laugh sounds through the door as I hear him moving around inside, and not a moment later, he's back, standing right by the door. "You can use every fucking toy you've got, but not one of them will be a suitable replacement for me. They'll never make you feel how I can."

"Oh yeah, big guy?" I murmur, the very thought of how he makes me feel leaving me desperate for his touch. "Pretty confident there."

I can almost hear his cocky smirk. "Damn right, I am," he says as I hear the distinct sound of metal against metal.

"Tanner?" I question, my brows furrowed. "What are you doing?"

"Wouldn't you like to know?" he laughs. "These are some nice hangers you've got in here. Nice and bendy, a bit like you."

The sound gets louder and my eyes widen, realizing he's using the wire hangers to unlock the door. My heart lurches as I whip around to grip the handle, but it's too late, the door tears open and I fall inside the open door. Tanner's arm whips out and braces my waist.

He presses me up against the wall of my walk-in closet, his hips pinning me against it. I wrap my legs around his waist, holding onto him as those dark eyes stare right into my soul. "Can your toys do this?" he questions, his chest right up against mine as his breath brushes over my skin. He grinds his cock against me, making me groan. "What about that?"

"Mmmm, maybe," I murmur. "I'm going to need more information. What else can you do?"

Tanner leans in, capturing my lips with his, the hunger pulsing through him and right into me. It's criminal to make me feel like this, so desperate and full of desire. I need him inside of me. I need him to fuck me until I'm shattered.

Unable to wait, I grip his shirt and yank it over his head, needing to feel his defined muscles beneath my fingers. Tanner's body pulls back just an inch, his hips keeping me pinned enough to free his hands.

Without hesitation, he tears my tank right off my body, leaving it in tattered scraps on the floor.

"Holy shit," I pant, pushing my bra strap off my shoulder, needing to feel his touch over every inch of my skin. He reads me perfectly, stripping me naked, and before I can scream in desperation, he slams that thick, veiny cock deep inside of me.

My head tips back against the wall, my hands gripping onto his shoulders as he fucks me hard. Hell, I can't even be sure that he took a second to wrap his equipment, but I trust him with everything I am. He'll never cross my boundaries.

His cock stretches me, filling me to the brim as his pelvis grinds against my clit, sending a wave of overwhelming pleasure rocking through me. "Killer," he grunts, thrusting into me again. "I could fuck this tight little pussy until I die."

I bite down on my bottom lip, his words making me feel like the most desirable woman who ever lived, and just to show him how much I appreciate them, I clench around him, each of us groaning at the instant satisfaction.

His fingers bite into my skin, holding me so damn tight it's as though he'll never let me go. "Tanner," I pant, a low groan rumbling through my chest. "So good."

Tanner pulls back and thrusts harder again and again, forcing soft moans of pleasure to escape my lips. He watches me for a moment, but it's not enough, and just like that, his lips are crushing down on mine as he gently pinches my nipple.

I gasp into his mouth, my body worked up and ready to explode.

He does it again and the build up becomes so fucking intense, I could cry. My hands roam over his body, needing to feel every inch of him. "Faster," I pant. "More."

He obliges without hesitation, and I cry out, my fingers digging into the firm muscle of his perfect ass. "Give it to me, Killer. Let me feel that tight little cunt coming around me."

Tanner slams into me again, his pelvis grinding against my clit, and it's all I need to throw me right over the edge into oblivion. My body explodes, my pussy convulsing around his thick cock as fireworks burst through my vision. I clench my eyes, gripping onto him with everything I have. "Fuck, Tanner."

His eyes flutter with absolute satisfaction. "That's right, Killer," he mutters breathlessly, his cock feeling every last one of my wild spasms as he comes hard. He doesn't stop moving, thrusting in and out of me as my high works its way through my body. "I bet those toys will never fuck you like that."

My head falls forward onto his big shoulder, barely able to catch my breath. "I don't know, that was impressive, but so are they," I tell him, still panting as my pussy convulses around his heavy shaft, my eyes rolling back in my head. "I was too worked up. Couldn't concentrate. I think you'll need to do it again, just so I know for sure."

Tanner laughs as his arms curl around me, pulling me away from the wall. "Oh yeah?" he asks, striding out of the closet and through to my bathroom. "I'm not sure you can handle it."

His eyes sparkle as he looks back at me, and I can't help the grin that stretches across my face. "Is that a challenge, Tanner Morgan?"

Tanner throws me into the shower, pressing my chest up against the cold tiles as I cry out, the chill shocking my body as he presses in behind me. "You bet your fine ass it is," he declares, twisting the faucet and letting freezing cold water rain down over me.

CHAPTER 20

TANNER

Venom burns through my blood, poisoning my mind as I stare across the field at the Hope Falls football team. Colby Jacobs has a lot of fucking nerve showing his face around here.

My hands twitch at my side, balling into tight fists. I'm about ready to throw away the whole goddamn season, my whole fucking football career, just to cut across the field and end his miserable life.

"MORGAN," Coach Wyld roars, forcing my attention back on him as my teammates huddle around, every single one of us more than prepared to beat these motherfuckers. After all, this game is personal. "If you don't fucking got this, I'll take your ass out of this game so damn fast, so help me."

Riley gives me a hard shove and shoots a sharp glare at me, a silent message to pull myself together. "I'm fine," I spit, clenching my jaw and trying to draw my attention back to my team.

"Get your head in the game, boy," Coach demands. "You're not fine. You're letting your personal shit stand in the way of the game. Jacobs shouldn't be here, we can all fucking agree on that, but you're not throwing away your future for that piece of shit. Hold your head high and win the fucking game respectfully, then handle your shit off my field. Is that understood?"

My gaze cuts up to Brielle in the stands. She sits with Arizona and Ilaria, and I'm sure they're doing whatever they can to keep her ass planted right where it needs to be, but the look in her eyes is murderous. She wants his blood just as much as I do.

Dropping my stare back to Coach Wyld, I give a sharp nod. "Understood. I got this."

He holds my stare for a moment too long, silently considering if he should trust me, but I've been giving my all for this team since my freshman year, and I've never let him down before. He has no reason not to trust me, but damn it, I barely trust myself right now. I've given him my word, and I have no choice but to stand by it. Besides, if I can't beat the living shit out of him right now, the least I can do is make him look like the fool that he is out on this field.

This is my fucking home, my field, and he won't be walking away unscathed. My team has got my back, and they'll make sure Colby Jacobs gets his ass handed to him. No college will want him when we're through. Though, it shouldn't matter. His ass is going nowhere but the slammer.

Addie has been out of her coma for close to two weeks now, and while she's doing well and getting stronger every day, she's still suffering. The cops haven't done their part in arresting Colby, and I can't help but wonder if a big part of that is due to Orlando Channing. Because of that, Addie spends her days living in fear. She rarely leaves the house, terrified that Colby will come looking for her, and when she does find the strength to leave, it's never alone.

Hudson has been hanging out more, and while he's been playing on this ruse of coming over to see me, he's been spending every minute of his time with Addie. As much as I want to beat his ass for it, the fucker has been putting a smile on her face and respecting her boundaries. There's nothing romantic about it. He said he was there to be her friend, someone to lean on while she heals, and that's exactly what he's doing. I can't fault him, but that doesn't mean that I won't kick his ass the second I get a chance.

There's no denying it though, the look in Hudson's eyes is just as vile as mine. This motherfucker is all in, and the second the final whistle blows, he'll be right by my side with our boys at our backs. We've been waiting for this moment since the second Coach told us we were going up against Hope Falls. Don't get me wrong, I was hoping Colby would have been arrested and charged by now, but if the fucker is dumb enough to show up on my field, then by all means, he'll be getting his ass handed to him.

The buzzer sounds, and with an almighty cheer from the crowd, both teams make their way onto the field, more than ready to get this shit over and done with.

"Morgan," Coach calls after me. I turn back to find his stare locked on mine. "I'm not fucking around with you, head in the game."

"Yes, Coach."

Jogging out onto the field, I catch Hudson's stare as he nods and Logan moves in beside me. "You good, bro?" he questions, glancing across the field to where Colby moves into position, his stare already locked on mine. "I don't know what Hope Falls is doing. They should have suspended him during the investigation. I bet they're not even doing an internal investigation."

"Hope Falls is nothing but a bunch of dirty pricks, you know that," I comment, stopping as I reach where I need to be. "But Colby is their best player. They're not giving that up for anything, which is why we need to prove that he's nothing but shit under my shoe, you feel me?"

Logan moves past me. "I feel you, and then after the game …"

I nod, confirming what he already knows. "After the game."

Not a moment later, everyone is in position and with the sound of the buzzer, the game starts with Bradford immediately pushing through on the attack. We race ahead, each of my teammates looking sharp as Hope Falls comes in with dirty tackles, only just legal enough to keep them from being penalized.

I'm not going to lie, we're barely thirty seconds in and the game is already messy.

This is going to be a shitshow.

The ball moves seamlessly from player to player, and I keep my eye on it, doing everything I can to not think about the way Addison screamed for help or the bruises he left on her skin. Even though we're playing by the book, the Hope Falls assholes aren't easing up on their dirty tackles. My boys are getting screwed over, and all it's doing is pissing me off.

Jax takes off with the ball, sprinting forward into their defense. He dodges two guys, weaving like a fucking pro, and as Riley moves into position, Jax hands the ball off to him with a perfect pass. He gets another few steps when a big fucker slams into Jax, taking him down with a brutal blow, despite being clear of the ball.

The crowd roars in protest as Jax pushes the asshole off him and the whistle blows. Jax gets to his feet and shoves the guy hard. "What the fuck?" he spits as Logan darts between them and shoulder charges Jax, pushing him back a step. He grabs Jax's helmet and shoves his right up against it before saying something that has Jax finding control.

The asshole who tackled him gets nothing but a slap on the wrist, and as he turns to get back into position, I notice the name *Hargrove* written across the back of his jersey.

Motherfucker. It's the asshole who texted Brielle last week. With all the bullshit going down with Colby, I'd almost let this asshole slip through my fingers, but now that he's on my field playing right alongside my sister's rapist, it'll be a two for one deal.

The thought has my gaze lifting to Bri, and I can't help but notice how pissed off she looks. She's not enjoying this game even a little bit.

Coach hollers something from the sidelines and not a moment later, the ball is in play again. We go hard, and when we throw an interception and are suddenly on defense, I couldn't be more thrilled.

My boys go just as hard with their tackles, taking those assholes down one by one. The ball moves from one player to the next, and when Colby finally gets his hands on it, I move like fucking lightning.

With every step I take, I hear Addie's screams, hear Brielle's cries, feel their pain, but nothing is stopping me now. Coach Wyld's piercing tone roars from the sideline, knowing damn well what's about to happen, but I'm well within my rights. Besides, what kind of player would I be if I just let him pass?

Colby shoves past two of my teammates, and there's no denying just how fast he is, but he's no match for Logan. No one is a match for Logan. I push myself faster, and the closer I get, the further my control begins to slip. Anger boils through my veins, and I don't give a shit if this gets me sent off the field or fucking suspended. Nothing can stop me now.

Colby's gaze flashes toward me, and just as his eyes widen, I barrel into him with the force of a fucking freight train. His feet lift right off the ground, and I send him back a few feet before slamming his ass down with a brutal blow, all of my weight coming down with it. He's visibly winded and gasps as it takes everything I have to push myself off the bastard and take an innocent step back.

A short-lived victory pulses through me, and I hide my smirk as everyone on the Bradford grandstand gets to their feet and cheers, screaming my name. I laugh to myself, that response usually only happens when someone has scored a touchdown or made the best play known to man, but Addison is Bradford's princess, and there's not a soul in those stands who doesn't know what this bastard did to her—even the stands on the opposite side of the field.

Bradford is coming for blood.

Chanel flies to her feet in her ridiculous little cheerleading outfit and screams, throwing her pom poms into the air and doing one of those insane high kicks, prompting the rest of the squad to get up with her, celebrating this win, despite how small it may be.

I put myself back into position, hoping like hell that I caused some type of damage. I don't get called out for it, and as I glance back toward Coach Wyld, the rage in his eyes tells me that I'm going to get my ass handed to me as soon as the game is over.

Hudson moves in beside me to get into position, and as the crowd begins to settle, he smirks at the way Colby discreetly rubs his chest. "Next time, go for the throat."

My tackle only angers Colby as the game goes on, prompting him to keep coming at me, with or without the ball, but I'm un-fucking-touchable. I put him down four more times while the rest of my team does the same, not allowing the bastard to get through our defense. It's not even halftime yet, and the fucker is quickly wearing thin. Hell, I even get to take Roxten Hargrove down, and it's some of the best fun I've ever had out on this field.

There ain't no stopping us now!

The ball lands in my hands, and as Logan takes off at a sprint, I rear back before letting it fly. He stays ahead of the ball, and I watch the game play out like pieces on a chess board. Riley runs after him, ready to have his back at a moment's notice, but Logan won't need it. Not today.

Logan launches himself into the air, collecting the ball with ease, while Hope Falls races after him, desperate to save themselves and what's left of their game.

Riley and Logan effortlessly get to the endzone, dodging every tackle until Logan slams the ball down in a clean touchdown just seconds before the halftime buzzer sounds over the crowd's roar. Riley barrels into Logan, the two of them celebrating as the rest of our players catch up, and just as I go to take off after them, Jax yells out. "TANNER! WATCH YOUR BACK."

I spin around just in time to be thrown to the ground, Colby's weight coming down on my chest as his fists barrel toward me. "You fucking piece of shit," he roars, hitting me with a face full of spittle. "I'll end you, and your little bitch too."

Hudson is the first to reach us, launching himself at Colby and tumbling with him into the grass. He gets one good hit on Colby before the rest of our teammates race in, tearing us apart. Two of my guys hold me back as Roxten pushes himself in front of Colby, blocking him from coming at me. The crowd's noise seems to be closing in, and when I glance up, the field is swarming with people.

Coach Wyld storms in, his familiar tone roaring over the crowd, but just when I think he's about to bitch me out, I realize his anger is focused on the Hope Falls coach. "Pull your boys in line, August. They're playing just as dirty as you did."

August takes a swing at Coach Wyld, and he swiftly puts him down as the referees' whistles nearly blow my fucking eardrums. The cheerleaders scream, and it's impossible to tell what the fuck is going on. Fists and insults fly carelessly left and right. Half of my guys are working on separating the fight as the other half try to get their hands on Colby. The whole school has my back on this.

Even parents and teachers are involved, some trying to separate people, others only encouraging the chaos. It's not until one angelic voice tears through the crowd that I can finally see things clearly. "TANNER," Brielle screams, barging her way through the horde of people, ducking and weaving between stray punches.

Panic tears through me, certain she's about to get hurt, and I launch myself forward, yanking her into my chest just moments before Riley falls back into her. "The fuck are you doing out here? You're gonna get hurt."

"I had to make sure you were alright."

 Fucking hell. I love her, but she'll be the death of me.

"I'm fine," I tell her, trying to get her to move out of the crowd, though thankfully it seems to be easing up. "I've taken harder hits from your insults than that asshole is capable of."

We break out into a clearing, and I take her over to the Bradford sidelines to find Coach Wyld dragging Hudson back away from the crowd. I tear my helmet off and grab a drink from the cooler before taking a quick sip and splashing the rest over my face. This isn't exactly how I envisioned halftime, and something tells me the cheerleaders are going to miss their performance today.

Brielle looks up at me, her eyes full of concern, looking over every inch of my body as the field finally begins to clear. "You sure you're good?" she asks. "You could have a concussion or something."

"Trust me, Killer. It wasn't as painful as being wrapped around a tree. I'm good. Besides, I didn't hit my head," I tell her, glancing over her to see Colby's coach shoving him into a chair.

Anger flares through me, and seeing that something has my attention, Brielle whips around. She's like a fucking rocket taking off, and before I can even grab her, she's gone. "FUCK." I glance back at the sidelines, knowing I'm going to need backup if I'm walking straight into the lion's den, especially when Brielle is involved. "HUDSON."

Hudson's head snaps up, and when he sees Brielle, he's on his feet and racing after her with me. Jax and Riley break away from the field to have our backs. We reach Brielle just in time for her to clock the fucker right in the eye. His head swings and she launches herself at him. "You fucking rapist," she screams, trying to get her arms around his throat. "You should be locked up for what you did to her."

Colby throws her off like she weighs nothing, and she tumbles into my arms with a squeal. Without missing a beat, I shove her behind my back and into Jax's arms. Colby gets right back to his feet coming for me again when his coach barges in. "Get the fuck over to your own side," he spits, looking at us like we're nothing more than shit smeared across the sidewalk.

Brielle's not having it though. She launches out of Jax's hold, his arms too sweaty to contain her. She's like a little chihuahua with a nasty fucking bite. "Why the fuck is he still playing? You should have suspended him when he was first arrested. What kind of piece of shit coach are you?"

I grab Bri around the waist, dragging her back when Colby pushes forward into my girl. "Watch yourself, whore. I haven't nearly had my share of you yet."

I see fucking red, but I refuse to release her to put this motherfucker in the ground. Roxten moves in beside Colby, smirking at my girl, and despite everything I want to do to them, I drag Brielle away from Colby and back toward our side, my boys coming with us.

"The fuck is wrong with you?" I demand, gripping her arm tight so the little she-devil can't slip away again. "He's a rapist, Bri. I don't give a shit how fucking tough you think you are, you don't go demanding that type of attention. We'll deal with him, but not like that."

Tears spring from her eyes as we get back to our side, and I indicate to the bench for her to sit. "I … I don't know. I just saw him and all I could remember was the way his hands were tightening around my throat, and it was like I couldn't breathe again. I just … I can't sit here and watch him get away with everything he's done. He's right there and no one is doing anything about it. The cops are just fucking around letting him get away with it. He should be locked up."

Letting out a sigh, I crouch down before her, one hand resting on her thigh as the other brushes the tears from her face. "I know," I tell her. "Trust me, I fucking know more than anyone, but I swear to you, I'm not letting him get away with this shit anymore. We've got him right where we want him, and the second this game is over …"

I clench my jaw, letting her see the wild venom in my stare, and she nods, knowing this is how it has to be. "I don't want you getting hurt."

"I won't," I promise her. "But we have to be patient. Half of these guys have colleges looking at them, and while I'm willing to give it all up for justice, they shouldn't have to. I'm not fucking up their season and their future for that piece of shit, okay? We play out this game and win, and the second we're done, all bets are off."

"I wanna come with you."

"Absolutely not," I say, shaking my head as the cheerleaders run around the field clearing off anything left behind from the brawl. The school security officers usher people back to their seats, demanding everyone calm down, while other spectators take off, not wanting to hang around for the second half of the game.

Coach Wyld takes a sip of his drink, trying to calm himself as Brielle presses her lips into a tight line. "I'm going to be a part of this whether you like it or not," she says as Coach orders everyone to gather around. "He hurt me too, Tanner. I deserve this just as much as you do."

I press my lips into a hard line, knowing she won't back down, but Coach Wyld will have my ass if I don't wrap this up quickly. "Fine," I tell her, going against my better judgment. "Go with the girls and figure out a way to get the motherfucker alone after the game. If we can get Hargrove too, even better."

Brielle grins, and as she leans in to kiss me, her eyes darken. "We've got this. Now go win your game."

And with that, she takes off into the grandstand, the wheels in her brain spinning a million miles an hour.

Pushing my ass back onto the bench, I drop my head into my hands, feeling the weight of everything that just went down. "You good, Morgan? That was a big hit," Coach asks. I give a sharp nod and he watches me a moment, wondering if he should trust me. "Good," he finally says. "Jacobs will be out the rest of the game, so there shouldn't be any more problems. Hudson, you're out too."

"What?" Hudson demands, getting to his feet. "That's bullshit."

"What's bullshit is watching one of my senior players involve himself in someone else's shit. You could have put an end to it and walked away, instead you aggravated an already fucked-up situation. You're out for the rest of the game. Don't like it? Take it up with me on Monday."

When Hudson's ass drops back to the bench, Coach turns back to his team. "As for the rest of you, you better perform so well that I forget about the bullshit that just happened out on my field. I want a win at the end of this game, otherwise, you will all face the consequences, whether you were involved or not. Is that understood?"

Shouldering up next to one another in a huddle, we all chant, "Yes, Coach," and get right back into it, going over our plays and figuring out how to stay on top.

CHAPTER 21

TANNER

Colby's black Charger lingers under the light of the Bradford Private student parking lot, and we watch from the shadows, waiting for the perfect time to strike.

We end this tonight.

With Hudson out for the second half of the game, the girls utilized his knowledge on cars, and after slipping into the visitor's locker room and stealing Colby's bag—containing his phone, wallet, and keys—they were able to fuck with that car enough to make sure the asshole could never afford to fix it. That car isn't going anywhere fast, and that's the exact distraction we need.

The parking lot cleared out ten minutes ago, and we even went as far as driving our own cars out just to let the fucker think he was in the clear after our win tonight. But he should know better. When you fuck with me or mine, I won't rest until you're in the ground.

Roxten leans over the open hood of the Charger, braced against the cold metal while shaking his head as Colby paces back and forth in anger, kicking the tires every chance he gets. As he roars his frustrations, a grin kicks up the corners of my lips. This is going to be the best fun I've ever had.

Despite how badly they wanted to stay for the show, we kicked the girls out of here twenty minutes ago. I know Bri deserves to see this after everything she's been through, but she'll have to be okay with the fact it happened. I couldn't live with myself knowing she saw me like that. It's not going to be pretty, it'll be brutal and animalistic, but I have to do this for Addison and every other woman or girl this motherfucker has touched.

Swinging the baseball bat, it comes around in a perfect 360 before the metal shaft drops into my open palm. "You boys ready?" I ask, not bothering to look across at them, knowing damn well they wear the same expression I do.

"It's now or never," Hudson says, his tone filled with venom. "They called the tow company twenty minutes ago. We get in and get it done before anyone sees. If someone comes, we bail. Drop the fuckers and run, no questions asked. We're not going down for this."

"Agreed," Logan says. "Let's do this."

Without another word, we pull our masks down and step out of the shadows.

We have the silence and stealth of cats in the night until the very last moment when finally, we pounce. We make our way down to the student parking lot completely unnoticed. Roxten and Colby keep their backs to us, talking shit about how they're going to fuck me up, and it's cool, it doesn't bother me. But the moment I hear Addison's pretty name fall from his lips, he seals his fate.

We step up behind them, making a circle around them, leaving no way out but through us.

I rear back with my Louisville Slugger, preparing for the best batting practice of my life. I hold my position, a trick I've stolen from Jax over the years because let's face it, the prick is all for the dramatics. Not being the kind of man to drop someone with their back turned, I let him know his time is up.

"Hello motherfuckers," I say, mimicking that ridiculous sound from TikTok. Colby and Roxten whip around at the same time I swing the bat, letting the cool metal smash into the side of Colby's face. A loud crack sounds through the night as Jax and Hudson don't wait to jump Roxten.

Colby goes to fall, but I push into him, shoving him up against the side of his Charger for easy access. Grinning like a fucking maniac, I toss the bat to Logan, wanting to use my hands for every second of this. I want to feel his heart racing beneath my palm, feel his blood beneath my nails and know that this is the best kind of justice Addie might ever get.

Colby shakes off the hit, though there's no mistaking just how disoriented he is, or the fact he's rocking a brand-new broken jaw. He tries to shove me back, but the blow to his face weakened him, and

I easily overpower his bitch ass. "You like that, don't you?" I mock taking another swing to the exact same spot on his jaw. "You like when they can't fight back."

Colby cries out, falling forward and gripping his face in agony. "I'll fuck you up, asshole," Colby spits, blood staining his teeth.

A barking laugh tears from my throat, listening to the sweet sounds of Roxten Hargrove being jumped. "I'm right here, motherfucker. This is what you wanted, right? Come at me. Give it your best shot."

Colby tries to swing, but I take a step to the left, watching as the momentum of his missed hit sends him spinning to the ground. He drops to his knees and tries to pull himself up by gripping the side of his Charger, and even with the cover of darkness, the blue paint from Brielle's Honda catches my eye and sends a wave of fire pulsing through my veins.

I grab him by the back of his hair and yank him up, shoving him into his car so hard that the side panel crunches under his weight. "I should end you for what you did to my sister, but instead, I'm going to make you wish I killed you." I slam my fist into his gut and watch him double over with a low groan, giving me the perfect opportunity to ram my knee into his nose.

The sweet, satisfying sound of his nose breaking tears through the night, but the moment is quickly destroyed by the way his blood spurts all over my shoes. My lips twist in disgust, and I step back, watching as he drops to the ground like the pathetic sack of shit that he is, gripping his face and groaning with agony.

He curls into a ball, trying to protect what he can, but there's no hope for him, especially when I go in hard, giving it everything for the trauma he put my sister through, for the brokenness she feels in her soul, for the tears she cries every night when she thinks no one can hear.

Jax and Riley leave Roxten on the ground, completely out cold as my knuckles split and blood splatters across Colby's face and car. Hudson hovers around me, ready to tag team this bitch as Logan takes the bat to the Charger like a scorned *Carrie Underwood* who just found her man cheating.

I don't give up until Jax and Riley physically have to pull me off him, and even then, I'm fighting to get back. Colby is black and blue, and I'm gasping for breath, more worked up than I've ever been. His face isn't even recognizable, eyes swollen shut, brows and lips split, and a good chunk of that nose bent right out of shape.

"That's enough, bro," Riley says, placing a calming hand on my chest. "There's nothing more you can do."

I shake my head, pulling against the boys' hold. "The fucker broke Bri's ribs. I ain't going until this shit is done. I might not get another chance."

"I've got you," Hudson says, stepping in. He walks right up to Colby and kicks his shoulder, rolling him until he's flat on his back. My body finally relaxes, and I take a proper breath as Colby looks up through the slightest slit in his swollen eye, completely deflated. Hell, he looks like he wishes he were dead, and I realize I delivered exactly what I promised.

Hudson leans down, watching the motherfucker as though

committing every drop of blood to memory, and I can't help but wish I could take a photo. Addie would love this, and she deserves to see justice served, but I won't hold onto that kind of evidence. Hell, if this prick can get away with raping my sister, then I sure as fuck am going to get away with this.

"If you even *think* their names again, I will end you, and there's not a damn thing you can do to stop me," Hudson says, his voice thick with venom to the point a shiver of fear trails down my spine. And with that, he pulls back and lands an almighty blow to his side, the sound of his ribs snapping like a lullaby in the night.

Hudson turns and I don't miss the smile that lights up his face, the weight of this night finally falling off each of our shoulders. "Camping?"

Letting out a calming breath, the boys release me, and I grin right back at him, more than ready for this weekend. "Fuck yeah."

CHAPTER 22
Brielle

*H*OOOOOOOOONK!

"The fuck was that?" Ilaria asks, partially popping out of her walk-in closet, looking like a floating head, and if it weren't for half her tit also poking past the doorframe, I might have believed it.

I shrug my shoulders and hurry to her bedroom window as Chanel's phone blows up.

Ding. Ding. Ding. Diiiiiiing. Ding.

"For fuck's sake," Chanel mutters, searching through her things as I stare out the window, finding a familiar black Mustang and Silverado in the driveway. What the hell are they doing here?

Unlocking the window, I shove my head out into the night to

find Tanner sitting through his car window, his delectable ass perched against the frame as he looks up at me. "GET THAT SWEET ASS DOWN HERE," he yells up to me as Riley hangs out his passenger side window, slapping his hand on the side panel in excitement. "WE'RE GOING CAMPING."

"Tell me that twat was just talking to you because I am not going camping," Ilaria exclaims, panic tearing across her face. "There's no way in hell. Fuck that. The only stars I sleep beneath are five stars with room service."

"No," Chanel breathes, her eyes widening with horror as she glances up from her phone. "They wanna take us camping."

"No," Ilaria says. "No, there's no way. If they wanna go on some fucked-up camping trip so they can all get murdered in the woods, they can fuck each other instead. It can be a sausage train, or I can point them in the direction of some realistic sex dolls. They'll even suck their dicks for them. Win-win situation."

Chanel glances toward Ilaria, curiosity written across her face. "I wonder if you can program them to make gagging sounds?"

Ilaria shrugs and steps back into her closet. "Ask Jax, he'd probably know."

"BRIELLLLLLLLLLE," Tanner's low tone comes sailing through the window. "If I have to come up there and get you, I'm going to show everyone that video you sent me."

"Not before I show them yours."

"Hold up," Chanel says, eyes wide. "What kind of video are we talking about? Please tell me it's a cum shot video."

A grin tears across my face as I look back at her. "It sure as fuck is, and it's…" I kiss my fingers, "chef's kiss."

"Goddamn," she groans, immediately pulling her phone back out, hitting a few buttons and bringing it to her ear. She waits only a second before yelling down the phone. "Where the hell is my cum shot video, Logan Morgan? If Brielle gets one, then I want one."

She ends the call before Logan responds, and not a moment later, I hear his screechy roar flowing through the window. "Do you have any idea how fucking hard they are to get the right angle, Chanel? Of course you don't, because you don't have a motherfucking dick, you judgmental princess."

Chanel races across Ilaria's room and shoves her face out the window. "Are you sure you have a dick, Logan? Because I hear a lot of bitching coming from down there."

"That's it. I'm coming up there."

Chanel's eyes bug out of her head, and she hastily slams the window shut, narrowly avoiding crushing my fingers. She whips around, her face ghostly white. "Uhhh, well … they're coming up."

"They?" I ask, shoving her out of the way, only to find Tanner, Jax, and Riley following Logan while Hudson and Addie hang back in Tanner's Mustang. "Oh, fuck."

"Wait. What? They're coming up here?" Ilaria breathes in fear, moving in front of the closet door, her perky tits on full display as she gapes at us in horror. We hear them bust through the front door and hit the bottom of the stairs. "BUT I'M NAKED!"

She slams her closet door, the whole wall shaking just as the boys bust through her bedroom door, Logan in front. He darts straight for Chanel, and she screams, racing across the room, but she's no match for Logan. He's the fastest kid in school. He grabs her around the waist and hauls her up over his shoulder, smacking her ass in the process. "You're coming camping whether you like it or not," he says, spying her overnight bag across the room and grabbing it. "Let's go."

"I swear to God, you big ass—" the rest of her insult is lost as Logan strides out the door, leaving me to deal with the rest of them.

Riley stares me down. "Where is she?" he demands, referring to Ilaria.

I shake my head. "Getting dressed. Just give her a min—"

Riley barges right through the closet door and Ilaria screams, clutching her tits. "Well, fuck me," Riley says, striding right into her closet and shutting the door behind him. There's a strangled scuffle coming from inside before we hear Riley's amused laugh. "Come on, babe. It's nothing I haven't seen before."

My brows shoot right up as Tanner crosses to me, and I can't help but scan my gaze up and down his body, knowing all too well what's kept them away tonight. He's freshly showered, his hair still a bit damp. If he'd gotten all bloody, he's gone to big lengths to hide the evidence, though there's no mistaking his cracked knuckles and the way he seems so much lighter. "Don't make me carry you out of here," he says, those dark eyes eating me up.

"What happened to Friday night races?" I ask, taking his hand and looking down at his knuckles before bringing them to my lips and gently kissing them.

Jax scoffs from across the room, bored of our conversation, and beelines straight for the bathroom door, only it opens just before he can get to it. "What the fuck is—"

Arizona lets out a high-pitched squeal as Jax lunges and flips her over one of his shoulders. "Get your shit, we're going camping," Jax sings, smacking her ass.

"The fuck I am," Arizona says, pounding on his back. "Put me down, you big turd."

Jax just laughs and strides out of Ilaria's bedroom as though there wasn't an eighteen-year-old girl hanging off his shoulder.

I turn back to Tanner, unable to keep my stare from his bruised and broken knuckles. "Did … is it …"

"It's taken care of, babe. He won't be able to hurt you or Addie again."

My eyes bug out of my head, gaping at him in horror. "He's dead?"

"What?" Tanner laughs. "No, but he's fucked up, and he knows exactly what'll happen to him if he even thinks about coming near you two again. You're safe. I promise you."

My heart swells, and I push up onto my toes, brushing my lips over his. "Fuck camping," I murmur. "Let's hide out here until they're gone, then you can fuck me for the next few days straight."

"If I have to go camping, so do you, you fucking whore," Ilaria calls from the closet just as the door opens with Riley grinning like a maniac and holding Ilaria, who's completely tied up from head to toe, scarfs wrapped around her to keep her from making a break for it. Though, I have to give Riley credit. At least he let her put a top on first.

I snort a laugh and Ilaria glares at me as Riley carries her out the door.

"I wasn't kidding," Tanner says. "Put up even one argument, and I won't hesitate to carry your sweet ass out of here. What's it going to be?"

Then just to be a pain in his ass, I lean back against the wall and cross my arms over my chest. "If you want me to sleep in a tent, then you best pick my ass up because there's no way in hell I'm going to do it willingly."

And just like that, the big asshole scoops me into his arms and throws me over his shoulder, his hand slipping up my thigh and beneath the hem of my shorts to grab my bare ass. "Just you wait, Killer. There's nothing quite like getting fucked with rocks in your back and sand up your cooch. You'll fucking love it."

I've gotta give it to the boys, it's absolutely beautiful here.

As we sit out by the lake, the moonlight reflects in the still water and the soft sounds of crickets and owls break through the night. The campfire crackles, and I can't help but feel as though this moment right here is as perfect as it'll ever get.

Tanner's arm rests around my waist with his opposite hand drawing lazy circles on my thigh. "Would you quit moving?" I ask, trying to hold his hand still as I rest the cold beer can against his swelling knuckles. "If you don't ice it properly, you're going to end up with ugly ape hands."

"Don't knock the ape hands," Arizona says from her spot between Jax and Riley. "I could be wrong here, but it sounds like ape hands come with some thick fingers."

A laugh bubbles up my throat, which only gets louder when I notice Jax discreetly checking the size of his hands.

"Ewwwww," Addison says, pretending to block her ears as she sits closely huddled beside Hudson. "I don't want to know about my brother's thick ape hands."

"Sorry, little sister," Tanner says, a smirk across his handsome face. "But something tells me that you're going to learn a shitload of things about me this weekend that you'll never be able to burn from your mind."

"Ughh, you're going to make me sick," she groans, getting up from the old log and dusting the dirt from her jeans. "I need a drink. Anyone else?"

Arizona's hand shoots to the sky. "Ahh, you said the magic word."

Addie walks over to the flimsy tents and grabs herself a new drink before scooping up a bunch more, knowing damn well they won't go to waste.

She comes back, and just as she starts handing out drinks, Tanner's phone vibrates under my ass. He goes digging in his pocket, and as he pulls his phone out to see his mom calling, apprehension settles on his face. He hits accept and lifts the phone to his ear as everyone watches on.

"Hey Mom," he says, his gaze sailing across to Addie. "Yeah, she's right here. Why?"

He listens for a moment, his lips twisting with a wicked smirk. "No shit," he says with a fake gasp. "He got jumped? By who?" There's a pause as he waits for his mom's explanation. "Nah, we headed out right after the game, wanted to make the most out of our camping trip. They got any leads?"

Tanner hits the speakerphone button on his phone, and we all listen in with bated breath. "Not as of yet, but I'm sure the school will launch their own internal investigation. Though, after what happened during the game, don't be surprised if they look at you."

"I've got nothing to hide," he tells her, more for her benefit. "I'm sure the school surveillance system will be able to show me leaving right after the game anyway."

"Of course," she says. "Now, I wanted to wait until you two had come home to tell you but, seeing as though you'll be out for the night, I might as well tell you now."

Tanner's brows furrow as Addison creeps in closer. "What's up, Mom?"

"Oh, sweetheart, can you hear me?"

Addison rolls her eyes. "Yes, Mom. I hear you. What do you need?"

"The police have finally got what they need and arrested Colby tonight. I think it was sheer luck they found him after the game. Though Colby's currently being treated at the hospital, he's under the watchful eyes of the police. He won't be able to hurt you, baby."

Addison looks at Tanner, her eyes filling with tears of happiness.

"You're serious?" she asks. "He's been arrested?"

"Yes, darling. Charges will need to be filed, and I'm sure there will be some kind of court sessions we will have to attend, but we're one step closer to putting him away, and from what I can gather, they're also trying to make a case against that other girl … What was her name? That friend of Brielle's?"

"Erica?"

"Ahh, yes. That's the one. They're trying to draw connections and find physical proof of her involvement, but so far, they have nothing that will stick. We should hear more soon, though."

"Thanks, Mom."

"Of course, sweetheart. Now, go have a good night. This is a big win. Celebrate with your friends and try to have a good time, okay? I love you, and I can't wait to give you a big hug when you get back."

Addison smiles, a real fondness in her eyes. "Love you too, Mom."

"Okay, could you hand me back to your brother?"

Tanner grins as Addison rolls her eyes. "Yeah Mom, he's still here listening."

"Oh, right, umm … Tanner?" she questions as though she doesn't believe it.

Tanner grumbles and shifts beneath me before tightening his arm around my waist. "Yes, Mom?"

"You look after my baby now," she says, her tone still soft yet somehow filled with the type of authority that makes you terrified to step out of line. "I don't want to find out that you spent the night teasing her. Be a good boy. Oh, and Tanner?"

"Yeah?"

"I saw your bag by the door and slipped some condoms in there. I don't want you being unsafe, okay?"

Tanner closes his eyes as Addison and everyone else snorts with laughter, humiliation washing through him. "Fucking hell," Tanner mutters under his breath, taking the call off speakerphone and pressing it back to his ear. "Thanks, Mom." There's a short pause before he lets out a soft sigh. "Love you, too."

Tanner ends the call and barely pulls the phone away before the whole circle cracks into uncontrollable fits of laughter. He takes the cold can of beer out of my hand and cracks the top. "I need a drink."

An hour later, Arizona is dancing on the shore of the lake, looking up at the stars as everybody talks shit, having a great time. "I swear," Chanel laughs. "It's true. I've never been so humiliated. My period just came. No warning. Nothing. Just started and came gushing out of me like someone had opened the floodgates. It was dribbling down my leg, and when I tried to dismount from the top of the pyramid … it was a bloodbath. The other cheerleaders tried to be supportive, but I could see the horror in their eyes. I swear, they've never looked at me the same."

Jax howls with laughter, falling off his chair and into the sandy banks of the lake, holding his stomach as he tries to calm himself. "Alright then, Jaxon Morgan. What's your humiliating story?"

He rights himself and climbs back onto his chair, getting comfortable around the fire. "I'm Jax Morgan," he says, way too cocky. "I don't have hidden humiliations. I'm an open book. Every fucked-up thing I've ever done has been shouted from the top of the world."

"Nope, I don't buy that," Arizona says, glancing back at Jax. "There has to be one thing."

Jax shrugs his shoulders. "There isn't. You know me, Ari. I don't hold back."

"Alright then, how about this," she says. "We go around the circle and play truth or … truth or get thrown in the lake. There is no dare. You get asked a question, and you either answer it, or get thrown right in. No avoiding the hard topics."

"You're on," Jax says. "But if I have to play, everyone has to play."

Everyone else groans, knowing damn well just how dangerous this game could get, but when no one backs down, Arizona grins. "Deal, but you're up first, pretty boy."

"Hit me with it."

Arizona bites her bottom lip, trying to think of something she wants to ask, when Riley shouts out his question. "When the fuck are you going to realize that Ari is in love with you and actually date her for real instead of fucking her like a toy?"

"Fucking hell," Tanner mutters, glaring at Riley who looks all kinds of fucked up. "Did you really have to do that? Now it's gonna be weird."

Riley looks across at Tanner and the blank expression in his eyes makes me wonder if he's been smoking something. "Do what?" he murmurs before raising his hand, a joint resting between his fingers, confirming my suspicions.

Arizona's eyes bug out of her head, her midnight lake dancing coming to an immediate stop as she gapes back at Jax, looking all too uncomfortable, even more so when Jax starts stumbling over his words. "I, ummm, ahh …" he stands, cautiously looking at Arizona. "You're in love with me?"

"It's not my turn, Mr. *I'm an open book, ask me anything.*"

"Uhhhmmmmmmmm."

"THROW HIM IN THE LAKE," Riley shouts.

Jax's eyes bug out of his head as Riley barrels toward him, flying straight past Arizona and submerging both of them in the serene water, wicked laughter tearing out of Riley. He stands and faces the rest of us, giving an extravagant curtsey, and we applaud his efforts, all while Jax just sits in the lake, water rushing off him as he stares up at Arizona, never looking so confused in his life.

"Alright," Arizona says. "Someone else go before this shit ruins my night."

"Okay, I got one," Tanner says, an odd amusement in his tone that makes my blood run cold. Everyone glances his way, but I keep my stare locked on the fire, feeling his heated gaze shifting to my face. What the hell could he possibly have to ask? "Brielle Ashford, truth or get thrown in the lake," he starts, reminding me of the rules of the game. "I love every inch of your body, and when I say every inch, I mean every fucking inch—"

"Stop being gross. Just ask the question," Addison calls out, shuffling even closer to Hudson.

Tanner smirks and his fingers gently brush over my skin. "I've been holding my tongue for a long time, not wanting to ask in case it's something awful or just outright embarrassing, but you've got one very particular scar—"

I feel the blood drain from my face. "Oh, no."

"On that sweet little meat curtain of yours."

"Meat curtain?" I laugh.

"Meat curtain, hot box, the squeeze machine. Whatever you wanna call it, babe, but the question still stands, what the fuck happened? Every time I go down on you, I feel it on my tongue, and it just gets me thinking. Don't get me wrong, it adds to the excitement and the mystery that is Brielle Ashford, but not knowing what happened to those pretty little lips of yours is killing me."

My cheeks flame as Addison shakes her head and stands. "Nope. Tell me I didn't just hear about your experience going down on your girlfriend?"

Tanner scoffs and a smirk stretches across his face. "If you're not careful, I'll be forced to tell you about the time I fucked her on my bike."

"Well?" Ilaria says, reaching for another drink and cracking the top before leaning back and putting her feet up on Jax's vacated seat. "Let's hear it. What happened to the lady garden?"

I close my eyes and take a huge swig of my drink, feeling my cheeks flaming even hotter. "Hot wax," I admit, feeling the embarrassment washing through me. "I tried it myself, slathered that shit everywhere, and when I tried to tear it off, half my lip came with it."

"NOOOOOOOOOO," Chanel gasps, her hands dropping between her legs as though she can feel my pain. "What happened?"

"My brother heard me scream and barged in to find me spread eagle on the ground in pools of my own blood," I admit, breaking my one solemn vow to never repeat this story. "He took me to the ER, and they had to heat up the wax with a hair dryer to get rid of it, then I ended up with something like thirteen stitches."

"No fucking way," Ilaria says, staring at me wide eyed. "Can I see?"

"You wanna see?" I laugh, certain she's fucking with me.

"Me too," Arizona calls out as Jax's head perks up. "Wait, we get to see Brielle's cooter?"

"No one is seeing my cooter," I announce, though to be completely honest, if the girls wanted to see, I'm down with showing off my scar. But only if the guys aren't around.

Addison clears her throat, looking as though she's about to shit herself. "I have a confession," she says, spitting the words out as though it's some kind of race. All eyes turn toward her, brows arched with curiosity, waiting for her to go on. "I'll spill my confession if we get to see the cooter."

"What?" I rush out.

Addison shrugs her shoulders. "I'm curious. I wanna see what a torn-off lip looks like."

"It was only half torn off, but okay. If it's a good confession, I'll show my cooter, but only to the girls."

"What?" Tanner spits as Jax's face falls.

"Let's hear it," I tell her.

Addison lets out a shaky breath before nervously glancing at Hudson who looks apprehensive, though clearly doesn't know what the hell this is about. Not knowing where to look, Addison stares directly toward the campfire, her fingers fidgeting nervously. "Umm … so, the day I woke from my coma, there was about half an hour beforehand where I was semi-conscious and could hear what was going on around me." Addison pauses as Hudson's whole body stiffens, his stare awkwardly locking onto the fire as well.

She turns toward him and catches his eyes, swallowing hard before going on. "I … heard everything you said."

Hudson just stares at her, not knowing what to say and looking completely dumbfounded, just as the rest of us … though not Tanner, he seems to know exactly what's going on.

"What … what did he say?" Ilaria rushes out, her eyes wide, completely captivated by Addison's confession.

Addison bites her tongue, and I realize that whatever this is about has more to do with letting Hudson know rather than outing whatever secret he's been hiding

"Goddamn it," Ilaria says, focusing her attention on Hudson. "Yo, Hudson. Truth or get thrown in the lake. What did you tell her?"

Hudson doesn't take his eyes off Addison, swallowing hard as Tanner's hand tenses on my thigh. Silence surrounds us, even the crickets seem to shut up as we hang on Hudson's every word. "I told her that I've been in love with her for the past two years."

The girls gasp as the guys' jaws drop, having absolutely no idea he felt that way. I can't tear my eyes off the two of them, watching as a silent tear slides down her face and drops to her chest before hastily wiping it away. "I'm sorry," she whispers. "I'm just not …"

Hudson nods, his hand slipping into hers and holding it tight. "I know that," he says. "I'm not looking to be your whole world right now, I know that's not what you need. But if and when you're ready, I'll be here. Until then, you've got someone who'll do everything in his power to make sure you're happy and protected. That's all I want for you, Addie."

Another tear falls, and she leans forward, pressing a feather-soft kiss to his cheek before standing and walking away. Tanner goes to stand, but I press my hand to his arm. "Don't," I tell him before catching Hudson's concerned stare. "She just needs a minute. Give her five and then go talk to her. Trust me."

And just like that, Hudson nods, both of their worlds colliding.

CHAPTER 23

TANNER

The soft glow of the moonlight shines down on us, and I can't help but notice how it illuminates Brielle's messy hair, making it look like a halo around her head. She's so fucking gorgeous it kills me.

She sits down at the lake, her toes barely brushing the water as her and Ilaria talk about who the fuck knows what. Arizona and Jax disappeared an hour ago after Jax failed to keep his mouth shut about the whole *Ari is in love with you* bomb that Riley accidentally dropped. Pretty sure that means Jax is going to try to actually talk to her, which is bound to be entertaining. I don't think that idiot has ever actually talked to a woman before, you know, when his end game wasn't to get in her pants. This would be a real and raw conversation, something that could have Arizona running back here with a broken heart.

I was talking to Riley for a while, but he disappeared to pee about twenty minutes ago, and I haven't seen him since. The fucker probably fell asleep. We'll have to send out a search party at some point. However, knowing Riley, he probably found a hole in a tree he can stick his dick into and is currently being ravaged by a swarm of angry bees.

Logan and Chanel are about two minutes away from fucking by the fire, and with Hudson ducking away to talk to Addie, I feel the rest of my night should be focused solely on my girl. Though, with Hudson talking to Addie in her tent, I can't seem to let the frustration go. They've been in there for well over an hour, and at first, I could hear the soft discussion about what she wanted, but at some point, it slowly morphed into conversation about what Colby did to her, and while she's spoken to me about it over the past two weeks, she didn't quite give the same kind of details as she's sharing with him. I guess Hudson was right.

Addie has been holding on to all of this, and I wasn't the right person for her to confide in, despite how badly I wished she could. I'm her big brother, and though that will never change, sometimes the people we need in our life aren't always the ones bound by blood.

I can hear her soft cries, and they tear at my chest, but she needs this more than anything in the world. Sometimes you have to tear yourself apart, rebuild with what's left, and start over. I'm grateful she has Hudson to help her. Though, if the fucker thinks he's going to share her tent, he can think again. Over my dead fucking body. He can sleep outside her door for all I care, though I'm not going to suggest it because knowing him, he'll do just that.

Ilaria and Brielle trudge back toward me, and Ilaria looks as though she's going to fall asleep on her feet. "I'm gonna crash," she mutters through a yawn. "If Riley shows up, tell him to sleep in the back of the Silverado. I'm not sharing with him."

"You got it," I tell her, watching as she walks away.

Bri cuts past the fire to me and goes to drop down on my lap when I shake my head and stand, taking her hand in mine. "Wanna go for a walk down by the lake, see if it leads anywhere?"

She beams up at me, her bright blue eyes catching in the moonlight as she nods. "Oh my, Tanner Morgan, that almost sounds like a date."

I scoff and fold her in next to my body, hooking my arm over her shoulder. "Cheapest date I've ever had."

"And if you're lucky, you might even get a kiss at the end of the night."

"Only a kiss?" I tease as I lead her back to the water, walking away from the fire and our friends. "And here I was thinking I could turn your mouth into an overcrowded daycare center."

She laughs as she threads her fingers through mine. "Tell me you did not just say that?"

"Don't act like you don't like my crude mouth," I tease. "You seem to like it when I'm doing all sorts of crude things to you."

"Damn right, I do," Brielle says, not even the slightest bit embarrassed about it. We keep walking when she comes to a stop, catching her breath as she looks down the lake. She puts a hand to my chest, bringing me to a stop as she squints into the darkness. "Is that a bear?" she questions, her tone so quiet I can barely hear it.

"No," I say, my hold tightening on her in case I need to throw her over my shoulder and run. Hesitating, I stare out into the darkness, trying to make out the awkward shape by the water's edge. "It can't be. We don't get bears out here."

She doesn't move an inch, positive that what she's seeing is an animal, but I'm not so sure. I hear the soft lapping of the water on the shore, and the longer I stare at the shape, the clearer it becomes.

No fucking way.

"Oh, that's definitely not a bear," I tell her, pulling her along. "Come on. You've got to see this."

We keep making our way down the water's edge, and I don't dare stop until she figures out what it is and sucks in a sharp breath. "Holy fuck," she gasps, her eyes wide as she takes in Arizona on her knees, her ass high in the air and getting railed by Jax while Riley's down in the damn sand with his dick halfway down her throat.

Arizona looks our way at Brielle's shocked gasp and freezes, Riley's dick falling out of her mouth with a wet pop. Her eyes go wide as Riley trails his hand through Arizona's hair, trying to entice her to keep going. She reaches back and taps Jax on the thigh, silently asking him to stop as she gapes at her best friend. "I, ummm …" Arizona cringes before trying to give Bri an encouraging smile. "Would you believe me if I said it's not how it looks?"

Riley laughs. "It's really not," he says. "These two were fucking and I just wandered past and thought I'd join. It's not like we planned it or anything."

"Shut up," Arizona says, swatting Riley's chest. "You're not helping."

"Oh, and you are?" he throws back at her, casually gripping his dick.

Bri sputters and as if finally registering what she's seeing, she spins around, burying her head into my chest as though she can't believe what's right in front of her face. "Holy fuck, Arizona," she says, her words muffled by my shirt.

Arizona stretches up on her knees and tries to cover her bits as best she can while the guys really don't give a shit, all too proud of their manhood. Though, it's not like I haven't seen it before. We've participated in more than our fair share of group activities. "To be fair," Arizona says. "I got to see your cooter before, so I suppose now you got to see mine."

"Oh my God," Bri says into my shirt, shaking her head as I laugh.

"Hey, uhh, listen," Riley says. "If you guys aren't going to hang around and make this a party, then do you mind if we get back to business? I'm kinda losing steam down here."

Jax scoffs and smirks at Riley. "Losing your touch, man?"

"Fuck off."

"Okaaaay," Bri says, gripping onto my hand and yanking me back in the direction we came. "I'm going to go and bleach my eyes now," she says. "And Arizona? Promise me that we will never discuss this again."

"Promise," she calls after us.

Brielle drags me away until her legs start to get sore, and she pulls me down into the damp sand. "Can you believe those three?" she says with a laugh, completely baffled by what she saw, though to be honest, I'm not entirely surprised. I mean, I suppose I am a little considering the weirdness between Jax and Ari, but it's not left field for them, and certainly isn't the first time I've walked in to see that exact same trio, only a different background. "I thought Jax and Arizona were out here having some deep and meaningful talk about their feelings and if there was even a possibility for a future between them, but they're out here fucking like bunnies … and Riley. RILEY! Holy shit. My head is spinning."

I laugh and pull her onto my lap until she straddles me, and she immediately dives in for a kiss, her lips moving so effortlessly over mine. She pulls back with a thoughtful expression. "What's up?" I ask, cupping the side of her face, unable to believe just how lucky I am to have her in my life.

"Have you ever done that … a threesome, I mean?"

My brows arch and I hold her stare. "Do you really want to know the answer to that?"

Bri cringes before a cheeky as fuck grin tears across her face. "Yeah, I think I do. I want all the juicy details."

"This isn't some kind of trap is it? It's not going to come back and bite me if I tell you?"

"Ha," Bri scoffs. "I'm not like that."

"Yeah," I laugh. "You sure as fuck are."

She pokes her tongue out at me. "Then why bother asking?"

"Same could be said to you if you're going to get sore about it later."

"Tough shit. I'm curious, and I know I shouldn't admit this," she says, her cheeks reddening as she lowers her stare in embarrassment, "but after seeing that, I'm kinda turned on and wanna know about all the filthy things you've done."

"Really now?" I question, tipping her straight back onto the ground and coming down over her. "Is that what you want? Someone else to join us?"

She bites the inside of her cheek as her legs wrap around me, and I can't help but grind against her. Bri truly considers the question before shaking her head. "I'm not entirely closed off to the idea, but I don't like the thought of seeing someone else's hands all over you."

"Good, because the idea of another man's cock in your mouth is driving me insane."

"Are you sure?" she asks, a timid tone to her soft voice. "Because I know you were probably into all of that, and I don't want to wake up a few years down the track to find out you aren't satisfied with just me. Like, if that's something you need, I'm happy to think about it more, I just … I'm not some secret BDSM dominatrix who can handle four dicks flying at my face."

"I have every faith that you could handle it. You're a fucking spitfire and that fucking mouth of yours, goddamn. You know what the fuck you're doing. That tight little cunt can go all night and still be ready for more, so don't think for one second that you can't handle it. You can," I tell her before pressing my fingers to her temple. "This is what tells you that you can't handle it, and I'm telling you that it's wrong. I know your body better than you ever could, and believe me, if you wanna take a job as a BDSM dominatrix, you'll fucking kill it. I'll be the first client though. Actually, on second thought, how do you feel about role play?"

Bri blushes and it's fucking gorgeous. "I am so down for role play," she says. "But you didn't answer the question."

"Wait, which question?"

"A few years down the track, will I still be enough for you?"

I slip my hand between us and cup her pussy, feeling her heat through her shorts. "What? This old thing?" I tease, smirking down at her as she laughs and swats me away. "Babe, you're my fucking world. Yes, I might have indulged in threesomes every now and then, but they're overrated and not always as fun as it sounds. But if you want to explore and change things up, just say the word. There's plenty of things we can do that don't involve inviting someone else into our bed."

Bri beams up at me, her eyes lighting like Christmas morning as she loops her arms around my neck, pulling me in closer. "In that case," she says, the corner of her lip pulling into a sly, needy grin. "You know I've never had sex out in the open like this."

I stare down at her, my brows furrowed. "Babe, we fucked on my bike in the woods."

"And while that truly is one of my cherished memories, we were hidden by the woods. The chances of someone finding us were next to nothing, but here by the lake with a threesome going on down in the next parking bay and Chanel and Logan not sure if they want to fight or fuck in the other direction, it's a risk, and it's kinda exciting."

"Holy fuck," I murmur. "I went and got myself a little minx with a kink."

Her mouth drops open and she goes to berate me, but I've had enough of the back and forth. I want to give this girl what she's craving, and hell, if we get caught in the process, then fuck it. I hope she finishes hard, fast, and loud.

I kiss her deeply and her body responds, arching up off the sand and pressing into me. The softest moan slips from between her lips, and I grin against them, loving how she comes alive for me. Her arms tighten around my neck, holding me closer as her leg hitches high over my hip. I grind down against her and she pulls back from our kiss, sucking in a throaty groan. "Holy shit, Tanner." Her eyes darken with hunger, making my cock twitch with a carnal need.

Unable to stand a single second without my lips on hers, I drop them to her throat, my tongue working over her soft skin. She squirms beneath me as I slip my hand down her toned body and into the front of her shorts.

She's soaking wet, and the moment my fingers push between those pretty lips, her hips buck beneath me. "Patience, Killer," I warn, meeting her hooded stare and almost buckling under her intense desire. "You'll get exactly what you need."

I start working my way down her body, my fingers slipping under the cotton fabric of her tank and pushing it up over her head. I drop it into the sand and before my hands are even back on her body, her nipples are pebbled, needing all the attention in the world.

Away from the fire, it's not so warm, and Brielle clings to me, but it won't be long until that sexy little body heats up like a fucking inferno. At least, that's how she'll feel inside.

My lips roam over her chest, sucking a perfect tit into my mouth and flicking my tongue over her pebbled nipple. Brielle groans and pushes up against me, and I do it again, loving how her body reacts to my touch.

Moving down her body, I trail soft kisses over her stomach until I reach the waistband of her shorts. I glance up, a devilish smirk stretching across my face as I find her braced on her elbows, more than ready to watch the show. I suppose the idea of getting caught isn't the only kink she's got. This little she-devil likes to watch.

Her eyes flame, daring me to hurry up, and I don't wait a moment longer, digging my fingers into the waistband of her shorts and pushing them down her smooth legs, making sure to take her black lace panties right along with it.

A low groan rumbles through my chest. There's nothing better than seeing my girl laid out naked before me, starving for my touch and knowing she's all mine.

Taking her thighs, I push them over my shoulders, opening her wide. She's fucking gorgeous. My dick twitches painfully in my jeans, but I'll bear it just to be able to see her like this. My head dips low, and I close my mouth over her tight cunt, gently sucking her clit before swiping my tongue through her center.

Bri bucks under me, her head tipping back as the pleasure rocks through her. "Holy shit, Tanner," she breathes. "Again."

My fucking pleasure.

I give her everything she needs, flicking her clit and gently sucking as her body bucks and squirms beneath me. She pants loudly and every last noise that comes tearing out of her is like a trophy with my name on it.

I work her hard and as she gets closer to the edge, I slowly push two fingers deep inside her. Bri gasps, tipping her head back as her legs tighten around my shoulders. "Oh fuuuuck," she says, the word drawn out on a breathy groan. "Tanner!"

My tongue rolls over her clit, back and forth, again and again, sucking, nipping, teasing as my fingers curl inside her, massaging her walls and making her scream. I push my fingers deeper, and she cries out again, heavily panting until she can't hold on to it a second longer.

Brielle comes hard, her pussy spasming around my fingers, convulsing as I keep working her body. She arches her back, her fingers digging into the sand and the most satisfying type of pleasure rocks through my chest. I could eat this sweet pussy every minute of every hour for the rest of my life and still never get enough. Watching her come undone like this … fuck.

Brielle Ashford is my kryptonite.

She comes down from her high, her gaze locked on the show, and I lift my head, giving her a chance to breathe. "Holy shit," she murmurs, remaining down in the sand as I rise to my feet, my stare locked on her bright blue eyes. "That was—"

I shake my head, a smirk pulling at my lips as I reach over my back and shrug out of my shirt. I toss it to the ground beside her and she grips onto the fabric, bunching it in her tight fist. "Uh uh," I say, unbuckling my belt and allowing my jeans to fall from my hips, my cock springing free. Bri's eyes drop, watching with hunger as I take my straining cock in my hand and squeeze before slowly stroking up and down. "I'm not nearly done with you yet."

Bri's tongue swipes across her bottom lip and she pushes up to her feet, her eyes sparkling with a challenge. She steps into me, her fingers brushing across my chest as her chin tilts up. "Then what are you waiting for?" she asks, slowly turning, my cock pressed up against her firm ass. She glances back over her shoulder, her lips pulling into a wicked smirk. "Come and get me."

And with that, she takes off like a lightning bolt right into the freezing lake, and without missing a beat, I fly right in after her.

CHAPTER 24
Brielle

A piercing scream tears through the silence, and my head rips up off Tanner's chest in our cramped, army green tent. Tanner sits up, his eyes wide as his sharp stare trails over me. "You good?" he rushes out in a panic.

Hastily nodding my head, we scramble out of our tent, positive we're about to find someone torn to shreds by a bear … at least I am. Tanner is certain there are no bears out here, only three-headed people in ridiculous positions.

The mid-morning sun beams down over the lake, and I squint against its reflection on the water, but the second I see Riley darting across our campground, naked as the day he was born while screaming in horror, the brightness of the lake doesn't seem quite so important.

"The fuck is going on?" Tanner roars, trying to be heard over Riley's terrified screaming as we rush toward him, everyone else bailing out of their tents for the same damn reason. "What happened? Are you hurt?"

Riley stops running, gaping at Tanner wide-eyed as though only just realizing he has an audience. "My dick," he says, grabbing hold of his junk as Jax and Logan move in beside us. "It's falling off. Look at it, man. It's all … it's all … wrong looking."

All eyes drop to Riley's dick, and I gape at it in horror. I can't say I've ever seen Riley's junk before, but this isn't right. The skin is darkening and there's something definitely off, but I just … can't figure it out. My brows furrow and I lean in, trying to get a better look as the idiot wails in horror.

"I swear, something must have come and bit it during the night. Please, God, tell me I'm not losing my cock. How the fuck am I supposed to screw my way through Europe without a dick?"

Jax moves in as the girls come out around us, watching over the guys' shoulders. Jax bats Riley's hand away to get a better look. "Did you fuck something you shouldn't have?"

Riley shakes his head and goes to respond when Arizona screams. "What the fuck is wrong with your dick?" she gapes, her eyes bugging out of her head in a panic. "I had that shit in my mouth." She goes green and rushes to the edge of the bushes before doubling over and brutally throwing up as Ilaria and Chanel meet each other's confused gazes.

"Wait," Ilaria says, cautiously glancing toward Jax. "Why was Ari getting with Riley?"

"Awww, fuck, fuck, fuck, fuck," Riley starts to chant, not giving two shits about the bomb that accidentally just got dropped.

Tanner shakes his head and pulls back. "I don't know what to tell you, man, but I don't think it's falling off, and it doesn't look like it was bitten."

"How can you be so sure? Look at it! Are you not seeing what I'm seeing? It's fucking brown, man. I haven't seen your cock for a hot minute, but I'm pretty fucking sure it doesn't change colors like this. This isn't fucking normal."

"It looked fine when you were with Arizona and Jax last night," I supply, probably not helpfully though. "What did you do after that?"

"Nothing," he says.

I go to poke at it when Tanner captures my hand and discreetly pulls me away. "Is it hurting or just … brown?"

Chanel leans in even closer, her gaze narrowing as though deep in thought. "I wouldn't exactly call it brown," she muses. "More like a golden, shimmery bronze."

"Are you fucking with me?" Riley spits. "How is its bronze complexion important right now? The thing is falling off!"

Chanel gives him a hard stare and rolls her eyes. "Did you give that thing a little Riley loving in Ilaria's tent last night?"

"Of course, I did," he says, just as Ilaria's eyes bug out of her head, realizing what Riley had been doing in the tent beside her. "Arizona left me hanging. I had no choice, but how the fuck is this supposed to help? It's not like I jerked it so fucking hard it was going to fall off."

"Oh sure, bite my head off, why don't you?" Chanel throws back at him, tired of his bullshit. "Though I'm probably the only person around this fucked-up little lake that knows why your cock looks like it took a trip to Hawaii."

"Huh?" Riley says, his hand cupping around his junk, having enough of the lingering stares.

"That shimmery bronze glow is the exact same shade as Ilaria's suntan lotion," she deadpans. "You jerked off with Ilaria's lotion, didn't you?"

Riley's face twists with a guilty smirk as Ilaria gapes in horror. "Oh, fuck no," she cries. "Tell me you didn't use my suntan lotion? That shit was brand new. Do you have any idea how hard it is to get my hands on that brand? It sells out in like … two seconds. I was on a waiting list and now my summer suntan is smeared all over your dick? Fuck, Riley. Why couldn't you just go in dry?"

"Are you shitting me?" Riley hollers, throwing his hands up in the air. "First up, no one goes in dry, and second, this is the best news I've ever heard. My dick's not falling off." He barges into Ilaria, grabbing her around the waist and hoisting her up into the air before manically spinning around, his relief knowing no bounds.

"Oh fuck," Ilaria panics, her hand clamping over her mouth as she turns green. "I'm gonna be sick."

Riley being Riley assumes he can push the boundaries just that little bit further despite Ilaria's warning, and not a moment later, she blows chunks right down his back.

Riley squeals as the wet sloshing sound of Ilaria's vomit drops heavily to the ground, and I have to turn away, my stomach clenching at the sight.

"Ahhh, fuck no," Hudson says, watching the performance from the entrance of the tent he shared with Addison, despite Tanner's objections. Though if Addison were going to be safe with anyone out here, it would have been Hudson. "It's too fucking early for this shit. I'm out."

Hudson bails and pushes back into his tent as Addison darts into the bushes past the lake, screaming something about nearly wetting her pants. Tanner smirks and shakes his head as I start making my way back to our tent. There's a fresh morning chill in the air that has shivers sailing over my skin, and I'd kill for one of Tanner's hoodies right now. Bonus points if it smells like him too.

By the time his favorite hoodie is skirting around my thighs, and I'm inhaling Tanner's natural scent left on the material, my phone is buzzing from somewhere beneath the mess of blankets and pillows.

Tossing things over my shoulder, I scramble around until I find my phone hidden beneath the evidence of last night's activities, and I pick it up before immediately wishing I hadn't.

A text from my mother flashes on the screen and this chilled out, incredible mood I've been feeling since the moment we arrived at the lake dissipates. My ass drops onto the half deflated air mattress, and I let out a heavy sigh before opening the text and scanning over what I can only assume have been carefully put together sentences.

Mom - Brielle, despite our differences, you must know that you and your brother are the loves of my life, and it would make me the happiest woman on earth if you would stand by my side as my maid of honor while Orlando and I profess our love for one another in front of the world. I know we officially tied the knot in Paris, however

I believe a grand white wedding would simply be spectacular. What do you say? Jensen has so gracefully accepted Orlando's offer to be his best man, and I can only hope that Damien will be right there with us, assuming he can make it, of course. But having you as my maid of honor? Sweetheart, that would be a dream come true.

My mouth drops as I take a look at the attached e-vite, asking me to RSVP to the wedding of the year, all the fancy little details already sorted out as though she's been planning this for weeks.

A solid ache settles into my chest, and as Tanner watches me through the open tent door, his brows furrowed and eyes full of concern, I can't help but shake my head. "You've got to be fucking kidding me."

A bitterness rests deep in my chest the whole way back to Bradford and doesn't go away, even when Tanner helps me out of his Mustang and offers to walk me to the door.

"You sure?" he murmurs, his hands gripping my waist as his thumbs trail back and forth over my skin. "I can come in with you, or you can just come chill at my place. I don't wanna find you up on your roof in thirty minutes because the bitch put hands on you again."

Letting out a heavy sigh, I shake my head and tip my chin up to brush my lips over his. "No, it's okay," I tell him. "I have to talk to her at some point. I might as well get it over and done with, and trust me, I'm ready this time. She won't get the chance to touch me again."

Tanner presses his lips into a hard line, not liking this one bit. "I feel like I'm sending a lamb to the slaughter."

A grin pulls at my lips. "Oh, thanks for the vote of confidence."

Tanner rolls his eyes and releases me before stepping back to the Mustang and grabbing my overnight bag. "You know what I mean," he tells me, handing me my things.

Stepping into him again, I close my eyes as his lips press down on mine, ignoring the teasing gags coming from Addison as she makes her way inside her home. "Just as you know that I'm going to be perfectly fine," I tell him when we come up for air.

Tanner grumbles something before finally giving in. "Fine," he murmurs. "But the second you've done whatever it is you need to do, I want you in my bed so I can spread those pretty thighs and eat that sweet pussy until you come on my tongue."

A thrill shoots through me and a smile tugs at the corner. "My, oh my," I tease in my worst Tennessee accent, my hand falling to my chest in horror as I step back toward the house of doom. "And here I thought you were a gentleman."

"You're not wrong, Killer," he says, winking as he moves across his front lawn, looking back over his shoulder. "I'll be sure to feed you before I fuck you."

Wet. Fucking wet.

Retreating back into the house of doom before I throw myself across the lawn and jump my boyfriend in the front yard, I slip through the front door just as Jensen is coming out. He takes one look at me and rolls his eyes. "Run while you still have the chance."

My brows furrow, but before I can ask what the hell he's talking about, my mother steps out of the formal dining room in a flawless white dress that could only be described as bridal. "Ahh, what on earth have you been doing?" she questions, glancing at her wrist to double check the time. "We've been calling you to come down for hours."

"Wow, didn't even realize I wasn't home," I mutter under my breath, distantly noticing the way Jensen slips out the front door while the attention is on me. "Classy."

Mom ushers me into the formal dining room and my eyes immediately bug out of my head, finding the room overwhelmed with wedding stuff. Over-the-top floral arrangements line the back half of the room, while a spread of cakes is scattered on the table. There are table decorations, lace, organza, and silk everything, candles, gowns, and a flustered woman who looks as though she's being worked to the bone. I can only assume she's some kind of wedding event planner, but right now, I bet she wished she never accepted this job.

"What the hell is all of this?" I gape, intimidated by it all.

"Is that a poor idea of a joke?" my mother asks. "I saw that you opened your e-vite yet failed to RSVP. You are well aware that this wedding is next weekend, and I could have used your input hours ago."

"Trust me, Mother," I say, the ugliness in my tone shining through. "You don't want my input on any of this."

"What on earth is that supposed to mean?"

"Open your eyes, Mom. This is embarrassing. You've known this guy for less than two seconds. You moved us into his home, changed my school, changed my whole freaking life. You started acting like some kind of country club wife, threw away the jobs you worked your ass off for, and then let him whisk you away to Paris and married him. And now this?" I question, waving my hand around at the mess surrounding the formal dining room. "What is this even about? Do you actually love this guy or is this some kind of fantasy you're trying to live out, trying to prove to the bitches from your past that you can have it all? Shit, Mom, Damien hasn't even met the guy, and you can't be so naive not to see how twisted his morals are when it comes to the law. You're throwing yourself at him, and it's embarrassing. He says jump and you piss yourself in excitement."

Mom steps into me, her jaw clenched as she raises her chin, trying to appear taller. "You sound just like your father," she spits. "You better watch your mouth, or I'll have no choice but to—"

"To what, Mom? Hit me again?" Her eyes slightly widen, showing the tiniest hint of regret, but it's gone in a flash. I scoff, not giving her a chance to go on. "When are you going to realize what you're doing to our family? You used to be the first person I'd want to see after school, but since moving here, you're nothing but a stranger to me, and I don't want anything to do with you. I want my mom back."

Tears well in my eyes as my mother stares back at me. A painful moment of silence passes between us, and just when I think she's about to embrace me and tell me that everything is going to be alright, she turns her chin up. "The wedding is at 3 p.m. sharp next Saturday, and I expect you at the church standing at my side. You will wear the gown I pick out for you, and you will stand beside me as my maid of honor. You will smile at all the right times and boast about how much you love our new family and home. When people ask, you will tell them that Orlando has gone out of his way to make you feel welcomed and that you are so grateful for the life you've been blessed with. Is that clear?"

Clenching my jaw, I glare up at this perfect stranger, feeling my heart breaking in my chest. "Crystal."

"Good," she says. "I have included a plus one for you, not that you are deserving of it. Am I to assume you will be bringing that wretched boy from next door?"

Venom spews from my glare as my hands ball into fists at my side. "Tanner is the best person I have ever known, so if he's wretched, then that sure as hell says a lot about you," I spit, and with that, I storm right out of the formal dining room, determined to never see her again.

If only she weren't my mother …

Unable to handle the raging emotions running rampant through my body, I barge out through the front door and get only a few steps down the front path when a familiar yellow Beetle pulls to a stop on the front curb. The rage intensifies, and I hate that my tears begin to fall free. "You've got to be fucking kidding me," I growl, storming toward the car.

Erica pushes out the driver's side, her hands out as if terrified I'm about to beat her ass to a pulp. "Please, just—"

"Are you fucking kidding me?" I roar. "How dare you show up here!"

"Please, Bri," she begs, moving around until she's standing right in front of me. "Please, I know I fucked up, but I miss you. We've been friends for thirteen years. Surely you're not going to throw that all away. We can get past this. I was messed up and taking shit I had no business messing with, and I was a shitty friend, but I can't lose you."

A throaty laugh tears from deep within me. "You think I'm the one throwing this away?" I question. "You're the one who climbed into bed with my boyfriend. You're the one who stood by to allow an innocent girl to get hurt. You're the one who put the blame on me. You're the one who threw it all away, Erica. You didn't need my help."

"It's not like that," she says, moving closer, tears in her eyes. "I didn't know she was going to get hurt. We were just screwing around with pills and when she turned up, Colby was telling me that she was the sister of some dick who'd been fucking with him, and I thought it'd be funny to mess with her. I didn't know that he was going to go that far. I swear, Bri. You have to believe me. If I knew he was going to rape her, I never would have had anything to do with it. I'm not the monster you think I am," she urges, pushing into me and grabbing my hands as though they're her only lifeline. "Please, Brielle. We've been friends for too long. I need your help. I'm buried so deep, and I don't know how to save myself."

Tearing myself out of her grip, I stare at her with disgust. "You're messing with me, right?" I breathe, unable to believe what I'm hearing. "Am I just some stupid bitch you can walk all over? You gave me up to the cops. I was arrested and slammed down against my desk in the middle of class after Colby broke my fucking ribs. Do you have any idea what that's like or how fucking terrified I was? They were going to charge me with rape, Erica. Rape! I would have been locked up for years all because of you, and now you have the fucking audacity to show up here, thinking that I'm just going to shrug it off. Hear yourself, Erica.

A real friend would never have done the things you've done to me, and a decent human being would never have suggested messing with an innocent girl."

Hands fall to my waist, and I take a breath, watching the way Erica's gaze lifts to Tanner's behind me, her eyes filled with terror. She shakes her head, her tears falling freely down her face before lowering her stare back to mine. "Please, Bri," she murmurs, sobs tearing at her chest as she falls to her knees in the grass. "Please forgive me. Colby made me do it. He made me give them your name. He said if I didn't, he'd come for me next. Please, I had no choice, but I thought our friendship could withstand anything. I thought we were stronger than this."

I scoff, shaking my head and feeling every little piece of my heart breaking within me. I crouch down, meeting her shattered stare, and swallow over the lump in my throat. "I will never forgive you for this," I tell her. "You're on your own, and I hope to God that you're charged for every bit of the involvement you had, including the shit you did to me. There's a girl in the house right behind me who's struggling to hold on, struggling to deal with the memories and trauma both you and Colby have caused her, a family you've torn to pieces and destroyed. You don't deserve to walk free, Erica, and you sure as fuck don't deserve my friendship. We're done. Don't ever come here again, otherwise I will put you in the ground myself. Get back in your piece of shit car and leave."

My hands shake as she gapes at me in horror. "No, no, don't do this. You're my best friend."

I shake my head, pitying the cold bitch on her knees. "No, I'm not," I tell her. "Since moving here, I've learned what it means to have real friends. Ilaria, Chanel, Arizona, and Addison would never do the things to me that you've done. They'd sooner die than be anything like you. So leave, I have my friends and Tanner—the only people I need in my life. I don't need you, not anymore."

She swallows hard, looking at me as though I'm some kind of stranger, and I watch as she shakily gets to her feet, not uttering a single word. The tears don't stop, and I can't help but wonder what she was hoping to get from this, but before I can wonder long, she scurries around to her driver's side door and lunges back into her car.

Erica hits the gas and, sparing one last longing stare, takes off, pulling the car around in a reckless U-turn. Her tires screech against the road and, not a moment later, she's gone, leaving my life for good.

The overwhelming pain cripples me, and I fall to the ground, my face buried deep in my hands as I cry. Tanner's strong arms curl around me, scooping me off the dirty ground, and pulling me against his inviting chest. Then without another word, he turns and makes his way back to his house, not stopping until I'm cocooned in his bed, his body flush against mine and his lips firmly against my temple.

CHAPTER 25

TANNER

Clutching Addison's hand, we stare up at the courthouse, both of us nervous for very different reasons. Addison is terrified about seeing Colby in the flesh and dealing with the fallout that will come with that, whereas all I can think about is just how fucking slimy his lawyer is.

It's been two days since Mom's call out by the lake, and today's the day we finally get a move on Addison's case. Colby will stand in front of the judge, have his charges read out, and be asked how he pleads. It's not exactly a massive step for Addison, but at least we're moving in the right direction.

"You're going to be alright," I tell Addison, pulling her into my side and giving her a tight squeeze. "Hold your head high. You don't even have to look at him, hell I don't think you have to do anything at all. It's only the arraignment, they're just laying out the charges and asking him how he pleads, like in the movies."

She swallows hard and tries to hide the nervousness I see in her eyes. "I know," she says. "I'm just … nervous."

"I know," I say, glancing back down the stairs to find Mom and Dad moving in behind us with the court prosecutor, Eddison Bishop, right at their side. "Everything good?"

"Yes," Eddison says, looking between both me and Addison, explaining everything step by step, knowing we're both nervous and curious. "In ten minutes, we'll start making our way inside. Today is simple. Nothing is expected of you at this point, and you may sit with your family. You'll hear a lot of legal jargon which you probably won't understand, however you can take notes and we can have a lengthy discussion afterward. Today is a formal acknowledgment of Colby's charges, and he will be asked how he pleads. Most likely, he'll plead not guilty. The judge will notify the court of the details pertaining to bail and then a date will be set for trial. Did you follow all of that?"

"Yes, I … I think so."

"Wonderful," he says. "Now, if you don't have any questions, I need to make a quick call before court commences."

Eddison excuses himself with a polite nod, leaving us as a family. Seeing the terror in Addison's eyes, Mom steps into her and wraps her in her arms. "Everything is going to be okay," Mom promises. "Considering the charges, Colby will be refused bail. There's not a doubt in my mind, Addison."

Addison buries her head into Mom's neck and tries to find her composure as Dad's phone rings loudly through the silence. He cringes and double-checks the time before accepting the call. "You've got two minutes," he says, turning and heading back down the steps. "What do you need?"

Frustration burns through my veins. For just one fucking day, Addison needed her father to offer his complete, undivided attention, but that's too hard for the motherfucker. Is it such a stretch to turn your phone off for a few hours for the sake of putting your daughter's rapist away? Fucking hell.

I scowl down at my father as Mom does what she can to calm Addison when I notice a familiar black Aston Martin pulling up to the courthouse. Anger pulses through my veins at seeing the pretentious asshole getting out of his car, a fucking smirk sitting on his lips as though he's got this in the bag.

Orlando Channing will get what's coming to him, and when that time comes, I'll be all too ready to sit back and watch. Just the thought of that guy being Brielle's stepfather makes me sick. She deserves better, so much better, and I can't wait to be the one to take her away from it all.

Orlando skips up the stairs two at a time before disappearing into the courthouse, but not before sparing me a glance, that cockiness on his face enough to rock me right to my core. I don't trust that motherfucker one bit, and I don't doubt that he's got plenty of dirty cards up his sleeve, but it's nothing Eddison Bishop hasn't already assured us about.

Eddison says he's prepared, but that doesn't stop my gut from twisting with unease.

"You good?" Addison asks, reaching for my arm and giving it a gentle squeeze.

I roll my eyes and give her a stupid grin. "I should be the one asking you that."

She goes to say something and, judging by the way her eyes narrow and sparkle, it's going to be something equally moronic and sarcastic, only my father returns, cutting off whatever she was going to say. "I'm so sorry," he says, sounding almost out of breath despite having come from only a few steps away. "The Melbourne office is in crisis. I have to head back out."

I clench my jaw, resisting the urge to knock him out cold as Addison sucks in a broken gasp. "What?" she breathes. "But you can't go … not now."

"I'm sorry, honey. My secretary is working out my flights as we speak, but don't worry, I won't have to leave until after court. There's still time and perhaps after court lets out, I can take you for lunch."

Addison's gaze drops to the ground, and the pain in her eyes makes me want to scream. "Yeah … I suppose."

"Alright," Eddison says, returning to our group. "Time to head in."

Addison lets out a shaky breath, her disappointment in our father already long forgotten in light of what she's about to face. As one, we follow Eddison up the stairs and through the doors of the courthouse. After making our way through security, we reach the courtroom and Addison takes a moment to breathe.

"You got this, brat," I remind her.

She nods to herself as Eddison pushes through the big double doors.

I look around with wide eyes. I've never set foot in a courtroom before, but it's just as I imagined from all the movies. People are scattered around, and as we pass through the aisle toward the front, I see him—Colby fucking Jacobs.

If I could tear his head right off his fucking shoulders, I would.

He wears a cheap rent-a-suit and still looks like shit from the beating the boys and I dished out a little less than a week ago. His bruises are in fine form, and that shattered nose looks like a fucking treat. Pride seeps into my veins, but the moment I realize Addison has noticed him too, all I feel is cold.

We get seated and things are about to get started when a small body pushes in beside me and Bri's hand slips into mine. "What the hell are you doing here?" I question, my brows furrowed as I take her in wearing her Bradford Private uniform. "I thought you had a math test."

"Screw the test," she says, eyeing Orlando across the room and sneering. "I got a pass. I can do a makeup test tomorrow. I just ... I wanted to be here for you and Addison. I hope that's okay."

My father eyes Bri with irritation, and I block it out as I put my arm over her shoulder and pull her into my side. "Of course," I tell her. "I wouldn't have it any other way, and I know Addison will be relieved to see some friendly faces in here. Though, fair warning, Hudson is going to have something to say about it. He would have killed to be here—"

"Oh yeah," she cuts me off. "He's parking the car. Like hell he was going to miss this. The second he saw me bailing, he was right there with me."

Not a moment later, Hudson strides through the courtroom doors and Addison glances back, locking eyes with him. There's an odd intensity between them, but as Eddison leans into her side and murmurs something in her ear, the moment passes, and Hudson simply slides in on Bri's other side.

Glancing across to thank him for being here for Addison, I notice a timid set of eyes locked on mine from across the courtroom, and my blood turns cold. Not because of who she is or what I did to her, but because of the child in her arms.

Rachael Jacobs, Colby's older sister who was sent away right after shit went down, sits with her parents and a baby boy clinging to her side.

Noticing my stare, Rachael's lips kick up into a wicked grin as if to say *gotcha motherfucker*. Her arm tightens around her son, and my whole world flashes before my eyes. She's too fucking smug for this to be innocent, and as she turns her attention toward the front of the room, I feel my world slipping away.

My hands begin to sweat and my heart races, mentally doing the math while my brain short circuits, not even able to recall just how long ago I fucked her, but I'm damn sure that I was safe. I used protection, but that kid with his dark hair and even darker eyes … no. It's not possible.

This is all in my fucking head. That can't be my kid.

I fucked Rachael once with protection, but he looks the right age, and fucking hell, he looks like me."

Panic tears at my throat, and I can barely breathe when Brielle pushes in closer. "Hey," she murmurs, her brows furrowed as she steals my attention. "Are you okay? You look like you've seen a ghost."

"Yeah, umm … I'm fine. Just worried about the case."

She nods, but it's clear she doesn't buy my brush off, then before she can question me further, I hear the bailiff's deep voice booming across the courtroom. "All rise for the honorable Judge Willis Sanderson."

We get to our feet, and if I weren't wound so tight and invested in this case, I'd find the whole process fascinating, but as it is, I can't stop turning my gaze to the baby across the courtroom.

The judge enters the courtroom through the side door and I take her in, already deciding that I don't like her. She looks fine, professional and well put together, but there's something in her eyes that strikes me as odd, even more so when her gaze sails across to Orlando.

We're all seated, and I find myself clutching Bri's hand tighter, too nervous to even breathe. Despite only a few minutes passing, I feel like I've been here a lifetime before we finally start getting into the reason we're here.

Colby Jacobs.

He is asked to stand, and I listen intently as a list of charges are laid out. Judge Sanderson watches him closely, looking bored before shuffling a bunch of papers on her desk. "Do you understand what you are being charged for, Mr. Jacobs? These are serious offenses."

"Yes, your honor. I understand."

"How do you—"

"Your honor," Channing says, standing. "May I be so bold to approach the bench?"

"Mr. Channing, you know the rules of my courtroom."

"I'm very well aware, your honor. However, I feel there have been some severe misunderstandings during the investigation. My client is innocent of these offenses, and I can prove it quite simply."

The judge shifts her gaze over Channing and Colby before moving across to Addison who looks like she's about to collapse with horror. Sanderson considers Channing's bullshit and presses her lips into a hard line before silently motioning for him to approach.

My back stiffens, and I watch as they have a murmured conversation. A slip of paper is presented to the judge before her head shoots up. "Where's the prosecuting attorney?"

Eddison stands, immediately stepping out from behind his small desk, his brows furrowed. "Here, your honor," he says, buttoning his suit jacket, clearly not liking this unusual turn of events which were supposed to be the most straight-forward part of this whole thing. "May I approach?"

Judge Sanderson nods and I spare a glance at Addison as she watches everything that's going down before her. She looks sick at the thought of Colby wiping his hands free of this, and hell, I'm feeling it too.

Colby looks fucking smug, and I can't help but notice the same fucked-up smirk across Channing's face, the same one he had before as he entered the courthouse. The private discussion with the judge becomes heated with Eddison clearly being railroaded, and before I know it, the judge is standing. "We will take a brief recess and reconvene in fifteen minutes," she says, addressing the court before looking back at the two lawyers. "You two. My chambers. Now."

We're all asked to stand as the judge files out with the two lawyers on her heels, and the moment they're gone, the courtroom bursts into chaos. Colby leans back in his chair, his cuffed hands propped behind his head as Addison falls into Mom's arms, sobbing uncontrollably.

I clench my jaw, my whole body shaking with a violent rage. Bri grips my hand, squeezing it with everything she's got. "Calm down," she urges, panic in her tone. She's seen me like this once before and it nearly destroyed us, but I can't let that happen again. I won't lose her again. "The judge will see that whatever evidence Orlando has supplied is nothing but bullshit. It's going to be okay. Colby's not going to walk away from this."

I shake my head, my whole body vibrating with anger. "You don't know that," I tell her through a clenched jaw, seeing all my fears and doubts playing out right before me. "You don't know this asshole like I do. I've sat at barbecues and listened to him bragging about the way he's fooled juries and supplied false information to get his clients off horrendous charges. This is nothing to him, just a fucking ordinary Monday. Addison doesn't mean shit to him, not as a person and not as the little girl next door that he's watched grow up. All he gives a shit about is his precious reputation."

"Hey," she says, reaching up and taking my face between her small hands, forcing my narrowed stare to hers as Hudson gets up and makes his way down the row to Addison. "Just breathe. We're going to get through this, and if he does get let off, then we'll deal with that too. No matter what, he will pay for what he's done, I promise you that, Tanner."

Letting out a shaky breath, I try to find the calm in the storm and only find it while looking into Bri's eyes. "Promise me, Killer. If I end his life, you won't walk away from me."

She nods, squeezing my hands. "I swear to you, I'm not walking away."

Swallowing hard, the world starts to come back into perspective, and I can't help but notice the way Rachael watches me from across the courtroom again, but I don't have time for her shit right now. It's all in my head. That kid isn't mine, it's just a really fucked-up coincidence. Besides, she was pretty much engaged when we spent the night together, and I'm not even close to being the only guy she was hooking up with.

Hudson crouches down in front of Addison and she falls into his arms, sobbing into the base of his neck as he murmurs something in her ear. She nods and lets him pull her to her feet, hastily wiping her eyes and taking a few calming breaths as he leads her down the aisle and out the main doors.

Mom leans around Dad, her hand dropping to my bouncing knee. "It's going to be okay," she promises, though the confidence in her tone simply isn't there. She sounds as though she's still trying to convince herself.

The next fifteen minutes are the longest of my life, and when we get a warning that court is about to recommence, I fire off a text to Hudson, telling him to come back in. They return only a minute later, and I just about launch myself over the fucking rails when Colby catches her eye and openly taunts her about what's about to go down.

Hudson leads her back to her seat and stays with her, sitting right beside her and holding her hand just as she needs. When Channing and Eddison stride back through the side entrance, Eddison looks as though he's about to tear someone to shreds while Channing looks as though he just got a quickie in the bathroom.

Before we can even ask what's going on, the bailiff's tone cuts through the room once again. "Please rise for the honorable Judge Willis Sanderson."

The judge walks back in looking pissed off and motions to the court to take their seats, and I listen to every word with bated breath. She takes her seat before looking out at the court and glancing toward Addison with pity.

She takes a breath, and a mask of indifference slips over her face before she circles her fingers around her gavel. "The evidence provided in the case of Jacobs versus Morgan is overwhelming. There has been a dreadful occurrence of human error and it's clear that Colby Jacobs is, in fact, not guilty of the rape and attempted murder of Miss Addison Morgan." Her gavel comes down with a sickening blow. "Mr. Jacobs, you are free to go."

CHAPTER 26

TANNER

Red hot fury tears at my chest as the officer moves across the courtroom and releases Colby from his handcuffs, all while Addison's whimpering cries sound through the shocked room. He turns and catches my stare, a smirk pulling at the corner of his lips just moments before Channing ushers him through the small gate and toward the exit.

No. No fucking way.

That did not just happen.

Eddison comes storming back to us, his hands balled into tight fists. "That motherfucker," he spits between a clenched jaw, his voice barely audible to anyone around us.

"What the fuck just happened?" my father demands, getting right in his face as Mom desperately tries to comfort Addison. "You said we had this. How did you let that happen?"

I stand, unable to get a grip on myself, my control quickly slipping away as Brielle stands beside me, her face mirroring the horror I feel inside.

Eddison shakes his head. "I don't know how Channing did it," he says, almost to himself. "He's a piece of work, but I didn't realize just how dirty he was."

"What happened?" I spit through a clenched jaw.

"He switched out the results from the rape kit," Eddison explains. "The semen sample taken from Addison in the hospital is no longer a match for Colby Jacobs. There was some kind of mix up and now Channing claims it's proof enough that his client had no action in this, and the judge agreed. As for the attempted murder charge, the judge claims the footage from the hospital surveillance is not adequate enough to provide a positive identification. There were no obvious markers to suggest the man in that video was Colby, apart from an estimated height and weight. She said it could have been anyone. We require more evidence if we would like to pursue the charges."

"What?" Addison breathes from the bench, tears streaming down her face. "How is that possible? I saw him. *I felt him.* He held me down and forced his way inside me while I screamed for him to stop. It was Colby. How could she let him get away like that?"

Eddison shakes his head, not liking this outcome one bit. "I'm sorry, Addison, but my hands are tied. The evidence shows that Colby's DNA was not that of your rapist's, and if we were still able to get this to trial, no jury would convict him now. We might be able to get him on drug charges, but then again, it's his word against yours, and he will say that you took them willingly. Channing will drag you through the mud on this, and after everything you've already gone through, I don't recommend pushing right now."

"That's bullshit," she cries.

My hands clench, picturing the way Colby would be walking down the hall right now, free as a fucking bird, pushing through the doors and out into the fresh air to do whatever the fuck he wants.

He'll come after Addison for this, and then he'll come for Bri again.

Fuck that. Colby Jacobs will not hurt my family ever again.

His family celebrates loudly on the opposite side of the room, his mom sobbing about how she knew her baby would never do something like this, and it sends me right out the fucking door, my father and Bri desperately scrambling after me.

I see fucking red as I storm through the hallways, my sharp gaze flicking from left to right as Bri catches me and clings to my arm, trying to pull me back. "Don't do this, Tanner," she begs, but every word falls flat, and I push myself on, shaking her off. "Please, we'll get him, but not like this. *Not here.*"

"Tanner," my father's booming tone sounds behind me. "Think about what you're doing. Don't be stupid, boy."

Fuck him. Fuck them all. I'm not letting him walk away from this and I'm sure as fuck not about to give him free rein to come after the people I love. No way in hell.

People linger everywhere—lawyers in designer suits looking like the most arrogant types of assholes, while their guilty-as-fuck clients cling to their last hope at their side. There are officers scattered throughout and people who look like they're about to be sick with nerves, but none of them matter to me.

I reach security at the main entrance and slip past them, pushing out into the breezy fall air and flying down the stairs, my gaze shooting from left to right. Raised voices fire off behind me, but nothing is more important than getting to the two assholes standing down on the curb, lingering by the side of the most pretentious Aston Martin I've ever seen.

Fire burns through my stare as I race toward them, my hands already curled into tight fists, and hearing the commotion coming from behind me, both their heads turn up, only it's too fucking late.

Channing steps in front of Colby, determined to put on the best kind of show for his guilty-as-fuck client, but if I have to go through Channing to get what I want, then that's exactly what I'll do. "Think about what you're doing, Morgan," Channing spits, his hands flying up as if to ward me off. "You put one hand on my client, and I'll destroy you."

I reach them in a matter of seconds and my arm rears back. Not sparing a thought for Channing's bullshit pleas, I grip the front of his tailored suit and launch my fist clear into the side of his face. He goes down like a sack of shit, and I barge right past him, not sparing a single thought for the asshole who just helped my sister's rapist walk free.

Colby barely has a moment to react before I'm on him.

My hand grips his throat, and I throw him to the ground, pinning him beneath me as I let every last shred of fury fly free. My tight fist slams against his temple, his eye, his jaw, his lips. "You'll never fucking touch them again," I roar, no hope of saving myself now. "I'll fucking kill you, ya hear me? I'll end you right fucking now."

My fists continue in a rapid assault, but nothing is enough. I need to go harder, faster. I need to fucking destroy him.

"TANNER," Brielle's shriek tears through the madness. "STOP!"

I hear her, but nothing is stopping me now. Not until it's done.

Blood spurts across the front of my shirt as I re-break his nose, but all too soon, I'm being dragged away. "Get off me," I roar, fighting the tight grip.

Slipping free of my captors, I go for Colby again, but when my palms hit the ground and my face scrapes the pavement, the fog clears. There's a knee in the center of my back, and I go limp, letting the officers wrestle a cold pair of cuffs around my wrists.

Brielle drops down before me, panic on her face and tears in those bright blue eyes. "It's going to be okay," she promises me. "It's going to be okay."

And not a moment later, I'm hauled to my feet and shoved hard into the back of a police car while my father shakes his head. "Get him out of here."

CHAPTER 27

TANNER

The holding cell is nothing but a small cement box and a metal bench. I've paced the bars like an animal, rattling my cage and screaming to be released, but no one gives a fuck.

How can they hold me here when Colby Jacobs is out there, free as a fucking bird?

Gripping the bars tighter, the scabs over my knuckles split open again. It's a torturous cycle. It's almost as though the minute they start to scab over, I do something that tears them apart again, but I don't regret it. I'll split my knuckles a million times over if it means getting to Colby.

I lost track of time hours ago, but one thing is for sure, my parents should have had me out of here well before now. Eddison should have shown up, and I should have been freed, but for some fucked-up reason, I'm still rotting away. No one has come down here to let me know what's going on. The only human interaction I've had since yesterday is the asshole who got stuck with the job of offering me food and water. Hell, I shouldn't complain, during the middle of the night, he even offered me a blanket. It was scratchy and stank of piss.

Releasing the metal bars, I start pacing again, grunting in frustration.

Neither Bri nor Addie are safe out there without me. They're unprotected, left alone to fend for themselves. Bri will be alright. She's strong and will be able to hold her own long enough to call for help, but Addison … after the blow in court, she'll crumble. I guarantee that she's locked in her room right now, weeping in fear.

I have to get out of here.

The familiar buzz of the security door sounds through the cell and my head whips up, watching as the heavy door pulls back to allow space for two people to stride through—one being an accompanying officer while the other is the devil himself, Orlando Channing.

Rage burns through my body, and I clench my jaw, the only relief coming from the sight of the heavy bruising across the side of his face. That dirty motherfucker. It's one thing to push your case and do everything within the law for your client, but this? Fuck no. I always knew he was dirty and full of shit, but I never expected that he was capable of something so heinous.

The officer remains by the door as Channing strides toward me, dropping his briefcase on a table and looking like the biggest douchebag I've ever seen. His filthy gaze locks on mine, anger swarming deep in his stare. This motherfucker hasn't forgotten what I did to him, and he won't be forgetting it anytime soon. Hell, just the memory of my fist slamming into his face has made my stay in this cell almost pleasurable.

Channing continues until he's positioned right in front of me—a bold fucking move considering I can reach right through the bar and grab him. Though for now, I'll play his little game and figure out what the fuck he wants with me until I decide I've had enough. I might be locked behind bars, but that doesn't change the fact this motherfucker is playing by my rules.

I fix him with a hard, unnerved stare and watch as he stares right back, refusing to verbally acknowledge his existence until he finally cracks and gives in. "You put your hands on the wrong man, boy."

"You freed my sister's rapist without even a hint of regret. Looks to me like I put my hands exactly where they were meant to go."

"Miss Morgan had it wrong," Channing mutters, his gaze darkening with pure hatred. "She falsely accused my client, and I had a responsibility to him to ensure he didn't go down for your sister's inability to identify the man who attacked her. Colby Jacobs is innocent. As stated in court, the DNA from Addison's rape kit was not a match for my client."

My arm shoots through the bars gripping the front of his designer suit and yanking him to me, his face slamming against the metal bars. "You're going to fucking pay for what you did to her," I growl, watching his eyes widen with fear. "I swear to God, I'm going to destroy Colby and then I'm coming for you. Understand me, Channing. Nothing will stop me, not now."

The officer races in, panic torn across his face as Channing just stares back at me, the fear quickly fading and morphing into something much more sinister. "Release him now," the officer spits, gripping my hand and tearing my fingers back one by one until I have no choice but to either let go or lose a finger.

Channing stumbles back a step and makes a show of straightening his suit jacket as he keeps his stare locked on me. "Careful now," he murmurs, his tone low and full of venom. "For a boy whose girlfriend lives under my roof, you're being awfully bold."

"You fucking touch her and I'll slit your throat while you sleep."

Channing laughs. "Oh, please. So dramatic. Do you really think I'd be so stupid to lay a finger on Brianna? No, I have much easier ways to get what I want when it comes to that girl."

I scoff as a chill sails down my spine, hoping I'm imagining the sinister look in his eye as he refers to my girl. "You really are a self-centered piece of shit. You can't even get your own stepdaughter's name right. It's Brielle, asshole. Not Brianna. If you're going to threaten someone, the least you can do is learn their name."

"Her name doesn't matter. She is nothing but a careless woman, put on earth with the sole purpose of catering to a man. She belongs in the kitchen and the moment I've had my fill of her mother, she'll belong in my bedroom."

Yep. I'm going to fucking hurl.

I slam up against the bars, a loud roar tearing from the back of my chest, making him flinch. "Just fucking try and see what I do to you. Brielle is nothing like her gold-digging mother. She'd rather gut herself with a butcher's knife than have anything to do with you."

Channing simply laughs, his eyes sparkling as though I just set down some kind of challenge. "We'll see about that now, won't we?"

Fuck me. "Why don't you go ahead and take one more step toward me? I swear, I won't bite."

He watches as though I'm nothing but a pile of dog shit beneath his foot. "Here's what's going to happen, Morgan," he says, taking a step back and leaning against the officer's desk beside his briefcase. "You're on hour forty of your forty-eight-hour hold and the moment that clock ticks over and you're released, you're going to go home and continue living your life as the star of Bradford's football team. You're going to wine and dine Brianna until I deem otherwise, and you're going to forget about the name Colby Jacobs. This is your only warning, Morgan. Step out of line even once, and I will ruin you, but what's more, I won't even need to try. You see, I already have everything I need to make it happen. I've watched you grow up, watched you destroy your skin with those ridiculous tattoos, and I watched as you made mistake after mistake."

"What the fuck are you talking about? If you think I'm just going to sit down and let you get away with this bullshit, you've got another thing coming."

Channing laughs before unclipping his briefcase and holding out a bunch of photos. I take them and my heart immediately starts to race, my past staring me right in the face. My body goes cold as I let the pictures fall from my fingers, horror pulsing through my veins. Nobody should know about this, they can't … my whole fucking world will cease to exist.

Bri … fuck.

"Your father is a dirty man, Tanner, and I'm not surprised that his son has followed right in his footsteps. I couldn't imagine what would happen if those images got into the wrong hands," he says, glancing down at the scattered images at my feet, images I can't stomach to look at. "Your poor mother, such a fragile little thing. She'd never be able to look at you again."

I clench my jaw, unease rocking through me like never before, my whole future flashing before my eyes. "What do you want?" I whisper, stumbling back in my cell, lead sinking into my gut and weighing me down.

Channing just smiles. "I've already laid out my terms, Tanner, and as a sign of good faith, I'm not even going to have you charged with assault. But in return, you are to continue on as such, attend the wedding of the year as Brianna's date, and distract her enough so that her mother doesn't notice just how much her daughter despises her. Take her out, show her the world, and become Bradford's hero out on the field. You're to turn her into the perfect, doting girlfriend, teach her how to please a man, and when the time comes, you will willingly hand her over. No questions asked. Is that understood?"

Bile rises in my throat, and I struggle to swallow. "Oh, and one other thing," Channing adds, glancing at the photos again. "Forget about Colby. You go after him even once, and those images will become the next viral sensation. I will end you, Tanner, and I'll barely have to lift a finger to do it. You will lose everything, and you'll have no one to blame but yourself … oh," he adds. "And your father."

The fuck? My father? How the hell does he have anything to do with this? As far as I'm aware, no one knew about this, only those directly involved. Not even the boys know what happened that night.

No, he can't know. That's not possible.

I shake my head, feeling my world caving in on me, knowing just how much I'm going to lose if this shit gets out. "You're not going to get away with this," I warn him, moving back toward the bars and gripping them tight. "No matter what I have to do. You'll never get your hands on Bri, and I'm sure as fuck those photos will never see the light of day. You underestimate me, Channing. You might be a dirty lawyer with bullshit tricks up your sleeve, but you forget, I'm not the only one who's got something to lose."

Channing pushes off the desk, fastening his briefcase before settling his heavy stare back on me. "Isn't it fun to hold all the power?" he questions, his lips pulling into a twisted smirk. "Watch your back, Morgan. Who knows when it could all come crumbling down."

And with that, Orlando Channing strides out the door, leaving me gasping for air.

I fall back to my seat before glancing down at the images again. That night changed my life in the worst ways. I was a monster, a fucking stranger. I couldn't even recognize myself, and I sure as fuck have barely been able to live with myself since. If it weren't for football or the guys … fuck, I don't know where I'd be right now. They saved my life, and they have no fucking idea.

Hearing someone outside the door, panic tears at me and I fall to my knees, scooping up the images and frantically tearing them into tiny pieces, destroying any evidence of the horrific things I've done. But I know Channing. This isn't the only evidence. He'll have copies, and they'll be stored in a place where only he can get to them.

Fuck. What have I done?

Hours pass before another officer graces my cell with his presence and walks toward me. He meets my haunted stare and nods, shoving a key into the lock. "You're free to go, kid," he says. "Follow me and we'll get you sorted out."

The officer turns on his heels and I follow behind, too conflicted with what I need to do to even be aware of what I'm supposed to be doing. It takes twenty minutes to sign all the papers they throw at me, then I'm walking out past security into the afternoon sun. Riley leans against his car on the curb in front of the police station, hands deep in his pockets as he stares down at the sidewalk.

My small breath of relief fades when the thoughts of those images flood my mind again. If my past gets out, Riley won't want anything to do with me. But what the fuck am I supposed to do? There's no way in hell I'm about to let Colby walk away from this, and I'm sure as fuck not about to let Channing lay a damn finger on Bri. If I have to give myself up to save them, then that's what I'll do.

Sensing my approach, Riley's head whips up and a stupid grin cuts across his face. "Bout time your bitch ass showed up," he says, a dark and deep concern flashing in his eyes as he takes me in. "Do you know how fucking long I've been waiting for you to get out?"

Riley steps right into me and throws his arms around me, clapping my back quickly. "You good, man?"

He pulls away, trying hard to mask his emotions as I nod. "Yeah, I'm fine," I tell him. "But you didn't need to come and pick me up. I could have found my own way home. Besides, aren't you supposed to be in class?"

"Fuck school," he says. "I called your mom last night and offered. Hudson was saying something about your sister being a mess and your mom didn't want to leave the house because it makes Addie nervous … so, ya know. Here I am."

"Well thanks," I say, dropping down into his car, determined to get home to check on Addie and then shower.

"For the record," Riley says as his engine rumbles to life, "your dad is a piece of shit."

Letting out a frustrated breath, I glance toward my best friend as he pulls out into traffic. "What did he do now?"

"The fucker still took off to Australia," he explains. "Even with Addie begging him not to go and you in the slammer. The motherfucker didn't give two shits. Not to mention, he made a comment to the arresting cops to hold you as long as legally possible. I swear, that asshole has had it out for you for years."

My lips press into a hard line as Channing's words come back to me. *You'll have no one to blame but yourself … oh, and your father.* Maybe my old man really does know something about what happened that night. Maybe he really does have it out for me.

Shaking off the thought, I relax back into the chair and close my eyes. I'm so fucking tired. All I want is to get home and end this shitty experience, but something tells me I've barely even scratched the surface. I want to see Bri and hold her in my arms, demanding she move out of that fucked up house, but I can't do that without risking exposure.

I fucking hate this.

Despite Riley wanting to stop for takeout, he drives me straight home, and I bail out of his car faster than I stormed from the courthouse. Within moments, I'm flying through the door of Addison's bedroom.

She lies in her bed, snuggled under the blankets in as much darkness as her blinds will offer, and as she looks up at me, I see just how broken she is. Her eyes are red and raw, evidence of long days and nights crying, and it kills me. "I'm so sorry, Addie," I murmur, moving across her room and dropping to my knees beside her bed.

Her bottom lip wobbles and a lone tear sails down her face before soaking into her pillow. "He's going to come for me," she mutters over the lump in her throat.

"I'm not going to let that happen," I tell her, gripping onto her hand and squeezing it tight. "I swear, just because the courts failed you, doesn't mean I will. He'll die before ever touching you again. You've got me and Hudson and all of the guys."

She swallows hard and nods, doing her best to be strong. "Dad told the police to hold you as long as they wanted."

I nod. "Yeah, I heard something about that."

Another tear falls as her voice breaks. "I really thought he was going to stay."

"I know you did," I tell her. "But you've got me now, and I'm not going anywhere."

"Okay," she says. "But if you're going to hang out in here, can you at least have a shower first? You kinda stink."

A grin pulls at the corner of my lips, and I push to my feet before looking down at the irritating little brat who I can't help but love, and being the caring brother I am, I crash down on top of her, making sure she gets a face full of armpit.

Addison screams in disgust. "Get off me, you big turd," she wails. "You're going to make me gag."

"Tell me how good I smell first."

"You reek, asshole."

A manic laugh tears through me as I refuse to move. "Tell me what I want to hear, or I'll be using your bathroom to shit in for the next month."

Addison gags and latches onto my nipples, twisting hard. "Nobody uses my bathroom but me," she screeches as I roar in agony, her whole body lifting off the bed as I pull away, her grip so fucking tight I fear she's about to tear them right off my chest.

"FUCK! Okay, you win," I say, certain one more second will send me into a weeping mess on the floor. "I won't shit in your bathroom."

Addison releases me and gives me an innocent smile. "Glad to see you've come to your senses. Now fuck off out of here before that putrid tang seeps into the walls."

Rubbing my man-titties, I stride out of Addison's bedroom and make my way toward mine, feeling better about the situation. The past forty-eight hours have seriously fucked with my head, but seeing her laugh goes a long way in healing something inside of me. Colby might have hurt her, but he didn't take away her fire, and as long as that still burns, Addie is going to be alright.

Walking into my room, I come to a dead stop in the doorway, shaking my head as my lips pull into a stupid smile.

That fucking pocket rocket.

There are dicks drawn across the walls from one end of my room to the other. I never knew my girl was such a fucking artist. Hairy ones, smooth ones, large, and small. Cut, uncut, veiny, thick, and pierced. Some are dripping, some are spurting, and some even have Brielle's name tattooed across their shaft. Though, it doesn't take a genius to see that she's only written her name across the big veiny ones that look like they'll destroy anything in their path.

I shake my head, taking it all in but then right in the center, above my headboard, is her perfect handwriting, telling me exactly what she's been feeling since Monday afternoon.

I LOVE YOU, TANNER MORGAN!
YOU'RE A DICK, BUT YOU'RE MY FAVORITE DICK.
AND I LOVE YOU EVEN MORE THAN ALL THESE
DICKS COMBINED.

CHAPTER 28

Brielle

rudging through the house, I throw my bag down on the bottom step before making my way up. Today has been shit. Hell, the whole week has been shit. Tanner has been gone, locked in a forty-eight-hour police hold, and I've hated being away from him. Not going to lie, the idiot deserved it. He lost his cool and decided to beat the shit out of Colby in front of nearly every policeman in Bradford. He was all but asking them to arrest him.

Had it been me? I would have waited until I could get Colby alone in a back alley or knock him out cold so I could take him somewhere a little more private to take my time with him. Perhaps the desert where no one could hear him scream. Tanner though, he popped the lid right off his emotions and let them run rampant, but in that courthouse, I promised I'd stand by his side no matter what, and nothing is going to change that.

I've had the worst kind of anxiety, hating that anything could be happening to him in that cell. Was he being fed? Did he sleep? Were the monsters inside his head giving him even a shred of peace? What happened in that courtroom was complete bullshit and, though it's been a few days, I haven't been able to stop thinking about it.

Addison hasn't left her room, and from what I was able to get out of Tanner's mom, she's terrified of what could happen now. I don't blame her. Colby is unhinged. The way he rammed my car off the road and then pulled the tubes from Addison's throat in the hospital … fuck. I don't envy her. She has a battle coming her way, but with Tanner at her back, she can do anything she puts her mind to. I don't doubt that Colby Jacobs is going down, we're just going to have to get creative to make it happen.

Reaching the top of the stairs, I start making my way to my room, desperate to get a good look out my window. I haven't heard from Tanner yet, so I can only assume he's still locked up, but that's not going to stop me from checking his room anyway. It's well past the forty-eight-hour holding limit, so he should be home, or if not, at least on his way. I have no idea how these things actually work, but I could have sworn I heard Logan and Jax saying something about Riley skipping out on class to go and pick him up. Either way, when he gets home and sees his room, he's going to know that I've been thinking of him.

The thought of the million eyeliner dicks on his wall sends a filthy grin across my face. Hell, I even feel a little bad about the clean-up it's going to require, and just to be an awesome girlfriend, I'll even think about scrubbing his walls clean for him. Who am I kidding? The asshole will have me on my knees, scrubbing the walls before I even realize what's happening. Though, he'll be sure to reward me afterward.

A thrill shoots through me as I reach my door and turn the handle. I shove my shoulder into it, barging my way through my room, only to come up short, finding someone sprawled across my bed. "Where the fuck have you been, you little turd sniffer?" my brother says, his eyes shifting to me only moments before they bug out of his head and a burst of howling laughter follows. "Holy shit! Check out your uniform. You're one of them now."

A wide grin cuts across my face, my eyes beaming with excitement, not even giving a shit that the douchelord insists on calling me out for my ridiculous private school uniform. "YOU'RE BACK!"

I bound across my room, barreling into my big brother just as he stands, my momentum rocking him back against my bed. He catches me with ease and gives me a tight bear hug, his big arms wrapping right around my small frame.

Damien releases me almost immediately ... because he's far too cool to hug his little sister. Did I mention the guy is a twat? And yes, I mean both versions of that saying. He's a prick as well as a massive, loosey-goosey vagina, but what can I say? He's my big brother and I love him, though I'm not about to tell him that.

"So ... this is our new place, huh?" he questions, glancing around my ridiculously oversized bedroom with all its fancy things.

"Yup," I say, popping the p as I make my way into my closet to pick out something to change into. "Mom really leveled up this time. Though, I'm warning you, a new house and husband isn't the only new thing she's got."

"What's that supposed to mean?"

"When did you get back? Have you talked with her yet? She's a completely different person now, nothing at all like the mom you know. She's turned into this Stepford wife, wearing designer clothes. She quit all her jobs and joined the country club. Hell, she even hit me … twice."

Damien stands and turns to gape at me, his brows furrowed in confusion. "The fuck?" he says. "You're lying. Mom would never do that."

"Oh, she did," I say under my breath, picking out a comfy tank and a pair of sweatpants. "Did you hear about the girl who was raped over the summer at a party back home?" I pause, glancing up in time to watch him nod. "Well, this new husband—Orlando Channing—he's a criminal lawyer and was representing Colby—"

"Wait. Colby? That dickhead you were seeing?"

"Yep," I say, embarrassed to have to explain all of this to my big brother. "You always said I knew how to pick the good ones. He and Erica were getting together behind my back, and they concocted this plan to mess with this girl, who just happens to be the sister of my new boyfriend—but that's beside the point. They hurt her really bad and despite everything, Orlando still represented Colby. But the thing is, Orlando is a complete asshole. At first, he tried to get me to make a false statement to clear Colby, and then he went as far as to switch out the rape kits so that Colby would walk free. He doesn't give a shit about what's right or wrong, only cares about his reputation."

Damien just stares at me blankly as I pull my sweatpants on beneath my school skirt. "Literally none of that explained why Mom hit you."

I think back over everything I just said and realize the guy is right. "Oh, umm … well, a few weeks ago, Erica tried to save herself by claiming I was the one behind the whole thing. I was arrested at school, and they tried to drop rape and attempted murder charges on me."

"The fuck?" he demands, gaping at me as though he barely even recognizes me right now.

"Right? The whole thing was insane, but it's fine now. I was able to prove my innocence, but for those couple of weeks while I was waiting for my name to clear, Mom really thought I did it. Can you believe that? She didn't even give me a chance to explain that I was being set up before she slapped me."

Damien turns and starts pacing my room, running his hand back through his hair and I can't help but notice just how much bigger he's gotten since starting boot camp. "Fuck, Brielle. Why didn't you text me that things were getting this bad? I could have—"

"Could have what, Damien?" I ask. "You've been at boot camp, and I wasn't about to text you and make you worry over it when there's literally nothing you could have done. That would only make you feel like shit."

"You're right about that," he mutters under his breath before letting out a heavy sigh. "Look, I'll have a word with her, but I can't make any promises. I only get a few days off and then I have to head right back again. I can't guarantee that things will get better, but I won't leave without trying."

I shrug my shoulders and cross my room, aiming for my window. "Don't bother," I tell him. "There's no use. She's barely said a word to me since we moved in here and the few she has said haven't exactly been nice. She's changed. I miss our real mom because this imposter has really been fucking with my zen."

He drops down with a heavy flop onto the edge of my bed as I glance out my bedroom window, noticing the way Tanner's bathroom door is propped open with steam from a hot shower flowing out around the small crack. Relief burns through my veins, and before I can throw myself out the window to get to him, Damien's murmured question fills the silence. "So, what's the deal with this wedding anyway? Didn't they already get married in Italy or Portugal or some shit like that?"

I shake my head and turn around, propping my ass against the window seal. "Paris," I confirm. "It's just some big excuse to show off in front of all the other rich people around here. Just wait until you see the dining room downstairs. I wouldn't be surprised if they put you in one of those penguin suits."

Damien shakes his head as he looks at me in horror. "A tux? No fucking way. I'm not wearing that shit. Have you seen me? I'll look like a fucking moron in one of those. I can barely pull off a regular suit."

"We could always trade. I'll happily wear your tux if you want to go in my maid of honor gown with a pair of Spanx riding up your ass and sucking in all the important bits until you look as flat as a pancake."

Damien just stares at me. "What the fuck is a Spanx?"

I shake my head, rolling my eyes and trying to hide the smirk pulling at my lips. "Do me a favor. When you meet my new friends, try not to be so obvious about the fact that you're a twenty-two-year-old virgin."

Damien laughs. "You've got another thing coming if you think there's any chance in hell that I'm still a virgin," he says, a cocky smirk tears across his stupid face. "Where are these friends you're talking about?"

Terror fills my veins. "I swear to God, Damien Ashford, if you even think about screwing one of my friends, I'll make your life a living hell."

The idiot grins back at me, making a show of laying back on my bed and kicking his feet up. "And how exactly do you plan on doing that when I'll be back at boot camp, huh?"

"I—fuck," I screech, racing across the room and ripping my pillow out from under his head just so I can smother him with it. "You're so annoying."

Damien howls with laughter, effortlessly evading my every attempt to destroy his life with my pillow. "Go and find your own room, you big asshole," I seethe. "And while you're at it, how about a new personality?"

Damien grips both my wrists in one of his hands and tears the pillow out of my hold before turning my weapon on me. The pillow pounds against my face, and I drop to the ground, covering my head with my arms and screaming for sweet relief as the giant asshole drops down on top of me, keeping me pinned to the ground with his ginormous ass.

"I swear to God, Damien," I say, trying to reach for the sensitive skin at the back of his thighs to pinch it. "Get off me."

"Or what?" he sings, awfully chuffed with himself. "You gonna tell Mom on me? Oh wait … you can't do that anymore."

Ouch. That one stung.

A throat clears by the door and both our gazes snap up to find Tanner leaning in my open doorway. Amusement flashes in his dark eyes but there's a hint of hesitation, unsure about what's going down in here. His eyes linger on mine, roaming over my body. "Please tell me this is your brother and not some random dude who I'm going to have to beat senseless."

A wide grin tears across my face. I've missed Tanner so freaking much, and the fact that Damien still hasn't moved is only making that longing ache inside my chest. "I think the better question is who the fuck are you and why are you creeping into my sister's bedroom unannounced?"

I shove my elbow back into Damien's thigh, loving the soft groan that flows through the room. "Get off me, you giant prick. This is Tanner, the only reason I've been able to keep sane since moving here."

Damien still refuses to move. "I don't know," he says, looking my boyfriend up and down, taking in all the tattoos. "He looks like a criminal to me."

Tanner smirks, more than entertained. "Does it help that I only just got released out of police custody?"

Damien stands at that, purposefully keeping his body in front of mine, blocking Tanner's view of me as I try to scramble to my feet. "What for?"

"Beating the shit out of the fucker who raped my sister and wrapped yours around a fucking tree."

Damien's eyes widen and he whips around to gape at me. "What the fuck is he talking about?"

I cringe, having purposefully left that part out of my story. "When Colby realized that I knew what he'd done to Tanner's sister, he tried to warn me to back down by ramming my car into a tree. He broke my ribs and strangled me until Tanner showed up, but I'm fine now. Well, mostly. My ribs still hurt a little but they're nearly better."

Anger bursts through his stare. "You should have told me that things were getting this bad. If I knew you were in danger, I would have arranged to come home sooner."

"You and I both know it doesn't work like that," I remind him, walking around him and right into Tanner's arms. "Besides, I had Tanner hanging around and fortunately for me, the big asshole can't resist me."

Damien shakes his head, watching the two of us together. "I don't like this."

"You don't have to like it," I tell him. "But for me, you have to respect it. Tanner is … well, he's kind of everything to me. I love him, and it'd mean the world to me if you could get to know each other while you're here. There's a big party after the wedding and you'll get a chance to meet everyone I've gotten to know in Bradford, and I promise you, once you see past all the bullshit, you'll see that this place is really good for me. I have real friends here, people who truly care for me. I'm happy … like really freaking happy."

Damien scrunches up his face as he shifts his gaze between me and Tanner. "Shit," he finally sighs before focusing his stare on Tanner. "One wrong move and I'll fuck you up."

"Wouldn't expect anything else," Tanner responds, something serious passing between them.

Damien waits a moment before walking past me toward the door, when he pauses and glances back. "For what it's worth, I'm sorry about what happened to your sister," he says, his lips pressing into a hard line. "If Colby happens to show up while I'm here and you want another go at his ass, count me in. I wouldn't mind getting my hands on that piece of shit too."

"There's a long fucking line," Tanner warns him. "But you're welcome to whatever scraps are left behind when I'm through with him."

Damien watches Tanner a moment longer, his eyes narrowed as he tries to make his mind up about this over-protective, badass guy who I've chosen to care about, then finally, he nods. His eyes soften and the hard line of his lips pulls into a loose smile. "Rough around the edges, but you're not bad. Treat her like a fucking queen and you and I won't have any issues."

And with that, my brother walks away, leaving me to fall right into Tanner's arms and bury my face into his chest. He holds me tight, his hand brushing over my hair. "I'm sorry," he murmurs. "I shouldn't have lost control like that. I promised you that I'd work on my anger, and I let you down. Believe me, the last thing I wanted was to scare you."

I shake my head and glance up at him. "You didn't scare me," I say. "I was just worried about you. I hate not being able to see you or speak to you. I couldn't even text to check in and—"

"Hey," he soothes, moving his hands to my shoulders and holding me back enough to see my face. "I'm here now and I'm fine. Colby is … I don't know. We'll figure it out, but for now, all that matters is that you and Addie are safe."

There's a strange hesitation in his eyes, something hard that I can't quite decipher, but when he blinks and pulls me toward my bed, whatever I saw is gone.

I snuggle in beside him, my head resting against his warm chest. "How was Addie when you got home?" I ask, the weight of everything that happened at the courthouse bringing me down. "Late at night, once Hudson goes home, I hear her crying. The first night, I wasn't sure what to do, so I went over there and just held her hand so she could sleep, and the next night your mom beat me to it. But I just … I hate that this is happening to her. She's so broken and I don't know how to help."

"I know," he says, his tone thick with pain. "Addie is strong, and I think with the right therapist and good friends around her, she's going to be alright. That fear will eventually wear off and, once it does, she'll be ready to face the world again."

"Or at least until we put Colby in the ground."

Tanner's arms tighten around me, a silent confirmation of my words. "He won't get away with it," Tanner murmurs, his voice so low I have to strain to hear him. "Even if it costs me my whole fucking world."

"I'm with you, Tanner. There's nothing you could do that will make me walk away now. Especially when it comes to protecting the people you love."

Tanner lets out a breath, his fingers gently moving across my skin. "If only it were that easy."

CHAPTER 29

Brielle

Slight movement beneath me pulls me out of my sleep and my gaze locks on the clock across the room. 2:30 a.m.

A soft groan rumbles through my chest and I close my eyes again, determined to get back to sleep. I don't do well with sleepless nights, especially on nights where the little sleep I had was broken and restless. The only thing that even made it possible to close my eyes was knowing that Tanner is out of that jail cell.

We spent most of our afternoon with Addison and Hudson, just trying to give her some semblance of a normal life. They watched movies and fucked around while I tried to concentrate on my homework, but that all went to shit when Riley and the twins pulled up and it somehow turned into a Wednesday afternoon rager. Hell, I suppose it doesn't really matter what it turned into as long as it managed to put a smile on Addison's face and got her mind off her rapist walking free. The same could be said for Tanner.

It took nearly two movies and having to listen to Riley explaining in explicit detail about his latest sexual conquest before I could convince Tanner to let me clean up his knuckles. He had a shower when he got home and did the boy version of first aid on them following that, but let's be honest, he did a shitty job.

Tanner talked shit with the boys, and it didn't go unnoticed that the topic of his lock-up went unmentioned, though something tells me that was intentional. Tanner isn't a massive talker when it comes to discussing his feelings or the shitty things that happen to him. He'd prefer to lock it all down and move on, but I can't help but notice how distant he's felt all afternoon. Those few days in the police cell have scared him and, right now, I have no idea how deeply that runs. I don't know if it was all that time being alone with his thoughts, or if something happened while he was there, but seeing him this rattled and not knowing why is killing me. He'll talk to me when he's ready, though. Until then, I won't push him.

I feel that same movement beneath me and my head shifts on Tanner's chest before I nuzzle into him again. His arm tightens around my waist, holding me closer, and a soft moan slips from between my lips. There's simply nothing better than this. I could lay with Tanner Morgan every moment until forever and be the happiest girl who ever lived.

"You awake?" His soft rumbled tone flows through my dim room, nothing but the moonlight shining in through the open window I've always refused to close. You know, unless Tanner specifically did something that would have me yanking the blinds closed faster than Riley jumping at the chance to get his dick wet.

"Mmhmm," I murmur, hitching my thigh up over his hip.

There's a slight pause before his amused tone fills my room once again. "Interesting."

Huh? Interesting? What the hell is interesting about being awake in the middle of the night?

Pulling my head up off his chest, I look up at him and my heart leaps right out of my chest, embarrassment crippling me. A smirk pulls across his lips, and I know exactly what's on his mind as he holds not one, but two of my super-secret friends who live in the bottom drawer of my bedside table.

"Who would have known you were such a deviant little animal when fucking yourself?"

My face smooshes back into his chest, my cheeks flaming to the point of pain. Gripping the blanket, I pull it right up over my head, the embarrassment knowing no bounds, even more so when he presses the tiny little button on the vibrator and the soft buzzing sound fills the air. "Oh my God. Kill me now."

Tanner laughs and tears the blanket straight back off me, sleep completely forgotten. "Don't you dare hide from this," he says, adjusting me on the bed so that my back is flat on the mattress, and he kneels between my legs, looking down at me. "I want to see how you use them."

"What?" I question, my eyes widening while trying to remain quiet. After all, this isn't exactly a conversation I want the whole house to overhear. "No way."

"Come on, Killer. Don't try and tell me you're shy all of a sudden."

Biting down on my lip, I groan as his thigh grinds against my clit. "I … I don't even really use those ones anymore," I mutter, watching as he presses his finger to the tip of the vibrator, feeling the way it gently sucks.

His brow arches, knowing damn well what I would use that bad boy for. "Oh yeah?" he rumbles, his voice thick with desire as his eyelids drop, becoming hooded and telling me exactly what's on his mind. "Why not?"

My hips rock, a soft ache building between my legs as the corner of my lip kicks up into an excited grin. Heat floods me, and I can't help but wonder if I have the nerve to follow through with this, but then, if I can record myself getting off, surely I can do this too. "Because the pink one is better."

He drops the vibrator, and immediately dives for my bedside drawer. I drop my hands over my face, listening to the way he rifles through my vast collection. "Well, well," he says a moment later, dropping the cool toys against my bare waist. "I think this is going to be our best night yet."

Tanner peels my hands from my face and pins my wrists above my head, his body pressing down over mine and squishing the toys between us. His lips brush against my throat in a seductive tease and I tilt my head back, wanting more.

A soft sigh slips from between my lips and I close my eyes as he works his way up my throat. Shivers trail over my skin as he reaches the sensitive place below my ear, and I can't help but turn into him, needing his lips on mine. Tanner kisses me deeply and reaches up with his other hand, and it's not until my wrists are completely bound to my headboard that I realize what he was doing.

My eyes widen just a fraction as he pulls back from me, his gaze shifting over my body and noticing the way my nipples pebble beneath the sheer fabric of my tank. I pull against my wrist, testing its durability, and quickly realize just how screwed I am. Tanner smirks as he watches me, and I grin back at him. "Pick up a few kinks while in the slammer, huh?"

He laughs before reaching for my sheer tank and tearing it right down the center, the two fragile slips of fabric falling to my sides. "The only kink I've got is for you," he mutters darkly as his fingers trail down my ribs and back to the toys patiently waiting on my waist. "I changed my mind. As curious as I am about seeing how you please yourself, you and I both know I don't have the patience to sit back and watch."

My heart races as my gaze shifts down my body to the selection of toys he's gathered, and my brow arches. There's my favorite pink vibrator, my girthy dildo, a diamond-studded glass butt plug, and just to be on the safe side, a small tub of candy-scented lube.

Fuck. I'm in trouble.

Tanner grins at me as though reading my mind, and I don't think I've ever seen him so excited. "Just say the word and I'll put it all away," he says, knowing damn well I'm not about to back down from this, but he should know a combination like that is a guarantee that this is going to be quick.

"I'll make you a deal," I tell him, moaning as his fingers move down to cup my pussy, gently squeezing and making me gasp. "You can do *whatever* you want to me, but you'll be tied up just like this next and the same rules apply. *Whatever I want.*"

Tanner presses his lips into a hard line, considering my offer before gripping the dildo by the shaft. "You're not planning on shoving one of these up my ass, are you?"

"Do you want one of those shoved up your ass?"

His gaze narrows and I can't tell if he's trying to figure out what's going through my mind or if he's truly needing a moment to consider his response. "No ..."

"You don't seem so sure about that."

"Oh, I'm sure. You can fuck me any way you want just not ... that."

I struggle to hold back a laugh and as he watches me, it takes only a moment to realize I was screwing with him. He leans over me, hovering on his elbows as he keeps just far enough away so I can't reach up and collect his lips in mine. "You better watch yourself, Killer," he says, his hand moving down my body and slipping beneath the waistband of my sleep shorts. "You're at my mercy now, and you know I don't play fair."

His lips drop to mine, and he kisses me deeply just as his fingers push between my folds, gently grazing my clit. I gasp into his mouth but he's relentless. He does it again, this time applying pressure and sending a wave of pleasure rocking through my body. He explores deeper, pushing two thick fingers inside me, gently curving and massaging my walls.

Tanner pulls back just enough so that his lips hover above mine. "So fucking ready for me," he whispers before raising himself up until he's kneeling between my legs once again. His fingers pull back, catching on my sleep shorts and dragging them down my legs until I'm bare for him.

Tanner pushes in closer, his thighs forcing mine wider as hunger blazes in his eyes. He picks up the small tub of lube and begins uncapping it as his eyes come back to mine. "Are you sure about this?" he questions, his fingers dipping inside and scooping out just enough.

Biting down on my lip, I nod, the anticipation like nothing I've ever known. I need this. I need him, but most of all, I need to let go of everything as he claims every inch of my body as his own. I need to feel his touch, his desire, his pleasure. I need it all. Grinning up at him, I let him see the fire in my eyes. "Do your worst."

Tanner groans as he places the lube down on my bedside table and his gaze sails down my body, stopping on my needy cunt. He rubs the lube between his fingers before bringing it down over me, starting at my clit and slowly moving lower. He bypasses my pussy and I suck in a breath as he ventures right down to my ass.

Tanner's fingers tease me there, gently pressing against me as his other hand finds my clit, his thumb rubbing lazy circles and making me squirm. "Oh, fuck, Tanner," I breathe, already panting despite knowing just how much more is yet to come.

His soft, knowing laugh rumbles through his chest and speaks right to my soul.

Tanner doesn't let up, and when I start pushing against him, he scoops up the small glass plug and trails his fingers over it, spreading the candy lube and sending a thrill shooting deep in my core. His eyes come back to mine, and I watch as he moves the plug low enough that I can no longer see what he's doing, but damn it, I can sure as fuck feel it.

The cool glass tip presses against my ass, and as he continues rubbing lazy circles over my clit, he slowly pushes it inside me. My eyes roll, welcoming the dull burn until it morphs into nothing but undeniable pleasure. I suck in a breath, pulling against the binds as my back arches off the bed. "Holy shit," I pant, my chest rising and falling with rapid movements.

Tanner's tongue rolls over his bottom lip, the hunger in his eyes only making everything so much better. He presses against the diamond at my ass, and I gasp as it softly moves within me. "Fucking hell," he mutters, watching just how worked up I am. "You ready for more?"

I tug against the binds again and nod, eager for anything he's willing to give.

Keeping his torturous pace on my clit, he takes hold of the girthy dildo and presses the tip to my lips. "Open wide."

Not one to disappoint, I open my mouth and he slowly pushes it inside. My tongue roams over it, making it wet, and as he hits the back of my throat, Tanner groans, needing to adjust his straining cock inside his sweats. Satisfied that the silicone dildo is ready to go, he pulls it from my mouth and brings it down between my legs, letting it drop against my clit.

I gasp but it quickly turns into a needy moan as he uses the cool rubber to press against me, dragging it down through my folds before pushing it back to my clit. "Oh God."

"You like that, Killer?" he says, doing it again.

My pussy clenches and I ache for more, desperately needing Tanner to push it inside me, to fill every fucking inch of me. Tanner plays with it, teasing me relentlessly, and having way too much fun with it. I squirm and groan until finally, he takes pity on my needy body, and I feel the tip of the thick dildo at my entrance.

Tanner's thumb presses back to my clit, rubbing slow, torturous circles as he pushes the thick head of the dildo inside. He catches his breath, his eyes glued to my pussy as I push down the bed, desperate to take more.

He pushes further, inch by inch until the girthy motherfucker is as deep as it can possibly go, and only then does the real fun start. He draws it back, in and out, watching me squirm and clench around it as my body accepts its fate. It's got nothing on the real thing, but the fact that it's Tanner making me feel this way does something to me I wasn't expecting.

My body is right on edge and with each passing second, it only gets better. Then just when I think I'm reaching my limit, Tanner picks up the little pink vibrator and the soft buzz sounds through my room.

"Oh, fuck," I pant.

This little vibrator is the best thing known to womankind. It can get me off in 2.5 seconds flat, but add it to everything else Tanner's doing to me, and it's lethal. I won't be able to take it. It's too much.

The soft suction comes down on my clit, and I cry out before forcing myself to bite down on my lip. The intensity is so great that tears fill my eyes. I've never felt anything so powerful, so damn intense. The vibrations rock through me like never before, pulsing right through my core and sending molten lava shooting through my veins.

Tanner's eyes are hooded, watching the show as though he's never seen anything so erotic, and when a pained groan tears from the back of his throat, I almost come undone. "Fuck, Killer," Tanner rumbles. "I need to see you come."

A tear of pleasure sails down my cheek, and I pull against my binds just as Tanner levels up on that fucking vibrator. I tip my head back as my body reaches its limit. I arch up off the bed, a low groan tearing from deep in my chest as my world explodes around me.

Electricity shoots through my body, lighting my world on fire as I clench my eyes and cry out. My pussy convulses around the silicone cock as the vibrator goes to town on my clit. "Holy fuck," I pant, my orgasm completely claiming my body, shooting right through to my fingertips as my pussy contracts like never before.

Tanner doesn't let up, draining every last ounce of pleasure from my body, claiming it all just as I knew he would. He turns up the level on the vibrator one more time and my already intense orgasm becomes something beyond comprehension.

I yank against my binds, more tears spilling from my eyes, and only when I come down from my high does Tanner release me from the sweet agony. He slowly pulls the dildo from my shattered pussy before turning off the vibrator and discarding it beside me on the bed.

A grin tears across his handsome face and as he leans down, leaving the plug right where it is, his fingers effortlessly work the binds at my wrists, freeing me to throw them around his neck.

Tanner's lips come down on mine, kissing me with raw passion. "I fucking love you, Killer," he murmurs against my lips, his straining cock more than ready to be freed from the confines of his sweatpants.

"I know," I murmur, shifting to the side of his throat, letting my lips brush against his warm skin. "But I'm more interested in tying your ass up so I can show you just how much I love you back."

"Changed my mind," he murmurs. "After what I just saw, there's no way in hell you're about to tie me up. I need my hands on you."

I shake my head, pushing against his shoulder and forcing his back to the mattress. I awkwardly climb on top of him, regretting the decision not to remove the plug. Knowing my luck, I'll probably sneeze and accidentally shoot it across my room like a bullet.

I straddle his hips, feeling just how rock hard he is through his pants. "A deal is a deal, Mr. Morgan. Now let me tie those hands before I have no choice but to leave you high and dry. It's my turn now."

Tanner grins and without hesitation, he offers me his wrists like a lamb to the slaughter, and I take them eagerly, more than ready to rock his world.

CHAPTER 30

Brielle

With every step down the aisle, the stupid song rolls over in my head. I've been inside the biggest church on this side of the country for less than thirty seconds and it's already the most obnoxious thing I've had to endure.

The sheer number of people here is simply ridiculous. Mom must have invited every single person she's ever strolled past in Macy's because there's no way in hell an asshole like Orlando Channing would have this many friends. Enemies? Maybe. Friends? Hell no.

I put one foot in front of the other and keep my stare locked on the rose-petal covered aisle, the only thing getting me through this is the promise of booze at the after party … and Tanner. He promised some wickedly delicious things if I managed to get through this without insulting anyone. Though he didn't specify the terms of our arrangement, and seeing as though he can't read my mind, I figure he'll never know about the insults I've been throwing down all day inside my head.

The music sounds like a bird screeching. My dress is itchy and looks stupid. And the off-white of Mom's dress reminds me of a dirty, peeled potato.

Ahhh, fuck. That feels good to say it all out loud … from inside my head.

I can't lie, no matter how frustrated I am about this wedding and how strained my relationship with Mom has been, there's no denying that she actually looks stunning, you know, apart from the dirty potato factor. I always knew she'd make a gorgeous bride one day. I just never expected, or hoped it to be like this. But if she's truly happy … which I honestly doubt, then I'll be happy for her. Or in the very least, try to be.

I try to channel my inner Dory and *just keep swimming,* but this shit is near impossible. It's a sham of a wedding and a waste of all these people's time. This marriage has no foundation, no trust, no real love, and I still stand by the assumption that Orlando is going to tire of Mom at some point and send us packing all the way back to

Hope Falls. Besides, they're already technically married. This whole production is nothing but a show to rub in the faces of those Mom has always been belittled by.

Orlando watches me from the top of the aisle, and I've never felt so uncomfortable. His gaze roams over my body in this stupid form-fitting dress. My tits are on full display and every curve of my body can be seen in explicit detail. If this were my high-school prom, maybe I'd be excited about wearing this dress, I might even feel sexy in it, but here and now? Not even a little bit. Orlando's stare is a prime example of why.

Tanner sits right up front, and the moment I stepped out into the aisle, my eyes found his. A wide, excited grin tore across his face, but the moment he saw just how uncomfortable I felt, his hands balled into tight fists and his lips pressed into a hard line. He doesn't want to be here either, but there was no way he was going to let me attend this shit alone. Hell, all of our friends are here, their parents included.

I should clarify—anyone with money who lives within comfortable driving limits of Bradford is here.

Still so uncomfortable, my gaze shifts back to Tanner, and I take a shaky breath, loving how he has the ability to calm me with nothing more than his presence. Only a few more steps and I'll be at the top of the aisle. I'm assuming I have to stand to the side like they do in all the movies but, considering I skipped out on yesterday's rehearsal, I could be wrong. I can't say I've exactly been to a wedding before.

Three steps to go.

Don't fall. Don't fall. Don't fall.

Two steps.

One.

I made it without turning myself into the laughingstock of Bradford. Bonus.

The music changes and I do my best to force a smile across my face, but even a blind man would be able to see just how uncomfortable I am standing up here. So, I do what any girl would do and focus on the six-foot-four piece of tattooed man meat in the front row. Tanner went all out in a five-piece suit that rivals that of David Beckham at the royal wedding. My gaze roams over his body, taking in the way his shoulders and biceps strain against the designer material. One flex from Tanner would have him busting out of that suit Hulk style, and I fucking love it.

He winks. He fucking winks.

That rat bastard.

Does he want me wet in front of all these people? It's a silk dress. Does he know nothing? Though, I suppose I can't blame the guy. I knew what I was getting into when I was getting close to him. He's an animal, and it wouldn't be right to hold something against him that he has absolutely no control over. It's just the way he is, and when it's just us behind closed doors, that animalistic part of him is one of my favorite traits.

Mom nears the front of the church, and I do what I can to pay attention. After all, it's one thing looking like the laughingstock of this ridiculous wedding, but it's another to appear as though I'm not happy for her. I mean, I'm not. I couldn't be less happy, but I'd look like a complete bitch if anyone in the pews knew that.

Damien walks her down the aisle, doing his part in giving her away, and I bite my lip, forcing myself to keep a straight face. He looks like a penguin with a wedgie in that tux, and judging by the stoic, irritated look on his face, he damn well knows it.

Don't make eye contact. Don't make eye contact. Don't make eye contact.

My big brother looks directly at me, and I lose it. A loud snorting laugh bursts from deep in my throat and my eyes bug out of my head, trying to quickly mask it as a cough, but judging by the wicked stare I receive from Mom, I'm doing a really shitty job at it. Damien smirks. He'd do anything to appear as the golden child, but lately, that wouldn't be hard.

They get to the very top of the aisle and Mom stops as the priest and Orlando step forward. "Who gives this woman to be married to this man?"

Damien clears his throat, his head held high for the one job he has throughout this whole ordeal. "I do."

The priest nods for a job well done, and I watch as my mother's hand is physically taken from Damien's arm and placed into Orlando's waiting hands. They smile at one another, but I've never seen anything so forced in my life.

They move back into the prime position as Damien slips off to the side, taking a seat beside Tanner. I'm not going to lie, over the past few days, Tanner and Damien have spent far too much time together, and as much as I love that they're getting along and seem to be really chill with each other, I also kind of hate it. The two of them together can only mean trouble for me, and something tells me that trouble is heading my way tonight.

Mom holds out her bouquet of flowers for me and I quickly take them, freeing her other hand so that she can face Orlando directly and fully participate in this sham wedding.

The priest gets started and I quickly zone out.

There's some big spiel about the meaning of marriage and how two people coming together in the name of love is the purest form of blah, blah, blah … The dude drones on and I can't say I'm surprised. I wouldn't put it past Mom to pay him extra just for the opportunity to stand at the top of the aisle with all eyes on her for longer.

They move on to the vows and I dig my nails into the palm of my hand, giving me something to focus on while listening to their bullshit. Jensen hands over the rings and Orlando does his part perfectly, slipping the ring onto Mom's boney finger as though she hasn't already been wearing it for the past few weeks.

Mom is next, and she says her vows perfectly, loud enough for the church to hear but not arrogant as though she's giving some kind of speech. It's beautiful … fake, but beautiful. Hell, it even forces a smile across my face.

The whole congregation seems to notice just how deep her vows are, everyone but Orlando—whose gaze has shifted toward the front row. My brows furrow and I follow his hard stare to Tanner who's looking back at him with a disgusted glare. Tanner never liked Orlando but considering everything that went down with Addison's case, that mutual dislike of one another has morphed into something so toxic it's honestly terrifying. But I can't lie, I'm right there with Tanner. Orlando deserves to be despised. He's a self-centered piece of shit with no moral compass. I bet he didn't even lose a wink of sleep after setting Colby free. Hell, if anything, he probably slept better knowing there was one more win added to his long list of bullshit cases.

If Tanner hadn't socked him in the jaw, I would have tried myself. Though one thing is for sure, I haven't stopped hearing about it all week, and from the look of it, someone was put in charge of concealing the remaining bruises for today.

A smug smirk pulls at the corners of Orlando's lips, which only has the hatred in Tanner's eyes bursting from the seams. His hands ball into tight fists to the point Damien even notices something is up, but not a moment later, Orlando glances back at his new bride and the hostility fades from the air.

My brows furrow, unsure what the fuck just happened. All I know is that it was far too intense to be nothing more than mutual hatred for each other. Something else is going on here.

Sensing my stare, Tanner glances my way, and I can't help but notice his desperate attempt to calm himself. He takes a few slow breaths while staring deep into my eyes, and on the third exhale, his hands finally begin to unclench on his thighs.

"What was that about?" I mouth, my curiosity far too intrigued to wait until after the ceremony to dig into this one.

Tanner just shakes his head and gives me an encouraging smile, a smile that's faker than the Louis Vuitton bag Mom's been getting around with for the past few years. Though, I wouldn't be surprised if that's been updated to the real thing since moving here. After all, she wouldn't be seen dead around here with a fake.

Not wanting to push Tanner, especially not here and now, I let it go and try to focus on the rest of the ceremony, only the nagging feeling that something bigger is going on won't quit circling my mind. Tanner has been off since being released from police custody on Wednesday. There's been something on his mind, something he can't seem to shake, and I can't help but wonder if Orlando had something to do with it. It just doesn't make sense though. Apart from Addison's case and the fact they're neighbors, the two have absolutely nothing to do with one another.

The wedding drones on and I have to keep shifting myself from one foot to the other as my feet begin to fall asleep. Would it be rude to ask Mom how much longer? I mean, she's so wrapped up in her fancy ceremony that she might just respond on autopilot, not even noticing what it is I'm really asking.

Nah, too risky.

After what feels like a millennium, the priest announces that Orlando may kiss his bride, and the gathered crowd cheers as Mom leans in to receive nothing more than a quick peck on the lips. My brow arches and I do what I can to wipe the look off my face. If my man kisses me like that on my wedding day, I'm castrating him right then and there. I want to be wooed. I want him to kiss me as though he's been waiting his whole life for that one special moment. I want our priest to clear his throat because our kiss is so steamy that it's inappropriate for a church wedding. But most of all, I want that man to be Tanner.

I know we're only eighteen and the reality of us getting married is so far away in our future, but when it comes to him, I'm certain. He is where my life is going, and despite only knowing each other for a few short months, I've never been so sure of something.

Mom and Orlando go to sign the wedding certificate and I stand by the signing table with Jensen, both of us watching and listening to what we have to do while the congregation falls into murmured chatter. "So, it's official," Jensen says. "You're my stepsister."

Rolling my eyes, I smirk up at the guy. "It was official the second they got hitched in Paris, you idiot."

His brows furrow, thinking it over before grinning wider. "Oh yeah. I think I knew that," he says, grinning back at me. "I suppose this means I officially have to be nice to you."

My eyes widen in horror. "No," I say. "Please don't. It's already weird enough. I'd prefer if you just keep going about your days pretending I don't exist. But like, don't be a complete ass. If you're making food, make some for me."

Jensen scoffs, making it known exactly what he thinks of that plan, but before he gets a chance to shut me down, I'm asked to sign as a witness to this sham, and being the ever pleasant daughter I am, I do exactly what's asked of me. Jensen moves in next, and after an excruciating few minutes, we're all back where we started at the top of the aisle.

The guests quieten and then finally, the priest announces that the ceremony is over.

Mom squeals with delight and throws her arms around me, crushing me to her body. "Oh, wasn't that just spectacular?"

My heart races and I'm struck with an intense wave of emotion as I hold my mother close, soaking in every moment of her affection. She used to hug me like this every single day, but I don't think she's even touched me since the day we moved to Bradford. Except for, you know, the slapping incident.

She pulls away from me as Damien steps into our side and she quickly falls into his arms as Orlando shakes the hands of the people sitting in the front row of his side. Tanner gets up to join me, and I can't help but notice how Jensen hangs back, not comfortable with such a social setting.

Tanner's arm curls around my waist as he pulls me in close. "You okay?" he questions.

I lift my gaze to him and his thumb swipes across my face, wiping a tear off my cheek, a tear I hadn't even realized had fallen. "Yeah," I murmur. "It was just nice having her all to myself again, if only for a few seconds."

He drops his lips to mine in a gentle, lingering kiss. "I know."

Having embraced her two children, Mom shuffles over to Orlando, and just like that, they make the traditional walk back up the aisle. We follow behind and row by row, the wedding guests file out behind us until we're standing out in the afternoon sunshine.

Mom immediately pulls me back into her arms and once again, I soak it up like a child starved of affection. "You were great," she boasts, pure happiness in her tone, but it's almost impossible to tell if that happiness comes from the love she feels for her new husband or the fact that she just got to experience the wedding of her dreams. "Thank you. I couldn't have done this all without you, my love."

"Thanks, Mom," I murmur, struggling to keep hold of my emotions. "But it was all you."

She squeezes just a little harder before being dragged away by the crowd, leaving Tanner and me with Jensen and Damien, the four of us more than ready to get the hell out of here.

CHAPTER 31

Brielle

The tequila burns its way down my throat as I sit on Tanner's lap, his arms twisted around my waist, despite my brother's disapproving stare. I've had one too many drinks to be able to tell if his disapproval comes from the way Tanner so boldly holds me or the sheer amount of alcohol making its way into my bloodstream. Considering Tanner hasn't let go of me since the moment he got out of those handcuffs, I'm inclined to go with option number two.

Mom was nice enough to allow me to invite all my friends to the reception and even nicer to allow me to sit with them, rather than be stuck sitting at the bridal table, and so far, shit is going south real fast. Sure, it was a nice gesture on her part to allow this, but honestly, it was a stupid decision. Free booze, food, and close proximity between all of us means nothing but trouble.

The bar has threatened to cut us off four times, and if it weren't for the fact I'm part of the bridal party and the bride's daughter, they probably would have followed through with that threat.

I've been dreading this wedding since that e-vite lit up my screen, but having everyone here has made it bearable. Not to mention, Jax and Riley are the best kind of entertainment I've ever seen, much better than the fancy string quartet that's been sending everyone to an early grave.

"Holy fuck," Ilaria says, slamming down her third shot glass for the night as she sits way too close to Damien for my comfort. "That one burned."

Damien grins at her and her cheeks instantly flush, and just to rub salt in the wound, he then turns his stupid grin on me. He doesn't say a word, but I know exactly what's on his mind. "Tell me, Ilaria," he says, leaning back in his seat and turning his body to face her, his stupid penguin suit long gone and replaced with something a little more his style. "Are you hitched with any of these guys?"

Ilaria laughs. "Ha. They wish," she says, disgusted with the very thought. "Don't get me wrong, Riley's had me on my knees a few times more than he ever should, but then, I think he's had just about every woman in this room like that."

Riley grins from across the table, all too proud of himself, and I pinch a green bean off Tanner's plate before launching it at the idiot. "That's nothing to boast about, Riley," I laugh. "You're practically a walking STD."

"Got that right," Arizona laughs, reaching for her glass of champagne while trying to avoid looking directly at Jax who hasn't stopped staring at her all night. Hell, he hasn't stopped since finding out about her crush on him at the lake. Only it's not a flattering kind of stare, it's more … stumped. It's been a week since our camping trip, and he still hasn't been able to wrap his head around it. Though that hasn't stopped him from getting down and dirty with her, but the moment they're done, he goes back into his catatonic staring state. It won't be long until Arizona breaks though. There's only so much of his bullshit she can handle before she's forced to put the fucker in his place.

Riley shakes his head, leaning back in his seat. "Puuuuu-lease," he says, dragging the word out as he hooks his arm over the back of Chanel's chair, only to have Logan immediately shove it off. "I'm so clean I'm practically sterile."

Tanner laughs, the sound vibrating right through to my chest. "That's not the flex you think it is, man."

Riley's brows furrow, trying to figure out where the hell he went wrong as Damien starts chatting up Ilaria.

I can't help but smile. I love moments like this. Everyone is dressed up and looking incredible. They're all chilled and getting along. Even Chanel and Logan are getting along. Though, I wouldn't put it past Logan to pick a fight with her soon. After all, she looks incredible in her silver silk gown, and I can see the need in his eyes to tear it off her with his teeth. He's a fucking animal, but Chanel wouldn't have it any other way.

A hand lands on the back of Tanner's chair and the way his back stiffens has a chill sailing through my body. "I trust everyone is having a good time?" Orlando's tone cuts through our table, cutting off every last conversation.

My jaw clenches and my fingers twitch for the bottle of tequila, though I can't work out if it's to drink or to use as a weapon. Tanner stands, shoving his chair back to come face to face with Orlando, his arm locked around my waist as he settles me on my feet, keeping me at his side and away from Orlando.

They become locked in a heated stare, and I can't help but glance across the table to Addison. Hudson's hand is firmly on her, and judging by the look on her face, she's not happy about Orlando's proximity. Hell, I'm still surprised she showed up, but Hudson dragged her along, promising that a night out with friends was exactly what she needed. I agreed with him—right up until this moment.

"Walk away," Tanner warns. His hand shakes with rage against my waist, making it damn clear something more is going on between them. Damien takes notice immediately and pushes out of his chair. I don't know what Damien's been able to piece together, but he's intuitive, and more than that, he's protective. And right now, he'll have our backs despite not knowing what the hell is going on.

Orlando laughs, arrogantly holding his arms out wide. "This is my party, Morgan. If you don't like my presence here, then I'd be happy to show you the door."

Tanner's jaw clenches as something passes between them, and Tanner backs down, stepping away and reaching for his drink. He throws down what's left in his glass before loosening his grip around my waist. "Whatever," he says. "This party blows anyway."

Damien catches my eye, his brows furrowed, unsure what's going on. I shrug my shoulders, right there with him, all too aware of the way Logan, Jax, Riley, and Hudson watch the show, each one of them more than ready to bust out of their seats. The fact that Orlando is the groom isn't enough to deter them from beating the shit out of him, especially after the hell he's put Addison through. Orlando better watch himself; he's playing a dangerous game and these guys won't hesitate to put him in the ground.

"That's right, keep drinking my drinks," Orlando tells Tanner, trying to exercise some kind of power over him. "Enjoy your night … Who knows when it might all come to an end."

My gaze snaps up to Orlando and I shove myself between them, my ass pushing Tanner back a step. "What the hell is that supposed to mean?"

Orlando simply laughs as Damien moves in closer, more than ready to step in if need be. "Oh, sweet girl. I don't think I got a chance to tell you how breathtaking you look in your dress. Simply stunning. You should consider taking care of yourself more often. A pretty little thing like you would be a grand prize."

Disgust filters through my veins. I've never gotten a creepy vibe from Orlando until this very minute, and I sure as hell don't appreciate it, and apparently Damien doesn't either. He shoves a hand against Orlando's chest, forcing him away from me. "Where the fuck do you get off talking to my sister like that?" he spits, his tone low and threatening, reminding me of just how lethal he can be. After all, you don't grow up in Hope Falls without escaping unscathed. "She's a fucking kid."

"A kid?" Orlando says, his eyes flicking back to me. "I hardly think so. Look at her. She's a woman."

Tanner's hand tightens in mine to the point of physical pain, and I'm forced to pull my hand free. I step forward, deciding to handle this on my own before Tanner or Damien turns this wedding into something else entirely. "Listen here, you disgusting piece of shit," I seethe, speaking low enough for the rest of our table to struggle to hear. "You ever leer at me like a piece of meat again, and I will personally put you in the ground. No woman in her right mind would ever want to be with you, so don't fool yourself into thinking you're anything special. My mom is fucked in the head for allowing this bullshit to go on."

"Careful now," he warns, moving in closer, his dark eyes eating me up like his next meal. "You're toeing the line of a dangerous game you're not prepared to play."

I scoff. "Don't fool yourself into a false sense of security. After the shit you pulled during Addison's case, I have everything I need to end your career with nothing more than a flick of my wrist. Asking a witness to provide a false alibi … don't get me wrong, I'm no lawyer, but I know a criminal offense when I see one. Tell me, how many lawyers are out there who'd be happy to take a stand against you? How many victims still have rapists and murderers walking free because of the shady bullshit you pulled during their cases? How many dirty judges, cops, and payoffs? Don't fool yourself, old man. One statement from me is all it will take to get the ball rolling on your demise, and I would have a whole army at my back making it happen. When I am through with you, the whole world will know how much of a dirty fraud you really are. Your name will be destroyed, and you'll be the laughing stock of the twenty-first century. Not to mention, every case you've ever worked will have to be reopened. All of those assholes you allowed to walk free will be locked up, right beside you."

Orlando glares, rage burning in his eyes. "You don't want to play with fire, little girl. You've got far more to lose than I ever could."

His gaze flicks over my shoulder to Tanner and my back stiffens. I'm fine with him coming for me, but Tanner and his family have already suffered through enough. If Orlando wants to play, then we'll play, but the people I love are off limits.

"Brielle," my mother's shrill panic tears through the tension. Her eyes are wide as she glances around us, making sure none of her guests are aware of the bullshit going on here. "What the hell has gotten into you? This is my wedding day. If you cannot be pleasant, then you will be asked to leave."

I suck in a faux-horrified gasp. "And leave you with the embarrassment of an empty table?" I say, watching as her expression shifts from horror to threatening before deciding that enough is enough. "On second thought, that's exactly what we're going to do. I hope you enjoy the rest of your night, Mom, but one of us needs to have at least a shred of self respect, so I'm out."

As if on cue, every last person at the table stands, and the relief on Addison's face is like nothing I've ever seen before. I owe her for making the trip out here. It couldn't have been easy to sit through that, but with Hudson at her side, she almost seems invincible.

Mom gasps as every last person from my table strides past her, and it's sad because her horror comes from the thought of an empty table rather than her daughter walking out … and I suppose that means her son as well. Though to be fair, it's late. We made it through dinner and dessert, had a bunch of free drinks, and even danced a while. Most people will probably start to leave soon anyway. Call us the trendsetters for the night. Hell, everyone else is probably just waiting for someone else to leave so they don't have to be the first.

Without even a backward glance, our whole group moves out through the side exit, and I can't help but notice how Tanner's other hand is curled securely around the neck of the tequila bottle while everyone else still holds their glasses. "Am I the only one who didn't think to bring my drink?" I ask, more than frustrated with myself.

Tanner laughs and throws his arm over my shoulder. "You don't think I brought this tequila for me, do you? I figured you'd need it after that bullshit with Channing."

I groan and press my body closer to his. "Can you believe that asshole? Like who does he think he is talking to me like that? I'm his stepdaughter for fuck's sake. His wedding to my mom isn't even over, and he's already searching for his next piece of ass."

"Don't worry about him," Tanner tells me. "He'll be dead before he even thinks about coming for you. Besides, I don't like to share, especially with assholes like that."

I nod, a heaviness seeping into my chest. "Tanner …" I say slowly, worrying my bottom lip, trying to figure out how to broach the topic. "Are you alright? You've been off ever since getting out of police custody, and I can't help but think it has something to do with him. You'd tell me if you were in trouble, right?"

Tanner swallows and gives me an encouraging smile before pressing a kiss to my temple. "It's all good, babe," he says. "Channing came to have a *talk* while I was in lock-up. He said things, I said things. It wasn't pretty, but it's nothing you need to worry about. I'm fine."

"You sure?"

He nods as a wicked grin stretches across his face. "He's just salty about his face," he says. "But I get it. I can only imagine taking a hit like that would be embarrassing. Personally, I wouldn't know. No one's been able to land a punch like that on me."

Riley snorts a laugh from behind us. "Buuuuuuuuullshiiiiiiiiiiiiiiiit," he sings. "Maybe you've had a few too many drinks and it's fucking with your memory. I can recall at least ten times I laid you out."

Tanner spins, walking backward to take in Riley behind us. "Oh sure," Tanner scoffs. "Assuming your idea of a good punch is nothing but a little love tap. I've seen grannies at Walmart throw down better than you."

Riley tips his chin up, his eyes narrowing on Tanner as we hijack the venue's courtesy bus. "Is that a challenge, bro?" he questions. "Don't tease me. If you're throwing it down, you better be ready for me to pick it right back up. I'll knock your ass out cold. Just say the word."

"You're on, motherfucker," Tanner says. "Let's settle this. Here and now. I'm down."

"Hold up," I say, throwing my hands up between them, though despite their fighting words, there's not an ounce of tension between them. They're fucking around, but I wouldn't put it past them to start throwing punches just for the sake of seeing who has the biggest set of balls. "If we're doing this, we're doing it Jell-O wrestling style, and there better be baby oil involved."

Logan's face scrunches in disgust. "Awww, come on, Bri," he groans as we all pile onto the bus that was meant to take the wedding guests back to the five-star hotel Orlando booked out. "You made it weird."

I give him a guilty smirk, unable to stop the laughter rumbling through my chest. "My bad."

Jax pulls out a wad of cash and has a private word with the bus driver, and within the space of twenty minutes, the bus is pulling to a stop outside the twins' mega-mansion.

"What the fuck is this place?" Damien mutters, staring up at it with a strange, impressed kind of horror, just as I had when I first saw the place. "Who lives like this?"

"That'd be us," Logan says, clapping him on the back as he jumps down from the bottom step of the bus. "Now, we can either stand here and look at the house, or we can go and get fucked up. Your choice."

Damien nods. "Enough said."

Ilaria takes off to raid one of the many house bars and meets us by the fire pit, her arms overflowing with bottles. She drops them to the table and starts mixing drinks, assuming she's some kind of cocktail goddess, and I'm not surprised to find Damien right by her side.

There's no doubt in my mind that by some point tonight, he'll have her legs wrapped around her own freaking head, and when that time comes, I'll be more than ready to hurl into the pool again.

Ilaria starts handing out drinks and, judging by the smirk across her face, I know this shit is going to be potent. Upon taking my first sip, I realize just how right I am. The mystery mix hits the back of my throat and burns the whole way down, adding to the buzz I've already got from the tequila.

It takes two seconds for Tanner and Riley to get back into their usual bullshit and start knocking each other around while Jax disappears inside. Chanel and Logan start bickering, which I don't doubt will eventually turn into a full blown argument, and Hudson and Addison remain huddled together.

It won't be long until Addison realizes just how lucky she is to have him, though I don't think she's there yet. She's still working through a lot of shit, and it could be years until she's ready, but there's no mistaking the way she searches him out in a room and lights up every time he's near.

With Damien openly hitting on Ilaria, I kick off my heels and move across to the pool before hitching up the bottom of my gown and dangling my feet into the water, narrowly avoiding getting clobbered by Riley and Tanner. Arizona joins me and we talk shit while sipping on our cocktails that I can't figure out if I actually like or not.

We talk for ten minutes before a loud gasp is heard by the firepit, quickly followed by a booming laugh, and I spin around to find Jax, standing in nothing but a cheeky man-thong, his body covered from head to toe in what I can only assume is Vaseline.

Arizona's eyes bug out of her head, but she can't resist the urge to feast her eyes all over his body as the rest of us laugh, my tipsy state almost sending me back into the cold water of the pool.

"What the fuck, man?" Logan says, shaking his head, almost embarrassed by his twin brother, and I'm sure if he weren't so used to Jax's shit by now, he'd probably be dragging his ass back inside.

"So," Jax starts, knowing damn well we all need a thorough explanation, not even an ounce of shame on his handsome face. "I was sitting there, trying to take a dump when I got to thinking; how fast can I get from one end of the house to the other?"

Tanner shakes his head, coming up behind me, curling his arms beneath mine and hauling me up off the edge of the pool before dragging me back to the fire pit. "Yeah, bro, we're going to need more than that," he says. "How the fuck did you make the connection between trying to work out how fast you can go to slapping on a pair of your mom's panties and slathering yourself in lube?"

"Alright," he says, his eyes sparkling with silent laughter. "Hear me out …"

"Shit," Arizona says, coming to join us. "This is going to be good."

Jax goes on as though Arizona didn't say a word. "I figured, lube is slippery shit, right? And clothes, well, they're just slowing me down. So, what if I ran and then slid? I reckon I could beat my time by half."

"Wait," Arizona cuts in. "You didn't really cover yourself in lube, did you? I thought it was baby oil or some shit like that."

Jax winks at her. "Sure fucking did, babe. It's that edible cherry one you like. I stocked up on it after you went wild with it that one time."

"Bullshit."

"You're more than welcome to come and lick me from head to toe if you don't believe me."

Arizona stares back at him, hunger burning in her eyes, and if I weren't so desperate to see the asshole attempt this, I'd already be locking them in his room just so Arizona can get what she's so clearly looking for. "There's no way this is going to work," I tell him. "You'll end up with carpet burns, but like … the tile versions."

"Ahhh, how quick you are to dismiss me, Miss Ashford," he says, the confidence in his eyes knowing no bounds. "If I time this just right, I should be able to slide right across the tiles and into the pool just like how that vibrator came shooting out of Ari." Jax puts his pointer finger in his mouth and then pulls it out, making that stupid *pop* sound as Arizona screams in embarrassment, her hands covering her face.

"JAXON MORGAN!" she screeches as Jax just laughs.

"Come on, babe. You know that's exactly how it happened. You created a whole new definition for the term pocket rocket. It was like a bullet shooting straight from its chamber. If I wasn't paying attention, it would have taken an eye. You were so fucking wet it just like …. swoooooosh," he adds, making sure to add hand gestures, just in case Arizona's humiliation wasn't quite enough.

"I swear to God, Jax. Say one more word about that night and I'm going to strangle you with your own balls."

Jax grins. "Ahhh, cute. It'll be like a little ball sack bowtie. I should have worn it with my suit tonight. Though it would have sucked if I missed any of those naughty little hairs from underneath, you know those annoying ones right in the back that you have to half sumo squat to get to? They would have tickled my chin."

Riley nods, taking this all too seriously. "Amen to that, brother."

Jax nods right back as though this is one of those real issues that men have to face, but before he can go on, Riley is on his feet stripping out of his suit. "Where's the cherry lube? I want in on this shit."

Jax grins and within the space of ten minutes, every single one of us is stripped down to our underwear, our bodies dripping with edible cherry lube as we line up, ready to shoot across the tiles like slippery hot dogs.

Jax and Riley go first and, just as expected, they slide along the tiles like a bunch of naked penguins slipping along the ice only to fall off the edge and plunge deep into the cold water. They laugh like idiots, and as I barge my way through the line for my turn, Tanner hits me with another shot of lube, his hands roaming over my body, spreading it to every inch of skin and making sure to be as thorough as humanly possible. So fucking thorough that he gets me wetter than any pool could, and before I get a chance to slip and slide across the tiles penguin style, he's slipping and sliding us all the way back to the pool house with every intention to slip and slide a little more.

CHAPTER 32

Brielle

"Sorry, kid," Damien says way too early for a Monday morning, his uniform and bag already telling me exactly what he's about to say. "I have to get out of here, otherwise, I'll miss my flight and your bitch ass will be driving me all the way back to Fort Jackson."

"Noooo," I whine, slumping against the kitchen island, my half cut orange completely forgotten. "Do you really have to go so soon? I feel like you only just got here."

Damien smirks and rolls his eyes as he helps himself to my breakfast. "I got here on Wednesday. It's been five days already. Trust me, that's more than the usual handful of days anyone else gets. I'm lucky I was able to get away at all."

My face scrunches with disappointment. "You suck."

"Right back at you, little sister," he says, taking pity on me and moving around the island to pull me into a quick hug. "Bootcamp isn't even that long anyway. I'll be done in a few weeks and back here so you can annoy the shit out of me some more."

"You've been gone forever," I tell him. "At least, it feels that way now that I have to deal with Mom all by myself."

"Seriously," he says, stepping back to fix me with a hard stare. "You have a phone. Use it. If anything happens, I need to know. I'm not putting up with more of this *I didn't want to worry you* shit, alright? Especially if Orlando gives you more of that *you're going to make a grand prize one day* crap. Got it?"

"Yeah, yeah," I say, rolling my eyes and getting back to cutting my orange. "Got it."

"I'm serious, Bri," he says. "I don't like the shit that's going down in this house. If things get weird, go next door. Tanner will look out for you. I spoke to his mom. She seems cool and is okay to take you in if you need a place to lay low."

My mouth drops as my head whips up to gape at my brother. "You spoke to my boyfriend's mother about me? What the hell, Damien? Not cool."

He rolls his eyes as though I'm being a dramatic child and it's the most infuriating thing I've ever seen. "Chill out, it's not like I went over there to discuss your relationship with the guy. I just wanted to make sure you had somewhere to go if shit hits the fan here."

"You're an ass," I remind him.

Damien scoffs. "At least I've got one, Pancake. Ever heard of a squat?"

My mouth drops and I stare at him in horror, more than ready to take a bitch out. "Take that back," I demand, my hands twitching for a fight. "I've been working on my ass. It's juicy now. A perfectly suitable bubble butt."

He scoffs again. "Right. Sure you have."

"Don't you have a plane you need to catch?"

Damien's gaze snaps up to the clock on the wall and lets out a heavy sigh. "Yeah, I do. I better get out of here, actually. You good here? You got everything you need?"

"I'm fine," I say for the millionth time since he first got here. "You know I'm eighteen, right? I'm not a little kid. I can take care of myself."

The asshole just smirks back at me before fixing his bag over his shoulder and backing away. "You keep telling yourself that." He turns and starts walking out of the kitchen before stopping and glancing back at me. "Bri?" he calls.

My head lifts from my orange and I do what I can to not get emotional about him leaving again. The first time was hard enough, but I suppose with the line of work he's getting into, this is just something I'm going to have to get used to. "Yeah?" I say, my voice low to mask the lump that's quickly growing in my throat.

"Don't let Mom get married again," he says, a stupid grin on his face. "Oh, and keep away from hard wax. We don't need a repeat of lipgate, especially when I'm not here to laugh my ass off."

My mouth drops open, humiliation washing through me, and

before I can launch my orange across the kitchen, the fucker disappears. "We had a pact," I call after him, knowing damn well we shook on that. The great lip incident of ninth grade was never to be spoken of, but if the fucker wants to play dirty, then I'm more than happy to remind him about the time he sneeze-farted in seventh grade and accidentally followed through.

The only response I get is a booming laugh before I hear the front door slam closed behind him, leaving me with a heavy heart despite the need to pulverize him. It's only a few more weeks and then he'll be back to torture me some more. Until then, I'm sure I can convince Mom she needs an extended honeymoon seeing as though she had to cut her Paris trip short. She's always wanted to visit Italy and go skiing in Switzerland. Hell, I could come up with a six month plan if that's what she needs. A trip around the world to visit every popular tourist destination on Orlando's credit card? Consider it done.

Concentrating on breakfast, I get everything sorted, and as Jensen comes downstairs to eat, I make a point in sharing what I've made. After all, I'm already at war with both Mom and Orlando, I don't need that same bullshit with Jensen. Besides, he's really not so bad. He keeps out of my way and in return, I keep out of his ... ya know, unless Tanner's in a rage induced temper tantrum, and I just happen to have a set of broken ribs and no car. However, I'm hoping I won't be put in that same situation again.

"Was that your brother leaving?" Jensen mumbles around a bite of food, barely glancing up as he speaks.

"Yep," I say, letting out a heavy sigh. "He'll be back in a few weeks.

He's nearly through with training, but I'm sure the second he gets home and settled, he'll be sent right out again."

"That sucks," he says. "Damien's alright. Not what I was expecting."

"Dare I ask what you were expecting?"

He scoffs, trying to mask a smirk. "A shittier version of your mom."

A laugh bubbles up my throat, and for a fleeting moment, guilt consumes me. I shouldn't be laughing at comments like that. She's my mom, but I can't help but feel that Jensen is right. Mom has been a shitty human, and I shouldn't feel guilty for finding amusement in my own pain. We all process the shit in our lives in different ways, and me? I need to laugh. If I don't laugh, I'll cry, and if I start to cry, I might not be able to stop.

Finishing up with breakfast, I quickly throw everything into the dishwasher before taking off upstairs and grabbing everything I need. Double checking the time, I realize I'm late, and as if acting as a second reminder, I hear Tanner's bike roaring to life.

I shove my head out my window, grinning down at the sexy piece of tattooed man-meat. "Wanna give me a ride?"

Tanner glances up as he straddles his bike, looking like the most delicious kind of snack as his helmet rests under his arm. His eyes sparkle and, even from across the yard, I can tell exactly what kind of comment I'm in for. "And feel the heat of your tight little cunt pressing up against me? Fuck yeah."

My cheeks flame as I quickly duck back inside my room, yanking the window down as I go. I fucking love it when he talks like that, so crass and dirty. It makes me feel like his personal little whore, but in a good way, not a gross kind of way. Tanner knows how to be respectable when he needs to be, but I prefer him like this. It's raw and filthy and I love it.

Dashing downstairs, I grip onto the railing, certain that if I were to go just a fraction faster, I'll trip and land face first into the Italian marble tiles at the bottom of the stairs.

Making my way outside, I rush toward the rumbling motorbike, excitement filling my veins. I love riding with Tanner. It's so thrilling, even if it's only a quick trip to school. I distantly notice the garage door rising and pay no attention to it as it doesn't concern me, but when I get halfway across the drive, only moments from skipping over to Tanner's property, I hear Orlando's curt tone calling out to me.

"Brielle, a word before you take off."

Fuck.

I consider ignoring the bastard but, finding Mom moving into his side with a ridiculous smile plastered across her face, I find myself pulling to a stop, my eyes still locked on Tanner's as my mood plummets into the ground. Tanner's face scrunches at seeing Mom and Orlando over my shoulder, and I can't help but notice the way his expression darkens. Whatever Orlando said to him in that jail cell really got to him, and I hate that for him. I hate that he has to deal with Orlando's bullshit like this. Hell, apart from everything that went down with Addison, Tanner should have nothing to do with the guy. Sure, Tanner clocked him right in the jaw, but I doubt that's a good enough reason to make the trip down to the police holding cells and threaten my guy, especially considering he could have just waited until Tanner got home.

It makes no sense to me, but I want to trust Tanner. He told me Orlando was salty about the fact he got knocked out in front of the courthouse, and as much as I know that's true, I can't help but wonder if there's something more to the story. Tanner is constantly threatened by assholes. It's practically a requirement of being the most popular guy in school and the captain of the best high school football team in the state. They want to knock him out, they want to beat him to a pulp just for being better than them, and they let him know it with every chance they get. It's usual sports trash talk, so having Orlando do the same shouldn't rattle him this way.

Despite my better judgment, I hold up a finger. "One sec," I tell him before turning and taking in Mom and Orlando standing in front of a brand-new Maserati GT Convertible. My brow arches, and as they make their way out of the garage toward me, I find myself backing up, not liking where this is going.

"SURPRISE!" Mom cheers, holding a key in her hand, a beaming smile from ear to ear. "We couldn't wait. It came in last night."

I look between Mom and Orlando before glancing toward the car. "I don't understand," I say, my brows furrowed. "What's going on?"

"Orlando bought you a new car, sweetheart. Aren't you excited?" she questions, her hand against Orlando's chest as she glances back toward the Maserati. "We were going to wait until this weekend, but I was just too excited. I knew you would love it."

No. Fuck no.

"What—why?"

Orlando chuffs. "Why?" he questions as though it's the most ridiculous question he's ever been asked. "Because I can. Because your car was wrapped around a tree, and you've been driving your mother's old car. You are a Channing now, and I won't have my daughter driving around in anything less than respectable."

"*Stepdaughter,*" I clarify in disgust, the phrase *daughter* making me feel sick. "And I am not a Channing. I am an Ashford. Some sham wedding ceremony can't change that."

"Brielle," my mother gasps in horror, looking at me like I'm some kind of stranger. "When a man purchases you a Maserati, you say thank you."

"Are you kidding me?" I scoff. "Where's the self respect in that? If a man offers to fuck me on the side of the road, am I supposed to smile and say sure thing, how do you want me? Or how about if some old rich guy demanded I uproot my whole life and move into his mansion to become his little pet to show off to all of his friends? Oh, wait. You've already done that."

"I swear, Brielle," she seethes. "I have had it with you. You are the most ungrateful child I have ever met. How dare you be so disrespectful. Look at this amazing life you have. Orlando has just bought you a Maserati for Christ's sake. A Maserati. And you haven't even got the decency to say thank you."

"Are you kidding me, Mom? Who do you take me for? I'm not stupid. I know a payoff when I see one," I say. "You don't think it's suspicious that he wants to buy me a fancy new car only days after I threaten to derail his whole career, a move which would put him behind bars for the rest of his life? Come on, Mom. You're smarter than that. At least, you used to be."

"Listen here," Orlando says, stepping forward.

"No, you listen here," I say, cutting him off. "Thank you, but no thank you. I'm not interested in your blood money, or your payoffs, and I certainly don't want anything you bought with money made from dirty deals and accepting bribes. If you want my approval, then start acting like a real man. Until then, you can take your Maserati and shove it up your ass. Better yet, save it for whichever whore you inevitably start screwing when you get bored of playing house."

Done with Orlando's bullshit attempt of bribery, I turn on my heel and storm right for Tanner's bike, skipping over the small bushes lining the property. "Brielle," Mom roars, calling after me. "Get back here right this instant. I am not finished with you."

Stepping up to Tanner's side, I push up onto my tippy toes and brush a soft, lingering kiss to his lips. "Please take me away from here," I beg him.

"My pleasure," he says, before pointing to the back of the bike.

I don't hesitate, throwing a leg over the bike and scooting in close to feel Tanner right at my core. The rumble of the engine vibrates through me and excites me in a way it simply shouldn't. I pull the helmet over my head, fix my bag on my back, and not a moment later, Tanner hits the gas. We take off at a million miles an hour, more than ready to leave Mom and Orlando's bullshit behind me.

CHAPTER 33

TANNER

"You sure about this?" I ask, a smirk kicking up the corner of my lips as I watch Bri in the driver's seat of my Mustang, her hands shaking with nerves as the sheer power from the engine rattles the whole car. "You don't have to do this. I'd understand if you wanted to bitch out."

Her mouth drops and she gapes at me. "Bitch out?" she questions, more than offended despite the way she still sits there, refusing to hit the gas and get the show on the road. "Since when do I ever bitch out?"

I grin back at her. "Then by all means, let's do this shit."

"Right, okay," she mutters, her brows slowly ruffling as her lips twist with uncertainty. "Oh, God."

Laughter tears at my chest, realizing that we could be sitting here for a while, and just as I go to offer to switch positions, Bri hits the gas like she's running from the cops, and I fly back against my seat with a heavy *oomph*, desperately reaching for the holy shit bar.

The Mustang propels forward, flying around the track as the usual Friday night crowd cheers for their few minutes of solid entertainment. Although one thing is for sure, this should be the most exhilarating race they've ever seen, especially considering

Bri is racing against no one but herself.

I don't even know how we ended up here, but it is what it is, and the moment she said she was down, I was already throwing her in the driver's seat. Who am I to deny a goddess a night of dangerously reckless fun?

The Mustang jolts and my stomach clenches, but that doesn't stop the encouraging smile I give Bri as she stares wide eyed at the track before us. "Oh, God," she mutters, looking almost sick with her decision to do this. "This was a bad idea."

"You're doing fi—WATCH OUT FOR THE PEOPLE!"

Bri screams and hastily corrects herself, shaking her head in terror as she flies past the bystanders who are lucky to get away with their lives still intact. She eases up on the gas while still forging ahead. I have to give it to her, she doesn't back down from anything, especially when it's something she's already started, despite the way it might terrify her.

We make our way around the track, and compared to the speed I usually take these corners, this feels more like a Sunday afternoon stroll. Though I don't dare mention that to my girl in fear of her gouging my eyes out with a rusty fork.

Dust flies up from beneath the tires and the crowd cheers for Bri, making her feel like royalty, and the further she gets around the track, the easier she seems to respond. She relaxes into the corners, and by the time we're hitting the last straight, she's doubling down on the gas and we're shooting forward, sending us hurtling across the finish line.

"Holy shit," she breathes, her eyes wide. When she hits the brakes, the Mustang comes to a screeching stop, and people rush in to crowd us. Her head whips toward me, a smug grin stretching across her face. "What was my time?" she questions. "I totally beat your record, didn't I?"

I stare back at her, my eyes narrowing. "You're kidding, right?" I ask. "I can't tell if you're serious or not."

"I'm so serious," she declares with pride. "One more lap at that speed and your tires would have burst into flames. I'm the motherfucking king of this track. I'm sorry to tell you, Tanner, but you just became my bitch. I mean, did you see how you freaked out at that one corner? I didn't think it was possible for such a tough guy like you to squeal like a little girl."

Her eyes sparkle with laughter and I can't help but reach for her, curling my fingers around the back of her neck and pulling her into me until those gorgeous bright blue eyes are staring deep into mine. "You're bad news, Killer."

She grins back at me like a fucking she-devil, and the way my chest aches for her is nothing short of crippling. "Whatcha gonna do about it?"

Fuck me. This little brat. What I wouldn't give to see my perfect handprint against that fine ass.

My lips crush on hers, kissing her deeply as her tongue battles with mine for dominance, but who am I fucking kidding? She's got me exactly where she wants me. I might be able to feign having the power here, but when it comes to Brielle Ashford, I'm as fucking whipped as humanly possible. She's got me on my knees, and there's no place else I'd rather be.

Finally coming up for air, we make our way out of the car and through the crowd. I don't bother moving the Mustang. It's well past midnight and the races are finished for the night. Hell, they were finished over two hours ago, but that didn't stop Bri from wanting to take a crack at it. Let's be honest, she sucks. Like really fucking sucks at it. Racing simply isn't for her, not that she'd agree with that, but if she asks again, I'd still be the first fucker offering up my car just to see the way her face lights up with excitement. Who knows, maybe after a little practice, she might even surprise me.

Making our way up the hill to our friends, I can't help but notice the death glare Bri sends to Jules Macey. I laugh as the girl immediately backs down from whatever bullshit she was planning.

We reach our friends in no time and Bri jumps straight into her recap of her practice lap. "Did you see me?" she says, wide-eyed, the excitement on her face lighting up the faces of everyone around her. "I was on fire. I swear, I knocked all of Logan's and Tanner's records right off the board."

"You sure fucking did," Riley agrees with her, despite knowing damn well no one could ever come close to my times. "Though just between you and me, I'm embarrassed for them. How humiliating, having your time smashed by a chick on her first ever lap. If I were you, I'd be reconsidering my choice of men. Now, if you need a replacement, I could show you a good time."

Striding towards Riley, I smack him up the side of his head, more than ready to pick up where we left off last weekend. After all, I never got the chance to prove I could whoop his ass, though we both know it's true, no matter how many times he denies it. That night kinda got away from us. The moment the cherry-flavored lube was brought out and slathered all over my girl, I was a fucking goner.

Grabbing a drink for me and Bri, I drop down into my seat and she sashays over to me, the perfect amount of sway to her hips that has my cock flinching in my pants. She takes her place on my lap, her arm hooking around the back of my neck as I crack open her drink and hand it to her. "Why thank you, peasant," she says with a ridiculous grin before leaning in and pressing her lips to mine.

"Watch yourself, Killjoy. You'll leave me no choice but to remind you who has you by the fucking balls. Ain't no peasant can make you scream the way I do."

"You're right," she says. "Only a king can make me come like that."

"And don't you forget it."

"Question," Jax asks from across our group, sitting forward and propping his elbows against his knees. Arizona sits on the ground in front of him, leaning back against him with his legs on either side of her, practically using his dick as a headrest. "Anyone else curious about the art of pegging?"

"Oh, please no," Addie says, pressing her hands to her ears. "The last thing I need is a mental image of you getting railed by some chick wearing a strap-on."

I gape at my sister, my jaw slack in horror. "How the fuck do you know what pegging is?"

She shrugs her shoulders and indicates toward Hudson beside her. "He explained it to me last week."

"What?" I question, my eyes practically falling right out of my head as I turn my horrified stare on Hudson. "What the fuck are you doing talking to her about that shit?"

"Woaaaaaah," he says, his hands shooting up in defense. "This is way out of context. It's not like I've been explaining this shit to her in the hopes that one day I can convince her to strap one on and rail me while I'm on my hands and knees. What do you take me for? It was mentioned in one of the smutty books she likes. She didn't understand, so I explained and then moved on as fast as I fucking could, otherwise she would have googled it and you and I both know that can't happen."

A smug expression flitters across Addison's face and as she attempts to mask it, I realize I just fell straight into her trap. Hudson and I both have. That little brat. She had every intention of messing with me and it worked like a fucking charm. I give her a hard stare, narrowing my gaze. "Dead to me."

"Oh, please," she scoffs, knowing damn well that I'm all talk. "Pegging wasn't even the worst of it. Imagine what else I had him teach me. Next time, I'll be asking for demonstrations and diagrams."

Logan laughs, his hand gently roaming up and down Chanel's thigh. "Rule 34," he announces, making me shake my head. "When in doubt, check PornHub. Guaranteed any fucked up curiosity you might have has already been thought of and exploited in porn. If you can think of it, there's porn of it." He winks. "You can thank me later."

Fuck no. The last thing I want is my sister searching the endless pages of PornHub. "Somebody talk about something else before I introduce Logan's face to my knee."

"Okay," Arizona says, flying to her feet and turning on Jax. She gives him a hard stare, the slight bit of alcohol in her bloodstream making her brave. "I've got something I need to talk about."

Jax shakes his head. "Don't, Ari. You don't want to go there. Not now."

"Are you kidding me?" she questions. "It's been two weeks since you found out at the lake, and you've been tiptoeing around it ever since. Am I that disposable to you that this doesn't even warrant a conversation? I'm in love with you, Jax, and I have been for … I don't even know how long. I am the only consistent woman in your life and the only one who always sticks around through your bullshit. I've watched you go from girl to girl, jumping through hoops just to get between their legs, and every damn time, you come back to me. Every time, Jax. You can't tell me that this means nothing to you. You treat me like a fucking queen … but only when it suits you."

"Ari, please. Come on …"

"No, you come on, Jax. I'm sick of waiting around, hoping that one day you're going to see me for what I'm worth. Do you have any idea how much it's killed me these past two weeks with you being incapable of even acknowledging what was said? I love you, Jax. Hear me. I. Am. In. Love. With. You."

Jax stands, getting on her level before taking her waist, doing what he can to calm her, the hesitation in his eyes making everybody catch their breath. "Ari, you know it's never been like that between us. We're friends and we fuck. We have a good time together, but you have to understand that you caught me off guard. I never realized you felt that way, and I'm not about to start leading you on and making empty promises. I care too much about you to do that."

"What are you saying?" she murmurs, heartbreak thick in her tone. "That it's okay for me to spread my legs for you every second night and be your comfort, but that I'm not worth anything more to you?"

"Babe," he says slowly, seeing just how south this is going. "That's not what I'm saying at all. I just … I don't want things to change between us. We're so good together."

"Exactly, Jax. That's my point. We're good together. You and me just work, but things have changed, and I have too much respect for myself. I want more. What we're doing … this isn't enough for me anymore."

"But I …" he swallows hard, his hands falling from her waist and capturing her fingers in a soft, hesitant grasp. "I can't give you more."

Bri's hand slips into mine as she sucks in a soft gasp, feeling Arizona's pain as though it were her own and I pull her in, pressing my lips to her temple as we watch the shit storm brewing before us.

Arizona's gaze drops, her heart in shattered pieces on the ground for the world to see. "Then I can't do this anymore," she whispers, pulling her hand free from his. "I won't do it to myself."

"Ari," he murmurs, his eyes filled with concern as he tries to reach for her, but she's already gone, turning on her heel with tears streaming down her face.

Chanel and Bri stand, ready to go after her, but Ilaria puts her hand up. "Don't," she tells them. "This time is different. She needs to be alone."

Chanel lets out a sigh as Addison shoots a nasty glare at Jax. "Seriously? What the hell was that? Why did you say that to her?"

"What?" Jax argues. "Would you have preferred I lied to her?"

"No, but I'd have preferred if you were honest."

"What's that supposed to mean? I was honest. I don't want to lead her on, especially if it's not going to go where she's hoping it will."

Addison scoffs. "You really are an idiot, aren't you?" she says, putting her drink down and getting to her feet. "Are you seriously that blind? You have feelings for her, real feelings, but you're just too scared to act on them because it means you'll have to quit fucking around. So rather than face that, you hurt her instead, and now all you've done is push her away. You're going to lose a good thing before you've even had a chance to see just how good it could be."

Jax scoffs. "Like you would know anything about being in a relationship."

"Wow, deflecting back on me to avoid dealing with your own messed up emotions. Great move, Jax."

"Back off, Adds. I'm not here getting at you about your relationship with Hudson," he says. "Lay off."

Addison rolls her eyes before passing Jax. "Whatever," she mutters. "I need to pee."

Addison heads toward the crowd, making her way back down the hill, and for a moment, I consider going after her, hating the thought of her being alone. Just the smallest things set her off and making her way through a crowd of drunk teenagers probably isn't going to help. She's not ready for this, but at the same time, having her brother insist on walking her to the bathroom isn't going to help her mood right now.

My gaze flicks toward Hudson, seeing the same indecision on his face when Chanel shoots up again. "Wait up," she calls after her, dashing past Jax. "I totally broke my seal."

I relax back into my seat when Bri leans into me, her hand pressed against my chest. "Wanna go for a walk?" she murmurs, wanting to escape the bullshit.

Taking her hand, I nod, and she jumps up before pulling me with her. We head in the opposite direction of the track, out toward the thick trees covered in darkness. My arm settles over her shoulder, and she walks close to my side. "You good?" I question, Bri not typically being the type to want an escape like that.

"Yeah," she murmurs, her gaze locked on the ground, making sure she doesn't trip over any stray branches or rocks. "I just don't like when our friends are fighting. I feel bad for Arizona. She's devastated."

"I know," I tell her. "But I think Jax did the right thing. If he doesn't think he can be what she needs, then it's best he tells her now before she gets too attached."

Bri scoffs. "She's already attached," she says, letting out a heavy sigh. "You don't think Jax feels the same way?"

I press my lips into a hard line, really thinking it over. "I think it's a possibility, but I don't think he's ready to face whatever it is he's feeling. When it comes to stuff like this, he's the complete opposite of Logan. Jax … he likes to keep his options open."

"Even if it means hurting someone in the process?"

"To be honest, I don't think he's really taken a moment to consider how his actions have been hurting Arizona, but I think tonight might be a reality check for him," I explain. "Maybe he'll come around to the idea, or maybe he's already certain that it won't work. Jax isn't the easiest to read, but what I do know is that if he feels pressured into it, he's going to close off from her entirely."

We venture deeper into the thick trees, not stopping until Bri perches her ass against the trunk of a fallen tree. She leans back, her head tipping as she gazes up at the few lone stars visible through the thick branches. "These past few weeks have sucked," she mutters, briefly closing her eyes and giving herself a moment of peace, and while I know she's trying to relax and take it all in, all I can think about is how fucking beautiful she looks in the soft moonlight and how desperately I want to put my hands on her.

"They have," I tell her, moving into her and dropping to my knees, my hands resting against her thighs.

Feeling me here, she opens her eyes and brings her chin back down to meet my stare, and those gorgeous bright blue orbs are filled with hunger. She reaches for me, her fingers working the buckle of my belt as she leans in and drops her lips to mine.

I kiss her back, giving her everything she's asking for.

My hands slide higher on her thighs before curling around to her ass and yanking her forward until that sweet little cunt is pressed right up against me. Bri groans into my mouth. "Oh God."

Fuck, the way she needs me … I'll never get used to it. No matter how many times I fuck her, no matter how hard or fast, she always comes back for more, and I fucking love it.

Bri releases my belt and gets straight to work, opening my pants and freeing my straining cock from its confines. Her warm hand curls around my shaft, squeezing tight as she slowly works her way to my tip only to destroy me when her thumb curves right over it, just the way I like it.

I strip her bare, pulling her soft tank over her head and flicking the clasp of her bra between her tits, letting the fabric fall down her arms. She arches her back, tipping her head to the sky, and I take every fucking advantage as my lips come down on her breast.

Her nipple pebbles beneath my tongue as I work my hands down her toned body, taking her hips and lifting her just enough to pull her jeans down past her thighs. I tear them from her legs, panties and all before pushing those pretty thighs wide.

Bri gasps, feeling the cool, midnight air against her pussy, but that's not all she'll be feeling.

Too hungry to wait, I hook her thighs over my shoulders and she squeals as she tips back, having to catch herself against the log. "Holy shit," she laughs, but the laughter quickly morphs into a low groan as I bury my face between her legs.

My mouth closes over her clit, gently sucking as I flick my tongue over it, loving the way her whole body jolts as though a bolt of electricity just shot right through her system. I do it again and she buries her fingers into my hair, knotting them and holding on for the ride.

I fuck her hard with my tongue, working that little bud of nerves until she's wound so tight she can't help but scream. My cock strains, desperate to feel her slick pussy so tight around me, but there's no way in hell I'm about to rush this. Fuck what I need, this is just too good.

"Holy fuck, Tanner! More."

Exhilaration pulses through my veins as I bring my hand up and push two thick fingers inside her, curling them just the way she likes and grinning when her grip in my hair tightens. She gasps loudly, her back arching again and I give her more.

In. Out. Suck. Flick.

She cries out when her sweet pussy shatters around my fingers, convulsing as her whole body spasms. "Tanner," she groans. "Yes."

I don't stop working her until she comes down from her high and, even then, my girl is ready for more. I pull back, watching as she tries to catch her breath but the hunger is still there in full force. She takes my face, pulling me into her before crushing her lips to mine and tasting herself on my tongue.

"I fucking love you," she pants against my lips.

I grin. I'll never get enough of hearing those words. "Oh yeah," I tease. "How much?"

Her hand dives down between us, stroking my cock and curling her thumb over my tip again, feeling that bead of moisture. "Shut up and fuck me," she demands.

How the hell could any man deny her?

Pushing up higher on my knees, I grip her ass and pull her closer. Not wasting a damn second, I line up with her entrance and slam my cock so fucking deep inside her that I know the names of our first two children.

Bri cries out, throwing her arm around my neck and holding herself close, her tits pressed right up against my chest as I fuck her hard. Our bodies grow sweaty and I wouldn't be surprised if Bri's ass is scratched up from the log, but she's not complaining.

My balls tighten, feeling the way her tight pussy clenches around me. "Fuck, Killer," I grunt. "Your sweet little cunt is gonna be the death of me."

"Don't hold back," she pants, begging for everything I've got. So I go in harder, my fingers digging into her skin, drawing all the way back just to slam deep inside her again.

Bri throws her head back, barely able to hold on to me as she reaches her limits. "Fucking come for me, Killer," I demand, knowing damn well that if she doesn't come soon, I'll be going alone.

My cock flinches inside her as the raw sounds of our fuck fest does all sorts of things to me. "Tanner," she breathes, her lips coming to mine. "I can't ... I'm ..."

"Give it to me," I tell her and not a second later, she comes undone. Bri screams out my name, gripping onto me as though her whole fucking soul is trying to leave her body, and I come hard as her cunt squeezes around me, putting me in a fucking choke hold.

I don't stop moving, watching as the high takes over her body. Her nails dig into my skin, her eyes clenching as she struggles to breathe, but the way her pussy spasms is what kills me. She's fucking perfect, every last part of her.

We come down together, both gasping for air as she meets my heated gaze. "You can fuck me like that any time, any day," she tells me. "Just say the word and you can have me any way you like."

CHAPTER 34

TANNER

Looping our joined hands over Bri's shoulder, I pull her in tight as we make our way back to our friends at the top of the hill, only with every step we take, I slow our pace, knowing it's time to come clean.

I've been holding on to this horrific secret for far too long and I just know if I don't come clean now and she finds out some other way, that's it for us. She won't ever look at me again, despite her promises to always stand at my side.

I need us to have a real future, and there's no hope for us unless every last secret is laid out for her to see. She needs to know who I really am, what I'm truly capable of. Otherwise, I'm doing nothing but living a lie, and she deserves better. She deserves the whole fucking world.

My stomach churns as I pull her up, swallowing hard as I prepare to drop one hell of a bomb on her ass, knowing damn well that she would have every right to walk away from me, from us, from everything we've been building together.

"Killer," I murmur, my hands beginning to shake with unease. Bri stops and looks up at me, those big eyes so full of hope and love, it kills me to have to destroy this perfect fantasy. "I … I've been needing to tell you something and I can't hold on to it anymore. I don't want secrets between us, but this … I don't know how you're going to take this, but it's not fair to you."

Brielle's brows furrow, the dim light from the races mixing with the soft moonlight and giving me just enough to see the worry etched across her face. "I know," she tells me. "You've been off ever since the courthouse, and I've been trying to give you your space, knowing you'll talk to me when you're ready, but I think I've figured it out."

"Figured it out?" I ask, my heart leaping out of my fucking chest. There's no way. It's simply not possible.

Bri nods. "Yeah, I've been going over everything that happened in court, and I know you said Orlando visited you in that jail cell. At first, I thought it must have had something to do with him, but it just didn't make sense. Apart from being neighbors and Colby's lawyer, you guys don't have any other connection, so that got me thinking about what happened in court."

I stare down at her, unsure where the hell she's going with this. "What are you talking about?"

"Rachael," she says, unease in her tone. "She had that baby with her and I was doing the math. He looked to be the right age to be yours. He has the same dark hair and dark eyes, and the way she was smirking at you … he's yours, isn't he? You're his father."

I blanch, my eyes widening in horror. "I … no," I say. "Absolutely not. Though I won't lie to you, the thought did cross my mind, but I was careful. I wore protection when I was with her."

"So, if she shows up on your doorstep, claiming the baby is yours?"

"Then I'll happily do a paternity test, but I'm certain. I'm not that kid's father," I promise her. "I didn't know Rachael well, but I do know she was practically engaged at the time despite being a senior, and I wasn't the only guy she was fucking around with. And I'm not saying that to be an ass, it's just fact."

"You're sure?" she asks, that same hesitation in her voice.

"Certain."

"Okay," she says, swallowing hard. "That's not what you were wanting to tell me though, is it?"

I shake my head, my stomach aching with unease. "No, I—"

A piercing scream tears through the night, so loud and raw that Brielle gasps at the sound. "What the hell was that?" she rushes out, her eyes wide and filled with terror.

My grip tightening on her hand, I look out toward the party, fear rattling me as I see people starting to run and more screams fill the night. "I don't fucking know. Something's not right."

"Ilaria," Bri murmurs. "Your sister. Everyone is still there."

We take off at a sprint, racing back toward the hill, one foot slamming down in front of the other as I half drag Bri along with me. She stumbles beside me, panting as she tries to keep up, but I don't dare let go of her. If something is going down, I need to know where she is at all times. But my sister … fuck.

People run everywhere, shoulder checking me as they flee toward the parking lot, desperate to get out of here. I struggle to hold on to Bri's hand as she gets stuck behind me. People try to cut between us, but they'll have me to deal with if they even think about breaking my hold on her.

My gaze cuts from one end of the property to the next, searching out the threat while desperately trying to find Addison, but logic tells me she's already with Hudson.

Looking up the hill, I find all the guys' cars still here and my Mustang still sitting down at the finish line on the track. I know I should head toward it, but I can't, not before knowing everyone is okay.

We sprint up the hill and almost get to the top when I come to a screeching halt. Gripping onto Brielle's arm, I shove her hard behind me as Colby Jacobs stands at the top of the hill, a bloodied knife in his hand, facing off against my friends.

Jax stands front and center, holding Arizona behind him as Logan slowly creeps forward, holding his hand up in warning. "Get the fuck out of here, bro," Logan says, his other hand out in warning to Chanel to stay where the fuck she is.

My gaze darts around the circle, trying to figure out how to handle this as Bri holds her breath, trying not to make a damn sound. She clings to my arm, her nails digging into my skin, knowing damn well that whatever happens here isn't going to be pretty.

Hudson catches my stare from across the hill, his eyes wide and petrified. Addie is nowhere in sight. He shakes his head ever so slightly, telling me he hasn't seen her, and my heart races, a fear I've only ever known once before spreading through my veins.

"I'm not leaving until I get what I want," Colby spits. "Where the fuck is she?"

My stomach churns. There are only two girls he could be referring to and he'll have to go through me to get to either of them.

Riley scoffs, moving forward to stand in line with Jax and Logan. "You're fucked in the head if you think for even one second we're going to give up Addison to a fucking asshole like you."

Colby smirks back at them, spinning the bloodied knife between his fingers. "That bitch?" he says as a perfectly round drop of blood falls from the tip of his knife. "Oh, I'm already through with her. She was easy then, and easy now."

Fuck no.

Red hot fury blasts through my veins like a fucking drug, and I let out an agonizing roar, sprinting full blast ahead at the fucker. Colby spins to face me, his lips pulling into a twisted smirk, especially as he sees Brielle cowering back, screaming in horror.

The fucker comes at me, but Jax is closer, launching himself at Colby's back, locking his arm around Colby's throat, dragging him down. I keep running, determined to end his miserable life, Brielle sprinting after me in fear.

Colby wrestles out of Jax's grasp and my eyes widen in horror. In a flash of lightning, Colby plunges the tip of the knife deep into Jax's stomach.

Jax roars in agony as a blood-curdling scream tears out of Arizona and both her and Logan run full force ahead, desperate to get to him.

The knife has bearly been ripped out of Jax's stomach when I launch myself at Colby, taking the fucker to the ground with a heavy blow. His head slams against the hard ground and my fist comes down in a sickening blow before he even gets a chance to right himself.

Colby pushes back as Arizona's raw screams tear through the night. Hudson takes off at a sprint, running to find Addie, Ilaria and Chanel racing after him as Brielle barrels into my back, knowing damn well that if I don't stop, I'll fucking kill him.

From the ground, Colby wields the knife in desperation, and there's a vacant, manic look in his eyes as I pound into him. His blade rips into my arm, but I don't feel the pain through the blind rage and adrenaline coursing through me. Riley barges into me, and Brielle tries to pull me back, but I'm out of control. I only see red, and Brielle's screams seem so far away.

I shove Riley hard, forcing him back as I distantly notice Logan hovering over Jax, his bloodied hands pressing against Jax's wound, begging him to stay awake while Arizona cradles his head in her lap, tears streaming down her face.

Images of Addie, naked on the floor, her bruises, blood and horror flash through my mind, and the fury only gets worse.

Fear cripples me, the thought of Addie being out there alone after this motherfucker hurt her again is all I can think of, and the image spurs every last one of my hits. His arms stop flailing around and the knife falls to the grass beside him, Colby's body going limp, only I can't fucking stop.

"Tanner," Bri cries, trying to grip onto my arm, but I shove her off, not nearly finished with him. Nothing will ever make up for what he's done, no number of punches will make this okay.

"Riley, please," Bri sobs, looking up at my best friend, a last ditch effort to try and save me. "Don't let Tanner kill him. He'll never be the same."

Riley stands, shaking his head beside me as he looks over at Bri sprawled out on the grass. "It's already too late," he says, his sad eyes moving to me, watching as I beat the shit out of a corpse. "Tanner, that's enough. He's gone. You need to stop."

Clenching my jaw, I keep going, tears of anger welling in my eyes. "He fucking touched her again," I spit, my fist cracking against his cheek, splitting the skin with ease.

Riley moves in closer, his hand coming down on my shoulder. "You're done," he tells me. "Addison is out there somewhere and she needs you. Go find her."

"I ..."

"Please," Brielle cries, the sound of her sobs killing something inside of me. "Please stop. That's enough."

Riley gets a good grip on me and tears me back, throwing me down into the grass beside Bri, my body sprawled out as I stare back at Colby, waiting for him to breathe. Only it never comes.

I killed him.

I fucking killed him.

My eyes are wide and I stare up at Riley in horror. "What the fuck have I done?"

"TANNER," Hudson's panicked yelp tears through the night from the bottom of the hill.

I look back over my shoulder, seeing Addison cradled in his arms, her clothes torn and bloodied, her head lolling back as he desperately runs toward us. "Fuck," I roar, flying to my feet, Colby's lifeless body all but forgotten as I sprint past Logan and Arizona, watching in terror as Jax's blood seeps through the gaps between Logan's fingers. Jax is barely holding on.

Bri comes rushing after me, but I forge ahead, knowing she'll catch up, getting only a few feet away from Addison when Bri's pained gasps tear through the night. "Tanner," she cries out, something in her tone forcing me to stop and look back.

My eyes lock to hers, just in time to watch as she falls, her face clammy and pale as she clutches onto her side. Her knees hit the grass, her body slumping heavily to the hard ground as she brings her hands away, each one of her fingers coated with blood.

She looks back up at me in fear, realization dawning on both of us as I start to double back, and not a moment later, she fades away, her eyes closing as her soft murmured plea cuts straight through to my soul, breaking every last part of me. "Don't let me die."

THANKS FOR READING

If you enjoyed reading this book as much as I enjoyed writing it, please consider leaving an Amazon review to let me know.

https://www.amazon.com/dp/B0B2QBH8PX

STALK ME

Facebook Page

www.facebook.com/SheridanAnneAuthor

Facebook Reader Group

www.facebook.com/SheridansBookishBabes

Instagram

www.instagram.com/Sheridan.Anne.Author

Tiktok

www.tiktik.com/@sheridan.anne.author

OTHER SERIES

www.amazon.com/Sheridan-Anne/e/B079TLXN6K

YOUNG ADULT / NEW ADULT DARK ROMANCE

Broken Hill High | Haven Falls | Broken Hill Boys |
Aston Creek High | Rejects Paradise | Boys of Winter |
Depraved Sinners | Bradford Bastard | Empire

NEW ADULT SPORTS ROMANCE

Kings of Denver | Denver Royalty | Rebels Advocate

CONTEMPORARY ROMANCE (standalones)

Play With Fire | Until Autumn (Happily Eva Alpha World)

URBAN FANTASY - PEN NAME: CASSIDY SUMMERS

Slayer Academy